The vampire grinned ... exposed, the incisors ... the blood that trickled from the corner of his mouth.

On the ground was a beautiful young blonde, lying on her back. Her dress was torn away to expose her left breast; her muscles were completely slack.

She had been drained of blood.

Her neck had been savaged. Instead of the usual pinprick holes, there were two ragged gashes. Her killer must have locked on her flesh and then, with his incisors halfway through her throat, thrashed her about in an orgasmic frenzy while her blood gushed into his mouth.

The vampire knelt beside the woman, lowered his face, and licked the final bit of blood seeping from her torn neck.

He was standing again almost before I knew it, staring at me with the same mad grin as he stuffed something into the jacket of his coat without looking down at what he was doing.

I glanced at the girl and suppressed an urge to vomit. He had cut off her ear as a trophy.

Also by Michael Romkey
*Published by Fawcett Books:*

**FEARS POINT**

# I,
# VAMPIRE

## Michael Romkey

FAWCETT GOLD MEDAL • NEW YORK

A Fawcett Gold Medal Book
Published by Ballantine Books
Copyright © 1990 by Michael Romkey

Library of Congress Catalog Card Number: 90-93049

ISBN 0-449-14638-3

Manufactured in the United States of America

First Edition: August 1990
Tenth Printing: June 1993

For CAROL, RYAN, and MATTHEW

January 1, 1990


To: T. Jefferson
From: L. da Vinci
Subject: New archives material


The following journal recently was donated to the
*Illuminati* archives.

I think you will find it interesting. I read it over
the weekend and was struck by its many similar-
ities to the Beethoven document.

Of course this is a contemporary account of the
education of a vampire under our current system—which I continue to insist demands entirely
too much of the initiate. I realize you, with your
well-meaning but rarefied theories about the nobility of the Common Man, will disagree with me
on this point.

Please have your staff cross-index the information in the computer system before filing, flagging
the entries to David Parker's personal directory.
I expect we'll continue to update his dossier regularly during the foreseeable future.

*Pax vobiscum.*

# PART I

✧

# The Mortal

# Chapter 1

**PARIS, JUNE 1, 1989**—Women are my weakness.

Or to be more accurate, I should say they are my greatest weakness, for I have many. Travel. Books. Classical music. Art. Excellent wine. And, formerly, cocaine. I admit these things without a sense of guilt. I am, as my friend from Vienna says, a man with a man's contradictions—*"ein Mensch mit seinem Widerspruch."*

I am neither good nor bad, neither angel nor devil.

I am a man. I am a vampire.

I have found the perfect place to spend this warm spring evening.

I am in Paris, the City of Light, sitting alone in an outdoor café with nothing much to do until the Wagner Festival begins in Bayreuth. At the festival I finally will be reunited with Tatiana, and Mozart will introduce me to the *Illuminati*, who comprise the innermost circle of the secret race to which I now belong.

Paris is as beautiful as people say, yet there is one thing about it that repulses me: It is a city of ghosts. I am unaccustomed to the heavy atmosphere of history that surrounds me here. Everywhere I walk, echoes of the past come back to me with the sound of my footsteps.

Tonight I wandered through the Tuileries gardens, then down the Rue de Rivoli past the Hotel Crillon, where Benjamin Franklin had rooms, to the seventy-five-foot-tall Egyptian obelisk in the center of the Place de la Concorde. The pink granite stiletto is covered with hieroglyphics written 3,300 years ago. I did not understand the literal message inscribed in the falcons and jackals and other carved images, but the secondary message—

the one yearning for life beyond the few years allotted mortal flesh—cried out to me in the night. The obelisk seems as at home in Paris as it must have been amid the ruins at Luxor.

I walked on to the far end of the Champs-Elysées to visit Napoleon's Arc de Triomphe, which is crumbling and draped with netting to catch bits and pieces when they fall.

Such folly. Men contrive these artifices to cheat mortality, but no monument is permanent enough to stop time from washing away all traces of its builder's existence. Time is a scouring river that transforms the past into a smooth, featureless landscape where only a slight rise on the horizon betrays the place an indomitable mountain range once stood, until eventually even that disappears.

The gardens and palaces and fountains remain in this historical city, but the people who built them have long departed, their bones turned to dust, their public works left behind to delay a little longer the anonymity of the grave. These monuments to men's egos were made of mortar and stone and timber, but their builders were made of flesh and blood and bone. Flesh and blood and bone cannot resist time's ravages.

Except in the vampire.

**Paris, June 2, 1989**—I have never understood what motivates people to keep diaries, and I am not exactly sure why I have started this one. I suppose it is a way for me to work through questions that have troubled me ever since I fell in love with Tatiana on a night just like this one almost exactly one year ago.

What is a vampire? I have spent the past twelve months studying this question from the inside out, but still I do not know the answer. I can make a list of the vampire's primary characteristics—superhuman strength, fierce intelligence, great stealth, aversion to sunlight, the terrible need to consume fresh human blood. Yet to say that's what a vampire *is* would be like saying Paris *is* streets and buildings and a river.

I am not interested in a description of the vampire species, which I know well enough, but rather in its nature. What *is* a vampire? And *why*?

More than a man, less than a god. Possessed with a great sensitivity for beauty, driven by a compulsion to feast on blood sucked from living mortals. An artist dedicated to creating, a parasite ever watchful for the next victim.

How do such opposing elements coexist within a single being? Perhaps they do not coexist. Perhaps the vampire is more good than evil—or more evil than good, since some members of my race are *extremely* evil.

Until I met Tatiana, I never felt the need to ask myself whether I was good or evil. Now I wonder about it constantly. A few nights ago, as I lowered my lips to the neck of the woman I had just made love to—opening my mouth wide to make room for the blood teeth slipping down from their cavities in my upper gums—a section of William Blake's verse ran at random through my mind.

*When the stars threw down their spears,*
*And water'd heaven with their tears,*
*Did he smile his work to see?*
*Did he who made the Lamb make thee?*

What do good and evil mean to an ordinary mortal?

To the vampire, whose life is anything but ordinary, they mean everything.

**Paris, June 3, 1989**—I find French women to be feminine in some mysterious way American women are not. Maybe it is that they seem more at home in their bodies, floating past my table with grace and lanky elegance, distracting my attention as I sit, gold-and-onyx fountain pen in my right hand, writing in this journal.

A moment ago a young woman on the arm of her escort smiled at me and lifted an eyebrow, as if daring me to follow. She parted her full lips, so that I could just see the tip of her tongue, and raised her chin. A magnificent neck. The skin, smooth and pure as alabaster, throbbed with a strong pulse above her jugular vein.

I felt a pang of desire and, beneath it, a more powerful Hunger.

I restrained myself with effort.

If this journal is to serve as the chronicle of my journey into the world of the vampire, I should begin at the beginning and relate how I have come to be what I am.

The words at the beginning of my first entry—"Women are my weakness"—is the place to start. When I say that women are my weakness, I do not mean to imply that I blame them for anything that has befallen me, but rather to explain my principal shortcoming. If women have exercised an undue influence over my life as a mortal and as a vampire—one can argue that they have—it is only because I have allowed it to be so. Women always have been the guiding force in my life, and while they have led me to the edge of oblivion on several occasions, I can blame only myself for letting my heart rule my mind.

What is it about the woman at the next table that keeps distracting my attention? Is it the smell of her perfume, the rustle of silk against bare skin when she raises her arm or the sight of the curve of her breasts, so perfectly drawn?

Or is it the steamy aroma of the blood flowing through her veins?

She glances in my direction, then looks away, smiling to herself and shaking her head, so that her thick black hair whips against her cheek.

I wonder whether she is French. Her skin is olive-colored. Perhaps she is from Greece or Italy. Yes, that is probably it. One of the Mediterranean countries, where the sun is fierce and passions run hot.

What am I doing to myself? I do not need blood tonight!

I must force myself to ignore her.

My earliest memory is of a woman. I can close my eyes and recall with great clarity sitting on my mother's lap in the nursery, twisting a lock of her hair around and around my tiny finger, the repetitive motion soothing me into a state of bliss.

Recalling such innocent pleasures can be painful to someone who also knows how it feels to stalk a woman through the streets during the night's darkest hour, ravenous for blood. There is a dark side to vampirey. I know because I've lived it.

Fortunately I've been strong enough to resist my worst impulses. Vampires need not kill their victims. With one tragic exception I have not killed mine. I've tried to be good, knowing that I must work all the harder at it because of the double threat posed by my unusual *urges* and the power I have to satisfy them.

Six months ago Tatiana sent her friend Mozart to advise me. I had been right to guard against misusing my mental and physical strength to satisfy my most craven desires, he said. Before he left me alone, promising to meet me here in Paris, he told me that not every vampire possesses the willpower to resist temptation.

I know that, too. Temptation and I have become old acquaintances, and we contend against each other nightly.

It has not been easy.

The woman at the next table finally has succeeded in catching my eye.

She smiled at me openly this time, but I only nodded and returned to writing these words, hearing her sigh softly with disappointment.

She is lonely, I sense, and attracted to me. I can hear her heart beating fast with desire, and I feel desire of my own beginning to burn deep within me.

I can't. I mustn't. I won't.

No, it has *not* been easy!

This journal is the story of my odyssey into the refined, elegant, and often frightening world of the vampire. I shall tell all—from the horror I experienced when I looked down at the slack body beneath mine the first time I fed on blood, to my unfolding awe for the sublime creatures who make up the vampire race.

My tale begins, as all vampire stories should begin, innocently enough, once upon a time ago and far, far away.

But I must stop for tonight. The waiter hovers by my table, the expression on his face telling me that the café is ready to close.

I have leased a suite of rooms in the Ritz Hotel in the Place Vendôme near the Opéra district. The Place Vendôme, like the entire city, is quite haunted. I imagine the spirits of Dorothy Parker and F. Scott Fitzgerald walking the halls of the hotel, along with the shades of my other fellow expatriate. Ghosts are everywhere. The hotel is at No. 15. Chopin died at No. 12, and I play a little Chopin on the piano in my room every night in his honor. Dr. Mesmer, the hypnotist, lived at No. 16.

I rented a Peugeot to explore the countryside, but the traffic is so bad that I haven't ventured out. Besides, there is enough in Paris to keep me enraptured with the city for decades. I lack nothing but the company of others of my kind, though I sense from time to time they are nearby.

I wish they would contact me. I wonder why they don't.

Soon Mozart will arrive, and we will travel to Bayreuth. We will go to the opera to hear Wagner, he'll introduce me to the

*Illuminati*, and we will spend long nights playing the piano and discussing the many things I have learned since our last meeting.

And, best of all, in Bayreuth I shall at last be reunited with the woman I shall love for all eternity, the beautiful Russian vampire, Princess Tatiana Nicolaievna Romanov.

# Chapter 2

**P**ARIS, JUNE 4, 1989—I was born thirty years ago.
My father is a real estate developer in Chicago. Money is his passion, his only passion, and he has a great deal of it. He's not a talkative man. My personal theory is that Father affected his taciturn style out of the belief that silence often as not is mistaken for wisdom. Not that it matters. Like my mother, I can predict what he is going to say the moment he opens his mouth to say it. Perhaps that is why he prefers to keep his silence.

Father's opinions are inflexible. His personal habits are compulsive. His politics are Republican, his religion the passionless brand of Episcopalian they practice on the North Shore. The suits that hang in his closet are all dark blue, and the shirts are all white oxford cloth, with button-down collars and heavy starch.

He is seldom seen without two props, a cigar and a copy of *The Wall Street Journal*, and that includes weekends and holidays. I would not be surprised to learn that his will instructs the undertaker to place a Cuban cheroot and the latest edition of the business newspaper in the coffin with him before burial.

The man is incapable of surprise.

Well, almost.

My mother comes from old money. She is sweet and loving, but it is impossible for me to imagine her being anything except a rich man's wife. It is not her fault. It is the profession she was trained for. Like many women of her class and generation, she does it well and seems to find fulfillment in it.

Mother's family goes back to colonial Virginia. Her maiden name—Alden—has been a fixture on the Philadelphia social roster since before the Revolutionary War. Wealth has always stayed

11

in her family, by hook and by crook, although fortunes have been lost nearly as often as they've been made by her people.

I never knew my grandparents on my father's side. My mother's parents, who died when I was a child, were the sort of pampered rich you see now only in pre–World War II Cary Grant movies. Grandmama refused to travel without her maid. Grandpapa carried a silver-headed cane and wore boutonnieres. They divided their time between homes in New York, Newport, and Palm Beach, migrating with the polo ponies, a full complement of baggage, and Grandmama's *fille de chambre* in tow.

Mother's family never forgave her for marrying mere money. Civilization as they knew it stopped west of the Hudson River, and my mother's decision to accompany my father back to Chicago was regarded as treason to their class. In my parents' defense, Grandmama and Grandpapa were insufferable snobs. I remember that they considered the Kennedys *nouveau riche*, and my grandmother never missed an opportunity to remind me that I was "just a little aristocrat." Even at the age of five, it seemed a bit absurd. Whoever heard of aristocrats in America?

My grandmother left her money to me, her only grandchild, when she died. It was meant as a final way of punishing my mother for her choice of husbands, but if Mother cared, she hid it very well. My inheritance is sizable enough to keep me comfortable for several lifetimes, freeing me from having to worry about how I'm going to finance the next century.

My childhood was happy. I had everything I needed and wanted, and I considered myself fortunate to have neither brothers nor sisters to compete with for my mother's affections.

I demonstrated a faculty for music at an early age. I used to pick out nursery rhyme melodies on the grand piano that sat in the corner of the drawing room, nearly hidden behind a forest of giant potted ferns. My first real musical accomplishment was to learn a simple Haydn melody by ear. I harmonized it, playing the third above the melody with my right forefinger.

When I was four, my mother retained Dr. Franz Terrapin, Chicago Symphony Orchestra pianist emeritus, as my piano instructor. From that young age on music became my entire life. While some boys become interested in sports or building models or other pursuits, I devoted all my attention and energy to the piano. To take a sheet of paper covered with cryptic dots and lines and convert it into something as lovely as a Bach prelude or Scarlatti sonata—it seemed like nothing short of magic to me.

I was no musical genius. At least that is what Dr. Terrapin told me with characteristic abruptness after six years of twice weekly private lessons. However, he said encouragingly, I was a good student with a promising career ahead of me if I continued to work hard. I would, of course, attend Juilliard or one of the better conservatories in Europe, Dr. Terrapin said; perhaps the school in Switzerland where he had trained as a student.

I assumed that was exactly what I would do.

One night at supper during my fourteenth year, my father announced I would leave for prep school at the end of the summer. As if this news were not shock enough, he went on to outline my entire future. After Exeter, I was to spend four years at the Ivy League college of my choice—as long as it was Harvard, Princeton, or Yale—and then proceed to law school. My father admired lawyers even more than developers, and he had decided that I was going to become one.

It's funny how you remember insignificant details from the crucial moments in your life; as my father delivered a lecture on the merits of the legal profession, I watched his gold collar clip move up and down each time his Adam's apple bobbed. The clip held his tie around his fleshy throat so tightly that I thought his head might explode like an overripe tomato.

I took the silence that followed the end of my father's lengthy declamation as an invitation to voice my views on the matter. "I have always thought I would continue to study piano," I said, conscious of how weak my voice sounded in our paneled dining room after my father's baritone.

"Continue taking piano lessons, if it suits you," Father said. "Just remember that music is a hobby, not a profession."

My mother, I was astounded to discover, had joined the enemy camp now laying siege to my future. "Being able to play the piano is all very good for making yourself popular at parties, my dear, but we do want you to make something of yourself."

Performing with The London Philharmonic or the Berlin Philharmonic Orchestra would not be making something of myself?

"Son," my father said carefully in a low voice, balancing his knife on the rim of his plate, "musicians are not even *in the game*."

I did not understand at this point in my life exactly what "game" it was that my father sometimes mentioned, but I gathered that it must have something to do with making money.

"There are only two kinds of people in the world, my boy: people who are players, and people who aren't players. If you want to be a player, you have to get in the game. With the way this country is going, being a lawyer is the best position you can to play. It's getting so that you can't even go to the bathroom anymore without a lawyer."

"Henry, please!" My mother turned to me and changed her frown into a smile. "No nice girl is going to want to marry somebody who is always getting on the plane to fly somewhere and play a concert," she said, taking a slightly different tack but one that was no more appealing to me at age fourteen. "You'll want to have a family someday."

All I could think of was the times Mother had sat for hours beside the piano, listening with a dreamy smile while I played Chopin, Beethoven, and our favorite, Mozart. It made me want to cry. These hours we shared had been the happiest part of my life. Now it was as if she were taking it all away.

"I want you to be a realist, not a dreamer, David. Listen to your father."

"Your mother is right: I'm right."

I looked at them and saw a seamless wall of stubbornness I could not hope to break through. The matter, was, therefore, settled.

Dr. Terrapin accepted the news with a curt nod. This, apparently, was a phenomenon he had witnessed before. He agreed to continue instructing me during my visits home. He died during my last year of prep school. I've always felt bad about him. Although he was much too well mannered to ever mention it, I knew I'd let him down.

I went off to Exeter, and Harvard after that, and the University of Chicago School of Law after that. I did it because it pleased my mother. I didn't want to disappoint her.

The ironic thing about my interest in music was that the more involved I became in the vocation my family had chosen for me, the more I depended upon music to keep me sane. By the time I started law school and plunged into its bottomless gray sea of drudgery, looking forward to a few hours at the piano was the only thing that kept me going. It became my escape, and without its release I think I would have gone mad with frustration and boredom.

I was living at home again, and when I returned from studying at the library late every night, I'd get something to eat and then go to the piano and play whatever came into my head for an hour or two. Studying law made me feel as if I were trapped inside someone else's existence; only when my fingers touched the cool ivory keys did I break free and take possession of my real life.

An acquaintance from law school heard me play one night at a party. We started talking about music, and before I knew it, he asked me to audition for his band, a jazz-rock ensemble he'd been playing with since his undergraduate days at Northwestern. I had little interest in popular music, but the idea of spending Friday and Saturday nights in nightclubs seemed like a good way to rebel against the monotony of my weekday life. The next day I bought a Yamaha electric baby grand piano and attended my first rehearsal with The Committee.

Going back and forth between the worlds of law and music during the next year was a schizophrenic existence, but I liked it. During the week I was a diligent law student in a blue Brooks Brothers blazer, bow tie, and horn-rimmed glasses. But when the weekend arrived, I changed into Levi's, a T-shirt, and sunglasses and retreated into a blue haze of cigarette smoke, Jack Daniels, and the comforts of more seductive and dangerous anesthetics.

I met my wife while playing with The Committee. It happened in a New Town nightclub named for its owner, Juanita Wong, a half–Puerto Rican and half-Chinese woman.

Like me, Clarice Luce was wealthy and bored, but she also was attracted to danger in a way that was completely foreign to me. She traveled in a fast crowd that included both millionaires' children and hardened felons. Not long before we met, her boyfriend was shot dead on a yacht off Barbados during a drug deal that went sour.

Clarice liked musicians. She'd come to Juanita Wong's with some people who had worked with The Blues Brothers. We were introduced during a break, and I offered to buy her breakfast. When I got to know Clarice better, I was amazed she'd ever agreed to go out with me a second time after learning I was a law student. I might have been playing in a band, but I was straitlaced compared to the sort of men Clarice kept company with. Later I decided there was something Freudian about her attraction to me. Her father is a lawyer, a partner in one of the top downtown firms.

It would be a lie to say I didn't love Clarice Luce. The way she betrayed me before it was over makes it hard to acknowledge, but I did love her. We were wrong for each other, like one of those doomed couples you see glaring at each other across the dinner table who make you wonder why they even bother trying. I knew this from the first, and I think she did, too, but it didn't seem to matter. In romance, opposites attract.

The early days were good for the two of us despite our differences in temperament. Clarice and I decided to get an apartment near Wong's, where The Committee had become the house band. I finished school and made the law review, a miracle considering the demands Clarice and the band made on my time.

After passing the bar exam, I spent some time drifting. One major part of my life—law school and my education in general—was ended. The part that came next—my career—had yet to begin, and I was in no hurry to see it start.

I had offers from several good firms. My parents were after me to accept a position, but pressure from them only made me more reluctant to decide. I bought an answering machine and used it to screen calls, deciding in advance not to return any from my parents for the time being.

Clarice's father had invited me to discuss a position in his law office, but I was reluctant to have that conversation. I suspected the offer was contingent upon my marrying Clarice.

Marriage was a touchy subject. Clarice seemed unwilling to make the commitment, complaining that marriage made people "middle-class." I suspected the truth was that she was not ready to take responsibility for herself as an adult. I didn't point that out to Clarice; she was not someone who could be easily made to recognize errors in her thinking.

And so I continued to sleep late and sit around the apartment, drinking Scotch, reading Barbara Pym novels, and playing the Steinway I'd bought myself as a graduation present. Weeknights I followed Clarice and her friends around to parties and the fashionable clubs they frequented, and we fortified ourselves with cocaine and alcohol and whatever else came along.

Time has a way of providing solutions, or at least eliminating options. After a month of vegetating, my future began to come into focus.

It was a Friday night. The band had finished its third set, and we were sitting at a round table that might have once been in a Victorian dining room, with carved claw feet at the bottom of a central pedestal and almost continuous cigarette burns running the circumference of its thickly varnished top.

The five of us were drinking Coronas and talking about taking a hiatus from playing. Tommy, the friend from school who had invited me to join The Committee, was about to start work for the district attorney; he proposed putting the band on inactive status for six months while he got his feet on the ground. I was going to need the extra time, too, he said, and I shrugged agreement.

We'd all known this moment was coming. We'd had our fun playing at being musicians. Now it was time to be adults. Reality time, Juanita used to call it when she told customers to hit the streets so that she could lock up at the end of the night.

The bass player, who sold drugs to supplement the money he made working in an auto supply store, produced a Tupperware container from the fishing tackle box where he kept his guitar cords and removed a rock of cocaine nearly the size of his fist.

Spirits in the room were elevated instantly.

"I'd better do it while I still can," Tommy joked. "Next week I'll be on the other side of the badge."

"That don't mean nothing in this town," Steve said, sliding the mirror to Tommy so that he could do the honors. We all laughed.

I'd just inhaled an enormous white line when there was a heavy knock on the door. The drugs were hastily hidden, and Juanita entered with an urbane black man wearing a beautifully tailored English suit. Peter Washington was a producer for Atlantic Records, who had come to Chicago looking for new talent. He thought The Committee had potential, with the right management. Were we interested in flying to Los Angeles? He would introduce us to some industry people and produce a demo tape. If everything went well, there would be a contract, a record, and a tour to promote it.

We stared at each other in stupid amazement. This was the sort of opportunity thousands of weekend bands like The Committee would have killed for.

The chance to live out every musician's rock and roll fantasy—and the cocaine draining down the back of my throat, numbing my jaw—made my heart race. I took a breath and grinned, then took a long pull on my beer, hoping the alcohol would slow my pulse.

I could hardly wait to tell Clarice. We would have to relocate to California, but she and Los Angeles were perfectly suited to each other. Mercedes Benz convertibles, hot tubs, movie stars, parties where hors d'oeuvres were offered by servants carrying mirrors—it seemed the perfect synthesis of everything she valued.

Clarice hated the idea.

"The band is fun now, but it would be pathetic for you to turn forty and still be dancing like a monkey in front of a crowd," she said, possessed for the moment by the spirit of common sense, which visited her but rarely. "You think you might become a star, and you might, but you also could end up playing in a Holiday Inn lounge somewhere in Nebraska."

That scenario seemed remote, thanks to my grandmother's trust fund, but the image of myself playing piano for three drunken salesmen in a motel bar was disturbing.

Clarice told me she wanted a husband, a home, and security. Had I been to see her father yet? Didn't I want to join one of the city's largest and most influential law offices?

I wouldn't have been more surprised if she'd said she wanted to move to Idaho and take up potato farming. It was so unlike Clarice to be responsible that I had no choice but to believe she actually meant it.

"When it really comes down to it," Clarice added, "what is of any less significance to the real world than a rock star?"

"A football star?"

"You understand my point. Pop music is so, so—" Clarice grasped for the right words, gesturing with her glass of Campari and soda. "It's so completely *on the surface*."

She was right. It was all on the surface.

I had expended a good deal of time training to become an attorney. It seemed senseless to turn my back on that just to have a chance—a *chance*—to become something as superficial, as inconsequential, as temporary, as a pop star. What had I been thinking? Tommy, who was no fool, had been the only member of the band to say he needed a day or two to think about Washington's offer. His instinctive caution served him well. His priorities were in order.

This is what I told myself, trying to talk myself out of doing what I wanted to do more than anything else in the world.

When I looked at Clarice, I could see that she loved me, and that she wanted to stay with me always—at least at that moment. With a woman as beautiful and spoiled as Clarice, that is as good as it gets.

I knew what I was going to do.

* * *

I joined Rappenoecker, Murdoch, and Luce and threw myself into the eighty-hour workweek of a young attorney at the launch of a brilliant career with a topflight law firm. Clarice and I were married and bought an elegant old town house near the lake. We hired the city's most expensive, most exclusive designer to remodel it from roof to basement.

The Committee never played again.

It took Clarice several months of matrimony to discover that she was less interested than she had imagined in settling down to a husband, a home, and security. She gradually went back to being a drug-addled former debutante, staying out until dawn most nights with her socialite friends, vacationing with them— *sans* husband—in Jamaica and Greece, interested in little else than the eternal pursuit of *la bonne vie*.

I went in to the office every day of the week, worked late, and went to bed early. Clarice and I seldom saw each other.

We tried hard to delude ourselves, but it was clear after less than a year that we had nothing in common but an address. I knew that at some point in the not-too-distant future we would have to face reality and declare our attempt at making a marriage a failure.

But now I must set this journal aside for tonight. I have ten minutes to walk to the café where I was last evening, just time to make my rendezvous.

I am meeting the same woman who tempted me so much last night, the one I said I would resist. She was so lovely and so lonely, and without Tatiana or Mozart in Paris, I am lonely, too.

Besides, women are my weakness.

As I guessed, Ariel Niccolini is Italian. She is from Florence, where she is the curator of one of the many museums in the city that was the birthplace of the Renaissance. I have never been there, but it sounds as if it would be wonderful to visit. Florence might even rival Paris for romantic atmosphere.

I acted the proper gentleman last night. I bought Ariel a drink, then put her in a taxi—alone—and sent her back to her hotel.

Tonight will be slightly different. It has been exactly two weeks since I have been with a woman, and I am feeling amorous. Besides, there is something else I need even more urgently.

Tonight, dear diary, I need blood.

# Chapter 3

**P**ARIS, JUNE 5, 1989—I am not alone.

I've known all along that there must be other vampires in Paris, but they have left me to myself. Until now.

Tonight I met one. I wish to God I hadn't.

I stumbled onto him moments after he'd butchered a young woman, apparently for no other reason than watching the life drain out of her—and enjoying my horrified reaction to his crime.

The killer's face, flushed with the fire of fresh blood, turned upward toward me from her neck with a leering smile, his incisors extended beneath his sardonically twisted upper lip.

There are no words to describe my reaction to seeing an innocent person so brutally slain. It is even more impossible to describe the repulsion and fear I felt at watching a killer take such fiendish joy in the murder and savage mutilation of his victim.

I was no accidental witness to this act. I was present because he wished me there. For some reason I do not understand, he wanted me to see him in his moment of predatory triumph.

I wish Mozart were here to tell me what to do.

Even the graveyards in Paris are steeped in history. Outside Montmartre Cemetery's gates, boys hawk maps to help tourists locate the graves of the famous, the *crème des morts* of French society.

Strolling among noble marble monuments, crumbling sepulchers, and more modest grave stones, you can pay calls to the final earthly residences of people who were once the toast of European culture: Dumas, Zola, Degas, Stendhal. There also are more modern tenants, including a few startling names. Jim Morrison, late of The Doors, is buried in Montmartre, his tomb-

stone defaced with the graffiti of the misguided who, like their
fallen idol, look upon death with romantic delusion.

I stopped at Morrison's grave tonight, pausing to watch the
breeze rustle the withered rose petals a lovesick fan earlier had
scattered across its surface. It made me think of Anna Montoya
and the lines of a poem she recited to me from memory once
after we'd made love:

> Darkling I listen; and for many a time
>   I have been half in love with easeful Death.
> Called him soft names in many a mused rhyme,
>   To take into the air my quiet breath;
> Now more than ever seems it rich to die . . .

I did not intend to visit Montmartre. I most certainly am not
"half in love with easeful Death"—not even in John Keats's
poetry.

Every two weeks the Hunger brings me and the Reaper so
close together that I can feel his icy breath upon my face. Only
the strongest expression of my will prevents me from helping
him harvest another life every time I feed.

I left my hotel tonight after sunset and walked aimlessly
through the streets, thinking it too early to stop at my favorite
café to drink a glass of wine and write in this journal. I did not
pay particular attention to where I was going, nor was I even
much aware of my surroundings. My mind was occupied with
remembering the night before, which I'd spent with the delicious Ariel Niccolini. I was crossing a street when the wind
stirred some leaves still remaining in the gutter from winter.
They swirled round me, and my eyes followed them as they
looped drunkenly down the street until they were captured at
last in the spike-topped iron fence that surrounds the Montmartre Cemetery.

The graveyard seemed so quiet, so peaceful, so filled with
interesting shapes and shadows, that I decided to enter.

I regretted my decision almost immediately. It is impossible
for the typical person to visit a cemetery without thinking about
his mortality. I am no different, even if my perspective on death
is anything but typical. The fear that haunts me is not that the
future will be too short, but that it will be too long—that I will
be forced to watch, from a discreet distance, as my loved ones
and family one by one grow old and die. My skin will not

wrinkle. My step will not slow. My eyes will not grow dim. At least not for many, many centuries.

It frightens me to think about the vast expanse of empty time ahead of me. Facing such a future without Tatiana is beyond considering. Mozart has promised to reunite us, but my slow walk through the graveyard reminded me that not every promise that is made is fulfilled.

The name on the marker at my feet belonged to someone I knew. He was a famous violinist. I had his records in my collection back in storage in the United States. I checked the date. Dead not ten years, but I was sure he was already forgotten by most of his former audience. What was it like, I wondered, to know the absolute peace of the grave? Or was it not peace at all but something else—perhaps even the Heaven or Hell talked about in Sunday school?

Only the dead know for certain.

I found myself morbidly wishing the resting souls could rise up from their coffins at moonrise and entertain me, over glasses of ghostly wine, with secrets only they could tell.

The last bit of day was dying on the horizon, a bloodred glow the night pressed small between the silhouettes of buildings outside the cemetery's distant walls. I walked on, pausing beneath a willow to read on a slab of weathered marble a name that belonged to a man whose birthday was the same as mine: May 13. Except the man whose name was carved in rock at my feet had been born exactly two centuries before me, in 1759.

Was there a body beneath this stone, quiet bones sleeping the sleep of ages, or merely an empty coffin, its assumed occupant a vampire like myself, whose "death" was contrived to hide the truth? If he were indeed like me, he might be alive and in Paris. He could even be on his way to Montmartre Cemetery at that moment to make sure the sexton had been taking proper care of his grave.

The thought gave me chills. I will never visit *my* grave when the time comes for me to have one.

I glanced over my shoulder, thinking for a moment that someone else might have come into the cemetery. I was wrong. I was alone, and all was quiet. The sounds of the city did not penetrate the graveyard.

I walked on, continuing my tour with a growing melancholy, kept company only by the bats that fluttered through the darkness like drunken sparrows.

The deepening twilight was no impediment to my wanderings. The rods and cones in a vampire's eyes are sensitive enough to see by the dimmest light. The stars alone throw enough illumination, although the colors become thin, like faded watercolors. Even absolute darkness provides little obstacle; in the complete absence of light, my other senses can detect the objects around me—especially living objects—with great accuracy.

Walking around a mausoleum, I again was overcome with the sensation that I was not alone, that I was being observed. A vampire seldom is caught unaware, so the sensation was doubly disagreeable.

I stopped and looked around carefully. I was unable to identify the source of my intuition, but I nevertheless *knew* I was not the only one in the cemetery—and that whoever else was there was somehow able to elude my detection.

In front of me was a white marble tomb of a bastardized design, something intended to strike a style someplace between the temple of Nike on the Acropolis and an Egyptian mortuary. The frieze depicted Osiris, the jackal-headed god of the dead, driving a chariot across a battlefield littered with bodies.

A shiver went up my back.

Someone *was* there! I was sure of it. It had to be another vampire, I thought, my pulse quickening.

The next perception struck me with the force of a sharp, unexpected slap: It was the scent of hot blood.

It did not frighten me, not at first. My initial reaction was to be both astonished and impressed. The other vampire had been able to conceal his presence from me, but even more surprising, he had masked the presence of the mortal, whom I should have easily detected even from outside the cemetery's walls. He had to be a powerful member of my race—more powerful than I, at least—to accomplish such a feat.

I broke into a smile. Perhaps it was Mozart!

I raised my head and breathed in deeply, gathering the sensations and vibrations that floated toward me on the warm night air. It was the blood spoor of a young Caucasian female. I judged her age to be twenty-one or twenty-two.

The blood scent suddenly became strong—much too strong. There was far too much blood in the air. The woman was hemorrhaging.

The first thing I saw as I rushed around the corner of the mausoleum to help—it seemed more hallucination than reality—was a disembodied head hovering in the shadow-filled graveyard. His face was thin and handsome, but contained an unmistakable decadence. The hair was black and longer than had been fashionable for more than a decade, at least in America. The moon was just breaking over the top of the trees, and his iridescent blue eyes gathered in the yellow light until they smouldered like two burning coals. His complexion, otherwise pale, was flushed over high, sharp cheekbones. I knew that he was experiencing the ferocious rush of energy that comes after gorging on blood.

The vampire grinned at me, his jugular teeth lewdly exposed, the incisors wet with the blood that trickled from the corner of his mouth. But his eyes—there was madness in his fiery eyes, and when I looked into them, I found myself too frightened to move a step closer.

On the ground was a beautiful young blonde, lying on her back. Her dress was torn away to expose her left breast and pushed up over her thighs. Her muscles were completely slack, both knees lying to the left, her head to the right. Her hands were on the ground at shoulder level, as if she had raised them to push away her attacker, but then suddenly lost the will to resist, letting them fall limply to the grass. Even from where I stood, I could see that there was no pulse in her pale and already cooling body.

She had been drained of blood.

Her neck had been savaged. Instead of the usual pinprick holes, there were two ragged gashes. Her killer must have locked onto her flesh and then, with his incisors halfway through her throat, thrashed her about in an orgasmic frenzy while her blood gushed into his mouth.

Ghastly. That is the only word I can think of to describe the scene: ghastly.

The vampire knelt beside the woman, lowered his face and licked the final bit of blood seeping from her torn neck. When he looked up at me again, he wore a smile that made me want to turn and run. Except I didn't run. I stood and returned his stare, feeling the hatred growing inside of me.

We belonged to the same race, but how different we were, this vampire and I. Hunger also moved me to feed on fresh human blood, but there was no similarity between the depraved scene in the graveyard and what had transpired between Ariel Niccolini and me the night before.

The killer wiped his mouth on the back of one sleeve as he stood. When he drew his arm away, I saw that his blood teeth had retracted into his upper gums, where they would remain hidden from mortal eyes.

"There is something about that last draft of blood taken even as the heart, beating slow and weak, makes its final pathetic flutter," he said. He spoke with the voice of an educated Englishman, someone who had been to Oxford and knew about cricket and punting on the Thames. The contrast between his cultured manner and the evidence of his bestial savagery lying dead at his feet only made him appear more monstrous to me.

"So sweet, so precious. Like the sound of breaking crystal." His grin became wider.

"You bastard," I said in a low, chill voice. "You can't get away with this."

The killer's smile disappeared. He took a single step forward.

"Do not cross me, Mr. Parker. Your powers are insignificant next to mine. I will crush you like a dung beetle."

He ground his heel into the loose gravel path. The sound seemed to go right through me.

The vampire raised his right hand, smiling at the shock he saw register in my face as I realized what he held. It was a scalpel, a razor-sharp tool that could save lives in the hand of a surgeon—or be put to unimaginably horrific uses in the hand of a psychopath.

He turned quickly back toward the girl, swooping over her, his hands moving with a fast, deliberate motion. He was standing again almost before I knew it, staring at me with the same mad grin as he stuffed something into the jacket of his coat without looking down at what he was doing.

I glanced at the girl and suppressed an urge to vomit. He had cut off her ear as a trophy.

And then, his mocking grin in place, he simply vanished.

I rushed to the girl, but I already knew there was nothing I could do. She was clinically dead. Even so, the vampire's enzymes did their fast work on her damaged tissue. The neck wounds were less ragged than they had been only a few moments before. Within fifteen minutes, the wound would be completely healed, leaving the coroner to puzzle over how a young woman in good health could die of massive blood loss with no identifiable trauma except the surgically precise severing of her ear.

I left the body and rushed to a public telephone several blocks from the cemetery, where I made an anonymous call to the police to tell them about a woman who needed help. I doubted the poor woman's body would be there when the gendarmes arrived. The Englishman wouldn't be foolish enough to leave behind that kind of evidence. Vampires never did.

After making the call, I fled the quarter, coming here to the bar in my hotel for whatever slight comfort a drink and familiar surroundings could provide me.

I have been caught in an embarrassing and humiliating trap. I cannot go to the police. The most basic law of vampirey is to do nothing that will alert mortals to the existence of our race. But even if I were bold—and careless—enough to go to the authorities, it would be worse than suicide. My experience as a lawyer tells me their most likely response to a story about a woman murdered and mutilated in Montmartre Cemetery would be to lock me in jail or a psychiatric hospital while they investigated. Either would prove fatal, come sunrise.

There is nothing I can do but remain in Paris, inconspicuous, and wait for Mozart. My future is completely dependent upon his taking me to Tatiana.

I am not, however, content to let the killer get away with his crime. For a vampire living in a mortal world, justice must necessarily come at the hands of another vampire. I may not be able to involve the police in finding him, but if *I* find him, I will do what I can to keep him from killing again.

And if I can't find him, then I will have to learn to live with the dreadful memory of this night. A few lines of Hazlitt come to me as I write about this sorry episode, a proverb that has the disarming charm of a nursery rhyme:

*For every evil under the sun,*
*There is a remedy or there is none;*
*If there be one, try to find it,*
*If there be none, never mind it.*

I am going to put this journal aside and telephone Ariel Niccolini.

It is late, and I told her I was busy this evening, but I do not want to spend tonight alone. I have no need for any more of her blood, but her affection and the warmth of her soft body will sooth the fever burning inside my head. Wrapped in Ariel's arms, my face buried in her perfumed hair—it is the only way I can think of to temporarily blot out the memory of the horror I was forced to witness tonight.

I know Tatiana would understand.

# Chapter 4

**P**ARIS, JUNE 6, 1989—I spent tonight walking the streets, searching for the fiend from Montmartre Cemetery.

No luck.

Why did I bother? I have no idea what I would have done if I'd found the English vampire. His powers eclipse mine, and my efforts most likely would have ended up as a case of the hunter being captured by the game. Still, I had to try. The recollection of what he did to that poor woman eats at me like a bitter cancer. His victim might just as easily have been Anna Montoya or Ariel Niccolini.

The Hunger will drive you to kill unless you master it. That much I understand. But why the mutilation? The memory of that scalpel flashing through the air sickens me more than almost anything else. His macabre handiwork seemed to indicate medical knowledge. Had he once been a doctor? That somehow fits: a cultured Englishman, trained as a healer, sunken to the most depraved and perverse acts of violence.

Yes, that is consistent with what I saw reflected in his mad eyes.

I am in my rooms, seated at a writing desk just inside the French doors, which are opened onto the balcony overlooking the Place Vendôme. If the vampire comes through the square while I am here, writing in this journal, I will see him. I should have written I *might* see him, because he certainly had no trouble escaping my notice in the graveyard last night. But unless he purposely conceals his presence, I ought to be able to perceive him once he enters the plaza. Now that I am looking for him, trying to *see* him, perhaps I will be able to penetrate the cloak of invisibility he wrapped around himself last night at Montmartre Cemetery. After all, I am a vampire the same as he, and any tricks he knows I should be able to penetrate.

Perhaps I will be able . . . I should be able . . .

The words I have written betray my true lack of confidence. Am I deluding myself?

I pour another glass of wine and hope this slim optimism is not completely without foundation. The truth is that the killer possesses abilities I scarcely understand and cannot imitate.

If only Mozart were here!

But Mozart is not here. I am on my own in Paris, partly to witness unspeakable things my mentor hinted I *must* see as part of my education as a vampire. And, I suspect, partly to test my strength, to determine whether I am worthy of the *Illuminati*. My soul has been thrust into the hellish fire of the events in this place so that the impurities might be hammered out. I hope that Mozart was correct in assuming me pure enough to withstand the purging I must now endure to survive.

It would be easy to fall back into my old despair tonight.

Knowing that he may be out there in the dark while I sit writing these helpless words, slowly killing another woman, reveling in her terror as if it were an exhilarating narcotic, makes me want to hide my face in my hands—or jump up and smash something.

> *Ah! I'm fed up:—But, dear Satan, a less fiery eye I beg you! And while awaiting a few small infamies in arrears, you who love the absence of the instructive or descriptive faculty in a writer, for you let me tear out these few, hideous pages from my notebook of one of the damned.*

I understand how Rimbaud felt in "Une Saison en Enfer." This visit to Paris has turned into my own "Season in Hell." Rimbaud's stream-of-consciousness poetry, written from the depths of a hallucinatory stupor brought on by drinking absinthe, is closer to my present state of mind than the pastoral verse of Wordsworth's that I was reading before I went for my walk in Montmartre Cemetery.

This bleak landscape is familiar territory to me. A year ago I was so depressed that I very nearly committed suicide. Maybe my grim mood is fitting, in a discomforting way, now that I have reached the point in this journal where I must begin relating the darkest part of my life as a mortal—a period I would not have survived if it hadn't been for Tatiana Nicolaievna Romanov.

There is only another hour until dawn, when I must close the shutters, draw tight the draperies, and retire. I pick up my Chicago story where I left off. . . .

Clarice and I honeymooned in Hawaii, Hong Kong, and London. When we returned to Chicago, I stocked my wardrobe with white button-down shirts, red suspenders, yellow bow ties, and a dozen blue pin-striped business suits. I went to work in my father-in-law's office, attacking my career with the sort of fanaticism usually associated with religious hysteria. During that first year, I put in sixteen to eighteen hours a day at the office, brought home work to read in bed, was at my desk on Saturday and Sunday and every holiday except Christmas.

It was not that I had discovered I liked being an attorney. Quite the contrary. I loathed the profession. However, I found that if I worked very hard, I did not have time to think about how much I disliked my life.

I was born with music inside of me, and it lived there still, no matter what I did to kill it. But the never-ending song had become a dull fever, a delirium that required every bit of my strength to keep down. I had made my choice. The law was my master, and I its slave. I sat at my desk reading statutes, like a Buddhist monk reciting sutras to quiet and unify his mind. It turned me into a good attorney and helped me make partner after only one year, but it was a cold, unfulfilling existence.

I had no special talent for the law, but I did apply myself. Mediocrity is as common among attorneys as it is in any profession, and the person who tries hardest is the person who succeeds.

I worked to become the best. I learned the law inside out and also made a detailed study of logic and debate, the artistic elements of the profession. I spent so much time getting to understand Greek and Roman rhetoric that, like a jazz player effortlessly improvising on a melody, I could stand up in court and riff a pari, a fortiori, a contrario, interrogatio, and gradatio arguments. Much of what I did in front of the juries was legalistic sleight of hand, but my job as an attorney was to represent my client, not the truth. I won cases, and that was what mattered.

That is what you tell yourself when you're a lawyer.

Sitting at a conference table in my law office, I saw the worst of mankind, an endless parade of liars, thieves, cheats, adulterers, and miscreants. The first casualty in the battle for the young lawyer's soul is the optimistic fiction that people are fundamentally good and that, given the choice, will do what is right. After a month in practice, I began to suspect people are essentially self-serving, scheming, duplicitous toads. After a year I was certain of it.

I began to have a drink to help myself relax at night. One Scotch gradually became four or five. I celebrated my second anniversary with the firm by renewing my dalliance with cocaine, a treat I had put aside as too risky for a respectable young attorney, my wife's continuing enthusiasm for illicit substances notwithstanding. There was always cocaine around the house, and I simply decided after a few drinks one night when I was home alone, why the hell not?

There was nothing unique about what, over the course of the next few years, became a serious addiction to alcohol and cocaine. It's an old story, especially among members of my profession. I drank to counteract my growing depression, and took cocaine to counteract the alcohol and give my mood a brief, chemically induced boost. The more controlled my behavior appeared during the day, the deeper I sank at night. One or two people at the office might have noticed a change in my behavior, but if they did, they kept quiet about it. And Clarice didn't guess anything was wrong. Now I was just like all her friends.

Toward the end of my mortal life, three in the morning often would find me sitting at the piano, a vial of cocaine, a glass of Scotch, and a nickel-plated Colt 9mm semiautomatic side by side on the Steinway. I'd do some coke, take a swallow of Scotch, and play a little Mozart.

Mozart kept me alive through that benighted period, breathing enough life into my parched soul to keep me going. And when not even Mozart could lift me up, I would sit, pale and shaking, and stare at the gun.

Marriage did little to change Clarice, who continued to invest her time and interest in what passed for a sophisticated social life among Chicago's idle young rich. Her days—which is to say her nights—were dedicated to parties where people talked about their clothes, their yachts, their lovers, and their homes in Palm Beach, but most of all about themselves.

The fact that I was constantly tied up with my practice did

not seem to bother Clarice much. I think she saw it as a convenience. We grew apart quickly. We lived in the same town house, but we saw each other infrequently, usually for a few minutes around midnight. That was about the time I dragged in from the office, and Clarice dropped in at home long enough to change into something suitable for dancing.

Our late-night meetings grew increasingly strange as time passed. One night I came through the front door and was startled to find a woman in bra and panties in the living room, leaning over a mirror with a razor blade and a rolled up hundred-dollar bill. The stranger was in fact my wife, whom I had not seen in more than a week.

During the brief matrimonial interruptions in our separate lives, we would have the sort of disjointed, non sequitur–laden conversations strangers have in bars and airports, neither party certain he understands or is making himself understood. Often we would forsake our lame attempts at communication and simply make love—on the bed, the piano, the kitchen table, wherever we happened to be when we stumbled into each other. I was more than a little concerned with our increasing estrangement, yet I confess, it did add something to our lovemaking, turning it illicit in a way that was exciting. It was as if I were seducing a stranger rather than my wife.

Looking back, I realize I knew about her affairs long before I admitted them to myself. I shut my eyes to many things in those days, careful not to confront unpleasant realities. I had built an elaborate house of cards to live in, and I did not want to be the one to bring it falling down around me. But sometimes things collapse of their own accord.

I had promised, in front of our friends and families, to be faithful to Clarice. And faithful I was, even as our love cooled and our paths diverged. Everyone lives his life according to certain rules, and mine left no room for adultery. (How that word has lost its sting!) I no sooner would have shoplifted a pack of chewing gum from the grocery store than had an affair with another woman while I was married.

Clarice, however, was like a cat. She had no loyalty and went, if it suited her whim, to whomever would stroke her. Her promiscuity reduced sex to the level of something commonplace, like a handshake or a pat on the back that could be dispensed to friends and acquaintances without a moment's thought.

Clarice's affair—which I eventually discovered was only the

latest of many—was a double betrayal. She had taken as her lover Michael Byron, a partner at my law firm, who sometimes took us sailing on Lake Michigan in his Choy yacht. She couldn't have hurt me any worse than by sleeping with a friend *and* a law partner, although I think the significance of that sort of action was beyond her ability to comprehend.

My first idea that something was going on between Clarice and Byron came at a cocktail party. I went into the kitchen for ice and found them there, alone, talking. Clarice was leaning against the counter by the Cuisinart, staring up at Byron earnestly, as though she could barely wait for the next syllable to fall from his lips. When they saw me watching them from the doorway, they looked at each other in a way that implied an understanding that went beyond the bounds of ordinary friendship.

I told myself I was being paranoid.

A few weeks later a client told me she had seen Clarice exiting the lobby of a hotel in the middle of the afternoon. The client, one of my wife's cattier friends, was not someone I was inclined to believe, especially since she had let it be known that she was available if I were interested. Still, I might have shrugged it off as coincidence if Byron hadn't bragged to me about taking his conquests there for afternoon trysts when he told me how he'd seduced his dentist's wife. Byron had not been in the office on the afternoon in question. He said he'd taken the day off to work on his boat.

My secretary ran into Clarice and Byron entering an Italian restaurant known for its intimate atmosphere. When I asked Clarice about it, she laughed and said there was nothing wrong with meeting a friend for lunch.

Clarice dragged me to a reception downtown one Saturday afternoon, and afterward we went into Lord & Taylor so that I could buy a new raincoat. As the clerk filled out the charge slip, Clarice admired a Hermès scarf. It would make a nice birthday present for Byron, she said.

I asked rather pointedly how she knew his birthday.

Clarice shrugged and walked away.

That night I freebased so much cocaine that even Clarice warned me to stop. We had an argument about it, and she ended up storming out of the house, screaming obscenities at me over her shoulder, slamming the door behind her. I went into my study, put a Wagner opera in the CD player and drank the better part of a fifth of Scotch trying to slow my pounding heart.

At dawn I was still sitting there, my red eyes staring out the window at the sky as it turned light. Clarice had stayed out all night, but she often did that, even when we hadn't had a fight. I finally dragged myself upstairs, thankful that it was Sunday and I didn't have to go into the office. I threw my exhausted body onto the bed and sometime in the middle of the morning fell into a dreamless sleep.

Opera was one of the few musical indulgences I still allowed myself while I was married to Clarice. The more unhappy I was, the more I enjoyed opera. The music and high drama always left me feeling cleansed and rejuvenated. For a day or two after each performance I would be almost at peace with myself.

Clarice hated opera—she disliked any kind of serious music, but she especially disliked opera—and I was in the habit of going alone.

I invented a game to play while sitting alone in my box waiting for the overture. It involved studying people in the audience and inventing little stories about them, mental sketches of the lives I imagined they led. An innocent enough diversion, though my characterizations tended to eviscerate rather than elevate their subjects.

This man is a wealthy stock broker, I would say to myself. He comes from a family of Iowa farmers. His business skills and intelligence are only average, but he's a wizard on the golf course, the man everybody wants as a golf partner. Instead of turning pro, he golfed his way into a vice presidency at his brokerage, shrewdly marrying the president's daughter to consolidate his position. He forces himself to come to the opera—which he enjoys about as much as he does swapping an Izod polo shirt for a tuxedo—because he thinks it enhances his social standing, about which he is insecure.

The night I finally admitted to myself the truth about Clarice and Byron, I had gone to the opera to hear *Don Giovanni*. While the orchestra was tuning up, I began playing my game with a lovely young woman seated below me in the orchestra section. I was able to study her closely and without, I thought, being noticed.

She wore almost no makeup, and her skin was a pure, silky white, except for the natural blush in her cheeks and her cherry-red lips. Her eyebrows were delicate convex lines, her eyelashes long and dark. She wore a pearl-colored gown, and her jet-black hair was pulled up on her head in a style reminiscent of the fashion at the turn of the century. She reminded me of one of the nineteenth-century European bluebloods whose portraits hang above drawing room fireplaces in English country houses.

But there was something different, something special, about this woman that I could sense even from my seat high above her. The antique impression she created went beyond her hair and classic beauty. Perhaps it was the way she held her head, for she had a noble, almost regal, air of self-possession. She truly seemed to belong to another time. Perhaps a sorcerer had cast a spell over the bewitched-looking woman in Whistler's *Symphony in White* that allowed her to step down out of the painting and leave the museum to spend an evening at the opera.

The lights dimmed for a moment, signaling the members of the audience to find their seats for the performance. As the room dropped into darkness, the woman in white—turned in her seat as if looking for a friend she expected to arrive late—relaxed her carefully composed expression. When the lights came back up, her green eyes seemed fixed upon some secret hurt far removed from the murmuring crowd in the concert hall.

In that brief unguarded moment when she let her pain show, her eyes expressed a sadness that seemed to extend forever.

*Don Giovanni* is half comedy, half tragedy—in other words, a perfect representation of real life. Consumed with insatiable lust, Don Giovanni, as Don Juan is known in Italian, tries to bed every woman he encounters, even attempting to seduce a peasant bride at her wedding. He makes love to the commander of Seville's daughter, then kills the father in a duel. When he sees a statue of the slain commander, he jeeringly invites it to come down off its pedestal and accompany him to a feast. The stone man comes to life and drags the unrepentant Don Giovanni down to Hell.

As Mozart's opera began, my own dark thoughts closed in on me. I forgot the woman in white and sank deeper into a funk. I had brought a glass vial of cocaine with me, but soon it was empty, leaving me even more depressed as I crashed from the high. Instead of following the opera, my mind was filled with profane visions of Clarice and Byron in each other's arms. Some of the unpleasant truths I had worked so hard to ignore refused to be ignored any longer. I had been such a perfect ass, I thought, watching the figures move back and forth on the stage.

Elvira had just convinced Zerlina, the peasant bride, that Don Giovanni was a seducer.

*"Ah! fuggi il traditore!"*

It was all crystal clear.

*Traditore!*

Betrayed by my wife.

*Traditore!*

Betrayed by my friend and partner.

*Traditore!*

And worst of all, betrayed by myself.

*Traditore! Traditore!*

When the crowd rose to give the performers a thundering ovation, I alone sat trembling in my seat, deaf to everything except the single word echoing again and again inside my head.

*Traditore!*

I stared at the railing at the front of my box, trying to erase from my mind the image of Clarice and Byron. It was impossible. They were probably together at that very moment!

I felt my hands grip the railing. My sweat-soaked palms slipped against the wood.

I was a lawyer, and I hated it. My passion for music had been relegated to the status of a hobby, which my friends and family condescended to indulge as an eccentricity.

I pulled myself forward with my arms. I felt myself rise from the seat.

Why struggle against an indifferent fate? I had everything—wealth, success, status, a beautiful wife—and I was miserable. And, the worst, my wife was unfaithful, betraying me with a friend and colleague.

*Traditore!*

Several thousand people stood around me, cheering their hearts out, but I was utterly alone.

All I had to do was lean a little farther forward. The curtains on either side of the box would keep me hidden until it was too late.

I bent slightly at the waist. My box was directly above the aisle. There was no reason at all not to do it.

Just a little farther.

All faces were turned toward the stage, where the performers were assembling to take triumphant bows.

I'd reached the balance point. Another inch was all it would take.

The woman in white turned sharply and fixed me with her piercing green eyes.

I froze. My motive was obvious—I was halfway over the railing—and I expected her to scream. Instead she continued to look up at me, the expression on her face completely neutral, except for her eyes.

Her eyes. They were the saddest eyes I had ever seen, and yet they were filled with an uncanny understanding, as if they shared my pain and understood it perfectly.

I looked into her eyes, and something I found there seemed to reach out across the distance and touch me gently on the forehead.

I fell backward into my seat. When I recovered sufficiently to look down again from my box, the woman in white was gone.

# Chapter 5

**P**ARIS, JUNE 7, 1989—I returned to Montmartre Cemetery tonight shortly after sunset.

From my work as an attorney I know it is true that criminals sometimes return to the scene of the crime. But witnesses and victims also may find themselves compelled to go back to the place where violence has occurred, blindly seeking to exorcise the haunting memories. This I know firsthand.

There was no sign of the English vampire in the graveyard, although the psychic residue from the killing lingered in the air like the smell of burned plastic. Only the faintest traces of forensic evidence remained, dim patterns on the ground, imperceptible to all but a vampire's keen senses. I leaned against the mausoleum and studied the single strand of the victim's golden hair lost in a patch of moonlit grass a dozen feet away.

It made me wish I had returned to Montmartre sooner, when I might have been able to pick up the killer's trail and follow him back to his lair. But then what? Perhaps my real concern should be his finding me, not my finding him.

There has been nothing in the papers the past two days about a woman being killed in Montmartre Cemetery. I'm not surprised. I'm sure he disposed of the body in a fashion calculated to escape police attention. The poor girl's family will never know what became of her.

I can't stop wondering why he forced me to watch him commit a murder. Was it an insane and meaningless gesture or the opening gambit in an evil game I do not wish to play?

I am sitting on my balcony, writing by the light of the street lamps in the square below, wishing I knew if what I saw in Montmartre Cemetery two nights ago has some terrible significance or means nothing at all. Perhaps it was only a flash of the random savagery that occurs in the world. Even mortals are capable of such depraved acts. It is easy to list only a few of countless murderers whose sadistic brutality has shocked the public—Charlie Manson, the Nightstalker, Jack the Ripper, John Wayne Gacy.

None of them were vampires.

At least none that I know.

I ended up the night in my favorite café, wanting to escape my worries for an hour or two.

When the waiter came to the table for my order, I asked for a bottle of Beaujolais. It's a simple wine, but simple sensations are all I can tolerate. Vampires are sensitive creatures, whether the stimulation is taste, sight, sound, smell, or touch. That is why, in folklore, garlic is said to ward off vampires. To the younger, hypersensitive members of my race, a strong aroma such as garlic is as overpowering as tear gas.

I'm building myself up a little at a time, and I think I'll eventually be able to enjoy the rich foods and drinks I loved as a mortal, but for now, complex flavors send me into sensory overload.

There's no embarrassment in ordering a simple wine, even in France. Yet for the waiter, to whom I was simply another ignorant American tourist, my order proved to be an invitation for insult, a red flag waved in front of a Gallic bull.

"Beaujolais? *Très bien.*" He sneered.

I glared at him narrowly and felt the dull ache of my blood teeth pushing against my upper gums.

The waiter lost his voice and stood pale and trembling, unable to command his feet to back away. Like all mortals, his mind was quite open to suggestion. I sent an image flashing through his head to show him what could happen to someone who was rude to the wrong individual. Horror spread across his face.

I instantly regretted my behavior. I was abusing my power. This was something the killer from Montmartre Cemetery might do. Mozart would have been appalled.

*"Excusez-moi,"* I said, glancing at my watch as I stood quickly. I gathered up my notebook and pen and explained that I had forgotten an appointment. I requested that he kindly consider my order canceled.

I walked toward the street.

The waiter spun on his heels and practically ran inside the café.

I shall not want to return there again.

The sky is growing light in the east. I am tired emotionally as well as physically. The past few nights have been difficult. I must regain my inner composure. As Tatiana told me before we parted, I must be brave.

I wish I'd agreed to meet Ariel Niccolini for dinner this evening. It would have been a more pleasant way to spend the evening than I found, left to my own devices. Unfortunately the beautiful Italian girl is falling in love. I must not allow that to happen. A serious affair between a mortal and a vampire would be doomed from the start, and I would never consider taking the responsibility of transforming her. Even if it weren't for Tatiana, it wouldn't be fair to Ariel. She has her own life to live, and nothing about her indicates that she is marked for vampirey. And as I'm only beginning to understand, this is a hard life—much harder than I ever suspected.

Besides, there *is* Tatiana.

Not an hour that goes by that I don't feel a stab of anguish from being separated from my Russian princess. Being apart from her these long months has been the worst part of the ordeal I've had to endure in becoming a vampire. But soon we will be together again. Mozart will meet me here in Paris and take me to her, and then not even our race's dark faction will be able to come between us.

These friendships I form with mortal women are matters of convenience, temporary liaisons made necessary by the peculiar *needs* I must satisfy every two weeks. I seldom see a woman more than once or twice. Occasionally, however, I meet someone who is special, a woman I could love if it weren't for Tatiana. First there was Anna Montoya, the poetess, and now, Ariel Niccolini.

No, I must not allow Ariel to fall in love with me.

But perhaps it would do no harm to see her just once more before she returns to Florence. . . .

I wonder what she's doing now. I close my eyes and see her in bed in her hotel room, wearing a black silk nightgown, oblivious of the night around her as she slumbers, a half smile on her face, dreaming of her vampire lover.

More tomorrow.

# Chapter 6

**P**ARIS, JUNE 8, 1989—I spent the evening with Ariel Niccolini. It was her final night in Paris, and I made reservations for us at an excellent restaurant. When I met her outside the hotel, however, she held herself tight against me and said the only place she wanted to go was back up to her room.

Some women are slow to ignite with passion, like damp matches reluctant to catch fire. For others lovemaking comes on like a spark struck into gasoline—the fierce combustion a virtual explosion of heat and flame.

Ariel Niccolini is this latter type of lover. Once kindled, her rapture burns with searing intensity until we both collapse, drenched with sweat and deliciously exhausted. Sex is not merely important to Ariel, the way it is with most people. With Ariel I think it is *the* force that moves her. Although there is nothing cheap or lewd about her, she seems to have been created expressly for love. The earthy Italian is a virtuoso in the way she uses her body to bring pleasure to herself and her lover, as much an artist in bed as I am at the keyboard of a piano. And yet she has a wonderful mind, filled with arcane knowledge about the Renaissance, on which she wrote her doctoral dissertation at the University of Rome. In sum she is an ideal lover—at least to someone with my tastes.

After three hours of nonstop pleasure we dozed for a brief time in each other's arms. When we awoke, I called room service and ordered champagne—an old habit of mine—and we propped ourselves up on the big feather pillows, sipping Dom Perignon and smiling at each other in the darkness.

*"Credo che tiamo,"* Ariel whispered in my ear, then kissed it.

"What does that mean, lover?"

Ariel nuzzled her body close against mine.

"It means I believe I love you," she said. Then, in a more cautious voice, she added, "I hope it does not upset you to hear me say that."

I stroked her face. "No. It makes me feel good, here." I touched my heart.

"I realize we've only known each other a short time, my darling, and that we both have separate lives to live in different parts of the world. But still . . ."

She kissed me on the lips this time.

"Do not reach too far for the words. Words are unimportant," I said. "It is feelings that matter, and I know exactly how you feel, because I share your emotion perfectly."

Ariel put her head on my shoulder and sighed, partly out of contentment, partly out of sadness. She knew that her life in Florence and mine in Chicago (I had told her I still lived there) created obvious complications.

"You are going back to Italy tomorrow. Give it time. See how you feel in a week or two or even three. Time will help us understand our true emotions." I put down my glass and took her in my arms. "All we know for sure tonight is this fire that burns inside of us whenever we are together. How can either of us be rational when the only thing we can think about is making love?"

She returned my kiss hotly, and we resumed where we had left off.

I feel a little guilty for having let things progress this far with Ariel. However, she is an intelligent, educated woman, and the decision to have this affair was hers as much as mine, even if I did need her blood. I'm sure that once she returns to Florence and her career at the museum, she will begin to realize what we shared was a magical interlude in our separate lives, a sweet memory that practicality will prevent from becoming anything more.

It would have been easy to use my hypnotic powers again on Ariel before I left her, to *make* her forget me the way I had made her forget the climactic part of our lovemaking the first night we spent together, when the Hunger was so strong in me. But I see no need to be heavy-handed. Besides, I think it would be wrong. Let her keep her memories, and me mine. Love is sometimes bittersweet; who am I to try to rearrange another person's heart?

There were tears in Ariel's eyes when I kissed her good-bye an hour ago. I may have had them in my own eyes, too.

I shall miss Ariel Niccolini. I could have just as easily said to her: *"Credo che tiamo."*

*To resume my earlier story:*

I went home after *Don Giovanni* to confront Clarice, but she was not there.

I sat up all night waiting, tortured with images of her and Michael Byron together, cradling their adultery between them like two pagans squatting before a golden idol. She still wasn't home when I had to leave for the office the next morning. I instructed the housekeeper to tell Clarice I urgently needed to speak with her and headed out the door exhausted and emotionally spent, hefting a briefcase filled with unfinished work, like a convict dragging a ball and chain.

I called home in midafternoon after court. Clarice had gone to aerobics, but the housekeeper told me I could meet my wife for supper at our favorite restaurant at eight if I needed to see her before the weekend. Rosa was to relay my answer back to Clarice, who would in turn call her girlfriend, Mignon—if it were *absolutely* necessary—and cancel their plans to attend the opening of an avant-garde pottery show at an Old Town gallery. Even with the message delivered in Rosa's fractured English, it was evident that meeting me for supper was an annoyance my wife preferred to avoid.

The last thing I wanted to do was run into Michael Byron, so I stayed shut up in my office for the rest of the day, spending the time alternately pacing and napping on the couch. At seven-thirty I went straight to the restaurant from work without stopping home to change; my blue pin-stripe suit would show Clarice I meant business.

It was eight o'clock when I turned the BMW over to the attendant and stepped into Bernard's. Even with my life in a tailspin, I'd be damned if I was going to be late. That was one character flaw I would not stoop to share with Clarice.

"Good evening, Monsieur Parker," Maurice said. "Your table is ready." The maître d's real name was Ernie; his French accent was good enough to pass in Chicago.

"I don't suppose my wife has arrived yet?"

"No, *monsieur*, I regret to say the lovely Madame Parker is not here yet. You would prefer to wait in the lounge?"

"You read my mind, Maurice."

Clarice arrived forty-five minutes late, which wasn't bad for Clarice. I'd managed to lubricate myself pretty well by then, and when my wife met me at the bar, she gave me a glare that could have withered a steel rod. Clarice is better than anyone I know at looking sober when she isn't, and she seems to believe that makes her morally superior to those of us who begin to become loose around the seams after a half dozen doubles.

We trailed Maurice into the dining room and sank into a white leather Jean Harlow banquette.

Bernard's balanced on the precarious line separating high luxury from utter tastelessness. Crystal chandeliers hung from the ceiling, and the waiters wore black satin knee breeches and powdered wigs. The coffee boys were made up like raj elephant attendants, and when they served you (a hint of perspiration evident around the edge of their plumed turbans), they looked at you with eyes that said they hoped your BMW broke down in their neighborhood on a night they weren't working at Bernard's.

Though the prices at Bernard's were ridiculously high, the food was excellent. So was the service. You could hardly finish a course without somebody appearing at your elbow to take away the plate. A wave of the hand would bring a functionary hurrying over with a white telephone so that you could call your stock broker or cocaine dealer to arrange a transaction over supper.

As Clarice and I stared at each other across the table, frowning with mutual distaste, I was struck by what perfect cynosures of yuppiedom we were. We were young, rich, good-looking, expensively dressed—and hedonistic, self-centered, and curiously unfulfilled. The other people in the restaurant were exactly like us, or pretended to be, and outside Bernard's was an entire city filled with young professionals who would have happily sold their souls to be like us.

I picked up my tumbler of Scotch and drained it in a single gulp.

The vigilant cocktail waitress had her eyes on me. I barely had to nod.

"So." Clarice slouched against her seat.

I looked at my hands. The speech I'd prepared seemed absurd now that the time had come to deliver it. I also knew I was about two drinks too drunk to trust my performance to strike the proper tone of righteous indignation.

Clarice jabbed a cigarette into her mouth and gazed at me through the blue jet of flame that spewed up from her gold butane lighter. I hated her smoking, which probably explained why she always made lighting up seem like a gesture of open defiance.

The cocktail waitress delivered a fresh Scotch, but I took a sip of lemon water instead. A water boy materialized before I put the glass down to refill my tumbler. Yes, the most annoying thing about Bernard's was that the service was too damned good. That's the one thing they lack in many of the best restaurants in America—the sensitivity to know when to leave you alone.

"This isn't easy for me to say," I began as the water boy retreated after bowing absurdly, "so I'm just going to say it."

It was difficult to get my consonants out without slurring. I concentrated hard on enunciation.

"I have reason to suspect you're having an affair with Michael Byron."

Clarice laughed. I suppose I should have expected her to laugh, but it caught me off guard. I lost my temper, something I seldom do—and the one thing I had wanted to avoid during our discussion that night.

"This is hardly a laughing matter. Are you sleeping with Byron? I'll settle for a simple yes or no."

Clarice pouted and twisted her cigarette in the ashtray.

I knew it. She didn't even have the decency to make a token denial.

"How long has this been going on?"

"Months," she finally said in a weary voice, as if the subject were extremely boring. "I'm surprised that you're throwing it up in my face now. It's so unlike you."

"What is that supposed to mean?"

"You've always been so agreeable, David. It's been one of the few good things about being married to you. I don't apologize for being selfish. It's who I am. You know that I always get what I want. I always have. But you've never challenged me before."

"I sure as hell am challenging you now. We're married. You can't simply go to bed with another man whenever the whim strikes you. I won't stand for it."

"Won't stand for it? Who do you think you are?"

"Your husband!"

"Listen, David, it's too late for you to make these demands." There could have been a hint of regret in the way she said it, but I doubt it. "You might have gotten me to settle down if you'd tried when we were first married, but you were more interested in spending twenty-five hours a day at the office. I got bored, David. You know how easily I get bored."

"How can you expect to be anything but bored? You don't do a thing except go to parties and fly back and forth from the islands, perfecting your tan. Why don't you get yourself a life instead of acting like a spoiled little whore?"

"Get a life? Like yours?" She shook her head, as if she were astonished. "You really don't understand what a drag you are, do you, David? Ever since you quit the band, you've been an incredible nothing. That's why I've been sleeping with Michael Byron. He's got a boat. He plays polo. He's exciting."

It was my turn to be astonished. "Since I quit the band? You were the one who wanted me to stop playing with The Committee and buckle down in your father's law office."

"I guess I was wrong," Clarice said, and shrugged. "I never knew being married to an attorney could be so dull, David. That's the only word for it: dull. I don't know how my mother stands it."

"Being an alcoholic helps."

"Say rude things about my mother if that makes you feel any better. She knows you don't care for her."

"But why Byron?"

"Why not Byron?"

"He's from the firm. My firm. Your father's firm. Do you mean to make asses out of us all?"

"I don't understand what this has to do with Daddy."

And the sad thing was that she didn't. She had no morals. *Right* and *wrong* were only words to Clarice.

"Do you want to marry him?"

"Marry him?" She burst into a fit of juvenile giggling that made me want to slap her.

"You've got to make up your mind. You can't have us both."

"Why can't I?" she demanded, sitting up straight. "You're too old-fashioned. All my married friends have lovers."

"Your tramp friends are hardly relevant to this discussion. Having an affair is bad enough, but having one with my supposed friend and a law partner is bloody well intolerable."

"I don't have to keep sleeping with Michael Byron, if that's why you're so upset. But I have no plans to go through life having sex with only my husband, like some middle-class suburban housewife who has two-point-three kids at home in a split-level ranch and a minivan parked in the garage. It would be like keeping my left hand tied behind my back all the time.''

Her eyes became slits, and I knew she was about to go on the offensive. I braced myself. She could be brutal when she wanted.

''You realize that Michael isn't the first man I've had an affair with since we've been married.''

''Not the first?''

For a moment I thought I was actually going to hit her. Instead I stared down at the salmon-colored tablecloth. I couldn't bring myself to ask the obvious question. I didn't want to know who else my wife had been taking to bed.

''The only real issue is whether you can loosen up enough to give me the freedom I need to breathe. I need my own space, David. You've got too many hang-ups. You should be in therapy. My psychiatrist has helped me tremendously.''

''Don't make me vomit.''

''All right then, why don't we just forget it?'' Her voice was genuinely angry. ''All you really care about is your career and the fucking opera. I'd say that you have the life-style of a seventy-year-old man, if you weren't so strung out on cocaine. God, David, look at yourself. You're a mess. You're the one who needs to get a life!''

Clarice raised her eyes to the chandelier as if appealing to an invisible god perched there. ''I just want to have fun. What's wrong with that?''

''That's a pathetic ambition,'' I said without much conviction. I already knew I was defeated, that I was fighting for something I didn't really want. Did I care if Clarice left me for Michael Byron? Forced by the situation to be brutally honest with myself, I had to admit the answer was no.

''You're the one who's pathetic, David. Your life is pathetic and boring, and I want out of it.''

''You don't mean that,'' I said. I still don't know why. Force of habit, I suppose. You have something for so long that you automatically hold on to it. Even if you no longer want it. Even if it hurts you.

Clarice stood up with her purse.

''I'll show you exactly how much I mean it,'' she snapped.

I was unable to speak. I could not force my eyes to follow her. I stared at a hairline crease in the white leather banquette and listened to the click of Clarice's three-hundred-dollar spike heels as she stalked across the terrazzo floor in the lobby and out of my life.

* * *

I retired to the lounge without eating. I was so depressed that even breathing seemed to require an enormous effort. There was only one thing that could make me feel better.

"Sammy! Phone, please."

Mark answered on about the sixteenth ring. Come on up, he said. His man had just come by, and it was party time. I ordered a double Remy Martin, drank it, ordered another, and threw it down my throat before hitting the road.

The visit to Mark's lasted only long enough to score. I drove over to the lake, parked and did up the better part of a gram. The buzz didn't make me hurt any less emotionally, but it fixed it so I didn't care.

I climbed out and leaned against the fender. The sky had clouded over. Beyond the last line of lights out on Navy Pier was only blackness, an expansive, unfathomable nothingness.

My nose was running. I sniffed and felt another cocaine rush sweep through my body.

I got back into the car and unlocked the glove box. The black Python 357 magnum was there, just where it was supposed to be. I put two big spoonfuls of cocaine into my left nostril—my right nostril was hopelessly sealed. I could have put the gun against my head and blown my brains out right there. I was so numb that it would have been easy.

But I had a different idea. Another two spoons of coke into my head while I thought about it, and I decided it wasn't just a good idea, it was a *great* idea.

I jammed a Doors tape into the deck, cranked the volume up full on "Roadhouse," slipped the car into gear, and proceeded to break traffic laws. The green light flashed yellow. I downshifted and punched the gas pedal to the floor, feeling the acceleration push me back in my seat as the light turned red and I rocketed through the intersection.

I knew exactly what Jim Morrison was singing about. No matter who you were or how well you were set up, the future was uncertain and the end was always near.

The BMW shot down Lake Shore Drive, past the Prudential Building, and on toward the Chicago Yacht Club, where I expected to find my rival in the master cabin of his sailboat. I left the glove box open so that I could glance over every few moments and see the magnum nestled there like a snake ready to strike.

Ahead of me was the Field Museum, its imitation Greek columns awash in floodlights. Something in the structure's stodgy, borrowed authority mesmerized me long enough to miss the harbor turnoff.

A fluttering movement caught my eye.

A woman was running barefoot through the grass past Buckingham Fountain, her long black hair and white chiffon gown billowing behind as gracefully as the boughs of a willow bending in the breeze. It was a picture of surreal beauty: the woman, the elegance of her motion, the fountain—like an advertisement for an expensive perfume in *Vanity Fair*.

She looked in my direction, and the jolt of recognition was like a 220-volt line laid against the base of my spine. It was the woman I'd seen at the opera the night before, the beautiful woman in white with tragic eyes. Her face held the same fathomless melancholy but also a sense of kinship, as if we had been lovers a long, long time ago.

Who *was* this woman?

She beckoned to me with a languid wave as she continued to run, the motion as fluid as in a ballet.

I jerked the BMW into the right lane. If I hadn't been watching the woman in white, and if I hadn't had so much to drink, I might have seen that the lane was occupied by a police car stopped at the red light at the intersection of Balbo and Lake Shore Drive. I remember feeling a spike of terrible surprise for the fraction of a second it took for my car to slam into the rear of the other vehicle. And in that brief flash of awareness I felt a cry of sympathetic anguish in my mind that told me the woman in white shared my frightened realization that I might be about to be killed.

The police said I was unconscious for less than a minute, but when I lifted my bleeding head off the steering wheel, the woman in white was nowhere to be seen.

# Chapter 7

**P**ARIS, JUNE 9, 1989—He's back.

I've sensed his presence off and on during the past few nights, but it was so faint that I wondered if it were real or imagined.

Tonight it was different.

I didn't see him, but he was there, stalking me, testing me, toying with me.

And, worst of all, tempting me.

I'd gone to the Louvre after closing.

When Mozart and I parted company, he instructed me to develop my powers. Although I make it a habit to respect mortals' rights while conducting my ordinary nightly business, I regularly practice the talents vampirey has given me, honing my skills at stealth, mind control, and thought reading. I still am only a novice, and I know next to nothing compared with Mozart and Tatiana—and the English vampire who has dogged me here in Paris—yet bit by bit, I am learning.

If I understood how to perform even a fraction of the incredible things Mozart has shown me . . .

My greed for power is a weakness I need to guard against. The vampire in Montmartre Cemetery, and again tonight at the Louvre, seems intent upon impressing me with his capacious abilities. For whatever strange reason, he wants me to envy him, to wish I could be like him.

That must never be.

While I was still in America, I got in the bad habit of passing the long nights in places that kept hours better suited to mortals than vampires. Museums, galleries, libraries—though they locked their doors when night fell, these were the scenes of my haunts during the lonely time between sunset and dawn.

The alarms and guards made my visits interesting at first, but as I became more polished, these anti-intrusion measures posed little challenge.

(I can float into a locked room as quietly as a shadow and stand behind you while you read this without your knowing it.)

Tonight, as I dressed and waited for the sun to drop below the horizon, I decided to continue exploring the city, to see what I could of Paris before I have to leave.

My visit to the Louvre started just after midnight, when the guards take their midshift meal break. I began in a gallery filled with magnificent Impressionist art, walking slowly, admiring the Manets, the Van Goghs, the Lautrecs.

I came to a Degas painting of a ballet rehearsal and paused to admire it. The exhausted dancer in the painting reminded me of Tatiana, my own ballerina. Degas's model even had green eyes, like hers. It wouldn't be long now, I reminded myself, looking forward to Bayreuth. Mozart could arrive at any time to take me there to be reunited with the woman I love. I smiled to myself. He might even be waiting at my hotel when I returned.

I tilted my head to listen.

A guard making unscheduled rounds, I thought, straining to hear.

No sound came back to me.

I reached out fully with all my senses, opening them to detect the nearly imperceptible flow of energy that emanates from all living beings.

There was nothing. And yet, I knew I had sensed *something*.

I turned and peered into the next exhibition hall. From where I was, I could see through five identical galleries. It was like standing with my back to a mirror while looking into another mirror in front of me, the same images reflecting themselves over and over again, each time a little smaller, a little farther away.

I dilated my pupils and emptied my mind, making myself receptive to the slightest vibration.

Someone was definitely there. Holding my breath and slowing my heart until it almost stopped, I was able to feel it—a presence so faint that it was weaker than the guards in their faraway lunchroom drinking coffee, weaker than even the two lovers strolling down the opposite side of the street outside the Louvre. And yet it was also very near.

It had to be another vampire, I knew, feeling a mixture of excitement and fear.

The presence suddenly grew alarmingly strong. The instantaneous surge of energy shocked my system so badly that I stumbled backward, my hands over my ears in the futile attempt to block out the pounding beat of the vampire's heart, thundering like an enormous drum inside my head.

And then, just as quickly, the presence was gone.

"Who is there?" I asked in a voice that was low but still loud enough to carry through the deserted galleries. There was no answer, but I again sensed the dim presence somewhere in the distance. It was weak now and flickered like a candle sputtering in the wind.

Doing everything I could to mask my own presence, I glided silently into the next gallery. No one was there.

The presence remained the same distance from me.

I paused, then slipped into the next room. It, too, was empty. The presence remained unchanged: neither stronger nor weaker, neither nearer nor farther. The other vampire was moving in perfect concert with me, maintaining a constant distance between us.

While I stood in the darkness considering what to do, my awareness of the museum dimmed, and I found myself—or rather the seven-year-old memory of myself—in a swimming pool filled with shouting, splashing children. I could not swim well enough to keep my head above water, but I had mistakenly jumped into deep water. I was conscious of that much before the memory took over completely, as real as if I had been projected back in time to relive the dreadful experience:

*I scream for help when I get my head far enough out of the water, but my voice will not carry above the others. I struggle to get to the side of the pool, but it is hopeless. As my head sinks beneath the surface, I realize I am going to drown. I claw at the water. I can feel the air with my hands. Then—miraculously!— my head is free. I cough and gulp in air at the same time. I see the lifeguard across the pool, sitting on his white scaffold, casually scanning the water. I scream for help again, but he doesn't notice. I slip back under the water. When I break the surface after what seems like an eternity, the only thing I can think of is that you're supposed to come up three times before you drown.*

*I scream with every ounce of strength I have. The lifeguard's expression changes slightly. Thank God! He sits forward and studies the swimmers. His eyes do not find me. Water spills into my mouth. The chlorine burns my eyes. I slip below the surface a third and final time. I know I am going to die. . . .*

The hallucination ended as abruptly as it began. I found myself back where I had been before blacking out, looking into the next exhibition hall—a room filled with medieval paintings of saints being tortured. Although I was drenched with perspiration, my throat was too dry to allow me to swallow.

The other vampire had reached into my mind and triggered the recollection of one of the most terrifying—and helpless— moments in my life, a childhood memory I had not thought of for many years.

I took a step backward.

Laughter rumbled toward me through the darkness.

It was *him*.

I was terrified of the other vampire, but at the same time I envied his superior powers. To be able to reach into my brain and pluck out the script of a memory that I had buried so deeply I would have had difficulty recalling it—was there no limit to what he could do?

Still, a more recent memory I could not forget—the murder and mutilation of the woman in the graveyard—kept me from experiencing too much awe for my nameless adversary.

A second hallucination flashed through my mind. This time, it was me, not the woman, lying at the vampire's feet in Montmartre Cemetery. I was forced to watch in mute horror as the fiend bent near with his scalpel—and cut off my ear!

With an enormous effort I shook the vision out of my head, grabbing at my ear to reassure myself it was still there. It was, but the pain!

There was no place to run in the Louvre at twelve-thirty in the morning, and no one to cry to for help against a supernatural monster. I was at the killer's mercy, and I knew him to be merciless.

"I am not afraid of you," I said in a loud voice, trying to make him believe I meant it. "Come out where I can see you, and tell me what you want."

"Join us," said the disembodied upper-class English voice, echoing through the darkened rooms.

"Who is 'us'?"

There was no answer, only the queasy feeling that I was very near to a source of pure evil.

"Who is 'us'?" I repeated.

There still was no answer. I sensed the other presence receding until, after only a few moments, it was gone. I did not move for a long time, no longer confident in my ability to judge whether he really had left or was only concealing himself.

I cautiously walked through the gallery and looked around, but the only faces I saw were the ones that hung from the walls.

The killer had vanished.

# Chapter 8

**P**ARIS, JUNE 10, 1989—I could not sleep, so I spent the afternoon sitting up, with the shutters closed tight, calling every hotel in the telephone directory, asking for Sebastian Wolf—the name Mozart uses when he travels. Nobody had a Mr. Wolf registered, and I was unable to find a hotel holding reservations for a man with that name. It didn't surprise me. A three-hundred-year-old vampire ought to know at least one person in Paris who would give him lodging. For all I knew, he owned a house here.

If it weren't for the fact that Mozart was going to take me to Tatiana and the *Illuminati*, I doubt anything could make me stay in Paris another night. Not with the English vampire stalking me.

I wish I could describe what I sensed lurking in the darkened museum. It was hatred, violence, jealousy, and pride, as well as the complete absence of mercy you would see in the face of a predatory insect, a creature driven exclusively by the need to hunt and kill. In short, *evil*.

The noisy café where I am sitting now creates the reassuring illusion that I am surrounded by friends. I know why some animals travel in packs. There is comfort in the herd, especially with a carnivorous enemy stalking unseen through the surrounding shadows.

I'll spend the time it takes to drink this carafe of wine retreating into the past. My mortal life was painful to live, but recalling it in this journal provides the only refuge available to me. . . .

After I smashed up the BMW, I spent two hours sitting in the shift commander's office, trying to work myself out of the jam. I was spared the embarrassment of being shown a cell, the benefit of being a member of a wealthy family and an influential law firm.

By the time the captain put me into a taxi for home, I was four thousand dollars poorer and owed a favor to an alderman I was certain would one day ask me to commit a felony, or at least a gross breach of professional ethics. Still, it was better than being led before a night court judge in handcuffs to enter pleas on charges of driving while intoxicated, carrying an unregistered, concealed weapon, and possessing illegal drugs The pendulum had started to swing back, and the courts were beginning to be unusually harsh with drug offenders, especially when cocaine was involved.

I tallied the score during the cab ride. I'd gotten myself into the sort of mess that only a complete fool gets into. I feloniously compounded my errors by bribing my way out of jail. The police had kept my gun and what was left of my cocaine. The BMW was a total loss. I'd have to buy a new car and pay for the damage to the police cruiser out of my own pocket, since an insurance claim would raise too many ugly questions. In the coming days, the two policemen in the car I'd hit undoubtedly would develop whiplash. That would be another thousand dollars apiece at the going rate. My own body felt like one massive bruise, although the doctor in the emergency room had said nothing was broken.

And as long as I was adding up disasters, I could hardly forget to count the fact that my wife had left me.

The cab stopped at a light. A street person came up to my window and tapped on it, asking for spare change.

"Get outta here, ya friggin' scuz bag," the cabbie shouted.

The derelict didn't seem to hear. He stood at my window until the light changed. He jumped back as we pulled away, the cab's tires screeching.

As absurd as it may seem, my mind kept going back to the woman in white I'd seen again just before the accident. I couldn't get her out of my mind. Every time I closed my bloodshot eyes, I saw her running through the park in her long white dress.

I scanned the sidewalks for a graceful woman who looked as if she had just stepped out of the nineteenth century. She was not among the people hurrying toward work, as fresh and eager as I was pale and wasted after a night of humiliation and disgrace.

Perhaps if I returned that night to the fountain . . .

It was dark when I awoke.

I pulled on a robe and went downstairs into the library to

outline my divorce papers on a yellow legal pad. I wanted to follow through before I lost my resolve.

The air in the town house was stale, so I threw open the living room windows and built a roaring blaze against the night chill that seemed to penetrate my body and settle into my heart. When I was finished making notes on the dissolution of my marriage, I sat in front of the fireplace with a book about the Civil War, not seeing the words, not turning the pages.

I wondered about the woman in white. Where was she? Would I ever see her again? Knowing that I almost certainly wouldn't plunged me into the same despair I'd suffered the previous evening, only this time it was not Clarice I was depressed about but a woman I'd never even met.

I had to be losing my mind. I was obsessed with a woman I'd *never even met*! Clarice had been right. I was strung out on cocaine.

Cocaine. Just thinking about it filled me with the craving. I rummaged through my desk in the study and found part of a gram folded up in a square of paper Mark had cut from the pages of *Penthouse* magazine. I carefully unfolded the packet. There was about a quarter gram of the white powder nestled in a crease that ran directly through a magnificently perfect breast.

My hands shook so badly that I spilled the contents all over the desk. Cursing myself, I licked the desk, then got on my hands and knees. I was about to put my tongue against the carpet when the extent of my degradation hit me, along with the rush of the cocaine I'd already ingested.

I *was* strung out.

"Fuck this!" I said angrily, and got up, grinding the white powder deep into the carpet with my foot. The time had come to stop. My life still had not yet truly hit bottom, but I decided I was finished with cocaine.

And I meant it. I never touched it again.

I thought Clarice might change her mind and come home, but she didn't. I didn't feel a sense of loss, only a peculiar emptiness, as if I had just realized that there was nothing inside of me. I was like one of T. S. Eliot's hollow men:

> *Those who have crossed*
> *With direct eyes, to death's other Kingdom*
> *Remember us—if at all—not as lost*

*Violent souls, but only*
*As the hollow men*
*The stuffed men.*

When I went upstairs, I discovered Clarice had been by to pick up her jewelry, confirmation that she had no plans to return. Her clothing was still there, but that didn't mean anything. She would simply use this as an excuse to buy a new wardrobe.

Our bed looked especially inhospitable, so I got a jacket and spent the rest of the night walking the streets, searching for the woman in white whom I had no real hope of finding.

The first streaks of dawn were showing in the sky when I returned home. Exhausted, I threw myself onto the couch without getting undressed and fell into a dead sleep.

My first appointment Monday was with LuAnn Swiskowski. Mrs. Swiskowski's husband, Sam, was a self-made millionaire who owned a chain of appliance stores in the suburbs. He had bowlegs and a fondness for cowboy boots and plaid polyester sports coats. Sam Swiskowski became famous throughout Chicagoland when he cast himself in a series of television commercials that were so obnoxious that they actually had a certain charm.

Mrs. Swiskowski was a few years shy of thirty, which made her at least twenty years younger than her husband. She was a tall redhead with a lusty laugh that always sounded as if it should be coming from behind a bedroom door. She was a little overweight but in a way that made her voluptuous rather than plump. She was like Ariel Niccolini in that she seemed to have been created to fulfill one particular human urge, a fact that must have figured prominently in her bedding and wedding the Maytag magnate.

Mrs. Swiskowski had been in to see me two months earlier to inquire about how she might expect to fare in a divorce. She had been careless enough to sign a prenuptial agreement, and after studying the document, which had been drawn up by an attorney who knew what he was doing, I had told her I regarded her prospects as slim.

Seeing her again made me think about my own wife. Even though Clarice had her own money, I knew that, as a matter of principle, she would try to soak me when we got into court. I had to hire a good divorce lawyer for myself, I thought, somebody who knew how to fight dirty. She would.

Mrs. Swiskowski was dressed in a black business suit. That surprised me. Her tastes ran toward low-cut red dresses with slits and silk stockings with seams that climbed to a garter belt—at least in my imagination.

"Mr. Parker!" she said in a choked voice and came toward me. Something told me she was about to throw herself into my arms. When I didn't move out of the way, that's exactly what she did.

"It's Sam," she said as I steered her into a chair. I sat behind the relative safety of my desk.

"You've had a disagreement?"

"You haven't heard?"

"No."

"Life can be cruel, can't it?"

I was hardly in a position to disagree, but I still didn't know what she was getting at.

"He was walking along the sidewalk yesterday, minding his own business, when it happened. God, I'm going to miss him."

"Sam is . . . ?"

"Dead."

"I'm sorry to hear that. His heart?"

"An air conditioner."

"I beg your pardon?"

"An air conditioner." She dabbed her eyes with a lace handkerchief. "An air conditioner fell out of a window and hit him on the head."

She leaned forward, rested a gloved hand on my desk, and dropped her voice to a confiding whisper. "It will be a closed-casket funeral."

"That's simply awful. You have my deepest sympathy."

"I know I talked to you before about leaving Sam. But every couple has their fights, don't they?"

I nodded, restraining the impulse to correct her bad grammar.

"I never could have left him. The talk about divorce was just my way of getting his attention. I was jealous. He spent all his time at work. I felt neglected. You understand, don't you?"

I winced. "Men who are successful in their careers sometimes have trouble making time for their families," I said, my voice sounding a little defensive. "In a way their work becomes their family."

"Sam and I would have worked things out."

"I'm sure you would have," I said, but I was being kind rather than honest.

"You don't have to tell anybody I was thinking about divorcing him, do you? I would hate to make it any more difficult for his family at this time."

I looked at her closely. She was up to something.

"Conversations between client and attorney are privileged, Mrs. Swiskowski. I would get into a good deal of trouble if I mentioned anything about what we have discussed in private. Of course there are exceptions even to confidentiality. If I had direct knowledge of a crime that had been committed, I would have an obligation . . ."

I let my voice trail off. She let that pass and steered the conversation toward safer territory.

"Sam had a lot of life left in him, and now he's gone. I should sue the hell out of the people who own the building." She sighed dramatically. "But that wouldn't bring him back."

My eyes narrowed. "Then you do not wish to pursue civil action against the responsible parties?"

"What's the point? Sam left me all the money I need. Would suing bring him back? Certainly you can appreciate the fact that I don't want to prolong my grief by dragging this out in court."

"I understand perfectly," I said.

And I did, which was why I hated being a lawyer. People like LuAnn Swiskowski *never* have all the money they need. If she didn't want to sue, it was because she had something to hide. I had no proof, of course, but I would have bet she had gotten a lover or a hired thug to drop that air conditioner on her husband's head. The surprising thing was that they'd managed to pull it off. It was elaborate, as murder schemes go, which made it stupid: The more complicated the crime, the greater the likelihood you'll get caught. Murder by air conditioner. Christ! But the more I turned it over in my mind, the more I liked it. The police would have a hard time imagining a murder conspiracy in which the weapon was a one-hundred-and-fifty-pound appliance. Maybe it wasn't so stupid after all.

"I'd like you to represent me during probate, of course. I could use Sam's attorneys, but I'd just as soon have my own. I know I can trust you, David."

I smiled thinly.

To hell with it, I thought. The police could either figure it out or not. It wasn't my problem. And if they guessed the truth, they could arrest LuAnn Swiskowski or shake her down for money and whatever other favors they could get out of her.

Divorce, probate, or murder trial—what did it matter to a lawyer, as long as his fee was paid up front?

"Now that my husband has passed on, there is the matter of his will," she said, watching me carefully.

"Yes, Mrs. Swiskowski," I said and settled back in my leather chair. "There is the matter of your late husband's will."

I was getting ready to leave for home when my father-in-law summoned me into his office.

He met me at the door and ushered me to a wing chair with the elaborate display of courtliness he reserved for people he was about to chop off at the knees. When it came to dealing with associates in everyday situations, Frederick Luce was as curt and rude as only the wealthy and powerful can be. That is, unless he was going to drop a ton of bricks on them. When that was the case, he became the very model of gentlemanly comportment.

Would I care for a Scotch?

"Yes, thanks." A bad sign. He never offered younger partners drinks in his private office. I wondered whether I was going to be eviscerated because of his daughter, or because of my encounter with the police.

A cigar to go with my Scotch?

"No, thank you." Now I knew it was going to be bad, maybe fatal.

"I wanted to have a little chat with you, son."

I tried to look politely interested. He had even called me "son"! I braced myself for the worst.

"I understand you want to divorce my daughter."

I was actually relieved that it was that, rather than the more embarrassing matter.

"I'd like to explain. . . ."

"My dear boy," he interrupted, "you needn't explain a thing to me. You know that I believe in intellectual honesty, so let's not equivocate. It's a hard thing to admit about one's daughter, but the fact is that Clarice is nothing but a—" he stopped himself—"is not a very loyal person, if you get my meaning."

"Yes, sir, I do."

Frederick Luce puffed thoughtfully on his cigar.

"I should have put my foot down with Clarice when she was younger, but I wanted her to have every advantage. Things didn't work out as I planned. She was a selfish, spoiled child, and now she's a selfish, spoiled adult. I blame myself."

I kept my mouth shut and my head motionless, but it required an almost superhuman effort to stop myself from agreeing with Old Lucifer, as the younger lawyers in the firm called him.

"My daughter has everything and appreciates nothing. Worse, she has no moral center. It's not an endearing trait in women, you know, and it becomes even less so as they grow older. Without moral glue, women fly apart when their looks start to go. Take her aunt Helen: the Whore of Palm Springs, they call her. *Non compos mentis*. We'll have to put her away someday if she doesn't screw herself into an early grave first."

The old man used his forefinger to smooth his white moustache, first on the right side, then on the left.

"So, you know about Clarice and—"

"I'm not blind. Goddamn Michael Byron!" Old Lucifer's face turned bright red, and he shook the fist holding his cigar so hard that an ash went sailing into one of the potted palms. "He thinks he's getting away with something now, but when Clarice is finished with him, I'll have his ass."

Good, I thought, but why wait until Clarice lost interest? No wonder she had grown up to be such a bitch!

Old Lucifer put his cigar in the ashtray and folded his hands in front of him, the perfectly manicured fingers interlaced. Even though they belonged to an old man, the hands looked capable of accomplishing whatever job needed to be done. They could sign a document, pat a shoulder, put a knife between somebody's shoulder blades—coldly, efficiently, without interference from anything as silly as a conscience.

"Be that as it may, Clarice is still my daughter. That is why I have to ask you to resign your position with the firm."

I nearly dropped my glass.

"I want you to know that it's nothing personal, but it might prove uncomfortable to have you stay on."

"I am perfectly capable of controlling my emotions, sir," I said, struggling to do just that. "And as for Clarice, she's not the type of woman to make scenes."

Oh, yes she is, I said to myself. I could tell from Old Lucifer's expression that he was thinking the same thing.

"I'm sorry, David, but my mind's made up. I like you as a person, and you're a damn fine attorney, but it's been decided. Everybody will be happier in the long run if you make a clean break. You've done excellent work, and you'll have no trouble getting started somewhere else. Turn this problem into an opportunity. As my father, Judge Luce, used to say, 'If somebody gives you a lemon, make lemonade!' I'll help you find a position with another top firm. A good friend on La Salle Street is looking for someone young and aggressive. When those boys put together a merger, the billings run into the millions.''

A wistful expression crept over Old Lucifer's face.

"If I were a young man again, I'd go into arbitrage. That's where the real money is today.''

I was too much in shock to speak.

"I'll help you set up your own firm, if you prefer. Be your own boss. I'd expect you to take your clients with you, of course. And we have more work around here than we can handle; I'd be happy to refer the overflow to someone as capable as you. You'd have a fine practice established in no time and would continue making the kind of money it takes to keep yourself supplied with BMWs and magnum revolvers.''

I took a big pull on my Scotch to mask my reaction. So he *did* know! What he was really saying was that he had just cause to give me the boot, even if it weren't for Clarice—who I was certain put him up to this out of sheer malice. My accident made it impossible to fight being squeezed out. Not unless I wanted to risk disbarment and worse. I started to open my mouth, but he spoke first.

"Yes, I heard about your problem with the police,'' he said without a hint of rebuke in his voice. "I know this is a difficult period in your life. I won't censure you for losing control temporarily. However, I do advise you to be a bit more careful in the future, especially about drugs. I have nothing against drugs per se. Coffee is a drug. Scotch is a drug.'' He snapped a fingernail against his crystal tumbler, so that it chimed. "But they're *legal* drugs. A little illegal fun is one thing, but too much of it can ruin a lawyer's career, even in Chicago. Besides, this crack-cocaine thing has made everybody hysterical. It reminds me of the fifties, when everybody was terrified that there was a communist hiding under their beds. Today, it's a crack dealer instead of a red.''

"Is the accident the reason you're asking me to leave the firm?''

"Good Lord, no.'' Old Lucifer leaned toward me and lowered his voice, not because he feared being overheard but out of years of habitual secretiveness. "There isn't a partner in the firm who doesn't have a skeleton or two in his closet. Believe me, David, you're a Boy Scout next to most of us.''

\* \* \*

I went back to my office, shut and locked the door, took off my jacket, and lay down in the middle of the floor.

A tremendous weariness had taken possession of my body. I felt as though my muscles and tendons were unhooked from my skeleton, making it impossible for me to support myself against the pull of gravity. I pressed my spine against the carpet and closed my eyes.

My depression seemed without limit. I was a ship sinking into icy depths. I was going where there was no light, no sound, no warmth, nothing but a crushing pressure that squeezes the life out of everything and makes it silent, cold, and dead.

# Chapter 9

**P**ARIS, JUNE 12, 1989—I awoke tonight after dreaming of Ariel Niccolini.

I miss her more than I have missed any mortal woman since Anna Montoya. I wonder if Ariel is sitting in her apartment in Florence at this exact moment thinking about me the same way I am thinking about her.

It would give me much pleasure to send her a large bouquet of roses to demonstrate the affection I feel for her and to thank her for the pleasure she has given me during what has turned into a difficult time of my life.

Would flowers create the wrong impression? My intention is to express gratitude, not encouragement.

I think I'm going to do it.

I'm sitting at a table outside a Latin Quarter café.

I did not make an entry in this journal yesterday. There was nothing to report. I remained locked in my rooms, obsessed with bitter thoughts, and did not go out.

Anger gradually took the place of the fear I felt for the English vampire after the episode in the Louvre. Neither emotion is healthy. It got to the point last night that I just wanted to *hit* something. That was when I realized I had to get a grip on myself. If I lose control of my emotions and let the dark side take hold, I surely will be lost.

I've decided to adopt a fatalistic attitude. I have no control over whether I'll see the killer again, so I might as well stop brooding about him until he makes his next move.

The idea that my one apparent option is to leave Paris, hoping the killer will remain behind, makes me wonder if that is his real motive—to force me out of the city. I do not know why he would want to do that, unless he intends to prevent me from meeting Mozart and going to join Tatiana and the *Illuminati*.

If that is his game, he has already lost. I will not run.

This possible scenario creates an entirely new set of questions I find deeply disturbing. Why would the vampire want to keep me from meeting Mozart? Or is it Tatiana or the *Illuminati* he wants to keep me apart from?

There is, I fear, at least the possibility that the killer is not a lone madman, as I first assumed. He may be working with Cesare Borgia, leader of the faction of vampires that Mozart said symbolizes everything evil and corrupt about our race. If the killer is hounding me through the streets of Paris on Borgia's orders, I am in very grave danger indeed.

I remind myself that I do not know this to be the case. I must remain fatalistic—and realistic. It is not time to panic, which, in any event, could only lead to disaster. I pray Mozart will be here soon. He will know what to do.

I admit I envy the English vampire's powers. However, I will not allow my envy to lead me to fall under his influence. Sad as it is to say, I am fortunate he has expressed such sadism in his activities here. If he had used subtler means, he might have succeeded in disarming my apprehensions long enough for me to be drawn into his spell.

Intuition tells me he wants to get me under his influence or, barring that, to frighten me away from Paris before Mozart arrives.

To *hell* with him!

Neither part of his scheme is going to work.

I am drinking chilled German wine in honor of Mozart. Perhaps it will help bring him to me sooner.

The lights on this side of the street are dim, and I can look up and see the moon and the stars keeping it company in the spring sky.

*The Moon and all her starry fays.*

The line of Keats's—Anna Montoya's favorite poet—comes back to me as I sit here, studying the heavens. The Parisian moon, a thumbnail of yellow against the blue-black sky, provides me with the inspiration for a haunting melody. I'm suddenly anxious to finish scribbling tonight's entry in this journal so that I can hurry back to my suite and work out the sonata taking shape in my head.

But there's no real rush. I can take my time. I will remember each note as it came to me, for the vampire's memory is prodigious.

I take a sip of wine and look around me.

No amount of menace from my English enemy could prevent me from knowing in my heart that this is *the* place I was meant to be tonight. Everywhere I look I see the ordinary miracles of everyday life. The beautiful hair that belongs to the woman at the next table. The shutters hanging askew on the old building across the street, making it resemble a cubist painting. The light glimmering in the glass of golden wine beside this leather-bound journal. Even the pale hand that holds my gold-and-onyx fountain pen.

*When I have fears that I may cease to be*
*Before my pen has glean'd my teeming brain . . .*

That's Keats, too.

I came so close to death before Tatiana Nicolaievna Romanov pulled me back from its shadowy grasp.

I think of the other vampire, the killer with the scalpel whom I have not seen for two nights. He's still out there somewhere, perhaps secretly watching as I write these words.

Perhaps I am close to death still.

My God, it's good to be alive!

When I got home after being sacked from my law firm, I filled a water tumbler with Glenlivet, pushed Wagner's *Götterdämmerung* into the CD player, and sat in front of the fireplace staring at the cold ashes of an earlier night's fire, wallowing in depression and self-pity.

My life was a comedy. No, worse, a farce.

There was only one solution.

Horns swelled louder as "Twilight of the Gods" boomed out of the Bose speakers, building toward the Wagnerian crescendo that I had heard a thousand times but that always seemed to take me by surprise.

The only things left to decide were how to do it and where.

I've heard that men favor a bullet in the skull and consequently enjoy a higher success rate than women, who prefer pills. I saw merit in the gentler method, but the last thing I wanted was to have paramedics drag me up from the depths of a barbiturate stupor just so I could spend the next decade as a brain-damaged vegetable in a nursing home.

A gun seemed logical and efficient, if messy.

I'd have to do it someplace else. I loved the old town house too much to damage its charm for future owners with my suicide.

I picked up the telephone and made a reservation at the Wharton, a hotel built in the twenties that redevelopers recently had restored to its original ersatz-art deco splendor. In an overnight bag I packed a bottle of one-hundred-year-old brandy, an L. L. Bean nylon knapsack and a pearl-handled Smith & Wesson .38 that belonged to Clarice. Killing myself with Clarice's revolver would make an appropriate statement, I thought stupidly.

I intended to be neat about it. I'd pull the knapsack over my head, inhaling that nylon smell that always made me think of camping in the Rockies during college days, lean over the bathtub, put the barrel in my mouth and pull the trigger. At least I'd spare some sorry wretch the trouble of scraping my brains off the walls.

I would leave no suicide note. I didn't want to risk writing a farewell message that might sound pathetic and self-serving despite my best efforts to strike a note of high tragedy, of love scorned, of musical genius thrown away for nothing.

My room at the Wharton was on the fourteenth floor, which was really the thirteenth, but the owners had adjusted the numbering to minimize problems with superstitious guests. It made no difference to me. I didn't believe in superstitions. In fact, at that point in my life, I didn't believe in anything.

The first thing I did was tear the cellophane off a water glass and fill it with brandy. I pulled a chair to the window and sat staring down at the people and traffic on Michigan Avenue. I did not move except to bring the glass to my lips or refill it. My breathing slowed, and my thoughts seemed to slow, too.

Afternoon turned into night. I sat and examined my life in agonizing detail, identifying each mistake, each misstep. There was hardly a wrong turn I had not taken, I thought.

It was nearly midnight when I went to the dresser like a sleepwalker and picked up the revolver. I opened the carriage. There were six bullets in the gun, six shiny silver circles snugly fitted into holes machined in the steel cylinder.

I looked toward the bathroom door, a rectangle of deeper darkness in the darkened room.

I needed one more drink. The brandy bottle had been empty for an hour. I'd nursed it dry without managing to get very drunk.

I looked at the gun again. I had to have another drink first. I put the gun back on the dresser and unchained the door.

The lounge was empty except for the bartender. I bought a double whiskey and took it to the white baby grand piano. The bartender watched me closely for a moment, then turned his back to me and went back to washing glasses.

An echo of music to carry in my head to my death, I thought. But what should it be? I took a sip of whiskey and thought about it for a moment.

Without making a conscious decision, I began to play my arrangement of "Eine kleine Nachtmusik." The opening figure leapt out of my fingertips as they flew across the keyboard, the music as crisp as sparks thrown by metal striking flint. Then came the slow counterfigure. Achingly beautiful, sublimely sad, the music seemed to bleed from my dying soul.

When I finished, I sat with eyes closed and fingers poised above the keyboard, waiting for some signal, some inspiration, to continue.

Silence and the feeling of painful resolution filled the room.

It was finished. There was no more music left in me. I was completely empty. The time had come to step into oblivion. I braced my hands against the piano bench to push myself up and opened my eyes.

"That was very beautiful. And very sad."

I tried to blink away the hallucination, but it was real. It was the woman in white, the haunting vision from the opera, from the fountain in the park. Standing so close to her, I realized she was even lovelier than I had thought. And when she spoke, the Russian accent transformed her low, melodious voice into an exotic song.

I knew without question she was a ballerina. Her legs were long, and she stood with that distinctive posture: chin and chest held high, arms and hands graceful as a swan's wings in motion or at rest. She moved with the awareness that her body was an instrument capable of great artistic expression, and she could no more have hidden it than a violin could have disguised its purpose. I had the impression that if I allowed my fingers to find the keyboard and begin to play again, she would dance through the room and out of my life.

I did not touch the piano.

And those sad eyes! Her large eyes were the color of emeralds, and they seemed to express fathomless tragedy. I wondered what her life had been like to make her eyes reflect so much suffering.

Her jet-black hair was drawn back in a bun, her face aristocratic and extremely pale, with well-defined cheekbones, a straight nose, and full red lips. She wore little makeup. Her eyebrows were sharply drawn but by nature. Her skin was as smooth and white as polished Cararra marble—the result, I thought, of too many days away from the sun in rehearsal halls and dance studios.

She wore simple diamond earings and a long sleeveless dress made from a gossamer material. The dress was white, of course, as in the Whistler painting, but more alluring. When she turned to put her arm softly on the piano, I saw that the dress split into two straps behind her neck, which crossed and attached to their opposite sides, leaving her back bare.

"Will you play more for me?" she asked, and gave me a melancholy smile.

"I'm very tired."

"Yes, I know."

She came a half step nearer and brushed her hand along the keys, not quite touching them. Her fingers were long and narrow and could have been carved from ivory, art objects contrasting the perfect whiteness of her skin with the bloodred lacquer on her fingernails.

"Please play. For me." Her voice was barely more than a whisper. "I'm feeling rather sad tonight myself, and I would love to hear Rachmaninoff. It would remind me of my home and my family. It has been a long time since I've seen any of them. Such a very long time."

Her emerald eyes held mine.

"Please?"

My God, I thought, I am in *love* with this beautiful stranger!

"I know Rachmaninoff," I said, my voice shaking.

The pale, raven-haired woman favored me with another sad smile and leaned languidly against the piano.

"Paint for me the music of Russia in winter," she whispered, her eyes slowly closing. "Paint me wrapped in furs in a sleigh racing through the night toward my uncle's dacha. Make me feel snowflakes melting on my face. Make me hear the bells on the horses and the rush of wind in the trees. Make me remember my home so long ago and far away.''

I lifted my hands and began to play.

# Chapter 10

PARIS, JUNE 13, 1989—Everything about my life changed after meeting Tatiana Feodorovna—as she called herself in Chicago—in the lounge of the Hotel Wharton.

Simply put, she made me happy. No longer did I slog grimly through life, my head down and my shoulder to the wheel. I awoke each day filled with anticipation—even if my Russian ballerina only would come to me after nightfall. The change in me went beyond mere happiness. There was an impenetrable air of mystery about Tatiana, and it served to add an element of magic to my life that I had never known before.

I have the most delicious memories from the early days of our love. . . .

I remember sitting at the piano one night, playing Tchaikovsky in the dark. The windows were open, and the breeze coming in from the lake made the curtains billow into the room. Outside, the night was clear and warm. There was a moon, and its light reflected on the water. As I played, my eyes half-closed, the shadows seemed to wrap themselves sensuously around me. The smell of my lover's favorite perfume, Coty's Jasmin de Corse, filled the air.

Tatiana had a way of coming silently into a room, but tonight the perfume betrayed her presence, running ahead of her. I stopped playing and sat with my eyes shut, smiling.

Cool lips brushed my neck.

"Hello, my love."

"Hello, David." Her accent gave my name special richness: "Dah-veed."

I took her in my arms and carried her into the bedroom, where we made love until she left me at the usual time, just before dawn.

71

* * *

Meeting Tatiana made me realize that I had been sleep walking through my life, repeating empty routines, mimicking emotions I no longer felt. I had become an actor, and everything I did was an act. But with Tatiana's first kiss, the sleeper awakened. I left my trance and began to live again.

There were important concrete changes in my life. For instance, I did not waste another hour practicing law. I didn't even bother to return to my former place of employment to collect my files and personal belongings.

The career I'd detested out of the way, I devoted all my energy to the piano. With Tatiana's encouragement, I began to prepare myself again for a career on the concert stage. I was starting late in life, as classical musicians went, but there was time. Inspired by my beautiful green-eyed ballerina, I felt as if I could do anything.

Tatiana became my muse. She was the source of the passion in my music and in my life. When we made love, our hearts literally beat as one; when we were parted, I lived for the moment we would be reunited.

I was too filled with bliss during those early days to be much concerned about my lover's eccentricities. She had many strange routines and habits, and she was obsessively secretive about her past. If I'd thought about it very hard, I might have at least partially guessed the truth. But I was in love, and what lover is cold enough to see the imperfections in his newly beloved?

Tatiana always came to me after the sun had set, and she left before the first light of the new day. She was a ballerina deep in her studies, and she told me she spent her days locked in a rehearsal studio, practicing furiously. Nevertheless, her energy at night was indefatigable. After being up with me nearly until dawn every night, she would rise after a little sleep and leave to dance. I, however, would sleep until afternoon.

She would neither tell me where she danced, nor allow me to visit her studio. She would not even reveal where she lived—a secret that would have driven me insane with jealousy had she not spent every night in my arms. When I asked why she kept so much of herself secret from me, she said she wanted to remain mysterious to prolong the passion of our new love. I went along with her, enjoying the mystery while, at the same time, thinking that sooner or later I would learn the details of the life she kept from me during those first wonderful weeks.

One topic Tatiana flatly refused to discuss was her family. Her reaction when I asked her about them made it plain that the memories were extremely painful. During a moment of candor one night, she mentioned that she would have been a grand duchess if there hadn't been a revolution in Russia. That bit of information led me to surmise that the communists had persecuted her family because of its royal bloodline, but of course I didn't really know.

One thing that was obvious was that she deeply missed Mother Russia. Tatiana was the sort of person who, exiled from her native country, became consumed with those parts of it a traveler can carry into exile—its music, its literature, its art. Her enthusiasm was infectious. It wasn't long before I began to share her appreciation for Russian culture. I began with music, the point where our individual interests intersected most directly. She taught me to adore Tchaikovsky, Rachmaninoff, Rimsky-Korsakov, and Moussorgsky, all composers I had only passing interest in before falling in love with the beautiful Russian. And her favorite Russian writers became my favorites. When we were apart, the time I didn't spend practicing was used to read Pushkin, Dostoyevsky and Tolstoy.

Though her conversation was remarkably bare of personal detail, Tatiana often spoke of her native country in words that drew precise little sketches of the land she loved.

"Nothing is the same in Russia," she told me once. "Not the light, not the time, not the seasons. Winter evenings begin in the early afternoon and last until halfway through the next morning. And in the summer the sky is still silver at eleven at night."

Sometimes Tatiana's secrecy cracked. It was during those few brief glimpses into her past that I began to suspect the things I did not know about my lover were much more disturbing than I could possibly imagine. One night, as we sat in front of the fire drinking ice-cold Stolichnaya vodka, she began talking about her father. I sat very still. It was the most she ever had said—or would say—about her family during the time we spent together in Chicago.

"My father took his vodka cold like this," she said and smiled sadly to herself. "I can almost see him. He was like a picture in a fairy tale. He wore a tunic that always looked crisply ironed, even when he came to have breakfast with the family after being up all night with the generals. His shiny black cavalry boots went to his knees. And his beard—he had a magnificent Edwardian beard, with a neatly trimmed mustache that he waxed so it curled up a bit on the ends. He was very dashing.''

The smile was still on her face, but I could see she was on the verge of crying.

"My brother, Alexis Nicolaievich, had his own little version of Papa's uniform. Alexis was an invalid.'' She blinked back tears. "The awful bleeding.''

"Bleeding?''

Tatiana gave me a startled look, as if I had just thrown cold water in her face.

"My brother was a hemophiliac. There was only one person who could help him. He was a scoundrel, but he was also a great friend of our family. Everybody tried to convince Mama to send him away. Poor Mama.''

Tatiana stared silently into the fire.

"Your family is still in the Soviet Union?'' I asked gently after many minutes had passed without her looking away from the flames. It was a question I'd asked before. I'd never got an answer, and I didn't expect one now.

"They're dead,'' she said, her voice very low. "They're all dead. Papa. Mama. My sisters. Harmless little Alexis.''

Tatiana flinched when I touched her shoulder, but she did not pull away from my hand. I studied her face in the firelight. Her expression was the mask of someone who had worked very hard to learn to hide her emotions, but there was no way to disguise the depth of tragedy she had seen.

"They shot them,'' she said before I dared ask.

I'm not sure whether I heard the words or merely saw them form on her lips.

"They?''

"The Bolsheviks.''

"You mean the communists?''

She did not answer but went on staring silently into the flames.

It was neither curiosity nor jealousy that finally drove me to follow Tatiana to learn where she went each night in the final hour before dawn. Rather, it was my concern for her mental well-being.

As our affair stretched into its second month, I began to take note of a dozen small things she said, which, combined with her obsessive secrecy, led me to wonder if the tragedy of her earlier life had damaged her in a way that might benefit from some form of psychological treatment.

We had spent every night for nearly eight weeks in each other's arms, yet she still refused to tell me anything whatsoever about where she disappeared to every morning just before dawn. And the few comments she made about the past began to strike me as sounding increasingly bizarre.

It was the last in a series of similar instances that led me to act.

We were sitting up in bed after making love. I was hungry, and Tatiana went to the kitchen and brought back a tray with caviar, crackers, and champagne. As we ate, we began talking about Chicago society. It was an unusual topic, not the sort of thing we usually discussed. The conversation wandered from here to there until Tatiana, pausing after a sip of champagne, got that strange light in her eyes that told me she was thinking about her past.

"The social season in Petrograd began New Year's Day," she said. "It was an unending series of balls, operas, parties, and ballets that lasted until Lent. We danced until dawn every night."

As she spoke, she kept the arm holding the champagne glass at an odd angle between her mouth and the tray. It reminded me of someone in a hypnotic trance who had been commanded to keep one arm rigid.

"I'm surprised there still is a social season in the Soviet Union. I suppose I thought all that stopped after the revolution."

Tatiana returned to the present with a start.

"And wasn't Petrograd changed to Leningrad after the czar was overthrown? Does everybody really still call it Petrograd?"

Her glass hit the tray and broke, splashing champagne across the bed.

"I'm sorry!" Tatiana cried and leapt up to get a towel.

I pretended to sleep when Tatiana arose a few hours later. She put on her clothes without turning on the light, pulling the long red silk cape around her shoulders as she went out the door.

I was out of bed and dressed in a matter of seconds in Levi's, a polo shirt, and loafers without socks.

I had to know where Tatiana went when she left me, whether she was all right, or if she faded into some sort of half-mad Victorian fantasy during the daylight hours, believing she was back in Petrograd before the revolution that brought a permanent halt to the Russian aristocracy's "unending series of balls, operas, parties, and ballets."

The predawn air was chilly. As I watched Tatiana disappear around the corner at the end of the next block, I wished I'd brought a jacket. There was no time to go back for one now.

I ran after Tatiana Feodorovna, hurrying into the night.

# Chapter 11

PARIS, JUNE 14, 1989—Good news at last!
    As I was leaving the hotel, the concierge called me over to her desk and handed me a telegram. It read:

David:
Am leaving Kathmandu tomorrow night. Expect to be in Paris within the fortnight, barring unforeseen complications. Be ready to travel. Regards, S. Wolf
P.S. Tatiana sends her love.

The telegram made me so happy that I danced a little jig in the middle of the lobby, much to the concierge's amusement.
Tatiana—and within two weeks!
Mozart is certainly full of surprises. I wonder what the devil he's doing in Kathmandu. Maybe sitting at the feet of the Dalai Lama—although I suppose it's just as likely that the Buddhist holy man is sitting at the feet of the wise old vampire!
Tonight, I'm drinking champagne while I work on my journal. If Tatiana were here to share it with me, my happiness would be complete.

There is a district in north Chicago near the lake, not many blocks from my town house, filled with sprawling mansions built during the late nineteenth and early twentieth century. The neighborhood is a relic of the Gilded Age, a place where railroad magnates, stockyard owners, and land speculators contrived to display their newly gained wealth with all the ostentation money could buy. The houses are colossal, many of them occupying entire blocks with their surrounding grounds—a lavish use of land, especially considering today's real estate prices in the city.

Many Gold Coast homes are grand to the point of vulgarity. My parents' house in the neighborhood, a relatively tasteful fake Tudor, sits across the street from an Americanized version of Versailles that the publisher of a well-known soft porn magazine recently bought. The next house on that side of the street, a mock southern plantation great house, belongs to the physician who owns one of Chicago's most prosperous plastic surgery clinics, a place where wealthy matrons go to cheat time. One of the largest mansions in the Gold Coast belongs to a Pakistani, a tiny, dark-skinned man whose legs were twisted by polio. He came to the United States a penniless student a decade ago, started a software company, and quickly became one of the richest men in America.

There's old money in the neighborhood, too, but it is generally a nouveau riche district. Money tends to stop in Chicago for a generation or two, then move west, south, or east, migrating to socially greener pastures. For all its wealth Chicago has never been fashionable. Beverly Hills, Palm Springs, and Palm Beach are exclusive. New York is the cultural mecca and has a certain chic decadence. Chicago, however, has never quite had *it*, whatever *it* is. One theory is that the city's importance as an early meat-packing center—which attracted hoards of non-WASP Eastern European immigrants—lingers on in the elephantine memories of America's Brahman caste.

Chicago always has been a city where money is made, as opposed to being a city such as Boston, where wealth is simply possessed by those who, like generations of their ancestors before them, have more of it than they can possibly spend.

I followed Tatiana to the Gold Coast, trying to hang far enough back that she wouldn't notice me.

I remember it startled me to realize how quiet the city gets in the final hours before dawn. There was nobody else to be seen, and the usual noisy fixtures of the street scene—traffic queued up bumper to bumper; buses disgorging passengers before pulling away in a roar of diesel smoke; taxis blocking lanes to let out their fares; people hurrying along the sidewalks—were missing at 4:00 A.M. Except for the muted rush of the wind off the lake and the electronic clicking as traffic signals changed colors, the street was completely still.

I found it a bit eerie.

The blocks of town houses and apartment buildings along the lake gave way to increasingly expensive single-family houses as we headed toward the neighborhood where I grew up. I had no intention of following Tatiana any longer than it took to discover where she was staying, but perhaps it would be near someone I knew, and I would be able to make discreet inquiries.

Tatiana paused to draw up the hood on her red cape in front of a rather tasteful traditional mansion built in the restrained Federal style, a house that seemed a bit out of place between a scaled-down replica of Horace Walpole's Strawberry Hill on the left and something resembling Chiswick House on the right.

I stepped behind a tree and waited for her to continue. When she was in the next block, I went after her. She turned right in the center of the block and vanished.

I hurried toward the spot and found a heavy iron gate barring my way.

I looked over my shoulder. The street was still deserted, but I was certain someone was there. The hair crawled on the back of my neck. My sixth sense was warning me that danger was near.

Chicago is not a place where it is safe to go walking alone late at night, no matter how up-market the neighborhood. In fact, the nicer areas tend to be the scenes of the more brutal assaults, since muggers, like businessmen, go where the money is. But when I thought about it—as I searched the deserted streets without being able to identify the source of my anxiety—I decided my imagination had to be getting the better of me. If I were going to be held up, it already would have happened. Any streetwise thief worth his felony-flier Nikes would know I might be about to pass through the iron gate and slam it locked behind me.

I thought of Tatiana. If someone *was* watching me—I still could feel it!—then perhaps it was really my lover they were following.

It was easy to make that supposition fit what I knew of Tatiana's life. The communists had killed her family. She had survived, I assumed, only because she was able to escape the country. She would have been a grand duchess but for the Russian revolution. Perhaps that was enough for the Soviets to want her dead. It was not beyond imagining. The Iranian secret police were still after the late shah's son, so would it be surprising if the KGB were trying to exterminate the last remaining members of the deposed Russian nobility seventy years after the killing first began?

It did not seem entirely probable, yet who could say what

strange orders might be given in a police state on the brink of collapsing into anarchy?

I turned back toward the gate, wondering how many secrets my lover carried inside her breast. The house was difficult to see from the street. A twelve-foot brick wall surrounded the compound, and glass bottles had been set in the capping layer of concrete and broken off, leaving a jagged ribbon of glass along the top to discourage intruders. It scarcely would stop a burglar, but it served as a clear signal that uninvited guests would be dealt with harshly.

Beyond the wall was the house, a mansion almost hidden in the center of a thick stand of oaks, ancient specimens that stretched their gnarled limbs in all directions and made it impossible to see much of the structure. Here and there, through small breaks in the branches, I caught glimpses of the place, which seemed to have been patterned after a Norman chateau. The towers were set at irregular intervals, with narrow vertical windows from which defenders could shoot arrows or pour boiling oil on invaders—at least in the original version.

I had no intention of trying to get to the house. I did not want to put too much pressure on Tatiana. Besides, Gold Coast homes all had excellent security systems, some even with guards, closed circuit TV cameras, and halogen spotlights activated by pressure-sensitive plates buried in the lawn. And there were the barkless dogs—surgically muted Dobermans that came up on you silently, all teeth and quiet savagery. They were the most effective, and brutal, security device of all.

Behind me!

I spun around and lifted my fists. No one was there.

I laughed weakly at my bad nerves and dropped my arms. I tried to shake it off, but the feeling that someone menacing was very near wouldn't go away. When you live in a city like Chicago, you develop a sort of psychic antenna that tells you when you're in dangerous territory. My psychic antenna was sending a screaming alarm to my brain, telling me to get the hell out of there.

I turned toward the house and put my hands on the iron bars. To my astonishment the gate swung away from me, opening onto a brick sidewalk that ran through a formal flower garden to the house. I did not hesitate, but hurried in and slammed the gate behind me, shaking the bars to be sure that it locked.

Thank God! I thought, breathing a great sigh. I was safe from whoever—or whatever—was out there. It may seem a little foolish to have got so worked up over an assailant I hadn't even seen, but I *knew* in my heart he was there.

As I stood there, considering what to do next, the irrationality of my situation became clear. I had not meant for Tatiana to know I followed her, for I expected it would make her very angry with me. But now I was locked inside her garden because I was afraid of—well, I couldn't say exactly what I was afraid of.

I looked out through the bars. There was only the empty street. No thug. No boogeyman. But still, the sense of violence, of *evil*, lingered in the air.

The locked gate settled the matter. There would be no going out that way.

I looked around the grounds, heavy with shadows from the thick growth of trees and bushes. Being Tatiana's lover would not prevent a zealous security guard from shooting at me with an electric stun gun—and it certainly would provide no protection against barkless attack dogs.

Perhaps I could climb back over the gate. . . .

No sooner did that thought pass through my mind than the fear was upon me again. I tried to fight it back, telling myself there was nothing to be afraid of, but it was no use. The intense, nameless dread I felt for whoever or whatever was on the other side of the wall refused to be vanquished by mere rationality. The dangerous presence was out there. And I felt it drawing nearer.

I began to hurry toward the darkened mansion. I'd go to Tatiana and honestly explain my concerns about her. She would understand why I followed. And perhaps she would be able to explain who, besides me, was following her.

Irises in the flower beds along the walk reached out for me, the breeze rustling their long, narrow leaves like fingers that strained to touch my legs. I followed the walk around to the front of the house and took the steps of the mansion two at a time, past the stone gargoyles perched on pedestals.

The massive wooden front door was big enough for four people to walk through side by side. The heavy planking was criss-crossed with iron studding and appeared stout enough to withstand a battering ram. The handle was a massive iron ring that would take a man both hands to lift and turn. In the center of the door at eye level was a silver double-headed eagle, the coat of arms of the Russian imperial family.

"Jesus," I said under my breath. Maybe the Soviets really were after Tatiana.

The door had been left ajar. I put my fingertips on the wood. The grain felt rough, even through the heavy varnish. A little pressure from my hand, and it swung away from me on well-oiled hinges.

The entryway was larger than a small house. Against the far wall was a parquet table with a marble top. Two candles sat upon it, their golden flames refracted in the cut glass crystal bowl positioned between them. The walls reached up to a point at the apex of the vaulted ceiling, and a chain descending back down held a chandelier. A pair of gilded mirrors fourteen feet tall stood across from each other against the side walls, white sheets draping them, hiding their reflective surfaces.

I pulled the big door closed behind me.

Two towers flanked the entry, each joining it with a door. The doors were open, and inside I could make out a spiral staircase that must have led to rooms on the second and third floors, and down to whatever was in the cellar. As I crossed the room, each footstep on the bare stone floor echoed against the walls. It was like being alone in a chapel—or a crypt.

I paused to look into the glass bowl between the candles. It was filled with dried flower petals, and when I ran my fingers through them, they were like tiny scraps of silk. Disturbed, their scent filled the room with a preserved smell, like a bouquet saved from a long-past wedding.

The hall that ran to the left was dark. Down the one to the right, I saw a dim light shining through a partially closed doorway at the end of the corridor.

I went toward the light, my footfalls silenced by the thick hallway runner. It seemed to take an eternity to get through the long passageway. I stopped in front of the door and held my breath. The air was electrified with the moment. Something important was about to happen, I knew. Whatever it was, I sensed it would bring Tatiana and me together forever or drive us apart.

After taking a deep breath, I opened the door and stepped inside.

The room was filled with hundreds of candles. Candles were lined up on the tables, along the fireplace mantel, even pushed into corners on the floor. The combined light of their individual flames gave the room a strange luminosity, a muted brightness that seemed to glow from within the objects in the chamber.

Heavy velvet curtains were drawn across the windows. That explained why the house appeared dark from the outside.

The room was decorated with antiques, a rich clutter of objects that might have been found in the crowded parlor of a Victorian palace. Tatiana's portrait hung above the fireplace. That is to say, I thought it was Tatiana, but when I examined the picture more closely, I realized it had to be her grandmother or great-grandmother, for the surface was checked with cracks that come as oil paint dries and separates over the course of many decades. The painting's naturalistic style belonged to an earlier generation, and even the pose was dated: The woman in the portrait, who wore an old-fashioned white gown and a diamond tiara, sat stiff-backed, her pose regal. It was the sort of painting that must have been done by a court artist, to hang beside other noble heads in a royal gallery.

The resemblance between the woman in the portrait and Tatiana was striking. It is not unusual for a child to resemble a parent or grandparent, but this was something more. I would not have been able to tell the two women apart, were they not already separated by so many years.

The portrait provided another clue. Tatiana's bloodline entitled her, depending upon who else still survived, to the Russian throne. But equally important, she bore an uncanny resemblance to a woman who must have been part of the last generation of royalty to rule Russia before the revolution. What more dangerous symbol could counterrevolutionaries have, now that opposition to communist rule was finally beginning to stir in the Soviet empire, than a grand duchess who appeared to be the very reincarnation of one of the members of the royal family?

My head reeling with ideas about fantastic KGB plots, I turned away and let my eyes roam over the crowded room. Everywhere I looked, it seemed, was an icon. The paintings—miniature portraits of the saints executed in bright enamel and gold leaf and held by frames of exquisite craftsmanship—were outnumbered in the room only by the candles.

I was, I realized, in the middle of a museum of antique Russian Orthodox religious art. The impression made on me by these strange little art objects, illuminated by the flickering candlelight, was altogether bizarre.

Feeling as if I were in a dream that might at any moment become a nightmare, I picked up an icon from the table nearest me. It was Saint Sebastian. His eyes were cast toward heaven, and his expression peaceful despite the dozen arrows jutting from his bound and bleeding body. Sebastian's eyes held an expression that was not so much pious as doomed.

I returned the macabre portrait to its place and frowned. This sort of art, intended to be inspirational, gave me the creeps.

Jasmin de Corse perfume filled the room, its familiar odor mingling with the smell of hot wax.

*Dah-veed.*

Tatiana spoke my name before I could turn to see her pass through the doorway. The way she said my name made it echo strangely inside my head. It was as if I had heard it without really hearing it—which I knew didn't make a bit of sense. I blinked to clear my mind. I felt dazed, as if I'd just been awakened from a deep sleep. God, I thought, please don't let me make a fool out of myself with this woman.

"David," Tatiana repeated, her voice no longer seeming so other-worldly to me.

I wanted to speak, to apologize for my intrusion into her privacy, but something about the strangeness of the moment made it impossible for me to find the words.

"This is one of my favorites," she said, picking up the icon I had just put down. "My Sebastian. He's very special to me. He once belonged to Rasputin. You know of Rasputin?"

"Do you mean the Mad Monk?"

"Please do not call him that. I know what the books say about him, but they lie. Rasputin was a good friend to my family. He helped us more than I can ever say." Her half smile vanished. "It was a very long time ago."

"You're doing it again."

"Doing what?"

"Talking about the past as if you were part of it, as if you had been there. You said Rasputin helped 'us,' as if he had helped you personally."

I looked into her green eyes and again felt light-headed.

*Haven't you guessed the truth yet, Dah-veed?*

This time, I was sure she had not spoken, at least not using her voice, though I clearly heard the words in my mind. I must have looked frightened, because she began to speak in a soothing voice.

"Do not be afraid, my love. How could you possibly understand? I knew you were following me tonight. I've known all along that you would have to know the truth if I continued seeing you. The fault is mine. I never should have allowed you to fall in love with me."

"Don't say that. You're the best thing that's ever happened to me."

"Do not be so certain. You do not understand what I am."

"And what is that? A political exile? Someone the KGB is hunting? Someone with"—I searched for the right word—"telepathy, or whatever you call the power that allows you to speak inside of my mind? Is that why they won't let you alone or is it your royal blood?"

"You assume too much and understand too little. Which is how it must be," she added sadly. "I am afraid that if you learned the truth about me, you would be—"

"What?" I asked.

*Terrified.*

She had not spoken, and yet her voice was there again inside my head. I went to her and took her hands.

"Tatiana, my love, you have a fabulous gift. It's not something that frightens me."

"You still do not understand," she said, pulling away. "It was a mistake to involve you. My motives were selfish. I behaved irresponsibly, and we fell in love. We are wrong for each other, for reasons you can never—must never—understand. This cannot continue."

"Don't say that."

"It can't ever be the way you want it, David. If you really love me, leave here now and never return. Please. I beg you."

"Are you in danger?"

"Yes." She looked at me closely. "And so are you."

"I know. I felt him—or is it them?—outside here tonight. Is that why you want me to go? I'll help you face them, or escape them, if that's what it takes. I *can't* lose you, Tatiana. You're the only reason I have to live."

Tatiana seemed close to tears, but she would not allow herself to cry.

"You have so many reasons to live, David. You're a wonderful pianist. That's why I kept you from taking your own life."

"You knew I was planning—you knew that?"

Tatiana nodded solemnly.

"Because you're telepathic?"

Her emerald eyes opened wider, and I had the sense that she was coming into me, mingling her thoughts with my own.

*Because I have powers you scarcely suspect*, she said, speaking inside my mind.

"None of that makes a difference. I love you. I want us to be together forever."

"You don't know what forever means, my love."

"I only know what I feel." I took a step toward her, even as she took a step away from me. "I want to be with you always, no matter what that means. I will love you forever."

"Do you really mean that?" One tear became too heavy to remain behind her eyelashes. It spilled down her cheek, leaving a wet trail that I wanted to kiss dry. "Do you really want to be with me forever? Do you mean that with all your heart?"

"Yes," I said simply, and looked deep into her eyes. There was so much sadness and pain there; I wanted only to wrap Tatiana in my arms and protect her and love her. "I would do anything for you," I whispered. "I would even die for you."

"No matter what I am?"

"No matter what you are."

Tears were streaming down Tatiana's face as I pulled her close to me.

"You really mean it, don't you?"

"More than I can ever express with mere words."

"I love you so much, David."

"And I love you."

"I have been so alone."

"And I never really knew what it was to be in love before I met you. I don't want to lose you, Tatiana. I would rather die."

"Then let it be so," she said, her voice shaking.

I kissed away her tears, running my hands through her rich hair, pulling her head down to rest upon my shoulder.

She brushed her lips against my neck in a butterfly kiss.

And then she sank her teeth into my jugular vein.

# Chapter 12

**P**ARIS, JUNE 15, 1989—My dreams were filled with sinister images after that night at Tatiana's.

*I stood at the edge of a dry lake. Two men knelt on the ground beneath a dead tree, playing a game of dice. One of the men was completely anonymous, but the other wore the purple robe of a Roman Catholic cardinal. It was hard for me, in my dream, to imagine that anyone who had so much hatred in his eyes could be a man of God. His gold signet ring flashed in the sun as he scooped up the dice. The ring was decorated with an ornate B. Something about the ring troubled me. What did the B stand for?*

*I heard a dry rattle, a stone-against-stone sound. The hand with the ring—now fleshless bone—opened. The dice came tumbling out of the dead man's hand in slow motion. They rolled straight at me, coming closer, closer. . . .*

I sat up in the dark and looked around in confusion. I was in my bed. It was early morning, judging from the diffused light coming through the windows.

I fell backward, asleep again before my head touched the pillow.

A jumble of half-formed images, some benign, some threatening, raced through my mind. Tatiana's face materialized out of the chaos. The second dream took shape:

*I put out my hands to touch the transparent barrier surrounding my sleeping lover. The ice that encased Tatiana was so pure that it was almost invisible. I pressed my hands against its surface and felt my palms become instantly numb.*

Dah-veed! *she cried telepathically.* Help me!

*Her pale skin was already turning blue.*

*Frantic, I threw myself against the frozen cocoon, clawing with my fingers, fearing she would be dead within moments. Although it was worse than futile, I clawed at the icy prison holding my doomed lover.*

*The ice silently caught me in its fatal embrace, weaving itself into the fibers of my clothing, sending frozen runners over the backs of my legs and up my sides. I tried to push myself up from the frozen block. It was already too late. I was trapped.*

*The ice enveloped my arms, my legs, my back. The spreading coldness crawled up my body and gathered me into its frigid embrace.*

I sat up again in bed, this time fully awake.

The light was like knives in my eyes. I shut them tight, but the brightness stabbed through, triggering an explosion of pain in my head that raced through my entire body until I felt as if the blood in my veins were boiling. Shielding my face, I stumbled to the window, closed the blinds, and drew both sets of draperies shut tight over them.

The darkness was like a sudden hush in the room. The pain gradually ebbed out of me, and my breathing slowed from frantic gasps to something more nearly reflecting the exhaustion that had taken possession of my body. I shuffled to the nearest chair and collapsed.

As I sat there, staring through the gloom with unfocused eyes, the nightmares came back to me in twisted fragments.

The cardinal with the signet ring. It seemed as though I should have recognized that sinister figure, but I could not place his cruel, hawklike face . . .

The nightmare about the hellish ice . . .

And then, the strangest dream of all, the one about following Tatiana home . . .

The sense of dread I'd experienced standing outside Tatiana's estate came back to me, the sensation that a fathomless evil was creeping toward me through the darkness, reaching its spidery fingers closer. I'd fled inside, where the smell of dried flowers mixed with the heavier scent of melted wax in a room filled with icons of martyred saints.

The sound of my own weak laughter came back at me through the darkness.

A vampire!

Absurd.

Yet my stomach tingled to remember the pleasure I had felt in my dream at the instant Tatiana bit into my neck. We had become one, and together we rode a wave of bliss beyond anything I'd ever experienced. . . .

I opened my eyes wide and stared into the silent darkness.

My God, I thought, grasped by the truth's inescapable jaws.

The room began to spin. I had to shut my eyes and concentrate on breathing to keep from hyperventilating. I forced the idea out of my mind as long as I could, but it would not go away. What I remembered was no dream; then, Tatiana Feodorovna *was* a vampire!

Incredible—and horrifying.

I felt myself slip sickeningly toward the edge of complete panic. What I was thinking was completely outside the bounds of reality. I'd certainly had reason enough to question my sanity before Tatiana came into my life, but where did this impossible experience leave me? An ambulance ride away from a mental institution?

I sat in some of the deepest anguish my soul has ever known for nearly an hour before the simple power of my own conviction slowly won me over, reining in my runaway emotions. The fact was that I *knew* what had happened to me the night before. The truth might have made me mad, but it was the truth nevertheless.

My watch told me it was four in the afternoon. I'd slept through the day.

I walked into the bathroom on shaky legs. The face I saw staring back at me from the mirror was sallow and drawn. The skin on the side of my neck was still tender, but the mirror revealed no marks to prove I actually had been bitten by a vampire. Either the wounds were too fine for the naked eye, or something in the process had caused the wounds to heal with unusual speed.

How much blood had I lost? Wondering made me lightheaded. When the room began to spin, I shut my eyes, thinking that would make it stop—but it only made me lose my tenuous grip on consciousness. I crumpled to the bathroom floor.

As the black sea of nothingness washed over me, the horror and disbelief all coming back in that final moment, I surrendered instead to the one emotion that was strong enough to overpower all others: I was in love.

* * *

After an hour of sleep, I awoke feeling completely unrested, with my face pressed against the cool tile of the bathroom floor. I staggered downstairs and pushed a chair around to face the door. There I sat, waiting for Tatiana.

Part of my strength slowly returned as I waited for nightfall, and with it a strange curiosity. The best way to sum up my beliefs at that point in my life is to say that I didn't have any. It's not that I didn't want to believe in God and all the rest of it, just that I didn't. We were simply here, I thought, and if anybody tried to tell you they understood more about it than that, they were lying. Or, as Chekhov more succinctly put it, "A carrot is a carrot, and nothing more can be known."

But the existence of vampires blew a hole in my smug rationality. The existence of one supernatural being opened the door on an entire realm of possibility I had been quite certain did not exist. What other mysteries and wonders might Tatiana reveal to her mortal lover?

I sat and pondered the intoxicating possibilities as I waited. And waited.

The time Tatiana customarily rang my doorbell passed without her arrival. Ten o'clock came, then eleven.

My anticipation gradually gave way to the fear that she wasn't coming—not ever. Tatiana had been reluctant to reveal her world to me, but I had been fool enough to force her to share the secret that she guarded most. Now, for the first time in months, she had broken her habit of visiting my town house after sunset. I took it as a bad sign, a very bad sign.

The hands on the clock moved toward midnight. My anxiety grew until, as the clock finally began to chime twelve, I jumped to my feet and raced out the door. The cool night air felt good against my feverish skin. The wind off the lake was strong, and it blew ragged white clouds low over the city, the lights shining up from below turning them the color of dirty cotton.

My legs were uncertain and my head light, but I found the determination to force myself to walk to Tatiana's. My lungs were heaving when I finally got there, and I had to grab on to the iron gate to keep myself from collapsing.

This time the gate was locked.

Guard dogs waiting on the other side of the wall were not barkless, but that failed to make them any less savage as they hurled themselves against the bars, snarling and showing their teeth. The ignorant, vicious beasts seemed unable to comprehend that they could not throw themselves through the metal rods no matter how badly they wanted to tear me apart.

The mansion was dark, though I knew that was no indication of whether Tatiana was inside. It hardly mattered. I wouldn't get three feet past the dogs.

I dragged myself home and fell into the chair to resume my vigil.

Tatiana did not come to me that night. Sometime before dawn, I closed my burning eyes and dropped into a deep, dreamless sleep.

Exactly two weeks passed without a visit from Tatiana. I almost gave up hope of ever seeing her again, although if it weren't for the slimmest chance that she would come back to me, I would have gotten out Clarice's .38 and finished the job I'd gone to the Hotel Wharton to do.

I slept during the day, rising at sunset to sit slumped in the same chair and watch the door, my eyes locked on the unmoving brass handle, while I brooded over my absent lover.

It was curious that I did not resort to my former vices during this bleak fortnight. I did try to drink whiskey once, but the smell when I uncapped the bottle sent me running to the bathroom, retching. Although I didn't know it, my body was undergoing subtle changes and was sensitive to anything I put in it—including food, which made me nauseous regardless of what I put on a plate. Unable to eat or drink anything except water, I simply wasted

I was stretched out on the couch one night, feeling a dull ache in the starved muscles in my arms and legs, when the familiar smell of Jasmin de Corse perfume drifted into the room. I jumped to my feet with an alarm that belied my starved condition. Tatiana was standing behind the couch, smiling her sad smile, seemingly unaffected by my appearance.

"Don't say a thing," I said, walking around the couch and taking her in my arms. I held her for a long time, afraid to let her go. I should have been furious with her for disappearing, but I was so glad to see her that I was unable to bring myself to be angry with her for abandoning me.

"You look simply awful, my love," she said when I finally loosened my arms enough for her to look into my eyes. "But then, that was to be expected."

"Where have you been?"

"Away."

"Why did you leave?"

"Remember my saying we were in danger? I know you sensed it that night. The threat was more real than I can tell you. I had to draw the danger away, so I took a trip to throw them off track, and then I disappeared. They won't be fooled for very long, but you're safe for the present."

"Who is threatening you—us?"

"Please do not ask."

"But I'm worried about you."

"I can take care of myself," she said, and smiled. "You, on the other hand . . ."

"I've been sick," I said, realizing that I hadn't shaved in two weeks. "I'm sure I'll be better now that you're back."

Tatiana looked away from me without replying.

"Promise you'll never leave again."

Tatiana walked slowly to the window and looked out at the night. It had started to rain.

"I cannot do that, David. I've come to say good-bye. Now that you know about me, surely you can see that this was all a mistake. It will be much better for both of us if I return to Europe alone."

"No!" I was appalled at the desperation in my voice. "I won't let you leave."

"You could hardly stop me, my love."

It was true. I lowered my eyes as she turned to look at me.

"This never should have happened. You have no idea what it's like to be one of us. There are so many risks. And this life can be so . . ." Her voice trailed off, and her eyes seemed to reach out to me even as her words tried to push me away. "This life can be so lonely."

"Like mine was?"

"Yes, David, but much more so."

"We'll never be lonely as long as we're together. Before we met, we were both tired of living. Don't deny it. I saw the pain in your eyes as surely as you recognized it in mine the first time we saw each other at *Don Giovanni*."

She took a step toward me, then hesitated. "You are very perceptive, David Parker."

"I love you and want to be with you. I'll gladly take the rest of it, no matter what it's like, if I can be with you."

Tatiana ran into my arms. My mouth found hers, and her passion seemed to infuse new strength into my weakened body.

We made love slowly and tenderly, as if we were finally and inextricably one.

"The light hurt my eyes for a few days. I've been very weak."

"Usually I don't take so much"—there was a self-conscious pause—"blood. But it is necessary if you are to undergo transformation."

I would be lying to say I wasn't terrified at what it would mean to become a vampire, but my fears were not half as strong as the love I felt for the beautiful Russian. I was ready to do whatever I had to do.

"No, I want it," I said, and took her hand in the darkness. "Does it mean that I must die?"

"Die to become a vampire? Only in the movies, my love. The transition from mortal to vampire is much more complicated—but much less melodramatic. What is it, David? I sense something else is bothering you."

It was true. I did have one major reservation. I was ready to die for Tatiana, but I was not nearly so certain that I could bring myself to kill for her. In fact, I was almost sure I couldn't.

"Will I have to kill? When I need blood, I mean."

"David, no," Tatiana said, appalled by the suggestion. "You need never take a mortal life, and I hope with all of my heart that you never do. Life should be as sacred to a vampire as it is to an ordinary human being. Morality does not change simply because you become one of us. Right and wrong remain the same regardless of race."

Thank God for that, I thought.

"You must understand that a vampire requires only a small amount of blood, hardly as much as it takes to fill a wineglass. There is no reason to permanently harm the mortal you take as your host."

She sighed in the darkness.

"But I must tell you the complete truth," she added. "There are vampires who kill. We have our criminals, the same way that mortals have theirs. Some vampires are inclined toward violence, toward the darker side of being. These individuals, because they possess our extraordinary powers, are particularly dangerous."

"Was it one of these vampires who you led away from Chicago when you disappeared?" It was a guess, but my intuition told me that I was right.

"Do not worry about it. I'll look after him."

"But I want to know. I want to protect you."

"Trust me, David," she said. "There are powers you cannot possibly understand at this stage—or contend with. A little knowledge can be a dangerous thing, even more dangerous than ignorance. When you are ready, I'll share everything I know with you. For now be glad for the innocence you have left. There are horrors enough in the world, and as your intellect and experience grow, you will come to know—and despise—them all."

I nodded.

"Have you any more questions about my race?"

"Yes. Why do vampires need blood?"

"We've studied that question for centuries without unlocking its enigma. Our bodies apparently lack some vital ingredient that we cannot produce. More than that we do not know. We do need blood to survive. Deprived of it, we die."

"Then nothing supernatural is involved?"

Tatiana laughed.

"The transformation involves a virus that modifies each cell's genetic makeup. That's why we do not refer to ourselves as human. Genetically we are a biologically distinct species. But you must remember that we do not consider ourselves superior to human beings—at least the wise members of our race do not. We possess some obvious advantages over mortals—longevity, strength, high IQs. But there are disadvantages, too."

"Sensitivity to light," I offered.

"That's one. Sterility is another. We cannot reproduce sexually. Our bodies are complete physiologically, and our functions are normal, but for some reason it just doesn't happen."

"What happens to me now? Is it already happening?"

"The transformation has started, but the process will continue only if we mutually agree that it should. The virus is not very aggressive. We usually only take a few ounces of blood at a feeding, and while infection does take place with every feeding, unless the host's system has been weakened—either through illness or because of the amount of blood taken—the virus is not able to withstand the body's natural immune system.

"There are three critical junctures, all of which take place within six weeks, if transformation is to be accomplished. The first is initial exposure, with the host left in an appropriately weakened condition so that the virus can take hold. After two weeks the virus's level in the blood begins to fall for a reason we do not fully understand, and it must be reintroduced."

I looked at Tatiana in the dark.

"It's been exactly two weeks since I followed you home."

"I know. If the virus is reintroduced two weeks after the initial exposure, two more weeks go by and the cycle repeats itself. If the host is infected a third and final time, the viral infection reaches critical mass and triggers the genetic changes. I warn you that it's not very pleasant to experience."

"And after that I'll live forever?"

"Not forever, but for a very long time. Because of enhanced regenerative powers on a cellular level, the aging process slows dramatically. Vampires have lived two thousand years and longer. However, it's rare for us to go on that long. One wearies of life after so many years. Especially if you're alone."

She touched my hand.

"Many of us become tired after only a few centuries, some even sooner. A vampire who no longer has the will to live can die quite quickly. We have no more than to wish ourselves dead for it to be so."

"You were tired of living when we met."

"Yes, David. Without you, I don't think I could have gone on much longer."

"And you saved me, too."

We looked at each other in the dark, our bodies close, our hands touching.

"Do you still want to join us, David? Are you willing to make the change?"

I kissed her gently.

"I'll do whatever it takes to stay with you."

"Have you any more questions before we proceed?"

"Only one. Who are you really?"

"My name is Tatiana. I have a long past. I'll tell you my story, when we have time, but the details are unimportant. The only thing that matters to me is you, David Parker. My life started again the night we met. I think you would say the same of me."

I pulled her body close to mine.

"I love you, Tatiana."

"And I love you David. With all my heart. Forever."

"I am ready."

Tatiana climbed onto me, her long hair hanging around her face, smiling as she lowered herself onto me. She kissed my ear and ran her tongue slowly down my neck.

This time, I barely felt her teeth pierce my flesh.

* * *

I remember little of the next two weeks. I stayed in bed lost in a feverish delirium.

One night I drifted back to consciousness, to feel cool air rushing over my body. It was enough to clear my mind briefly. I lifted my head. I was very weak, and it required all my strength to move even that much.

Tatiana was standing at the foot of my bed, the night breeze playing in the folds of her gown, swirling it around her legs.

"It has been two weeks, my love," she said in a low voice. "It's not too late to remain mortal. It would be easier for you."

At first I could not command my voice to speak. Finally, in a whisper forced through clenched teeth, I managed three words: "Do it now!"

Tatiana was at my side. Her cool hand was on my forehead. A sense of complete peace flooded through me.

"There is one small problem, my love. Our old enemy, the one I led away from us before, is back. He will destroy you if he guesses you are about to make the change. I have no choice but to leave again. I will lead him farther away this time, distracting him until you are strong enough to leave your town house."

Looking into her green eyes seemed to give me the energy to answer.

"I'll be all right."

"I wish I could be certain of that. I wish there was someone to guide you through the change. It will be difficult alone."

"I can do it." The room began to whirl around me. Yes, I could do it, I thought, as long as I didn't have to do anything except lie there helplessly.

"I will send someone to help as soon as I can. I have a friend who is very experienced and clever. He will find you wherever you are, so you do not have to worry about staying here. In fact, I advise you not to. It will not be safe. My enemy may return here to try to pick up the trail. Leave Chicago as soon as you are able to travel, and leave no trace of where you've gone. My friend will locate you, and I'm relatively certain the prince will not. The prince's talents are not great enough for such a feat, at least not without help from his more powerful allies. But leave Chicago. The prince will be savage if he finds you here and guesses what you are in the process of becoming."

I managed to nod, wondering what prince she was talking about but too weak to ask.

"I love you so much, David. A year apart will be nothing compared with the centuries we will spend together."

My eyes opened wide, but I no longer had the energy to speak, much less argue. A *year*?

"Many trials lie ahead of you. First you must endure the physical strain of transformation. There will be times when you think it's going to kill you. You will survive, David, as long as your will to live remains strong.

"But that is only the beginning. Harder still, you must learn what it means to be a vampire. The lessons will not be easy. You must prove beyond all doubt that your soul is ruled by good and not evil. Not one mortal in a hundred has the inner resources to control the powers—and the temptations—a vampire faces. But you are no ordinary person, *moi dorogoi*. I know you will prove that you truly deserve to be one of *us*. And when that happens, we will be reunited."

What was she talking about? I almost didn't care. I just wanted to get on with it. I felt miserable, and I knew my discomfort— to use a mild word for the agony I felt—would only increase over the next few weeks. The sooner the virus was reintroduced to my bloodstream, the sooner my suffering would end.

Tatiana stroked my burning face with her cool hand.

"Through all that happens, my beloved, remember this: Wherever you go, I go before you. Remember our love, and be brave."

Tatiana kissed my lips, my cheek, my neck. . . .

After that there was only blackness.

# Chapter 13

**P**ARIS, JUNE 16, 1989—I sensed *him* for a moment when I first sat down in this café.

It wasn't much. Just a flicker of awareness quickly gone.

It's been a week since my last encounter with the English vampire. Is he preparing the third round of his twisted game? I almost wish it were so. I still do not know his name, but I'm willing to go through another experience like the one in the Louvre to find out. I presently am unable to match him power for power, but someday I will be his equal and see that he pays for his crimes—if I can find out who he is.

Tonight, however, I have little inclination to worry about that miscreant. The Hunger is growing in me again. I should spend this evening looking for a woman, one who is young and pure and willing to help me satisfy a very special need.

The Hunger will not become insistent for two more nights, but I think I may break discipline and feed early. Because of *him*. The Hunger is not a force to trifle with, and I must not give the killer an opportunity to turn its power against me.

But enough!

I wonder what Ariel Niccolini is doing tonight?

I sent her flowers last night, hoping I'd delayed long enough to keep from giving the wrong impression. I wish I could fly to Florence and spend a night in her arms, satisfying the Hunger once again with a taste of her spicy Italian blood.

Of course, I must not leave Paris. I cannot risk missing Mozart.

But Ariel Niccolini—oh, how I wish I could see her just one more night!

\* \* \*

I fell into a delirium after Tatiana's final visit to my town house. For two weeks the virus raged inside my body. Foreign DNA penetrated each cell, ordering the genetic material to re-make itself in the image of a new species. The process was agonizing. My bones felt as if they were dissolving. My blood seemed to have been changed to acid that burned in my veins and rotted my internal organs. I spent most of the time mentally functioning on the level of a terminally ill animal, but in my few moments of higher consciousness, I thought that I would either go mad from the pain or die—or both.

My senses became extremely sensitive, so much so that many ordinary things became torture. Noise was the worst. The sound of traffic on the street came through the thick walls of the town house as a deafening roar that hurt my ears so badly that I some-times screamed. I tore out all of the telephones in a rage one night rather than endure their screeching. When the neighbors were home, their conversations blasted me as if each word were amplified through a gigantic speaker.

My aversion to natural light also intensified. The dull, dif-fused glow that filtered between the carpet and the bottom of the bedroom door during the day made my skin feel as if it were being peeled from my body. I stuffed towels under the door, covered every window in the town house with old newspaper, and permanently closed the shades and curtains.

When the fever finally broke, I was weak as a baby. I dragged myself into the bathroom and looked in the mirror, hardly able to recognize the scarecrow who stared back at me. My face was skeletal, with cheekbones pushing out sharply above hollow cheeks. I had a short beard, and my hair hung long over my ears and down my neck to my shoulders. My fingernails had grown so much that they had started to curl under. The virus had caused my metabolism to burn at a frantic pace. It was as though months had passed. When I weighed myself, I discovered I'd lost thirty pounds.

Moving my uncertain frame back into the bedroom—one hand against the wall for support—made me conscious of the empti-ness in my stomach that quickly turned into a desperate hunger. Except it seemed to be more than *just* hunger—much, much more.

Was it blood I craved? The thought threw me into a panic. My heart began to pound and my breath came in gasps. I had to sit on the bed and force myself to calm down. I would never be able to deal with whatever horrible demands my new condition made on me if I let fear overwhelm me.

I listened to my body as best I could. Did I need blood? The answer seemed to be no, not yet. At least I didn't think so. The feeling deep in the pit of my bowels—the nauseating sensation that my body was caving in on itself, devouring itself—was nothing more than the acute hunger any critically ill person experiences coming out of a long fever, I decided.

The only thing left in the refrigerator was a head of lettuce decomposing into a puddle of brown goo in the crisper. I stared into the empty cupboards and regretted firing the housekeeper, but her threat to summon a doctor had forced my hand. Where the telephone had hung on the kitchen wall was only a tangle of wire and exposed plaster. I regretted that, too. I was terrified to leave the relative safety of the town house, but if I was going to quell my aching hunger, I had no choice but to go out and get food myself.

I did not have the energy to shower or shave, but I also lacked the strength to care. The only thing on my mind was food. Unless I ate soon, I thought I would collapse and be beyond saving myself. I wanted a big, juicy steak—the biggest I could buy, cooked very rare, I thought as I dressed myself, my hands shaking so badly I could hardly button my shirt. I had to put on a beaded Indian belt Clarice had left behind; none of mine would cinch tight enough to hold up my pants on my emaciated frame.

I drove as fast as I could to the nearest market and hurried inside, moving at a walk that threatened to become a run.

The meat counter was at the far end of the store. I lurched down the aisle toward it, boxes of cake mix on the right, boxes of cereal on the left. A barrage of powerful sensations spilled into me. Sight, sound, smell—my senses were overloaded from the stimulation, making me stagger like a drunk. I stopped and closed my eyes while I fought the vertigo.

What I thought was the pounding of my heart was actually the heartbeat of the woman in the next aisle. Unaware of me she pushed her cart forward, one wheel squeaking. Between each heartbeat, I could hear the swoosh of blood rushing through her body—a rich red river whose current seemed to tug at my body, dragging me toward it.

"No!" I said out loud and shook my head violently.

The butcher stared at me with disgust. I knew exactly what he was thinking—another unwashed street person, a derelict who should have been locked in a mental hospital instead of being allowed to roam free, tormented by voices and visions that only strong medication could quell.

Ashamed, I turned away and pretended to study a box of Hungry Jack pancake mix. The avalanche of input continued to flood my senses, but I found that if I concentrated very hard on something—anything—I could tune out enough of the other stimulation, at least to function.

The woman came into my aisle, pushing the squeaking cart. Keeping my eyes down, I focused on the breath coming into my lungs, expanding my diaphragm. I held it for one count and then began to slowly let it out. Control, I told myself. Maintain control!

She came closer, making a point of ignoring me. You learn to see through degenerates in the city as if they were invisible, and that was what she was doing with me. She did not suspect the monster that lurked inside my disheveled appearance, the inexorable Hunger that threatened to break free of my control at any moment to satisfy its lust for blood.

Sweat trickled down my neck. The rope I was hanging onto was frayed almost to the point of breaking.

I could hear the blood circulating through her body. I could even smell it! Its intoxicating aroma steamed into the air from the delicate system of capillaries that ran near the surface of her skin. By God, I could almost *taste* it! Each beat of her heart was like an explosion inside my head.

A searing pain started in the top of my skull and worked itself lower until it was concentrated in two places in my upper jaw— one left, one right—just above my canine teeth. The pain was almost more than I could stand. It was as if ten-penny nails were being driven through my gums from the inside out.

I dared to glance up at the woman.

The moment our eyes met, she froze, a look of horror on her face. Although she could not possibly have imagined what I was, I knew that she saw the terrible Hunger in me even as I saw her fear. The survival instinct gives us all, mortal and vampire alike, the ability to know when our lives are seriously threatened. The same sixth sense that had sent me fleeing through the gate at Tatiana's gripped the woman now, telling her that what she saw facing her in the aisle at the grocery store was her own death.

I broke off eye contact. She rushed past.

The Hunger had its talons in my soul now, and there was no mistaking what my body wanted. I had to have blood, even though I didn't know how to take it—and desperately wanted *not* to take it. But still the Hunger howled inside me. *Satisfy me*, it said; every atom of my being cried out for fresh blood.

I looked around wildly, gaining a keen appreciation for how it must feel to be a starving wolf amid a fold of sheep. Blood spoor was thick in the air. I opened myself up until I could *feel* the presence of the woman with the shopping cart. She was at the cash register now, along with three other women.

*Take her!* the Hunger screeched.

I fought the impulse back. I couldn't do it. Not in public.

The Hunger was not interested in listening to reason. It cared nothing for my safety and continued freedom. It only wanted one thing, and it wanted it *now*!

I shot a look over my shoulder at the butcher, a balding middle-aged man in a white apron smeared with red. He had gone back to putting packages of hamburger out for display. Maybe I could drag him into the back room, I thought wildly.

He moved a few feet farther down the case and picked up another item from the supply cart. A thrill I can only describe as sexual ran through my body when I saw the bloody chunk of flesh.

The butcher put the meat in the display case. The eight-pound rib roast had been recently cut. Red oozed against the tight cellophane wrapper and collected in the styrofoam tray. It was the most beautiful thing I had ever seen in my life.

I took four bounding steps and snatched up the roast. The butcher was shouting something and coming after me. He evidently thought I meant to steal the meat. I ignored him and rushed past the register, throwing a hundred dollar bill at the startled cashier, and not waiting for change.

Outside, I spun in a circle, half mad with the Hunger. I could not wait to get home. It did not matter that the meat was uncooked. I would eat it raw. Yes. Raw was better.

I ran into the alley beside the store. There was a dumpster about twenty feet down the narrow, littered passage, just past the point where the circle of illumination from the feeble security light ended and the shadows began. I stumbled to the dumpster and cowered behind it, hissing at the rat that scuttled away into the filthy darkness.

I knelt in the loose garbage, breathing in the smell of rotting food as I ripped into the package. The alley reeked, but the stronger smell—blood, precious blood!—overpowered my other sensations until I scarcely knew where I was.

What was left of my human dignity asserted itself one final time. I held back for the briefest moment—staring at the cold, bleeding flesh in my hands, ignoring the pain splitting apart my upper jaw—and felt disgust for the wretched creature I had become. Knowing Tatiana had made me think of vampires as romantic, magical beings, but joining their race had debased me to the lowest sort of degeneracy. And where would my journey into the depths of self-abasement end?

In that moment in the alley, I finally realized how little I knew about what I had gotten myself into with Tatiana. But then, as I admitted at the beginning of this journal, women are my weakness.

Possessed completely by the Hunger, I tore into the raw meat with my teeth, sucking the cold blood into my mouth like a man lost in the desert who finally reaches an oasis and lowers his face into the life-giving waters to drink deeply—oblivious of time, of circumstance, of right and wrong, of what he has become.

The sour, rotten smell of the alley still clung to my clothing when I awoke the next night.

I put my head over the side of the bed and vomited.

I spent an hour soaking in the bathtub, shaved off my beard, and combed back my long hair—which was thicker and darker than it had been before. I put on an Arrow shirt, khaki pants, Clarice's belt, and Top Siders.

The emptiness in my stomach made me nervous, but a visit to a twenty-four-hour breakfast restaurant eased the pain in my belly as well as in my mind. The beef blood I consumed the night before had satisfied the Hunger for the moment. I knew, however, that it would not leave me alone for long.

My meal put me in better spirits. It was a beautiful night. People were out on the street, walking or sitting on their front steps. Simply to be a part of this scene was enough to make me feel almost human again.

I walked to the University of Chicago Library, which stays open until midnight for students, and went to the place in the stacks where books about the Russian revolution were shelved. I took down a half dozen volumes and carried them to a table.

Tatiana Feodorovna said she would have been a grand duchess if there hadn't been a revolution. Now that I knew she was a vampire, it seemed likely—judging from the portrait at her house—that she had in fact been a grand duchess before the czar was overthrown. If this were the case, I might be able to find references to the Feodorovnas in the histories of the period and fill in some of the many blanks in what I knew about her past.

I picked up the first book from the pile, a large leather-bound volume that had a section of pictures in the middle, sandwiched between several hundred pages of text. I was disappointed to find that the index had no listing for Feodorovna, so I began flipping randomly through the pictures, thinking I might get lucky.

It did not take long to find my lover's face.

The third or fourth page I glanced at had a reproduction of an old photograph of Czar Nicholas, a tall, bearded man wearing a military uniform, whose face held an unmistakable air of authority. At his side was a beautiful young woman—*my* beautiful young woman.

The caption said the photograph showed Czar Nicholas II and his daughter, Grand Duchess Tatiana Nicolaievna Romanov. I hadn't known it before, but in the parlance of the Russian aristocracy, grand duchess and princess were synonymous terms. Tatiana, my ballerina, was in reality Princess Tatiana Nicolaievna Romanov, heir to the Russian throne.

I sat without moving for a long time, lost in thought. The sadness that was always in my lover's eyes and her refusal to discuss the past now were easy to understand. To lose both family and empire—how difficult it must have been to endure such tragedy and continue living.

I looked Tatiana up in the index and read the listed entries to learn what I could about the czar's daughter.

Tatiana was the czar's second eldest child. Born to Czar Nicholas and Czarina Alexandra were Olga in 1895, Tatiana in 1897, Marie in 1899, Anastasia in 1901, and baby Alexis in 1904. Tatiana had been a quiet, intelligent, and well-liked girl, from what I found, although historians tended to pay little attention to the czar's four female offspring.

I checked the accounts in each of the six books. They all were quite explicit about one important point: Tatiana and the rest of the royal family were shot by communist revolutionaries in 1918, and their bodies were thrown down a mine shaft.

What the history books could not tell me was whether Tatiana had been a vampire before the executions, with superhuman strength that made it possible for her to survive, or if she miraculously had escaped the slaughter and underwent the transformation later, perhaps while in exile.

Looking through one of the books, my eyes settled on a photograph of Rasputin, with his long hair and beard and electrifying eyes. It reminded me of the icon Tatiana said Rasputin had given her. The notorious Mad Monk was said to have possessed strange, diabolical powers that he used to put the czar's family under his spell. Was Rasputin incidental in my lover's life story, or did he play a bigger role in her strange fate?

Whatever happened to Tatiana that made it possible for her to survive, looking not a day older after seventy-one years, I knew it would not be explained in history books about the fall of the house of Romanov. As far as the historians were concerned, she perished in a hail of gunfire in 1918.

I closed the final book and smiled sadly.

I knew something the historians did not.

I walked past Tatiana's house after leaving the library. I knew she was no longer in the city, that she had left to draw away our nameless mutual enemy, but I thought visiting the place she had lived would make me feel closer to her.

The mansion—dark, as usual—looked deserted. I rattled the gate and whistled. No dogs.

I bounced on the balls of my feet and looked up at the wall. The muscles in my calves were as taut as new springs.

Leaping over the twelve-foot wall was surprisingly easy. As I looked down and saw the jagged broken glass that topped the wall sail beneath me, I realized that such a vertical jump was impossible for a human. But then, I was no longer human.

I looked through the window where Tatiana and I had been the night I followed her home. The moonlight spilled past me into the large, bare chamber. On my previous visit the room had been a treasury of antiques and icons, brilliantly lit by the glow of a thousand candles. Now no evidence remained of the beautiful Russian princess who had lived there, surrounded with artifacts from her tragic past. It was as if she had never been there at all.

We would only be apart a year, I reminded myself, feeling the words echo in my aching heart.

Not a very long time for a vampire.

But for a novice vampire it seemed like forever.

# Chapter 14

**P**ARIS, JUNE 17, 1989—I've time for only a brief entry. I must leave within the hour for a date with Rachel Weir, an American woman I met last night.

Business brought Rachel here from New York, and I have promised to show her Paris. We'll have dinner and take a taxi tour of the city. And later, after we've returned to my room to linger over glasses of brandy, and kisses, and snaps and buttons, she will give me a small amount of her blood—hardly enough to fill a wineglass, but exactly what I need to keep the Hunger at bay.

I have learned to enjoy these interludes with mortal women, but I am not much in the mood for tonight's seduction. Ariel Niccolini telephoned this evening to thank me for the roses, which she thought I had sent to commemorate the two-week anniversary of our meeting.

"I miss you so much, *amore mio*. Why don't you come to Florence to visit?"

"I wish that I could."

"Please?" There was a hint of desperation in her voice. She had not yet decided that what we shared was over. And neither had I.

"I'm sorry that I cannot," I said with real regret. "It's impossible. But if things change, I promise to come."

Then I had an inspiration.

"Why don't you fly back to Paris? Do it as a crazy impulse. Don't even pack a bag. Drive to the airport and get on a plane. I'll buy your ticket. You can call the museum in the morning and tell them you're home sick in bed with the flu."

Now it was Ariel's turn to demur. She had to attend a dinner party the following night with her patron, a wealthy Italian whose donations practically funded the museum's entire budget.

"He's a tyrant," she explained. "If I don't show up at his party, he'll have a fit. But he invited me to bring someone if I wanted. I know you and he would hit it off. He knows more about opera than any two other people."

"Ariel, I really wish I could. . . ."

We discussed again how our different lives complicated what otherwise could have easily blossomed into a beautiful relationship. But of course I could not admit to her the biggest complication of all. Ariel sounded quite sad by the end of our conversation, and I felt much the same.

I must be careful in the future not to become so emotionally involved with the mortals I go to for blood. Extricating myself from these situations is too painful. My heart is too open, which I suppose is why women are my weakness.

In less than an hour I will go to meet my next conquest. I feel like a gigolo, but there is no alternative. The Hunger must be satisfied.

Two nights after the humiliating episode at the supermarket— and one night after I learned that Tatiana Feodorovna was Princess Tatiana Nicolaievna Romanov—the Hunger returned.

I was awakened by an insistent craving for blood that was as unpleasant as opening my eyes to find one of the Manson Family standing at the foot of my bed, holding a butcher knife and grinning. I sat up in a cold sweat, a metallic taste in my mouth. I knew I had to have blood, and instinct told me that nothing but human blood would quench my burning desire.

I spent half an hour pacing, trying to formulate a plan. The Hunger seemed to grow inside me with each step, threatening to become an uncontrollable frenzy if I didn't act soon. I had to find a mortal to give me blood while I still retained some small measure of control over myself.

There were plenty of places in Chicago to pick up an anonymous woman for the night. However, the exact process by which I would separate such a woman from her blood remained a complete mystery to me. The throbbing in my upper gums told me I soon would have teeth capable of puncturing a jugular vein. But how soon, and what of the rest of it? I had no idea how to convince a stranger to let me open her jugular and drink her blood. And then there was the matter of what happened afterward. What would prevent my victim from going to the police with an account of the attack and a vivid description of her assailant?

There had to be things that I didn't yet understand. My only hope was that instinct would provide me with the guidance I needed when the moment arrived. After all, I thought with bitter irony, how does a newborn babe know to suckle at its mother's breast? You didn't need to be shown some things: They were hard-wired in on the genetic level.

For insurance I tore through the town house on a scavenger hunt for things I might need if instinct failed me. In the event that the vampire physiology did not deliver me with the necessary means to take blood, I brought a razor and a package of bandages, thinking I could cut an artery and staunch the bleeding after I had what I needed. I found a pair of handcuffs Clarice had bought in a moment of kinkiness. I also got a length of nylon rope and a roll of black electrical tape from the utility room, and put the entire collection into a briefcase.

A cab took me to the airport, where I rented a car and drove to a place where money could buy almost anything.

It was a hot spring night, and I rolled both front windows down, an inadvisable thing to do in dangerous neighborhoods after dark—or during the day. Young men in leather jackets and an occasional female stood alone or in clusters on the curbs and sidewalks. Driving slow was the only thing I had to do to advertise that I was shopping for illicit merchandise. They came toward my car or yelled out as I rolled past.

"Crack, man!"

"Hey, bro, what you need is right here."

"Dose. You want a dose?"

A woman stepped out of the shadows. "Let's party," she called to me.

There was no mistaking what it was she was selling, and a glance in her direction was the only encouragement she needed. She appeared to be a woman of average appearance despite her garish makeup and clothing. When she came closer, I realized she might have been fifty as easily as thirty. She'd lived hard, and it was difficult to imagine anybody paying to have sex with someone who looked so beaten. The skin inside her elbows was scarred and discolored. I could see a long, purplish bruise along the ridge of one extruding vein where she had been shooting up most recently.

I shook my head and pressed on the accelerator.

"Faggot!" she screamed after me.

"Got crack here. Best quality."

"Yo! Mexican brown, man."

"Get out of here with that Mexican brown shit. I got China white, man. The real stuff. Come straight from the Golden Triangle."

I silently mouthed "No" to the dealer who stepped toward me from the curb as I rolled slowly by. Like most of the others selling drugs, he let it go at that. There were plenty of customers.

Stoplight.

From behind a purple van stepped a woman whose small frame made her breasts appear even larger than they really were. She wore a tight rayon blouse, a short leather skirt, and spike-heel shoes with straps around the ankles. She was young, maybe not much older than sixteen. Her face was pretty, and her café au lait skin smooth and fresh. The absurd thing—I suppose it was intended to be absurd—was her hair, which was dyed blond.

I kept the cool look frozen on my face. Inside me the Hunger screamed for blood.

"Hello, good-lookin'," she called out. I pulled into a no-parking space. She came around and leaned against my door to talk.

"What you want tonight, sugar?"

I didn't answer. The smell of her blood made me want to drag her in through the window, and it was all I could do to keep my fingers locked around the steering wheel. I drew in a slow breath, held it a count, then blew it out slowly, shaking.

"So you want to have a party with me?" she asked, slurring her words.

Something wasn't right. There was something in her blood—it wasn't alcohol, as I first thought—that didn't belong. The smell was cloyingly sweet, like too much cheap perfume. It reminded me of poppies. Her out-of-focus eyes looked right past me. Heroin, I guessed.

I wanted to tell her I wasn't interested, but the Hunger wouldn't let me. Any chance I had to be selective was in the past.

*Take her!* it screamed in my head. *The heroin will only make her easier to handle!*

"I know a hotel," she said. "It's twenty dollars for the hotel and thirty dollars for me."

*Snap!*

The steering wheel cracked between my hands. The sharp noise startled the hooker, but she didn't seem to know where it came from. She stood up from my window and took a wobbly step backward.

"Yeah," I said, my voice a hoarse whisper. "Get in. Let's have a party."

There was contempt as well as triumph in the way she leered at me while walking around the front of the car, shaking her hips with a slow, deliberate rhythm. She opened the door and slid in beside me.

I could hardly stand it. I had to have her now!

The door slammed. Her hand was on my thigh, sliding higher, going between my legs.

I'd intended to take her to a motel I'd picked out of the phone book that was near a public hospital. I wanted to be able to call for an ambulance if something went wrong. But all of that was impossible to think about now. It would be a miracle if I could hold off long enough to get off the crowded street.

She put her tongue into my ear. I moaned, but not out of sexual pleasure. The light turned green. I jammed my foot against the accelerator.

"Whoa, man, slow down! I'll get you there fast enough."

There was an all-night restaurant at the end of the next block. I skidded the rented Taurus to a stop in the space between a bread truck and the warehouse wall at the far end of the parking lot.

"You need it bad, lover man."

Yes, I needed it bad.

"It's all right," she said with a low laugh. "I'll do you here and save you twenty dollars."

The smell of the prostitute's blood filled my head like ether, but instead of making me unconscious it made me crazy. Surges of ferocious energy rushed through my body, giving me the physical strength to do anything I needed to get blood.

"How you want it? Thirty dollars is for the basic. For fifty, you can do anything you want to me for as long as you want."

I grabbed her blouse and ripped it completely off her body in an explosive frenzy.

She started to scream, but I locked my eyes onto hers and she fell instantly quiet. Instinct did not fail to give me the predatory tools I needed. She would submit to me because I *willed* her to!

What a sense of power! My will alone was sufficient to hold her there, silent and helpless, ready to take anything I wanted to do to her. She stared back blankly, as if her mind no longer registered what was happening. The hands that had tried to push me away dropped limply, and she slumped backward against the door, totally passive, her head rolling to one side to expose her pulsing neck.

The pressure behind my upper lip made me feel as though my jaw were about to burst. There was a wet, tearing sound as my gums split open, but I hardly felt it. Reflected in the car window, I saw the fangs jutting from my mouth, wet with blood from my torn flesh.

I lowered my eyes to the woman and felt a surge of animal pleasure. She was *mine*!

Opening my mouth wide, I lowered myself to her neck. The sounds of both our hearts pounded together in my head as I pressed my lips against her warm skin, her pulse speeding to catch mine until both were perfectly synchronized. My breath came in short, rapid pants as I ran my tongue along her neck, tasting the salty flesh.

And then I bit down—hard.

Rapture a thousand times more intense than anything I'd ever experienced—even greater than the times I'd fed Tatiana—flooded through me. The woman's hot blood gushed against my throat. I gulped it down greedily, not wanting to waste a single precious drop.

Beneath me, the hooker moaned and thrust her body against mine.

A wonderful calm flowed into me as I drank the sweet, heroin-spiced blood. The nerve-frying surge of power that had gripped me just before feeding subsided into an awareness of great strength in repose. With each swallow, I became increasingly conscious of the power growing within me that would bring more experiences and wisdom than a mortal could collect in a dozen lifetimes. And the key that unlocked it all was blood, miraculous, life-giving blood, which opened the door to an infinity of possibilities for the vampire.

I wanted to drink forever.

Forever . . .

Forever . . .

I suddenly realized what I was doing.

Horrified, I pulled myself away, knowing that I had already taken too much. The woman's body was limp, and her brown skin had a chalky cast. Her eyes were open, but unfocused, staring up at nothing.

I had to get help! Yet did I dare?

I jerked the mirror toward my face. My mouth was smeared

with blood, and the hideous fangs still jutted downward, dripping red that stained my shirt and jacket. How long would it be—a minute, an hour—before I could pass myself off as a human? And even then, the bloodstains were everywhere!

I flung open the passenger door in a panic and pushed the woman out onto the asphalt. She rolled out of the car limply, more like a large doll than a person, no tension in her slack muscles.

I started the car and threw it into reverse in a single motion. Six blocks later I skidded to a stop at a telephone booth. It wasn't enough, I knew, but it was all I could do at that point: I called the police.

"There's a girl in the parking lot of the Half Moon Grill," I said. "She's been hurt badly. I think she might be dead."

I was a murderer.

The vision of the prostitute tumbling limply out of the car played itself over and over inside my head until I thought I'd go insane with grief.

I had been unable to control myself. The Hunger had become my master, and as its slave, I'd sacrificed a woman to pay the first installment on the debt I owed for the purchase of my relative immortality. I hadn't meant to harm her. It had been an accident. But that wouldn't make my crime any easier to live with.

And what would happen the next time?

I could not imagine how Tatiana would react. I remembered her words as clearly as if she'd said them only the day before:

*"You need never take a mortal life, and I hope with all of my heart that you never do. Life should be as sacred to a vampire as it is to an ordinary human being. Morality does not change simply because you become one of us."*

I was a killer, a vampire too weak to control his worst impulses. I could not expect Tatiana to love the monster I had become. She thought I would comfort her through the ages, but she would not find shelter in the arms of a murderer.

I sat in the dark in my living room, the weight of my crime pressing down on me. There was no escaping what I had done and no living with it. How many centuries would I sit alone at night and think of that poor woman? How could I atone for taking a human being's life?

The only thing I had to look forward to was the Hunger returning to possess me again, compelling me to hunt down and kill another victim. That, and the pleasure I had felt in the midst of that criminal act—the inexpressibly delicious rush of ecstasy. Perhaps I would even become conditioned to enjoy killing.

It took no imagination to see where I was headed. For the sake of everything good I had to die before I fell any farther. The disappointment Tatiana would feel at losing me could be no worse than the experience of returning to meet a monster inhabiting the form she'd once known as David Parker.

The hands on the clock stood at seven-thirty. Though the town house windows were blocked shut against the light, I knew the sun would be climbing over Lake Michigan. I went to the front door, unlocked the deadbolts and unfastened the chain.

"I pray that God, if there is a God, will forgive me for what I have done and for what I am about to do."

I threw open the door. The sky was blue, the sun was golden-white, the light blindingly brilliant.

Searing agony exploded in every nerve as I stepped out into the cleansing fire of the new morning. My body was ablaze in the purifying flames that would burn away all traces of my crime, my weaknesses, my failures as a man and as a vampire.

I pitched forward onto the concrete landing and lost consciousness.

The darkness opened, and at its center, shining in the formless sea of nothingness, was a golden seed of awareness that was all that was left of me.

This, then, is death, I thought. I'd left behind the noisy, pointless world of the living. The only part of me that remained was that which was eternal. I was no longer body but pure spirit: good, light, diamond-hard.

Then came the pain.

It seemed that I was not dead after all but only very close to it.

Still, there seemed to have been an atonement in what I'd done, for I felt an inexpressible peace in place of the spiritual agony that pushed me to try to kill myself. It was as if the sun's cathartic fires had cleansed me, burning away the husk of my life until only the kernel, the essence, remained—and I knew without doubt that the essence was good in spite of the incidental failures and casual evils I had blundered into during my brief, unhappy life.

Now I was truly ready to die, not in despair but in joy. I had done some things well in my life, and I had made my share of mistakes. But I finally understood that none of it really mattered—the profit and the loss, the victories and the defeats, the strengths and the weaknesses. They were incidental. The only thing *real* was the spark of awareness that was perfect and complete in itself, the sense of peace that comes from existing in the moment, free from caring what had come before or waited ahead.

The peaceful darkness rolled back over me.

When I regained consciousness again, I was able to recognize my surroundings. I was sprawled on the tile entryway floor. I could just see my right hand. It was hideous, the skin blackened and broken with open blisters.

The survival instinct must have taken over after I collapsed. Apparently I had dragged myself inside and managed to push the door closed.

Mercifully, I passed out. The pain was still there when I reawoke, but it was a different sort of pain, one that was less intense. The skin on my hand was bright red, as if I'd suffered a serious sunburn, but certainly not as serious as the damage had appeared before. I pulled myself up onto the couch and sat there for half an hour, incredulous as the healing process completed itself. It took my body exactly two hours to mend burns that should have been fatal.

I went into the bathroom and stood in front of the mirror, running my hands slowly over my face. No trace remained of the damage the sun had inflicted, but I also discovered that an old scar above my left eyebrow had disappeared. Had my appendix and tonsils grown back, too? I wondered, marveling at the way my vampire body had regenerated itself.

Pushing back my upper lip, I ran my forefinger over each of the two slits high on my gums, one just above each canine tooth. The places where the incisors retracted into the upper jaw were almost invisible.

This is not someone you really know, I thought, staring at myself in the mirror. And it was true. David Parker the man was no more, and David Parker the vampire was a stranger who seemed to be capable of endless surprises.

It is impossible to come so close to dying without being changed by the experience.

For me it drew a line through my life. On one side of the line was my past, characterized by compromise, delusion, and self-pity. On the other side was the present and the future, which were filled with innumerable possibilities.

I resolved to put the past firmly and finally behind me. My old life had been burned away. Like a phoenix, a new David Parker had risen from the ashes of my previous existence. This life was totally new, and whether I made a success of it was up to me and me alone. I did not ask to be absolved for my earlier mistakes. I accepted responsibility for them. But I was determined not to repeat them.

And I would learn to master the Hunger and never kill again.

Tatiana, I thought, loved me enough to understand the tragedy that had occurred the previous night. Together we would find a way to go forward.

Cutting my ties with the past filled me with a tremendous sense of freedom. It made me feel like doing the one thing I enjoyed more than anything else. I went to the piano and ran my hand along its top. There was a thin film of dust coating the black finish. It would gather dust no more.

I sat down and lifted the cover from the keyboard and began to play all the Mozart pieces I knew by heart. I didn't get up for twelve hours.

# Chapter 15

**P**ARIS, JUNE 18, 1989—I met her for the first time in an art gallery on the Left Bank. She was frowning at a cubist painting. I stood beside her for a moment and frowned, too, trying unsuccessfully to discern any recognizable objects or ideas within the explosion of geometric shapes on the Braque canvas.

"I'm afraid I don't get it," I admitted.

She smiled up at me. Her eyes were hazel, the perfect color for her red hair, which was cut in the style that always makes me think of Cleopatra.

"I had a professor in college who said modern art is an inside joke. Unless you're in on it, you have absolutely no idea what is going on."

Her accent was pure New England Yankee, probably Massachusetts. Like Katharine Hepburn, she breathed right through her *R*s: *"I had a profess-ah in college who said mod-ahn aht is an inside joke."*

"What about this Matisse? I like it."

"It rather more suits me."

We moved to the next painting and then to the next and the next, viewing the remainder of the collection together. Our tastes were similar, and we found it easy to agree. When we got to the end of our tour, I invited her across the street for a glass of wine. She accepted without hesitation.

Rachel Weir was an investment banker on Wall Street. That surprised me. Her relaxed, confident manner was much more low-key than the manic, ulcer-ridden stock market types I knew. She was in Paris to renegotiate bond payments with officials from the bankrupt government of what is usually euphemistically referred to as a developing country.

"And you, Mr. Parker? What is it you do?"

I explained that I formerly was an attorney, but that I had given up law to devote myself to my real passion in life, the piano.

"You must be taking a considerable risk."

"I suppose that depends upon what sort of risk you're talking about."

"I mean giving up the security of a law career."

"Then you're talking about money."

Rachel blushed. "I'm sorry. It's an occupational hazard."

"Don't apologize. Except, no, the risk is entirely personal for me. I was fortunate enough to have a grandmother leave me a comfortable trust fund. However, the risk to my ego is risk enough. There are no half-successful concert pianists. You're either near the top of the field or you're nothing."

"So you're following your heart."

I looked into her eyes. She was a practical woman, yet she was not so practical that she was immune to the romance inherent in my career change.

We enjoyed several very pleasant glasses of wine, our friendship warming as the conversation wandered from music to banking to art to life in general. I escorted her back to her hotel just before midnight. The stroll up the Champs-Elysées was unhurried, even lazy. Neither one of us was anxious for the evening to end.

When we arrived at her hotel, Rachel invited me in for a drink. I surprised her by refusing. It was late and we both had business early in the morning, I said. But if she was free the following evening, would she care to see me again? I had tickets to the national opera. We could have a late dinner afterward.

"That would be lovely," she said.

I kissed her on the cheek. When she raised her mouth to mine, I tasted her delicious lips, holding her close for a moment, savoring the mingled aroma of good perfume, blood, and the hint of Château Margaux that lingered on her breath.

And then, ignoring the Hunger within me, I wished her a good night.

The time I spent with Rachel Weir last evening was equally charming—until the end, when the night quickly turned sour.

Rachel is exactly the sort of woman I'm attracted to most. She has brains and is a witty conversationalist, which is important to me, for my private ritual of satisfying the Hunger always begins with conversation. I may be a vampire, but I am still a gentleman. I prefer to charm women into giving me what I need, rather than using the indomitable power of my will to force them to submit.

Sharing blood is the most intimate act of all, even more intimate than love. It is a sensual experience, and in taking pleasure and sustenance, I appreciate the opportunity to give pleasure in return.

I usually meet my lovers at the opera, in the poetry section of bookstores, or, as it was with Rachel, in a gallery. Conversation, an evening at the theater or concert hall, a romantic dinner, soft music played by candlelight on the piano in my room—lovemaking follows its natural course, unhurried, unforced.

And when our passion heats toward its most satisfying conclusion, there is the final act that lifts our mutual pleasure to an even higher plateau.

We saw an excellent production of *Carmen*, and enjoyed an especially good meal at a little restaurant near the theater. We rode back to my hotel in a taxi, sitting close together, Rachel's head on my shoulder.

In my suite I poured sherry and sat down at the piano. She sat beside me. Electricity seemed to run back and forth between our two bodies as I played "Clair de lune," which I find irresistibly erotic.

I turned to Rachel, Debussy's final notes shimmering in the air, caressing us. The surrender was unmistakable in her dreamy smile. I kissed her, and she returned my kiss with equal passion.

"I want you to make love to me, Mr. Parker," she whispered.

Exactly what I had in mind. I swept Rachel Weir into my arms and carried her into the bedroom.

It was two hours before dawn. The city had finally gone to bed.

Rachel lay beside me, the soft light cast by a single candle on the armoire throwing an exquisite golden glow on her perfect body. Her breasts slowly rose and fell with the steady rhythm of deep sleep. I felt a sharp pang of desire as I admired her lovely body and listened to her faint breath and her strong heartbeat.

I would not disturb her. Not yet.

The windows were open, and the light breeze billowed the gossamer inner curtains into the room like the sails on an enchanted boat. It made me think of my own bedroom so far away in Chicago and the nights I had spent there with Tatiana.

It seemed as if Tatiana and I had been apart such a long time. Yet I did not miss her less. Exactly the opposite, in fact. The more time we spent separated, the more I loved her and ached for her to be returned to me.

I looked down at the sleeping woman in my bed and felt the sting of guilt. Two weeks before, Ariel Niccolini had occupied the same place beside me. I had slept with many women in the past year and developed serious affection for Ariel and Anna Montoya—although Tatiana was the only woman I really loved. Any of them, however, had good reason to accuse me of being an incontinent and opportunistic lover.

Unfortunately it had to be that way. Every two weeks the Hunger returned in me, and making love to women seemed infinitely preferable to picking victims out at random and forcing them to submit to the power of my will. Certainly Tatiana would forgive me the infidelities I committed to keep the beast within me at bay. After all, she had to have blood, too.

I sat up quietly in bed, careful not to disturb my newest lover. My robe was thrown over the sofa at the foot of the bed. I pulled it on. The silk felt good against my skin. The curtains brushed by my face as I stepped onto the balcony and looked down on the darkened square.

A figure in an ankle-length topcoat—they call them dusters, I believe—leaned against a lamp near the quietly splashing fountain. He wore a wide-brimmed hat and stood, hands in pockets, with his head tilted down, so that the shadows hid his face. By day the Place Vendôme was alive with crowds of people and flocks of pigeons, the birds swooping through the air and congregating in large, rotating circles around benches where people sat and fed them.

The man removed his hands from the coat pockets. Something about him was not right. I watched as he lifted a cigarette to his mouth. The feeling I had was really quite peculiar. I was unable to identify exactly what it was about him that disturbed me, yet there was *something* . . . .

Then it dawned on me: Even though I could see him perfectly well *with my eyes*, none of my other senses registered his presence. I should have been able to *feel* him in half a dozen ways, but instead it was as if he were not really there.

I opened my senses and reached out. The sound of the water in the fountain in the center of the square became a roar, but there was no heartbeat from the figure in the Place Vendôme mixed in with the sound. There was nothing there! It was as if he were a mirage, an aberration of light and shadow that had deluded me into thinking I saw a man leaning against a lamppost when no man was there at all.

Except that he *was* there! My eyes did not lie, despite what my higher senses told me.

Then I heard it, hardly louder than a whisper: the low, wicked laugh. I knew that laugh!

The vampire struck a match and lifted it to the cigarette as he tilted his chin upward so that I could see his face in the glow of the flame. The killer's sardonic smile was large enough for me to see his gleaming blood teeth shining in the lamplight, as white as new ivory.

What did this fiend want now?

I glanced over my shoulder at the figure sleeping in my bed. The answer seemed painfully clear. He wanted Rachel.

When I looked back down from the balcony, the English vampire was laughing and twirling a small shiny object in the fingers of his right hand. I didn't have to look at it directly to know it was the scalpel he'd used to cut off the ear of the woman he'd murdered in Montmartre Cemetery.

I spun on my heel and went back inside, closed and locked the windows, and drew the curtains. My anger rose, and with it came a hellish rush of energy that swept through my body, gorging my muscles with adrenaline and quickening my breath. Let him try to get into my rooms! I thought, opening and closing my fists. *Goddamn* him!

I was so eager for a confrontation that I almost went down to the street to meet the killer, but I stopped myself before I got out the door. That would have been exactly what he wanted me to do, I realized. I knew then that the one thing I had to do was stay with Rachel. In the murderous game of chess the aristocratic Englishman was forcing me to play, she had just become a pawn in an exposed position.

Rachel stirred in her sleep, touching the bruise on her neck with her fingers, kicking against the loose sheets as if they were a web she was ensnared in. She was having a nightmare. I knew—I don't know how, but I simply *knew*—that the vampire outside the hotel was putting terrors into her dreaming mind, tormenting her with visions of the twisted things he wanted to do to her body with his scalpel—before he killed her.

"Bastard!" I said out loud. I put my hand on Rachel's forehead, which was damp with a cold sweat.

"Sleep peacefully, my darling. All is safe. All is well."

The anxiety went out of her face as she relaxed against the mattress and dropped into a deeper level of unconsciousness.

Rachel awoke an hour later. I could see the soft forgetfulness in her eyes. She remembered the best parts of the evening—and had forgotten others. There was no longer any sign of the two faint red marks near the base of her neck. The powerful enzymes from my mouth had healed her completely.

I insisted on walking her back to her hotel. The fiend was no longer anywhere to be seen, but I knew he was there someplace, disguising his presence so that I couldn't pinpoint his location.

I kissed Rachel good-bye and promised to write her when I got back to America. She ran up the steps toward the lobby, turning at the top to wave one final time and blow me a kiss. She disappeared through the door.

I followed.

When she stepped into her elevator, I slipped from behind the post where I was standing and paid the desk clerk for two nights' lodging, inducing him to put me into the empty room next to Rachel's.

A taxi would bring my lost luggage from the airport later, I told him. However, under no circumstances whatsoever was I to be disturbed before evening. I had a bad case of jet lag and planned to take a sleeping pill and spend the day in bed.

Upstairs I listened outside Rachel's door. She was brushing out her hair, getting ready to return to bed for a few more hours of sleep.

I stood vigil at her door until the first light of dawn began to show in the eastern sky. When I was certain she was no longer in danger from my enemy, I rushed to my own room and blocked the window with the bedspread. I was too exhausted to sleep, so I sat down at the desk, found this paper and began these notes, which I will insert in my journal when I return to the Place Vendôme tonight.

It's almost ten o'clock in the morning. In three more hours, Rachel will board a jet and return to New York.

At least I've managed to frustrate my murderous rival this time.

# Chapter 16

**P**ARIS, JUNE 19, 1989—In the week that followed my first attempt to feed, I searched the pages of the newspapers in vain for a story about a woman who had been killed and dumped in the parking lot of the Half Moon Grill.

Murder is not big news in a city like Chicago. Nevertheless I thought the medical mystery of a dead prostitute found inexplicably drained of blood might have enough novelty to catch a reporter's attention.

My only recourse when the press failed to pick up the story was to turn to official sources, but I was not foolish enough to contact the authorities. Police are suspicious by nature, and it would have been stupid to ask questions that would have created a connection between me and a dead woman I had no legitimate reason to know or care about. The police might even be holding a description of a man the victim was last seen with, a man who looked amazingly like me.

Still, it surprised me that there was nothing in the papers about the woman.

Maybe an incompetent pathologist thought she'd died of natural causes, the body lacking any discernible wounds. Or maybe an overworked and cynical staff member at the city morgue didn't care enough to investigate the unusual death—just another dead junkie hooker Chicago was better off without.

One possibility was that the authorities had never recovered the body. There are plenty of sick people in the world, and one of them could have snatched the corpse off the street, for his own twisted reasons.

Or she could have miraculously survived. I didn't want to delude myself, especially since I'd been certain the woman was dead. But there was a slim chance that, in my panic and inexperience, I'd been mistaken.

Not a day goes by without my thinking about her. I didn't even know her name, and I spent less than a quarter hour with her, but our fates have become inextricably linked forever.

I only wish I knew what happened to her, and where she was buried, if she was buried at all.

Although the newspapers told me nothing about the prostitute I thought I'd killed, they did contain daily stories on a topic that caused me great anxiety. Health officials, I read, were becoming desperate over the number of AIDS cases the city had seen, and could see, as the epidemic spread. Thousands of infected carriers walked the streets, unaware of the time bomb hiding in their blood.

The stories I read talked about certain life-styles putting people at risk for AIDS. But whose life-style could put them any more at risk of contracting a blood-to-blood virus than a vampire? I knew that the Hunger was going to force me to drink the blood of strangers. That meant I would have a regular opportunity to become infected.

Though vampires' bodies are hardier than mortals', I did not know whether my system was strong enough to fight off whatever random diseases I might ingest drinking raw blood. If I fed from a woman who had the flu, would I then have the flu? The issue was more serious when I considered more deadly possibilities: leukemia, AIDS, and so on.

The possibility that I had infected myself with AIDS nearly drove me mad with worry for several days. I called a lab and found out how to get tested, but I didn't go through with it. Who knew what the technician would see when he smeared my blood on a glass slide and looked at it through a microscope? It might provide conclusive proof that whatever I was, it wasn't human. I couldn't afford that risk.

The only thing I could do was hope for the best and promise myself to be as careful as I could about choosing the people whose blood I drank. If there were high-risk candidates for the diseases I feared most, I would then turn to the lowest-risk individuals to serve as the hosts to my Hunger.

I finally put the chance that I had been infected with AIDS—and that I might in turn infect others—out of my mind. Time would prove that I was right to do so. My body has thus far proven immune to blood-borne diseases.

* * *

My powers grew at a steady rate.

I could see as well without my glasses as with them, so one day I took off the horn-rimmed spectacles, which made me look very much the lawyer I no longer was, put them in a drawer, and left them there.

I was always a fast reader, but my speed increased dramatically after I'd undergone the transformation. I could finish a five-hundred-page novel in less than an hour. More amazing yet was my retention. I could quote, word-for-word, passages four or five pages in length. (Since then I've gotten so that I can read a book and recall perfectly every word, comma, and period!)

Brain experts say we remember virtually everything we see, even though we can access only a tiny fraction of this stored information. The vampire, I've learned, is able to utilize much of the eighty or ninety percent of the brain that lies fallow in human beings.

In the days between when I first learned the truth about Tatiana and the time I joined her race, I thought about vampires in terms of immortality, strength, and the amazing paranormal powers that allowed them to drift unnoticed in and out of rooms and speak telepathically. But after I became a vampire, none of those things impressed me nearly so much as realizing the astounding capacity of the vampire's mind.

I do not believe our brains are physically different from a mortal's, but they are for some reason open to developing their full capacity. Good or evil, there are no *stupid* vampires. Perhaps this is why we are so attracted to art, why we are, among so many other things, creatures of high culture.

This has been the most wonderful part of my new life—feeling my mind opening like the blossom on an exotic flower. As time passes and I successfully meet new challenges, I feel myself increasingly capable of understanding my small role in the life of this planet, and better able to use the full range of my resources and experiences.

I no longer think of a vampire as a creature driven to drink human blood. I think of a vampire as a creature of the mind.

I began to feel the Hunger twelve nights after my first feeding. It was weak and distant at first, a sensation more remembered than experienced. Except that this time I knew my vague craving would grow until it overpowered my self-control and turned me into an unreasoning beast driven to serve its thirst for blood.

Never again would I be its slave.

This time, I would act before the Hunger could act upon me. I would satisfy my need while I still maintained reason enough to drink only the small amount of blood my body required.

My intention was to find a woman whose blood would be safe. I would find a woman whose sexual experience was limited, which would make the process more difficult. Prostitutes made the task of meeting and seducing a stranger relatively uncomplicated, reducing it to the level of a commercial transaction.

I dressed for the hunt in Reeboks, jeans, a black turtleneck, and a lightweight leather jacket. When I looked in the mirror, I saw the David Parker I used to be back in the days when I was a member of The Committee. Though I respected the Hunger enough to be frightened of its power, I was still more than a little excited about the evening ahead of me. It had been a long time since I'd gone out alone at night, looking for a lover.

After I was ready, I put a Pat Metheny CD in the player and sat down on the sofa in the living room with a mineral water, listening to the cool jazz and waiting for the day to end. I felt razor sharp and ready as the edge of night cut across the sky, drawing a line between the sober concerns of the nine-to-five world and the sensual pleasures that only flower in darkness.

The last bit of red was dying in the sky when I left home. Without a destination in mind I let my feet carry me to the neighborhood near Northwestern University. As I walked, I began to form the outlines of a plan.

I approached a dormitory, my pace an unhurried stroll. There were hushed footsteps on the sidewalk behind me. I stopped to read a flyer taped to a lightpole. A stage hypnotist was performing on campus that night, demonstrating his incredible powers of mind. I smiled. I could show him incredible powers of mind.

The young woman I'd heard behind me passed with the rustle of cotton against bare legs. I waited until she was a half block ahead before I followed.

She was dressed like many of the women you'd find on a college campus, which is to say inexpensively but with the expressiveness that comes from not having to pay the least attention to convention. Her shoes were canvas flats, and I could hear them whispering against the sidewalk a block in front of me now. She wore a long cotton peasant's skirt that reached within a few inches of her ankles. The skirt was loose but was cut to cling tightly to her hips. Her blouse was also cotton, bright yellow overprinted with a bamboo pattern. Instead of a purse she carried a nylon hiking pack slung over one shoulder.

She was a slight woman, little more than five feet tall. Seen from the back, her most prominent feature was her hair. Her head was crowned with a riot of black curls, inherited, I learned later, from a Gypsy grandmother.

I followed at a discreet distance, breathing in a delectable aroma she left eddying behind her in the soft night air, her scent a combination of soap, herbal shampoo, inexpensive cologne, and fresh, virginal blood.

She turned into a shop. It was one of those cramped bookstores—the windows plastered with notices announcing art shows, protests, and coffee house concerts—found near any university from Boston to San Diego. I went in and followed her between the densely packed shelves, past The Classical World, Psychology, and Women's Studies. She led me through the doorway to a back room so crammed with people and book boxes that it seemed much smaller than it really was.

About a dozen battered chairs had been set up in the rear, but most of the crowd leaned against the storeroom's outer walls or sat on the floor. They were a Bohemian crew, thin, pale, many of them smoking the Camels and—for those who could afford it—Gauloises I imagined sustained them, their diet of tobacco supplemented only by literature and innumerable cups of espresso.

The young woman sat down and propped her back against a crate with the THIS SIDE UP instruction pointing in the wrong direction. The only other space free was next to her, so I made myself comfortable and waited to learn why we were there. In the meantime I studied her intelligent face out of the corner of my eye. Undoubtedly Spanish. Her features were delicate yet well defined, a face that showed sensitivity as well as strength. Her smooth skin was olive-colored, and she wore no makeup. She had opalescent eyes that smouldered with an inner passion, but there was a hint of humor in her expression; it was plain that she did not take herself with the same deadly earnestness as was expressed in the other faces around the room.

*Anna Montoya.*

The name popped in my head when I turned my face toward her. She returned my smile.

Anna Montoya. Yes, that was her name.

She was not so much small as compact, I realized. Anna

Montoya radiated energy and a sense of will that distracted from the fact that she couldn't have weighed much more than ninety pounds.

Yes, I thought, Anna Montoya would be perfect for me.

A woman walked to the front of the room. She appeared to be in her late forties. The strands of her long, straight hair were equally divided between black and gray. She wore a loose-fitting black sweatshirt, skintight black jeans, and cruel-looking black shoe-boots that would have pleased a Victorian misogynist. Her body was thin to the point of gauntness, and she had a pinched expression behind her glasses, two perfect circles of glass framed in gold wire.

There was no introduction, apparently no introduction being needed. The position she took up made her the focal point against the far wall, which had been left clear but for two chairs. One of the chairs was occupied by a glass of water, the other by a young man with a goatee, and bongo drums perched on his knees.

A poetry reading, I guessed, and in the classic 1950s tradition I thought had gone out of style with the Beat Generation.

I repressed a sigh and ordered myself to remain open to the experience. Anna Montoya's dim smile showed that she shared my uncertainty over whether the coming performance was meant to be taken seriously or as parody.

The man with the goatee pounded his drums dramatically as the woman—still standing—began her recitation without the aid of notes.

*"Sixteen spinning spiders spinning webs."*

The drummer punctuated the pause with a loud *bop*.

*"Spinning skeletons, spinning steel wheels."*

*Bop! Bop! Bop!*

*"Kiss the steel wheel, kiss the spinning steel wheel of motherless night!"*

The reading went on in this fashion for nearly thirty minutes. At first it seemed funny, although I was careful not to laugh. But after a while it became merely boring, although occasionally a clever turn of phrase emerged from the stream-of-consciousness gibberish. Finally, in a crescendo of bongo beating and screaming—*"Eyeballs popping razor blades CIA sweating Republican war factory death machine!"*—the poetess bowed her sweat-soaked head, her creativity and energy both spent.

The audience responded enthusiastically. I applauded long

enough to show I was glad the reading was over but not so long as to encourage an encore.

I followed Anna Montoya out of the stifling room, my eyes stinging from the smoke and my head abuzz from the nicotine my sensitive body had absorbed from the atmosphere. I wished that she would stand apart from the others, who gathered beneath the street lamp to critique the performance. Responding to the force of my wordless suggestion, she moved away and stood by herself. Surprised at the ease with which she responded to my will, I followed.

"I won't forget *that* soon," I said, keeping my tone intentionally ambiguous.

She smiled. It was a beautiful smile, made more alluring by its shyness.

"America's best extemporaneous poet, according to *The Village Voice*."

"High praise for such—"

I stopped myself.

"Rubbish." Anna Montoya frowned. Even her frown was beautiful. "I can see that's what you think. Frankly, I agree."

I laughed, partly out of relief, partly out of nervousness. This business of picking up a woman was more difficult than I had remembered, now that it had come time to make a move. I could easily wind up sounding like an idiot on the make if I weren't careful.

"I was curious to see what it would be like," I began carefully. "It probably marks me as hopelessly unsophisticated, but my tastes lean more toward the traditional. I think I'll stick with Keats."

I managed not to cringe, even as I made the potentially fatal mistake of saying too much on a subject I knew too little about. Keats? What was I talking about? I hardly knew who he was!

Yet Anna Montoya's smile had brightened considerably. At least I had blundered in the right direction.

"Anybody who wonders why people don't read poetry any more should have been in there tonight. And I share your opinion of John Keats. It's pleasant—and rare—to meet somebody who likes the Romantic poets at one of these readings."

I simply nodded. I wondered if I could steer the conversation away from poetry. No, not too soon, I decided.

"I love the Romantics," she continued, "especially Wordsworth and Keats. They knew something about how language works."

She shook her head, making her long black curls whirl about her.

"I was born in the wrong century!"

"Why did you come to hear this tonight? Out of curiosity, like me?"

Anna Montoya blushed.

"I'm here for mercenary reasons. She's the head of my poetry workshop at Northwestern. I'm embarrassed to admit it, but it's politically expedient for me to pretend my tastes are something other than what they truly are. Fortunately part of the workshop ethic is that you never say anything especially complimentary about anybody else's writing. So I don't exactly have to lie, unless being someplace I'd rather not be is a lie."

"Your secret is safe with me," I promised. "That's the good thing about talking to a new acquaintance: you can't tell your deepest secrets to a friend, but a stranger is perfectly trustworthy."

Her laughter was musical, but it attracted the attention of a young man coming out of the bookstore. He obviously recognized Anna Montoya, for he smiled with his eyes as he came through the door and toward us.

*No,* I thought, pushing the thought toward him with as much force as I could muster. *Leave us alone. You do not know this woman.*

He stopped and looked at Anna with apparent confusion.

*Go away!*

He turned and headed down the street.

"A friend?"

"An acquaintance from school." Anna Montoya frowned, although it was more from amusement than displeasure. "That's odd. He's usually more persistent. I think he has a crush on me."

"I hope I didn't frighten him away."

"That's all right. Well—" She seemed suddenly self-conscious. "Well," she repeated, "I really have to be going. Good night."

"Would you . . ."

Her open smile told me she was glad I stopped her.

"I've enjoyed talking with you," I said, beginning again, afraid to ask her to go out with me quite that soon. "I'm David Parker."

Another blunder. I knew that it was a mistake to reveal my name, but it was already out. Besides, I liked this young woman too much to deceive her. I would just have to gamble that I could get her to forget the most peculiar—and frightening—thing about David Parker when the time came for us to part.

"I'm Anna Montoya."

She held out her hand. It was tiny, warm and firm.

"Yes," I said. (Just stopping myself before adding: "I know.") "Would you care to go across the street and continue our conversation? I'd be happy to buy you a cup of coffee."

She started to decline, as any prudent young woman would do. Before she could speak, I fixed my eyes on hers and reached out with my mind—probing gently, just enough to push through the hesitation I sensed there. *Friend* . . . I told her, putting the single word quietly and carefully into her subconscious mind.

"Yes, that would be nice," she said after a moment, apparently surprised to hear the words come from her own mouth. And then, with more certainty, she added, "I think I would like that very much."

Anna Montoya's parents were from Madrid. Her grandfather was the son of a wealthy landowner who scandalized the family by marrying a Gypsy flamenco dancer. He fought against the Fascists, was wounded, and spent time in prison. Her father was a physician, a strict autocrat who saw only the practical—or rather impractical—side of poetry. It was, he believed, his daughter's ticket to life on public aid.

Anna was not unlike me at an earlier stage in my life, except that it was poetry, not music, that sparked her passion. I urged her to be ruled by her own heart and not let her family turn her away from whatever path she knew was the one she must follow.

"I wouldn't consider any other way," she said, as if shocked I could imagine otherwise. She was stronger than I had been in my confrontation with my family. "I may have to teach or get a job as a clerk in a women's clothing store, but it won't make any difference. I'm a poet because I *must* write poetry. I'll die before I give it up. Do you write?"

"Poetry? No, but I do read it." This was not exactly true, although I'd already committed myself to the lie with my earlier remark about Keats. I had read some poetry, but it had been part of the assigned work at school. It was a mistake to compound the lie, and I regretted my words the moment I heard them ringing falsely in my inner ear. I was skating far from shore on what could be thin ice.

"Who do you like besides Keats?"

That question should have been all it took to unmask me as a fraud, but fortunately my vampire mind came through for me.

"Yeats," I said without missing a beat. Keats, Yeats—it was like word association, even if the two names were spelled a lot more similarly than they were pronounced.

"I like him very much, too," she said.

I began to rack my mind for the name of a Yeats poem I could drop from what I'd read years before in prep school literature class. I didn't intend to show off; the words began to come out of my mouth as if under their own power:

*"Turning and turning in the widening gyre*
*The falcon cannot hear the falconer;*
*Things fall apart, the center cannot hold;*
*Mere anarchy is loosed upon the world,*
*The blood-dimmed tide is loosed, and everywhere*
*The ceremony of innocence is drowned."*

" 'The Second Coming.' "

"Yes," I said, startled at my own "incredible powers of mind." For some reason, I also was quite excited that this wild-haired girl knew the poem. But then it was obvious: What we were sharing was more than just a few lines of verse; we were sharing an emotion, a sense of friendship in the midst of the crowd of strangers who make the world an inhospitable place for someone with an artistic temperament.

"That poem is an old favorite," she said, making little attempt to disguise her growing attraction to me. Her eyelids fell partially closed, and when the words came, it was as if she were speaking from the depths of a trance:

*"A gaze blank and pitiless as the sun,*
*Is moving its slow thighs, while all about it*
*Reel shadows of the indignant desert birds.*
*The darkness drops again; but now I know*
*That twenty centuries of stony sleep*
*Were vexed to nightmare by a rocking cradle,*
*And what rough beast, its hour come round at last,*
*Slouches towards Bethlehem to be born?"*

" 'What rough beast . . .' " I repeated absently. "The words go right through my heart. They make me feel as if they have a special message written just for me."

"But they have."

I looked at Anna Montoya carefully.

"Bad poetry is written for literature teachers, poets, and intellectuals, but good poetry is written for you, for me, for everybody. That's what makes it good. It has something unique to say to each of us." She lightly pressed three fingers against her breast. "It resonates."

The gesture was covertly sexual, and I felt a pang of desire—and, behind it, controlled but unmistakably present, the Hunger. She rested her hand on the table by her cup. Taking a long chance, I covered her hand with my own, my eyes never leaving hers.

"This isn't the sort of thing I do," she said, turning her small hand over beneath mine and clasping it.

"Nor do I. Do you want me to say good-night?"

I started to reach into her mind, but I forced myself to stop. I did not want Anna Montoya that way. She was too good for that. If I couldn't behave like a gentleman, I didn't deserve to have her.

The Hunger tugged at me hard enough to remind me of the stakes. If Anna Montoya rejected my overture, I might well wind up out on the street, desperately seeking a prostitute or whatever victim I could waylay in a dark alley.

She leaned across the small table until her face nearly touched mine. She answered in a low whisper: "No, I don't want you to say good-night."

And then, to my profound surprise, she kissed me before I could kiss her.

We went to my town house. Her dormitory would have provided us with too little privacy, and a hotel would have been too crude. I was as truthful with her as I dared to be. There was no hope, I said with genuine regret, of us becoming permanently involved.

"Are you married?" she asked, looking again at my left hand to see if I wore a wedding band—I'd noticed her doing the same earlier.

Divorced, I said. I went on to explain that I was about to begin a project which would take me away from Chicago for several years or more. I was leaving soon; in fact, I should have left already. And it was true. I hoped I hadn't waited too long to heed Tatiana's warning to leave the city as soon as I could travel.

Anna Montoya laid her hand on my shoulder, sighed, and said nothing.

"I've let my heart run away with my head, I'm afraid. I've already taken advantage of your affection. Let me drive you home."

She stilled my words by putting a finger against my lips.

"It doesn't matter," she said, turning her face up toward mine. She was the perfect image of innocence, and yet her Gypsy eyes burned with a passion that made me ache to run my fingers through her wild hair.

I gathered her into my arms, and her lips were suddenly again covering mine, stopping my words before they could escape my mouth.

We went into the bedroom, and I opened the windows so the breeze could blow through the curtains. I brought champagne in for us. We drank from the same glass as I undressed her.

So much of it was the same that night: the room, the Taittinger champagne, the white curtains billowing and falling back with the gentle sighing wind off the lake. It brought me up short for a moment, reminding me of the nights I'd spent there with Tatiana. She would understand the reason why I was determined to turn taking blood into an act of love. What I was about to do was so necessary, and in my heart it seemed so right, that I knew I could not possibly be making a mistake.

The Hunger was insistently calling me now, but I held back. I was in control this time. I was the master. Holding off longer was my way of proving I had cleared away the last obstacle that stood in the way of becoming a vampire without, at the same time, turning into a monster.

Anna and I made love slowly. And when our passion reached its crescendo, our bodies straining together to become one, I bit into the smooth, faultless skin on her neck and we were carried away on an ocean swell of inexpressible pleasure.

I prepared to leave Chicago.

Tatiana had warned me to leave, but I would have done so even without her advice. Too many people knew me, and that increased the chance somebody would question the peculiarities in my behavior, such as my flat refusal to leave my town house during daylight hours.

It would be all the better to be a vampire in a place where David Parker was totally anonymous, where he could easily slip away if there were complications.

One such complication was Anna Montoya. I had gone into her mind when she fell asleep and commanded her to forget one particular part of our evening. She awoke smiling and showed no sign that she recalled anything that caused her concern. Nevertheless I was anxious that the memory might come back to her over time. I had almost no experience with mind control—an ominous sounding phrase—and no assurance that she would not one day simply remember that I had sunk two particularly sharp teeth into her jugular vein and drunk her blood.

Anna Montoya knew my name. She knew my address. She might have been the one reason I wanted to stay in Chicago, but she also was foremost among the reasons I had to leave.

The only thing left for me to decide was where to go. After considerable thought I picked what I imagined would be the perfect city for a creature of my race. Once I decided to go, the rest was easy. I hired a property maintenance company to look after the town house. I owned it outright, having bought Clarice's share as part of the divorce settlement.

I wanted to give the house to Anna, so that she would have a comfortable place to live while she was writing her poetry, easing some of the material concerns I feared might damage her creative spirit. I knew she was too proud and sensible to accept it as a gift from a onetime lover, so my idea was to get her to move in on the pretense of keeping it safe from thieves during my absence. Given the time, I thought, I could devise a way to get her to accept ownership—perhaps as a bequest at whatever time I staged my "death" when I removed myself permanently from the scrutiny of those who knew me as a mortal.

(My plan has worked so far. Anna is living there now while she works on her master's degree. We correspond every month through an intermediary in Switzerland, where my mail is sent. Her letters remain warm. Perhaps I shall be able to see her at least one more time. Come to think of it, though, it's been two months since she's written. Perhaps she's met someone. I suppose I hope she has. I wish her a happy life, although if it weren't for Tatiana—and to complicate matters even further, Ariel Niccolini—I think I could be very happy with my young Gypsy poet.)

Except for a trunk filled with music and an album of photographs, I resolved to leave the material aspects of my former life behind in Chicago. I would buy new clothing, new furniture and whatever else I needed when I got where I was going. I was starting my life over in every way, and my hopes were focused on the future, when I would be reunited with Tatiana.

I spent several evenings saying good-bye to my friends and family and taking leave of the city. I found myself staring at things I looked at almost every day without really seeing: the stone lions on either side of the stairs in front of my town house; the shining brass handles on the entrance to the apartments across the street, which the doorman polished almost hourly; the wind-swept lakefront.

I was saying good-bye to the city that had been my home all my life. I found myself making many mental pictures and storing them away so that I could remember, in the years ahead, in the centuries ahead, the mortal life I left behind.

The last thing I did in Chicago was send Anna Montoya a farewell note, a dozen long-stemmed roses, and a first edition book of Dylan Thomas's poems. I was grateful to her for helping me in a way she could never know. The sense of rage and self-loathing I felt after my disastrous assignation with the prostitute had faded into the background, replaced by the infinitely sweeter memory of making love to Anna.

*Do not go gentle into that good night,*
*Rage, rage against the dying of the light*

But Anna had helped me learn that a vampire *could* go gently into the good night. For that, and for helping me tame my awful Hunger, I will always be grateful to her.

I returned a final time to the bookstore where Anna and I had gone to the reading and bought several slim volumes of poetry for myself. Some of the verses I'd read in school that Anna compelled me to remember were very much on my mind as I prepared to leave my house. I can't say whether there was some poetic essence that Anna transmitted to me in her blood, or if she helped awaken a sleeping interest, but I became aware of the fact that she had infected me with her love for poetry. I have not recovered, I'm glad to say, and along with music, reading it has become a regular pleasure for me.

My final errands finished, I returned to the town house and took one last walk through its rooms, remembering the bad times and the good times and the women who shared them with me there.

Then I telephoned a cab and rode to O'Hare Airport, where I boarded a jet for my flight to the city of eternal night.

# PART II

# The Pilgrim

# Chapter 17

**PARIS, JUNE 20, 1989**—The telephone rang tonight as I was preparing to go out. I eagerly lifted the receiver, expecting it to be Ariel Niccolini, the only person who has ever called me here. It would have been nice to talk to her—much nicer than the call turned out to be.

"You fucking pig."

It was a woman's voice, an American with a slight southern accent.

"Who is this?"

"You son of a bitch."

The line went dead.

I sat and stared at the receiver as if it were a snake that had just bitten me. I don't know any American women here. At least I don't think I do.

I have no clue why a woman—an *American* woman, no less— would phone me in my Paris hotel room, blurt obscenities, and hang up. A random event? It seems unlikely. There is very little that happens in the world completely by chance, I've discovered. Does the caller have some connection with the English vampire? A disturbing thought, even if I have no reason to think so. But who else hates me enough to be behind such an act?

I wish I could just get the hell out of this city. Except that I cannot. Not before Mozart arrives. Until then I'm forced to sit patiently and wait for whatever evil befalls me next.

Regardless of whether *he* had anything to do with the telephone call, I can feel him out there. There's no doubt in my mind that my enemy is planning something. It's only a question of what and where and when. And now, of whether he is acting alone or has another vampire to help him conspire against me.

\* \* \*

*Resuming my story . . .*

Everything I saw from the window of the United Airlines 727 was brown and lifeless. The full moon illuminated the vastness below with a shimmering silver-blue light. Ahead in the distance a feverish glow hung over the city, a city that never slept—my new hunting ground, my new home.

Beneath the wing were treeless mountains and rocky flats where nothing lived but a few scrub brush and cacti, and the lizards, rattlesnakes, and scorpions that hid beneath them.

An electronic bell chimed twice over the airliner's intercom system. The Fasten Seat Belts light came on.

Outside the window distant movement caught my eye. The headlights of a pickup truck came into view around a mountain. The highway made a beeline for the city, the concrete a shining line drawn through the desert in the reflected moonlight. The lights of town were at least twenty miles away. The truck and its driver seemed very much alone, traveling through the desert toward the city built where by rights no city should have been.

Las Vegas was a water spot for troop trains until a savvy gangster guessed the possibilities in a sparsely populated state. With legalized gambling, legalized prostitution, and easy money from the mob, the way station turned into a boom town.

My flight was all-coach for the trip west, one long stretch of seats from the back of the aircraft to the door of the cockpit. About a quarter of the passengers were business people continuing on to Los Angeles. They wore suits and read *The Wall Street Journal*, *Forbes*, and *Fortune*. The rest of the passengers were gamblers, dressed casually in jeans, jogging shoes, and nylon jackets with company logos on the back. They were in a party mood, and many talked and laughed too loudly, having already had too many drinks.

It was the gamblers, not the gambling, that brought me to Las Vegas. The casinos in town never closed, and the visitors slept as little as possible. They crowded around crap tables and roulette wheels at all hours of the night, filled with the relaxed comradeship that was part of trying to squeeze as much fun as possible into the few days they had before flying back home. In Las Vegas you let down your hair as well as your guard and forgot about being wary of strangers.

A perfect place for a vampire.

I rented a house on the edge of the city, a one-story ranch laid out in an *L*-shape, with a swimming pool and a careful arrangement of stones and cacti taking the place of a lawn. The house was furnished, and the only personal items I added were clothing, books of poetry, and a grand piano. On the piano I put the antique silver frame that held the photograph of Princess Tatiana I had cut from a book about Czar Nicholas II.

I behaved with the stealth befitting a vampire. I used my real name only on the lease and other official papers, doing so in those cases only to avoid complications. I used assumed names with the few acquaintances I made. My contacts with mortals were limited mostly to fortnightly feedings.

Music and books became my regular companions during my exile in the desert. Anna Montoya had awakened my interest in poetry, and I read everything from Eliot to Dante. It opened my sensitivity to the rhythm and melody in language, which helped me better understand music. (I was deeply into Lizst at the time, and I struggled to wring from the difficult scores something more than a display of technical mastery.)

For a time I was very happy. The solitude gave me the opportunity to sort out my life, and I made peace with my past, putting a lot of things behind me that had lingered just under the surface of my awareness, stoking the mild depressions that contributed to the sorry state I was in when Tatiana came into my life.

My powers continued to develop, foremost among them my intellect. I began to really *see* into the music I was studying, to have blinding insights into composers' unwritten intentions. These revelations were not restricted to music, but came to me from whatever direction I focused my attention. The music, the poetry, the quiet of the desert night—it as if they all were working together to unlock some wonderful secret within me.

And then one night the miraculous thing I had sensed building happened.

I'd run five miles into the desert to stretch my legs and clear the cobwebs out of my head after a long session at the piano. I climbed onto a boulder at the edge of a rock outcropping, took a poetry collection out of my backpack, and began reading Oscar Wilde by starlight:

> *Surely there was a time I might have trod*
> *The sunlit heights, and from life's dissonance*
> *Struck one clear chord to reach the ears of God.*

A night bird called from somewhere out in the desert, and suddenly it was as though a dam had broken inside of me, unleashing a flood of creativity. Those three notes—three *simple* notes—keyed a torrent of melody in my head that made it impossible to sit a moment longer. I stuffed the book into the backpack and ran back to the house as fast as my feet would carry me.

I sat down at the piano, holding back a minute to savor the realization that the remaining chains that had fettered my spirit had been unlocked at last, allowing it to soar heavenward.

I touched the cool ivory piano keys with my fingers and closed my eyes. For the first time in my life, I began to compose my own music. Within the first few bars I understood that something truly significant was happening. A new life—my life as a composer—had begun.

I had truly been reborn.

Every two weeks, when the Hunger began to press down on me like the sea upon a diver who has gone too deep, I would take a break from the symphonies and sonatas that were pouring out of me, pack a suitcase, and check into one of the many hotels along the Strip. I would find a way to befriend a couple, ideally one where the husband would be absent at a seminar or on business a significant amount of the time. It was easy. Las Vegas attracts a tremendous number of conventions. While it may not be wise to combine business with pleasure, many people do, and opportunities abounded.

For example, one time I had four tickets to the sold-out Sinatra show. I stationed myself near the ticket office and watched the steady stream of tourists stopping by thinking there might be a chance of getting in. I soon spotted the group I wanted: a man about forty; a woman who obviously was his wife; and a younger, unaccompanied woman who wore a wedding ring.

"Excuse me," I said, stepping in front of the trio as they were about to leave, disappointed, "but if you're looking for tickets to tonight's show, I can help."

"You have tickets?"

"Four. In an excellent location."

"Can't we get in trouble buying tickets from a scalper?" the wife whispered.

She was starved to fashionable thinness in a way that made her look almost skeletal, especially around her face, which was framed with a close-cropped haircut. The décolletage in her midnight-blue evening dress exposed the bony upper part of her chest, where her clavicle threatened to poke through her skin.

She looked as if she had leukemia. Her blood would be thin, like wine that had been diluted with water.

"You misunderstand. The tickets are not for sale."

"Not for sale?" The younger woman seemed eager to be entertained, as if the other couple secretly bored her. Her thick chestnut hair fell to her shoulders. She had a lush figure—full breasts, hourglass waist, sinuously curving hips that pushed against her red dress. She was voluptuous in a way the other woman, with her hungry leanness, could never be. She reminded me of Kathleen Turner. *She* was the one I wanted.

"What's the story, then?" the man asked, a little impatient.

"It's really very simple. My name is Michael Reilly. I'm an attorney from Evanston, Illinois. I came here on business with some people, and we were planning to see the show tonight. Unfortunately, a company emergency forced my clients to return to Chicago early."

"Ah."

"I decided to stay the weekend." I shrugged and tapped the breast of my jacket, indicating the inner pocket that held the tickets. "So, here I am, with four tickets to the Sinatra show and no one to share them with. If you'd care to be my guests, I'd be delighted to have you at my table."

"That's awfully nice of you to offer," the man said, no longer looking irritated. "But I insist we pay you for the tickets."

"Nonsense. My clients bought the tickets. It would be improper for me to accept money for them."

"It's a very generous offer," the woman in the red dress said.

"Not at all," I said, looking only at her. "You'd be doing me a very great favor by allowing me to be part of your evening."

"My name is Doug Sprague," the man said, holding out his hand.

"Michael Reilly," I repeated, returning his firm grip.

"My wife, Vivian."

"How do you do."

"And our friend, Margeaux James."

"How do you do."

I held her eyes a moment longer as I took her hand, reaching out with my mind to gently probe hers. There was a natural attraction between us, and I knew she could feel the same tingle of electricity when our hands touched. Her cheeks colored, and she blinked and looked up at me through her long eyelashes.

"Margeaux's husband, Bob, is ill and couldn't be with us

tonight," Vivian informed me in a casual way, but it was intended as a warning. Private property, no trespassing.

"Bob has migraines," Margeaux explained. "He insisted that I—that we go out anyway."

"That's too bad."

I felt Vivian's suspicious eyes on me. I smoothed my tie with my left hand knowing she and the others would see the wedding band on my left hand. I'd kept it for occasions such as this. When one wants to make oneself attractive to members of the opposite sex, sometimes nothing works better than appearing to be unavailable.

"Well," Vivian said, finally smiling, her mind made up that I was acceptable company to complete their threesome.

"We probably . . ." Doug began, glancing at his watch.

"Yes, let's go inside and find our table," I said.

And so the four of us set out, Margeaux and I leading the way, chatting, and Doug and Vivian bringing up the rear.

Doug bought two rounds of nightcaps after the show to repay my hospitality. Margeaux and I got on very well indeed, and when we parted, I sensed that peculiar guilty reluctance married people feel when they are drawn to an acquaintance of the opposite sex but wisely decide to honor an older, deeper commitment. (Had Clarice been so inclined, my life would be very different than it is today.) We said good-night, and Margeaux returned to her ailing husband.

My room in the hotel was six stories above Margeaux's. I waited until three in the morning; then I took the elevator to her level, stood outside her door, and stared at the number—422—concentrating hard.

I heard the soft rustle of sheets and bare feet on carpet. I could smell her perfume—Opium, she had told me it was called. Beneath it lingered the infinitely more subtle aroma of the essence she carried in her blood. The faint sound of the oiled metal gears worked in the door, and it swung silently open. Margeaux James stood before me, her body outlined by the darkness in the room. Behind her a man sank deeper into sleep at my wordless suggestion; he would not awaken now even if he were shaken.

Margeaux had removed her makeup, and her complexion glowed with soft radiance. Her lips parted slightly as she looked at me with dreaming eyes. Nothing was said. Nothing needed to be said. In the morning, she would remember nothing more than an erotic dream about an acquaintance.

I extended my hands a few inches from my waist, palms outward.

A tiny gasp slipped from her lips as she came to me. We held each other tight, and I slid my hands down the back of her nightgown, my fingers brushing lightly past the hollow small of her back and up over the luscious rising curve of her hips.

I swept her into my arms and carried her toward the empty elevator waiting at the end of the hall. Behind me the door swung silently shut and locked itself.

Despite the comfort I took in the arms of Margeaux and many beautiful women like her I found in Las Vegas, I began to grow lonely. I missed having someone I could talk to—really talk to, without the phony names and made-up details getting in the way. In short, I yearned for Tatiana, who was my friend as well as my lover.

I began visiting the casinos, even when I wasn't driven by the Hunger, simply to be around people. Inventing pretexts to make conversation with the mortals I met there, I began to feel like one of those sorry old men who have nothing better to do than waste other people's time in their pathetic attempts to maintain some thread of contact with the world.

And then one night, as if in answer to my unspoken prayer, another vampire arrived in Las Vegas.

I noticed him for the first time as he observed the gamblers at a blackjack table. He was a tiny, formal looking man—he held his chin in the air at a thirty-degree angle as he watched the chips change hands—with a well-tailored European suit. His thick hair was red almost to the point of being orange, and he wore it brushed straight back, tight against his head. When he turned slightly, I saw the hair was gathered in a tight ponytail that hung past his collar.

I did not realize he was a vampire the first two times I saw him. It should have been obvious, but he was clever. During our first encounter I made the mistake of glancing away from him while puzzling over what it was about him that gave me such a peculiar feeling. When I looked back, he had disappeared.

I saw the little man the next night in the Silver Dollar. I was on my way out, and I saw him loitering near the exit, feeding quarters into a slot machine. I meant to speak to him, but some wordless impulse told me to continue my purposeless ramble. The "impulse" was his, of course, planted in my head, to see if I had the strength to resist it. He *made* me walk through the doors. It must have disappointed him to find me so impressionable.

Two nights later I was playing roulette at the Sahara at the insistence of the woman I was with, when I had the unmistakable feeling someone was studying me. I turned around to see the redheaded man staring down from the balcony, smiling at me.

At that moment I realized what should have been obvious from the first: He was a vampire! When I opened my eyes and really *looked* at him, I saw that his aura was the same deep purple as mine and completely unlike mortals, whose were bloodred.

I hastily excused myself from the table, leaving my female friend with several thousand dollars worth of my chips. I began to cross the casino toward the stairway that led to the balcony level, but as if on cue, the crowd surged in front of me, stopping my progress. I saw him come down the steps, chuckling to himself. There might as well have been a wall between us now; the crowd formed a barrier I could not penetrate. By the time I finally made my way through the tide of bodies to the foot of the stairs, he was gone.

I ran outside and stood on the sidewalk, looking up and down in vain for a sign of the other vampire. The thing I wanted to know, now that the truth had finally dawned on me, was whether this was just another vampire, or if he was *the* vampire—the one Tatiana promised to send to bring me to her.

The only answer I got that night was the hot desert wind blowing in my face.

# Chapter 18

PARIS, JUNE 21, 1989—I'm drinking a double Scotch to steady my nerves. Although I've gotten to the point where my system can tolerate alcohol, it no longer affects me the way it does mortals. For once I wish I lacked the vampire's efficient physiology. I'm tempted to buy a case of whiskey, drag it up to my rooms, and see exactly how much liquor it would take to free me from the memory of this awful night. But even if I can't get drunk, the repetition of an old habit does have a slight calming effect.

This journal has taken on new significance, because I'm beginning to doubt I'll survive my visit to this city. Events have turned too sinister—and too violent—for me to have much hope of getting out untouched. If I die, these few pages may find their way to Tatiana, telling her of the last miserable days I spent here, and what befell me.

She was right: Her enemies *are* my enemies. They have chased me here, even as they chased Tatiana away from Chicago.

I've heard nothing more from Mozart. I have no idea where he is or when he'll get here—or even *if* he'll get here.

Mine is a classic case of being caught in the middle: I can't leave; I can't stay. And so I simply do nothing, waiting for the next horror.

My enemy has killed again. The crime was even more gruesome than the first, a work of consummate sadism. And such power—it appalls me to think of the strength concentrated in the hands of that fiend.

How many women has he killed? He's clearly much older than I, and he takes such elaborate, even artistic care in his crimes that I can only believe this has been going on a very long time.

147

He's been careful, though, and the authorities have no idea of the carnage taking place beneath their noses. If the truth were known, his crimes would make headlines around the world. Not since Jack the Ripper, another butcher who liked to do his work with a scalpel, has the world known such a monster.

There's a streak of exhibitionist in his personality, the need to have someone take notice of his handiwork. I can tell that he's frustrated at missing the serial killer's thrill of shocking the public with virtuoso acts of homicide. And so he has chosen me to be his audience of one, his sole witness.

The evening started innocently enough.

I took a walk, as I do nearly every evening. I visited a rare–book-dealer's shop in a medieval section of the city, where I was fortunate enough to find an early, hand-printed edition of Rimbaud. The owner wanted more than the volume was worth. We haggled, and I let him take slight advantage of me. It was worth the extra francs to see the victory in his eyes. Although it seems as though a century has passed since I stopped being David Parker the attorney, I remember well what it was like to be mortal, and the satisfaction that came from petty triumphs of the ego!

I walked down by the Seine and sat on a bench beneath a lamp to read. There's so much human suffering in Rimbaud's tortured words, and yet they might just as easily have been written for a vampire:

> *J'ai tant fait patience*
> *Qu'à jamais j'oublie.*
> *Craintes et souffrances*
> *Aux cieux sont parties.*
> *Et la soif malsaine*
> *Obscurcit mes veines.*

> *I've been patient too long*
> *My memory is dead*
> *All fears and all wrongs*
> *To the heavens have fled.*
> *While all my veins burst*
> *With a sickly thirst.*

I put the slim volume into my coat pocket after reading only a little farther. Better to leave "A Season in Hell" for a time when my spirits were darker, I thought. I bought a bouquet of flowers from an old woman with a wooden pushcart. A trio of girls came down the sidewalk, their schoolbooks under their arms, returning home from a study session. I handed the flowers to one of the girls, whose eyes were the same emerald-green as Tatiana's.

*"Pour votre maman."*

The old woman with the flower cart smiled and shook her head as I walked away. She was used to Americans wandering Paris on warm summer nights, their heads filled with romance.

I started back toward my hotel just after ten. Although it has been my habit to stay out each night until nearly dawn, some vague compulsion sent me back to my rooms early. There was nothing innocent about my whim, I've since realized. The Ripper—as I have come to think of the English Vampire, having to call him something—had planted the idea in my head; he wanted me to return to the hotel while it was still early enough for the twisted little game he'd planned to play with me.

As I walked along the street, my head was filled with thoughts of Tatiana. I did not know that the night was about to become ugly.

The fear was on me the moment I entered the Place Vendôme. The night, so mild and pleasant, turned all at once sinister. Dread grew in me with every footstep that brought me closer to the hotel. I stepped into the lobby and looked around, certain that some unspeakable horror awaited me, feeling as if I were moving in slow motion. There was no mistaking the fact that *he* was there, yet except for the concierge—a severe, middle-aged woman oblivious of anything except the receipts she was examining—I appeared to be alone.

I wanted to flee, but decided I would feel more secure in my rooms. There's something that draws us home in times of trouble, the comforting safety of familiar surroundings, even if they only are the hotel where one has been lodging.

A tingle raced up my spine as I passed a room where there was a writing table and stationery for guests. I had to force myself to look in. There was no trace of the Montmartre Cemetery killer, though I doubted my eyes. Previous experience had taught me that the Ripper could elude me easily enough.

I drew in a sharp breath and, telling myself to remain calm, started toward the elevator. I was stepping inside when the thought of being trapped in close confines with the fiend led me to veer toward the stairs.

I have not been so completely and mindlessly afraid since childhood. My imagination seethed with visions of things not quite seen in dark places, and I raced up the stairs, chilled by the notion that *something* was following just behind. The sensation was so real that when I reached my landing and dared a glance over one shoulder, I was certain that I glimpsed something, although I was not sure what—or who—in the shadows below.

I stood with my back pressed against the wall, trying to get hold of myself. The other vampire could terrorize me only if I let him. It was possible to resist the suggestions of panic he put into my mind, but I had to fight them. I fixed my eyes on the fleur-de-lis pattern in the wallpaper on the opposite wall and concentrated. The gold design seemed to become more clear against its blue background as the fear slowly ebbed out of me. It was all a question of mental control: mine versus *his*.

My hand went into my jacket pocket and found the room key. Feeling steady as a rock, I smiled to myself, believing I had beaten him. I thought of the figure below my window the night I'd brought Rachel Weir to my hotel: his gaunt face and, flashing in the light thrown from the lamp, the scalpel. A good thing I had spirited Rachel away before he could harm her—for that clearly had been his intention.

I slipped the key into the slot. Counting tonight, there were two wins in my favor, I thought, and turned the knob.

The reek of fresh blood assaulted my senses before the door was open more than an inch. In my mind I could see Rachel's body, her skin white and cold, stretched out on my bed, her throat viciously ripped out like that of the girl in the graveyard.

"No!" I shouted to force him out of my mind, for in my mind I had started to imagine seeing the Ripper as he bent low over my lover, ready to go to work with the scalpel. The mental picture dissolved with my shout, but the stink of cold blood did not leave the air. It was real.

I raced through the sitting room and bedroom without finding the body. The spoor came from the bathroom. I stumbled madly into the white-tiled chamber, almost senseless with grief at the thought of finding the broken body of the woman whose only sin had been to make love to me and let me take a few drops of blood. Fool that I was, I'd been arrogant enough to think I had won a senseless game with a killer, in which Rachel Weir was the prize!

There was no body. In the sink I found a cheap silk scarf. It originally had been white, judging from the single corner that was not soaked with the blood that trickled down the curving porcelain basin and into the silver-ringed drain.

I picked up the grim talisman and, tears in my eyes, held it to my lips.

The taste of the blood was so awful that I had to spit.

This was not the luscious summer wine that ran through Rachel Weir's veins, but a foul, almost toxic substance. The blood brought me the vision of a middle-aged woman who had abused her body to the point that it could no longer filter the poisons from its system, the liver and kidneys in the early stages of collapse. It was polluted with nicotine and a bitter, etherlike substance that made my lips at once tingle and burn. Amphetamines, I thought.

Outside in the hallway I heard him laugh.

"You bastard!"

The Ripper was gone by the time I'd hurled open the door, but I could detect the trail he left in the hallway. It was like swimming in a lake in early summer, when icy currents untouched by the sun lie hidden within the warmer water. The space where the killer had passed was cold enough to make me shudder. (Cold, not in temperature, but in vibration. These experiences are impossible to express in mortal vocabulary!)

I tracked him down the back stairs and out into the alley, knowing he could have hidden his trail better if he'd wanted. He had been careless. Or perhaps he didn't know I would have the power to sense where he'd been.

There was a third possibility. Maybe he wanted me to follow, and his apparent carelessness was, in fact, intentional.

It didn't matter. Rage overwhelmed my caution as well as my fear.

Despite its charm, Paris, like any large city, harbors decay in its poorest and oldest neighborhoods. The monster seemed to prefer decrepitude, for his path followed the thread of squalor woven through the city's fabric.

Hurrying down a refuse-strewn street, I kicked a battered garbage can out of my way. As I followed the killer, my own heart filled with hate, darkness was all around me.

A woman stepped out of a doorway. She whistled lowly to

catch my attention. Her vacant eyes held a weariness no amount of makeup could hide. The red lamp above the door did not reflect in those tired, lightless eyes but merely bathed her in an unnatural glow that held no warmth, only the promise of a few minutes of vague, simulated passion.

*I think we are in rat's alley,*
*Where the dead men lost their bones.*

I shook my head sharply at the woman, T. S. Eliot echoing in my head. She melted back into the shadows, disappearing like dirty water down a drain.

The killer's trail passed in through a battered door on a street too narrow for anything but foot traffic. The latch had been broken long before, and the unpainted door hung perpetually open several inches, admitting windblown trash and whatever wickedness happened that way, seeking its own grim fulfillment. I pushed it open with my foot and stepped inside.

Steep stairs climbed almost straight up into the darkness that could not conceal a hundred vile odors and at least as many corruptions of the human soul. This was *his* territory, my sixth sense told me. If the building did not conceal the killer's lair, it was, at the least, a place he much frequented.

Strength surged through my body as I clenched and unclenched my fists. The Ripper had tormented me long enough. Now the confrontation seemed finally at hand.

Adjusting my eyes to the darkness, I took the stairs two at a time. There was a landing and more stairs, then another landing and another flight of stairs. His trail led to the fifth and final floor. The stairs stopped at the end of a long, narrow hallway.

Against the left wall, at the far end, a door was ajar.

Bits of trash littered the floor. Plaster had fallen off the ceiling and walls in places, exposing the laths. The doors on either side of the hall displayed a flat number and an array of locks, including heavy padlocks of the sort one might use to chain a factory gate.

The same fear I'd felt in the hotel lobby washed back over me. The hall seemed to stretch visibly longer, the walls pressing in on me. I clamped my teeth together and forced the illusion out of my mind. It was easier this time. I was learning how to fight his tricks. I would not allow him to manipulate me.

Anger quickening my step, I walked down the hall, ignoring the high, wild smell of spilled blood. The stink of death was heavy in the air when I reached the door at the end of the hall. Ready, I thought, for anything, I put my fingers against the scarred wood and pushed.

My stomach almost came into my mouth at the overwhelming stench. It was the same rancidness that soaked the silk scarf left in my rooms, mixed with the stink of human excrement. I ignored the corpse, more concerned for the moment with where the Ripper was and what he'd do next. Feeling a distinct presence, I pulled the door closed behind me, yet I did not see him.

"Show yourself!" I demanded.

There was nothing. He was very near, but not in the one-room apartment—at least not as far as *I* could tell.

The woman's body lay on a mattress in the corner. She was damned hard to look at. The Ripper had neatly sliced the nose from her face, leaving two gaping nasal cavities. Her throat had been slit from ear to ear; beneath her chin there was a gaping crimson smile that mirrored the rictus grin frozen on her dead lips. The instrument of death, a surgeon's scalpel made of bright metal that managed to shine even through its thick coating of blood, lay on the floor nearby.

But that was only part of it.

She'd been so horribly mutilated that it's difficult to find the words to describe what he'd done. The flesh had been carefully cut away from one section of her left leg, as if she were a cadaver used for dissection in a medical school lab. The medical skill was evident in the disfigurement. It was like an anatomy lesson, the glistening muscle and veins carefully trimmed free of flesh and fat and left exposed.

I turned away, thinking I was about to be sick, when I saw the worst thing of all. It wasn't even part of her body anymore. . . .

I had to stop writing for a few minutes to get control of my emotions.

What happened was this:

I glanced toward the mirror hanging over the cigarette-burned vanity. When I did, I knew why the room smelled of excrement. The Ripper had cut out the woman's intestines and draped them over the mirror, looping them back and forth like so many feet of bloody rope.

The strange thing was that the corpse, which was shoeless but otherwise dressed, didn't appear to have been disemboweled.

Then I realized he must have stuffed the abdominal cavity with something to keep it from collapsing.

There was no sheet on the bed, and blood soaked into the mattress. There was not as much blood as there would have been if a mortal had been responsible for this butchery. Some of it was in the scarf back in my rooms, I thought, smelling the aroma of blood, nicotine, and half-metabolized amphetamines that clung to the corpse like poisoned perfume; the rest of the blood had been gulped down by her eager killer.

The thought of drinking from such a polluted stream made me nauseous. The Ripper obviously was insensitive to such distinctions. Or perhaps he reveled in base experiences, like people who receive sexual gratification from being beaten and humiliated.

I stared down at the dead woman, wondering whether he'd killed her first, or if he'd tried to keep her alive as long as possible to watch her suffer. Her arms were thin, the right one marked with the tattoo of a rose. The scars from past suicide attempts disfigured the insides of her wrists. Her cheap blouse was unfastened and pulled apart just far enough to reveal small breasts. Just above the right nipple was another tattoo, a cherry. She wore net stockings and garters, her working uniform. Her short leather skirt had been pushed up on her hips far enough to show that she wore no underwear.

The table next to the bed held a lamp, a washcloth, an ashtray spilling over with cigarette butts, handcuffs, and a zippered leather mask. A dangerous profession, I thought, guilty with the memory of my own encounter with a prostitute while trying to satisfy the Hunger. Except what I had done had been an accident.

A pool of blood collecting near the small of the prostitute's back caught my attention. Not from the neck wound, I thought. Overcoming my revulsion, I pushed the body onto its side. I wished that I hadn't when I saw the grisly hole in the woman's back and the bloody veins dangling from it. The killer had carved the woman's left kidney out of her body. The organ was missing.

Fighting the urge to vomit, I stumbled toward an open window, feeling as if I would faint unless I breathed fresh air.

The Ripper's presence was all over the windowsill. I hung my head out and looked down at the long drop to the street. I could see the direction he had taken as he'd descended the wall like a giant spider, his path leaving behind a peculiar greenish frost that clung to the flaking bricks despite the heat of the summer night.

I took several deep breaths. My head began to clear.

On the floor by the window was a torn piece of brown paper that still shimmered from his foul touch. On it, written in blood, was the following message:

> Your powers are pitifully weak. Join us, and we will help you discover your true strength. Defy us, and we will crush you like the worm you are. By the way, I left the bitch's other kidney for you. The one I ate was delicious!

I threw down the paper and thrust myself halfway through the window, determined to follow. Vertigo made my head swim. Fighting to maintain my equilibrium, I put one hand against the exterior wall and felt the blistering paint crack loose beneath my fingers. I tried to will my hand to stick, but nothing happened. I leaned farther out the window, straining to extend my energy. I lost my balance and only by a miracle managed to catch a knee against the window and save myself from plunging to my death.

I pulled myself back into the reeking apartment and slumped against the wall.

I couldn't do it. The other vampire was blocking me, making it impossible for me to follow him down the wall. I tried to clear my head, but it was no good. He'd broken my concentration, proving once again that his will was stronger than mine. He was right: My powers were weak! I was more mortal than vampire at a time when the situation desperately required the exact opposite.

Something moved on the blood-stained mattress.

Startled, I expected to see a rat already arrived on the scene at the first promise of decay. There was no rat. The movement I saw came from the dead woman's hand.

"My God!" I whispered.

The corpse jerked itself upright on the mattress as if controlled by invisible wires from the ceiling, and rotated on the bed until it faced me. Changing position released a fresh flow of blood, which gushed down her pale breasts, making them glisten with wet redness in the dark. Gravity held her chin against her chest, and her eyes were rolled up in her head so that only the whites showed.

The corpse's hands fumbled with the skirt, bony fingers finding the hem, hiking it higher. With an unnatural spasm, the legs jerked apart, exposing naked, dead flesh that was somehow the most obscene thing I'd ever seen.

*Fout-moi!*—fuck me!—the corpse croaked in French. While the dead woman's lips moved, I knew it was physically impossible for her to speak with her throat cut. The voice came from inside my head. And no matter how I tried, I couldn't shut it out. My defenses had been completely shattered.

*I said, fuck me!*

I'd pushed myself into the corner, but she still was no more than a dozen feet away.

*Haven't you ever wanted to savage some dirty little whore, to give her what she really deserved?* she said. *Wouldn't it feel good to let your rage run wild and be totally free?*

*He* was controlling her, I knew, using the corpse as his puppet from somewhere out in the night.

"Stop it!" I shouted. "I know it's you."

*I know it's you! I know it's you! Who cares what you think you know, David Parker? Come over here and fuck me!*

The corpse pointed at me. I held up my hands, as if that could shield me from the thing.

*I expected to find you when I returned to Chicago.*

It was no longer a woman's voice in my head but that of an upper-class Englishman—the vampire from Montmartre Cemetery, the Ripper. It was macabre: the dead woman's lips moved, but I heard *his* voice.

"It was you in Chicago? I should have guessed." My voice sounded surprisingly steady.

*You're lucky you were no longer in that city when I returned, although my attitude about you has, shall we say, been modified slightly since then. I should have guessed that the princess would be compelled to turn her little frog into a prince. It's the music. She cannot resist music.*

"What do you want?"

The corpse turned its head, as if to see me better, and cocked it for what was intended to be a coquettish effect. It was hideous.

*I'm impressed to find you in Paris. It shows a certain resourcefulness. We never thought you'd get this far without us. I say, you're not getting help from one of Tatiana's friends, are you? That would make us very angry. We're your only real friends.*

"Who the hell are you?" I demanded, shouting at the dead body, getting to my feet. "And who the hell is this 'we' you keep referring to?"

*Fuck me, David*, the corpse said, again a female voice speaking in French. The tone was pleading. *Fuck me. One last fuck before they put me in the ground. I'm dying for it.*

The corpse's hands went between her legs and made lewd motions.

*I know there's a part of you, a secret, hidden part of you, that wants to fuck me, that wants to do the wild things that only the strong dare. Go ahead. You're no longer bound by dull human morality. You're a transcendent being! Do it! Fuck me! You're a killer now, David Parker. Just like the rest of us. Vampire, killer—there is no difference.*

"Not to someone like you," I said, realizing the absurdity of arguing with a mutilated corpse as an intermediary. Absurd and horrifying. I'd had enough. I dashed for the door.

The corpse scrambled after me in the dark room, but I was too fast—almost.

As I threw myself into the hall, fingers locked around my ankle. I jerked my leg with all my strength and managed to get free. I slammed the door behind me, ran down the steps and didn't stop until I was nearly back to my hotel.

I shall never forget the horror of what I saw in the last frantic second before the door slammed. The corpse grinned up at me, mutely working her lips, her blouse pulled up enough to reveal the lazy-*S* curve of the autopsy incision the killer had carved in her abdomen, the halves of the incision pulling apart.

Back in the relative safety of my hotel, the first thing I did was destroy the evidence that might link me to the murder. I burned the scarf in a wastebasket on my balcony, then I flushed the ashes down the toilet. I would have liked to wipe the dead woman's flat free of my fingerprints, but nothing could induce me to return there as long as the corpse remained.

It was nearly three in the morning by the time I showered, changed clothing, and sat down with this journal.

I sense that events are moving toward an unavoidable crisis. Yet I remain here at my hotel, awaiting Mozart, apparently my only hope of being reunited with Tatiana.

A year ago, I was an attorney in Chicago, unhappy and unable to conceive of a reality beyond the severe limits of my small world. But I have learned this planet is a bigger place than I suspected. There are worlds within worlds within worlds, some of them good, some of them bad beyond imagining. And there are things that you think can never happen to you—until they do.

I came to Paris to be reunited with the woman I love. Instead I have found only bloody horror and an inexorably tightening circle of doom.

*O Rose, thou art sick.*
*The invisible worm*
*That flies in the night*
*In the howling storm*

*Has found out thy bed*
*Of crimson joy,*
*And his dark secret love*
*Does thy life destroy.*

It is almost dawn. I should draw the curtains and go to bed, but I am too depressed to move. To die in an hour, to die tomorrow or the next day—what difference is there except the amount of torment the Ripper will force me to suffer first?

# Chapter 19

PARIS, JUNE 22, 1989—I'm walking through the hollow motions of my usual routine. I do it numbly, awaiting the next disaster. Clouds obscure the sky, and the rising wind smells like rain. Even the wine tastes bitter tonight. The people at the next table, a couple who traveled to Europe to restore the romance to their failing marriage, just stormed out after an argument filled with vicious accusations.

The end seems very near.

The time I spent in Nevada was completely the opposite of what my life is now. In the desert I was in a state of creative bliss, my head swirling with melodies and lines of poetry that came together in the most satisfying combinations when I crossed the stony wasteland, past the cactus where a tiny owl made its home, to the outcropping of rock that had become my special place for thinking beneath the crystalline night sky.

But isolation, even in the presence of a magnificent flowering of creativity, eventually leads to loneliness. As the weeks stretched into months, my new compositions acquired an inescapable sadness. I'd been writing exclusively in minor keys for more than a week before I realized it. I missed Tatiana so badly that I was on the verge of despair.

It was at that fortuitous moment the redheaded vampire arrived in Las Vegas. However, the salvation I'd expected him to deliver did not follow quickly. A week passed after the night he revealed himself at the Sahara, and still we had not met, much less *talked*. Instead we played a game of cat-and-mouse. I assumed his purpose was to learn what sort of vampire I was before deciding whether to introduce himself.

159

I felt the vampire's presence wherever I went beneath the shivering neon that lit the night in that vulgar city. He was always there, watching from the distance, measuring me with his eyes and with his mind.

(It was not the way it is now with the Ripper. I never felt anything malignant about the redheaded vampire's presence, only an intense curiosity.)

Another week passed, and my frustration and impatience grew to new levels. I missed Tatiana more than ever, but the vampire I'd hoped was her emissary continued to remain aloof.

At night I went out and searched for the redheaded man I could always *feel* but never find. I spent the long days shuttered in my house, unable to sleep, pacing the darkened rooms like a caged animal that senses its mate is somewhere nearby.

This was waiting of the hardest sort. I read Edgar Allan Poe and composed brooding music filled with harsh, unresolved chord progressions. At this point the city in the desert seemed less a refuge than an Elba. The sense of enlightenment I'd begun to experience faded, slowly killed by longing.

I began to think of the redheaded vampire as Poe's Raven, a dark, intractable messenger come to deliver a pronouncement of doom.

*And the Raven, never flitting, still is sitting, still is sitting*
*On the pallid bust of Pallas just above my chamber door;*
*And his eyes have all the seeming of a demon's that is dreaming,*
*And the lamplight o'er him streaming throws his shadow on the floor;*
*And my soul from out that shadow that lies floating on the floor*
   *Shall be lifted—nevermore!*

The inevitable Hunger returned, forcing me out of my house and back into the casinos and cabarets, studying faces to find a woman who could give me the precious substance I needed.

For once, I could not feel the redheaded man's presence. I took it as a bad sign. He'd apparently gone away, leaving me behind with only my growing thirst for blood to keep me company. I feared the vampire's disappearance signified the same thing as Poe's Raven's croaking, "Nevermore!"

\* \* \*

I stood in the hallway on the seventh floor of the Tropical Hotel, holding the woman who had helped me keep the Hunger at bay for still another fortnight. I closed my eyes and kissed her tenderly, trying to imagine she was my Russian princess. Our lips brushed together, and I ran my hand through her thick black hair.

She was Japanese, my first Oriental woman. Her husband was off with his business partners from Osaka, attending one of the female-impersonator reviews that had suddenly become popular in hotel show rooms. The Japanese, who seemed to be present in the city in increasing numbers, had made drag queens suddenly in hot demand. A hotel manager told me the flood of Japanese tourists brought with them sophisticated international tastes, but it was simply decadence, in my opinion.

"Sleep, my darling," I whispered into my almond-eyed lover's ear. I didn't need to see her eyes to know they were softening with forgetfulness. "Tonight has been only a dream. When you awake in the morning, you will remember making love—but of course it was only a dream, a dream so vivid that you'll almost think it was real."

She turned from me on my mental command, opened the door, and entered her room. The door closed silently behind her.

The hair on the back of my neck prickled. I spun around and saw the vampire with the red ponytail standing in the opened fire door at the end of the hall. Of course it *had* to be another vampire: No mortal had the stealth to creep up on me unnoticed.

There was a half smile on the vampire's face and a cast to his eyes that reminded me of the way an adult looks at a child who has just done something precocious.

The vampire's right hand came up, touched his elegant tie, and traveled on toward his head. I thought he was about to put his forefinger against his lips to signal me to remain silent, but instead he gave me a brisk little wave and disappeared through the fire door. It happened so quickly that it was almost as if he had vanished into thin air, leaving me with the mental image of the sapphire ring he wore on the little finger of his right hand.

"No, wait!"

The only answer was the sound of footsteps fast receding down the concrete stairwell. The footsteps were especially peculiar. Even a novice vampire such as myself can move with a silence not even a cat could match. He was telling me, perhaps challenging me, to follow.

I raced after him.

The stairwell door on the main floor opened to the outside behind a stand of palm trees. To the left, the sidewalk went to the swimming pool. I went right and followed the walkway around the hotel to the Strip.

The unmistakable red ponytail was two blocks ahead of me. As I spotted the vampire, he stepped into the street and broke into a slow run. Cars slowed to let him cross the street, and he went through one of the glass doors beneath a giant neon sign designed in the shape of multicolored poker chips.

I followed him into the casino, plunging into the Saturday-night crowd. The gamblers jostled against my shoulders like choppy waves fighting a swimmer on a windy day.

Overhead a woman in a sequined bikini flew through the air in a wide arc, flipping head over heels before grabbing the wrists of her acrobat partner on the opposite trapeze. A net you had to look for to see kept the performers from falling into the crowd. One came upon such bizarre scenes so often in Las Vegas that they soon lost their ability to excite attention. Most of the gamblers were oblivious of the circus show. It was simply part of the Vegas sensory overload that bombarded tourists from the moment they stepped off the planes, to find rows of slot machines lined up in the airport lobby.

My eyes found the other vampire on the opposite side of the main room. A waitress carrying a tray loaded down with free hors d'oeuvres for the gamblers came through the swinging service door. The vampire waited for her to pass, then exited through it.

I made my way through the throng as fast as I was able and pushed through the door into the kitchen. The uniformed chefs and their assistants did not look up from their work; the large casino kitchen was a busy place, and the presence of strangers didn't generate notice. There was a screen door that opened onto an alley that ran behind the casino. I walked toward it as quickly as I could without actually running and made it outside in time to see the red ponytail disappear into a silver Jaguar parked just beyond the dumpsters.

The only other car in the alley was a black Crown Victoria. A hulking man in a dinner jacket leaned against the driver's door. He could have been a boxer, a football player, a bodyguard, or a mobster—none of them were rare in Las Vegas. He shot me a don't-bother-me look as I approached. It was difficult to tell whether he was really warning me off or if he had simply practiced the menacing expression so long that it had become his permanent mask.

I kept my eyes on the pavement until I was six feet away from him, then locked my pupils onto his. His eyes wavered as if he were having trouble focusing, then they were still, held by my stare.

"I'll take the car keys, please."

"They're in the ignition." His voice was flat and unemotional.

"Why don't you go inside and play the slots?"

"Okay."

"You can pick the car up in the morning at the municipal lot at the end of the Strip. You know the one I mean?"

He nodded.

"I'll leave the keys in the ignition and lock the doors, so bring your spare set. If anyone asks, you locked your keys in the car tonight. Got it?"

"Yes, I've got it."

"Sorry about this. It's an emergency."

"That's all right."

"And you don't remember this conversation or my face."

The man walked by me as if I were suddenly invisible, heading toward the kitchen door.

"Thanks," I called after him.

He didn't answer. He'd already forgotten I existed.

I spotted the Jaguar's taillights six blocks ahead at a traffic light. I caught up and hung a half block back. He made no effort to lose me, but he did not acknowledge my presence, either.

The casinos gave way to commercial development, which changed, in turn, to residential neighborhoods as we approached the edge of town. We reached the last subdivision, the place where the water lines ended and the desert began. The Jaguar kept moving, accelerating slowly as it passed the few remaining scattered houses and went out into the desolation.

I sped up to keep pace, watching the speedometer needle climb to eighty. I let the distance between our two cars increase correspondingly. I didn't think the other vampire would slam on the brakes, but it was impossible to know quite what he was up to. He surely knew I was behind him, but there was nowhere he could go to lose me now that we were outside of town.

The desert seemed to crouch, hushed and waiting, on either side of the road. At night the rocky defiles and dry wash gulches became pools of shadow that held creatures driven into hiding during the fierce heat of day. Half-seen things dashed, crawled, and flitted in the darkness.

The Jaguar's taillights streaked through the night like twin red comets. The highway drew a smooth, orderly line across the flats, running toward the ridge of mountains on the horizon. With no moon the mountains were only a jagged black silhouette against the glittering sky.

I checked my fuel supply. The tank was three-quarters full. I tried to estimate the car's mileage. It would be fatal to run out of gas and be stranded outside of town at dawn.

We reached the foothills, and the highway began to rise. The incline quickly became steep as the mountains came up sharply, ragged crags thrust up from the desert floor. There was nothing peaceful about these mountains: gazing at them did not inspire images of trout streams and aspen trees bending gently in the clean, crisp breeze. These were not mountains a hiker would visit, or a family would stop in for a picnic. We were in the high desert, dry and dead and inhospitable to all but the few creatures adapted to its extremes.

The mountains, like the flats, were mostly without vegetation. The peaks were wild rather than majestic, as if they had been made while the Creator was in a fury. Amid the foothills stood volcanic chimneys, massive towers of brown rock pushed up from the earth's core by the seething powers below. Eons of wind had softened the primeval shapes, transforming sharp angles into fluidly blending lines and surfaces that resembled flowing water more closely than solidified magma; it gave the landscape an air of unreality, molding it into what might have been a place where people went in their sleep to dream.

The highway switched back and forth as we got into the mountains, working its way toward the pass that was the gateway to the other side of the range. I frequently lost sight of the taillights ahead of me as the road twisted and writhed like a huge python slithering over the tortured rocks. I thought of a passage in ''The Waste Land'' that seemed to describe the territory through which we were traveling:

> Here is no water but only rock
> Rock and no water and the sandy road
> The road winding above among the mountains
> Which are mountains of rock without water
> If there were water we should stop and drink

*Amongst the rock one cannot stop or think*
*Sweat is dry and feet are in the sand*
*If there were only water amongst the rock*
*Dead mountain mouth of carious teeth that cannot spit*
*Here one can neither stand nor lie nor sit*
*There is not even silence in the mountains*
*But dry sterile thunder without rain . . .*

I had not seen the red lights ahead for nearly a minute. I pushed hard against the accelerator to close the distance. The motor in the big car moaned as the sedan seemed to lift itself and lunge forward. The Jaguar, parked along the shoulder of the road, flew past on the right almost before I saw it.

I jammed my foot against the brakes—a foolish thing to do. The wheels locked, and the car's rear end began to come around. I felt it in the pit of my stomach—a sick feeling, a coming-unglued feeling—the moment before the force that held the car in its sideways skid let go and the big Ford snapped into a crazy spin.

I'm not sure how many times the car turned around, but I was all too aware that the distance between the car and the cliff was diminishing. I tried mentally to will the vehicle from plunging over the edge. I don't know whether it had any effect, but the car shrieked to a stop with two wheels on the pavement—and two wheels on the gravel shoulder a foot from the precipice.

I could see part of the Jaguar in the rear view mirror, the front bumper and leaping chromium cat hood ornament. My shaking hand found the gear shift lever, and I backed the Ford around, slowly and deliberately—taking three cuts to avoid the edge of the road—and drove back down the highway toward the other car. I parked the Ford on the wrong side of the road, its radiator facing the Jaguar, and got out. The English roadster was empty of its occupant and any of his belongings. The keys were still in the ignition.

I stepped backward into the road, looking for signs of the driver.

"Nowhere to go," I muttered to myself.

No, I was wrong. The fact was that the vampire could have gone *anywhere*. I looked around again, this time somewhat more nervously. I had no indication that his intention toward me was friendly or even benign. He might have led me into the desert to do me in, for all I knew. Perhaps *he* was the reason Tatiana had fled Chicago. It was true that I'd sensed no hostility in him,

but maybe he was as good at hiding his evil intentions as he was
at hiding himself.

I studied the mountain. My guess was that he had gone up.
Did I dare follow? All I had to advise me was my intuition, and
my intuition told me the vampire with the red hair was not
dangerous.

"Hello!" I called.

"Hello!" My echo came back so fast that it startled me.

*Hello!* I called a second time, but this time I used my mind
instead of my voice.

My eyes ran up the side of the mountain to a ledge that pushed
out into the air nearly halfway to the summit. At the edge stood
the vampire, hands on his hips. We studied each other a moment
before he let his arms drop slack to his sides, then gestured with
his right hand, beckoning me to follow.

I wondered how he had gotten so far up the mountain in such
a short time. And if he wanted to make contact with me, I
thought, what could be the point of going even farther into the
arid wilderness?

As I hesitated, he waved again, then turned and disappeared.

If I was to discover who he was and what he wanted, I was
going to have to climb the mountain like a pilgrim seeking
knowledge from a reclusive holy man. And in a sense I was a
pilgrim. Finding Tatiana was not my only reason for wanting to
talk to the elusive vampire. Except for the brief conversations
with my lover, what I knew about the world of vampirey was
limited to the few things I'd discovered on my own. The other
vampire, clearly older and wiser than myself, might provide the
answers to many questions I had about my life.

It could be dangerous, but I seemed to have already decided
to risk it by following him as far as we had come.

The moon, the thinnest possible crescent of silver, glided up
over the peak as I stood pondering my choice. The celestial light
seemed to signal the way, rising over the place the redheaded
man had stood.

*The moon abiding in the midst of*
*serene mind.*

The line of Zen poetry floated through my head as naturally
and simply as a single white cloud moving across a summer sky.
In that moment I saw the torn desert mountain as it truly was—
not a hostile environment, but perfect in its stark beauty. And I

saw the other vampire in my heart for what he truly was: a friend.

The other vampire spoke to me then, his voice metallic with its German accent but possessing an unmistakable kindness. His words were from ''The Waste Land,'' later lines from the poem I had been thinking about as I drove up the mountain. He had reached into my mind and read my thoughts, and now he used lines from the same poem I'd been reciting to myself to achieve an exactly opposite effect, to point out the possibility of greater things abiding within the apparently mundane and inhospitable present:

> *In this decayed hole among the mountains*
> *In the faint moonlight, the grass is singing*
> *Over the tumbled graves, about the chapel*
> *There is the empty chapel, only the wind's home.*
> *It has no windows, and the door swings,*
> *Dry bones can harm no one.*
> *Only a cock stood on the rooftree*
> *Co co rico co co rico*
> *In a flash of lightning. Then a damp gust*
> *Bringing rain.*

This was a kindred spirit, bringing rain to quench my parched spirit.

I hesitated no longer but ran to trace his footsteps up the side of the mountain, ready to hear whatever sermon the vampire had to preach atop a peak cloaked in midnight's deepest purple-blackness.

Whatever the other vampire had brought me to the mountain to tell me, I knew it would be something wonderful!

# Chapter 20

**P**ARIS, JUNE 23, 1989—A few quick notes in case they arrest me . . .

I don't know which frightens me more: the corpse sprawled across my bed, or the likelihood that the police are about to kick down my door and arrest me for murder.

It's impossible to look at the body without thinking about what happened two nights ago in the red-light district, when the mutilated corpse of the killer's previous victim pulled itself upright in bed, staring at me with the lightless whites of dead eyes.

I must not think of *that*—not if I am going to keep my courage up to deal with the present problem.

He has killed his latest victim in my rooms, leaving the body on my bed. It was the last thing I expected. I should have known better than to underestimate his murderous creativity. He is, after all, a *vampire*.

He was unusually neat this time. He did not disfigure her, I was relieved to see. I still have to get rid of the body. An odious enough chore, even if it weren't for the additional worry of whether the dead woman will remain "dead."

Thank God something told me to return to the hotel early. The killer no doubt hoped I would follow my usual pattern and come back just before dawn—forcing me to spend the entire day locked up with the corpse, smelling it begin to decay, praying that it would continue to lie motionless on the bed.

What if my nemesis sends the police here with an anonymous tip about a slaying?

I would not survive long in jail if it came to that. There would be no place to hide when the sun rose. They would call for paramedics, but there would be little they could do except watch in fascinated horror as I ran around the cell in screaming agony, my skin on fire, for whatever short time I had before death claimed me.

It would be the end of David Parker.

I think.

Lying in a darkened police morgue, protected from the sun's ultraviolet radiation, my body's regenerative powers might prove strong enough still. The pathologist would have an expression of keen interest on his face as he entered the postmortem lab to investigate this curious case. He might have heard rumors about macabre, supernatural elements to the case, although, as a man of science, he would of course have laughed them off as absurd superstition. The surprise would come when he slid open the refrigerated drawer to remove my body for autopsy and found not a burned corpse but a living creature, awake and desperate to drink a deep draught of the hot liquid that flowed through the stunned doctor's veins.

It was a clever plot the killer concocted. Fortunately for me my intuition steered me back to the Place Vendôme early.

I must hurry. If he sees that I have prematurely sprung his carefully laid trap, he may telephone the police before I can get rid of the body.

Live or die, what happens to me as an individual is suddenly unimportant. It is my *secret* that must be protected. The mortals must not know that our race exists. It would be a tragedy to awaken the old hatred again after so many centuries. The last time, religious hysterics went out to hunt for my vampire brothers and sisters, to drive wooden stakes through their hearts. The memory has become part of folklore, something people now regard as the quaint fiction of unsophisticated times.

The police must never catch me. Even if it means that I must die. Even if it means some of them must die with me.

The corpse lies silent, yet still I sit here writing, stalling for time. I've got to pull my thoughts together. I've got to think out my next move. One misstep, and I'm finished.

The elevator stops on my floor. I hear two sets of footsteps.

The police?

There's nowhere to hide in my suite of rooms. I could go out on the balcony, but if the killer has sent them here to apprehend me for his crime, there will be police in front as well as in the alley. Perhaps they already suspect me for his earlier crimes.

My enemy could have involved the authorities in his game from the beginning, setting *me* up as a modern Jack the Ripper. That would be rich!

The footsteps pass my door. The dreaded knock does not come. I hear whispers and a subdued laugh. A man and a woman, the Swiss couple staying at the end of the hall, returning from a nightclub. I sniff the air. The juniper berries from the gin they drank leaves a bright, fresh sting in the air.

What was it the note said in the prostitute's apartment? "I left the bitch's other kidney for you. The one I ate was delicious!"

I don't know why it didn't strike me before now—perhaps the killer I've come to call "The Ripper" was blocking me, preventing my mind from accessing familiar information—but the historical Jack the Ripper wrote something similar in a note sent to taunt the police after one of his gruesome Whitechapel murders in 1888. I can remember now. He'd cut the kidneys out of one of his victims. One kidney was never recovered; its mate was mailed to police with a note saying, "I ate the other one. It was delicious!"

An appalling possibility creeps through me, a spider of an idea crawling up the back of my neck: What if the English vampire is not merely committing crimes similar to Jack the Ripper's, is not merely trying to imitate Jack the Ripper, but actually *is* the insane Victorian mass murderer?

The corpse remains in its place on my bed, absolutely still and lifeless. I have to get rid of the body.

Jack the Ripper . . .

My God, it makes perfect sense!

What kind of monster has the vampire race preserved for eternity?

I've got to get out of here fast. For once the advantage seems to be mine. I cannot conceive that he would give me the opportunity to extricate myself from this problem if he knew I'd come back to my rooms so soon. He must be busy elsewhere—busy doing I dare not wonder what.

There's no time to waste. Morning will come whether I figure out how to deal with this problem or not. And I've got to do *something*.

Jack the Ripper!

I glance again over my shoulder.

The dead body remains a dead body and not some hideous

meat puppet controlled by a creature who was—who *is*!—one of the most bloodthirsty killers in recorded history.

Be that as it may, I must get the corpse out of my rooms.

Until later, if there is a later for me . . .


Thank God that is finished.

It's 4:45 A.M. I'm in a hotel across the Place Vendôme from the Ritz. The police will not find anything when they search my old rooms, but I do not think he will bother to send them there when he realizes I've outmanuevered him.

I took my car out of the hotel garage and parked in the alley before coming back to my room for the body.

I had to keep reminding myself that the woman was dead, that no matter what macabre things Jack the Ripper—in my soul I *know* it is he!—was able to do using his powers of mind, her corpse still was nothing more than the shell of a human being and unable to harm me, with my superhuman strength. As long as I kept control of my emotions, I would be all right. It wasn't easy. There is an instinctive fear of the dead that does not disappear simply because one becomes a vampire.

When I came back to my rooms from moving the car, the body was as it had been, stretched out on its back on the satin bedcover. The woman could have been asleep except for the stillness. The dozen almost imperceptible movements that indicate life—breath, heartbeat, the rush of blood through the arteries, the red glow of a living human aura, the unmistakable presence of energy—all were missing.

There was no trace of blood left in the woman. Two purplish places the size of dimes over her jugular vein showed where the killer had fastened onto her, draining her blood and her life at the same time.

I pulled the contents out of my steamer trunk and threw them on the floor. Taking a deep breath through my mouth, I lifted the limp body into the trunk, half expecting it to open its mouth and deliver some dreadful message.

The body remained perfectly quiet.

I slammed shut the lid and snapped the brass latches. The center lock required a key to close, but I didn't bother with it. The other two would hold well enough. Then I paused for a moment, just long enough to reconsider. I hurried to the dresser for the key and locked the center latch.

The risky part was getting to the car. A hotel never really sleeps. Fortunately it was a time of the night when activity had slowed. The hallway was empty when I opened the door and slid out the trunk, pushing it along the carpet with one foot, hearing the soft scrape as it rubbed against the carpet's nape. I locked the door behind me and picked up the big trunk, holding it with a deliberate lightness intended to convince anyone who saw me that it was empty.

I reached out with my senses to detect any mortals headed my direction. There were footsteps on the floor above me and running water, but that was all.

The body moved in the trunk. While I saw the dead prostitute grabbing for me in my mind's eye, I kept walking, telling myself it was only the weight shifting to rest in a different position.

The elevator was free, but I passed it and took the steps to the basement and came back up the rear stairwell to avoid the lobby. At first I thought the steamer trunk would not fit in the back of the Peugeot, but I slid it around until I found a way to ease it just under the rear deck.

I drove without any particular destination, traveling first along the Rue du Faubourg Saint-Honoré paralleling the Champs-Elysées, skirting the Arc de Triomphe. The Avenue Charles de Gaulle led me out of the city. I passed the Bois de Boulogne, several thousand acres of forest parkland that almost makes you forget you're in one of Europe's largest cities. The woods seemed to go on forever when you walked through them, as I had one night after I'd first arrived in Paris. The Merovingians had hunted wolves there. The wolves are centuries gone, along with the Merovingian kings, but other predators remained.

There are two lakes in the Bois de Boulogne. I thought about visiting the larger one, which for some reason is called Lac Inferieur.

The turnoff was just ahead.

I could punch holes in the trunk to allow water in and weight it down with rocks.

The turnoff to the park came at me fast. Then it was gone, behind me, past.

I couldn't bring myself to dump the dead woman in the lake. Whoever she was, she deserved better than to have the water pick at her flesh until she bloated up with gas and brought the trunk bobbing to the surface. And even in the park at night there was no telling who might be watching. My senses are not infallible. They're quite adequate for finding my way through a darkened museum or listening for others in a hotel hallway, but in the forest? Too many distractions, too great a risk for a vampire determined to be, above all else, cautious.

I stayed with the freeway and drove toward Saint-Germain-en-Laye. At random I turned onto a smaller highway. I drove for fifty minutes, slowed to travel through a village, then pushed harder against the gas pedal as I headed back out into a stretch of countryside that I scarcely saw fly by my window.

I was in a mild state of shock, and my attention remained focused on the rear of the car, waiting for the dreadful sound of movement.

I turned off onto a secondary road just wide enough for two cars to pass each other. There was no traffic. I followed the road five miles, then pulled onto a country lane. The gravel road followed the rolling topography, with drives splitting off at irregular intervals to meet darkened farmhouses set far back from the road. The fields were separated by stone fences, and stands of timber occupied some of the hilltops and the more rugged defiles that sloped down to meet small streams that drained the surrounding fields.

I shut off the lights and continued in the dark for a few miles. The country folk were asleep in their beds. There seemed to be not a single soul awake to see me, the vampire, come to Provence to dispose of a corpse. I felt despicable, like some form of lower life, some vermin, that did not deserve to exist. It would be a long time before the families in this rural neighborhood turned out their lights at night without wondering if the killer was wandering their fields after dark, looking for his next victim. I regretted the fear I would leave behind me, exporting murder to this peaceful corner of the world, but I had no choice. I had to get rid of the body, not only to protect myself but to protect my race.

I pulled the car to the side of the road at the top of a lonely hill with no buildings for a mile or more and a clear view of the road in either direction.

The quiet seemed to swirl up around me when I turned off the motor. I'd become accustomed to silence when I lived in Nevada, where I often took long tramps through the desert at night, chanting poetry to the rhythm of my footsteps on the hardscrabble landscape. Since coming to Paris, returning to life in the city, I had quickly grown accustomed to the high level of background noise every city resident—mortal and vampire—learns to tune out.

Now, miles from the city, surrounded by the night and the

reality of the terrible task I had come to perform, I heard only the sound of my breath and, beneath it, the slow, steady beating of the immortal heart within my breast.

I directed my senses backward to the compartment behind the rear seat. I listened carefully, as carefully as only a vampire can. There was nothing but silence, deadly silence, in the car.

I opened the door, climbed out, and leaned against the car, feeling a single trickle of sweat run down the back of my neck and into my shirt collar. I stood there for five minutes, unable to make myself act.

As the night became accustomed to my presence, the darkness came to life with a thousand tiny sounds. There were crickets. Running unseen through meadow grass nearby, a solitary field mouse caught the attention of my acute hearing. The hushed breeze came across the fields and up the hill, rustling through the wheat below and the trees above me on the hilltop, whispering a message that served to remind me I had no time to waste.

I looked at my watch. I would have to hurry to beat the dawn.

It depressed me beyond measure to see how the Ripper had drawn me into his crime, enlisting me as an unwitting and unwilling accomplice. There was no escaping my role in his twisted plot, and the responsibility that went along with it, as I stepped onto the stage to play the part he had written for me.

He had killed a young woman in my rooms, and it was my role to dispose of the body, to become a part of his conspiracy.

It took a moment more to work up the courage to open the car and pick up the steamer trunk. It came out much more easily than it had gone in. I lifted it across the stone fence and carried it up the hill toward the stand of trees that threw down long shadows from the summit now that the moon was coming up.

I would have preferred to abandon the trunk with the body, but that would have meant leaving behind too much physical evidence—fingerprints, fibers from the carpets in the car and hotel, a possible trace to the luggage shop in Las Vegas, where it had been purchased. I had to take the trunk with me, but first it had to be emptied.

I undid the latch on the right.

The metallic snap seemed to ring out like a gunshot on the quiet hilltop. The crickets fell silent. I waited, listening carefully. No sound from within the container.

I undid the latch on the left.

Still nothing. I took out the key and unlocked the middle latch.

Fear tightened in my throat as I stood staring down. Nothing held the trunk closed—and nothing from within pushed it frantically open.

I took a step backward. My rational mind knew nothing was going to happen, but it required a conscious effort to fight back the illogical fear that the trunk was about to burst open and spew forth a gibbering corpse bent on getting its icy dead fingers around my neck.

The only sound was the wind, which seemed to be rising. It rustled through the trees, making the boughs creak in the darkness. Somewhere in a wooded ravine on the other side of the road a screech owl called mournfully to the night.

I touched a corner of the trunk with a thumb and finger and flipped open the lid, standing quickly upright, my hands in front of me, knowing as no one knows quite so well as a vampire that anything is possible.

The open trunk seemed to gather in the shadows and hold them the way it had once held the sheet music and poetry books I'd brought from America. From my angle I could see part of one arm and a single hand. There were discolored half moons across the palm where fingernails bit in during her final moments of terror as the fiend greedily sucked the blood out of her, not even bothering to blank her mind first to save her the needless horror of knowing she was about to die.

I moved closer.

The dead woman's posture was relaxed in a way that was unnatural in anything but a corpse. She looked uncomfortable, but I knew she was beyond such considerations. I could not bring myself to lift her from the trunk; making a silent apology, I tipped it forward and spilled the body out on the ground.

I stared down at the slack form dressed in a white nurse's uniform and felt profoundly ashamed to realize that I was only now seeing her as an individual human being—and not merely an unwelcome problem to deal with. The Ripper had scored against me again almost without my realizing it, I thought bitterly. He'd made me an accomplice in his crime, but worse than that, he'd put me into a position where my own selfish fears overrode my concern for the human being he had senselessly slaughtered. I'd driven to the country to dump the body without much more regret over her wasted life than he would have felt.

I had, in fact, participated in everything except the actual act of snuffing out the woman's life. What would be next? Committing the actual killing?

I felt dirty, as if there were a thin film of greasy oil coating my soul. I'd done what I could to resist the killer, but I was playing far out of my league. Bit by bit the Ripper was pulling me deeper into his dark world. I would rather die than slide farther into the bleak, brutal morass where he made his home—and dying seemed the only way to keep such a thing from happening.

Tatiana had been truthful when she said becoming a vampire would be more difficult than anything I could possibly imagine. I tried to swallow, but my mouth was too dry. I stood for a long moment and mourned the poor murdered woman, whose life had been cut short for some obscene game. And though it was a sign of my old self-pity, I also mourned the man named David Parker, who died without knowing it when he traded mortality for an eternal nightmare.

> And every tongue, through utter drought,
> Was withered at the root;
> We could not speak, no more than if
> We had been choked with soot.
> Ah! well-a-day! what evil looks
> Had I from old and young!
> Instead of the cross, the Albatross
> About my neck was hung.

I turned away from the dead woman and stared at the copse of trees on the hill.

One tree at the edge of the grove stood slightly forward from the others, intertwined with a heavy spider's web of vines that stretched across the gap to the other oaks, connecting them in a shadowy framework. The solitary tree was bare of leaves, a skeleton, its trunk rotted completely away six feet from the ground. The only thing holding it up was the vines—which had killed it and were now stretching to insinuate themselves with other trees, to kill them, too.

I was like that oak: seemingly alive yet dead, connected to the living only by the dark Hunger that fed upon them.

For the first time since meeting Tatiana, I felt a weariness with life and a desire to be free from it. But then, what of Tatiana? I had promised to protect her against the eternal loneliness that is the curse of the vampire race, a loneliness only love defeats.

She had told me I would have to be strong. I released a deep sigh and lifted my head. I would be strong. I could not give in to the killer.

The night air was sweet with the smell of blossoming clover. The poor dead woman. If I could avenge her and the others, perhaps it would absolve me for my role in this affair.

I straightened the woman and folded her hands over her stomach. I wished there was something to cover her face, but it would have been stupid to leave my jacket behind. The thought of leaving her there bothered me, but there was nothing I could do except stop on the way back to the hotel and call the police.

That is all I have to tell. The sky is becoming light in the east. It is time to close the shutters and draw the double set of heavy velvet curtains against the day. I welcome the escape that a few hours of sleep will bring.

I was fond of my rooms at the Ritz Hotel in the Place Vendôme, but I will never return there. I must not make it too easy for my bête noir. I can no longer afford the luxury of a casual attitude, not while I'm locked in a game of chess with a killer who snuffs out a human life for each of his moves. I must be on my guard constantly as long as I remain in Paris. There will be no peace for me while I am here until Jack the Ripper has either paid for a century of crimes, or I am dead.

I left a message for Mozart at the Ritz. I'll visit the lobby there every evening, looking for signs of his arrival. The rest of my nights I'll pass in cafés, surrounded by crowds. I'll check into a different hotel just before each dawn, and remain in my room until I check out the next night. That, at least, will prevent the Ripper from sacrificing any more mortals in my lodgings.

If I am to survive for Tatiana, I must use all my guile against the fiend.

# Chapter 21

**P**ARIS, JUNE 24, 1989—It was easy to follow the vampire's path up the Nevada mountain once I found his trail amid the rocks. His presence lingered after him as a faint melodic hum that resonated in my mind like the final note of a symphony after the music has ended.

Rocks jabbed the soles of my feet through my soft Italian loafers, but I hardly noticed. Upward I hurried, pulled along by the prospect that some great revelation was at hand, that unimagined secrets of our race soon would be made known to me.

The mountain was deceptive. From the highway—now receding into the distance below—it had seemed to present a fairly uniform mass that rose steeply toward three peaks that ran along the ridge dividing the range east and west. However, the mountain was much more complicated than the undifferentiated rock it appeared to be from afar. The terrain was creased with a network of lines, like the face of an ancient man.

The desert mountain was an unreal place at night. The stones absorbed the cool blue light that fell from the stars and thumbnail moon until they seemed to glow from within with the energy of distant galaxies. It was a lovely but eerie sight.

The trail skirted a series of deep rifts that appeared suddenly out of the darkness, places where the rock fell suddenly away to leave nothing but chasm. The other vampire was either extremely familiar with the mountain or a genius at finding his way across the crazy landscape. We had yet to double back after reaching a dead end, a significant navagational accomplishment in a place where, from any given point, there was perhaps one path that allowed continued climbing, and many that ended at box canyons, unscalable cliff faces, and abysses too wide to cross with anything but a helicopter.

The path followed a saddleback ridge, gradually narrowing to a ledge that shrank from ten feet wide to a space that left only the two or three inches needed to sustain a foothold—if I plastered myself against the cliff face.

I moved slowly, my back pressed against the rock, trying not to think about the yawning space that threatened to return me to the highway with all the haste gravity could provide. The parked cars looked like Matchbox toys, and seeing them seemed to set a large moth fluttering loose inside my stomach.

I traversed several hundred feet of trail with little more than luck preserving my life. Then the path widened, imperceptibly at first, slowly becoming broad enough for me to resume a faster pace. As I neared the summit, the trail leveled and began to travel parallel to the ridge of peaks, climbing no higher. The highway was no longer anywhere in sight, lost below and behind me.

I had reached a completely wild part of the mountain, a place no casual passersby ever saw. The territory I was trekking across pushed out from the rest of the range like the root of a tree reaching beyond the main trunk. In the distance I could see the change in shadows that marked the place the ridge turned back in toward the main body of the mountain.

My goal was not far away, intuition told me. Somewhere just past the bend I would find the redheaded vampire waiting for me.

I broke into a run but stopped after only a few strides, pulling myself back from a plunging gorge that was impossible to see until it was almost too late to save myself from falling to my doom.

With the abyss yawning past the tips of my shoes, I stood and stared dumbly at what I *saw* and *heard* in the darkness. Shimmering across the blackness, like a bridge built from the sound of a thousand tiny silver chimes, was the other vampire's path, its presence so powerful to my preternatural senses that I was almost tempted to try to walk across the gorge on it.

But what I plainly saw with my vampire senses had to be an illusion. The other vampire had crossed a gulf of nearly one-hundred feet to make it to the far side of the crevasse. Such a feat was clearly impossible. Muscles, tendons, and bones only can accomplish so much. There are physiological laws that cannot be ignored, by either man or vampire. No one, not even a vampire, could make such a leap.

Nevertheless the trail lingered in the air, as unmistakable to my hyperreceptive senses as the white vapor line a jet draws across a cloudless summer sky.

Music floated toward me on the still night air as I stood looking up and down the mountainside, trying to see a way around the chasm. It was the opening piano flourish in the allegro maestoso movement of Mozart's Piano Concerto no. 21. The lyrical scales sprinkled through the night air like the first raindrops of a warm spring shower, laughing, teasing, calling me playfully forward.

I smiled to myself in the darkness. What I heard was no recording. The music was being performed, live, on a grand piano somehow transported three-quarters of the way up the side of that desolate mountain.

And the playing! So perfect! At the keyboard this vampire had the touch of an angel. The music was so beautiful that it was easy to stand there and listen, enraptured, on the wrong side of the impassable chasm. His brilliant interpretation had an antique feel that I find hard to explain in words. His playing was so subtle, so rich—quite unlike anything I'd heard from my contemporaries, whose own performances seemed noisy and histrionic by comparison.

I must have looked like a befuddled old woman as I stood there dumbfounded, my mind running through the world's greatest keyboard geniuses, both ''dead'' and alive, trying to decide who the redhaired vampire could be.

I seemed to know that impish face, but I could not connect it with a name. I felt that the recognition was there, just beyond the grasp of my knowing. It was the first time since becoming a vampire that my perfect memory had failed me. It didn't take long to guess that the vampire was blocking me, using his infinitely more powerful will to prevent me from ''remembering'' him.

The desert breeze began to blow gently across the mountain, carrying on it the faintest hint of a scent I had not experienced for what seemed an eternity, even though I could never forget it. The aroma was pale at first, but it blossomed into a rich, unmistakable fullness.

Jasmin de Corse perfume. Tatiana's fragrance.

I took a half dozen fast steps back the way I had come, turned, and ran at the crevasse, throwing myself at the impossibly distant far side.

My body flew out over the blackness. I reached what should have been the apogee of the arc and something extraordinary happened. There was a tingling in my solar plexus, as if invisible strands of energy were shooting out of me, attaching themselves to objects on the far side of the gorge and pulling me forward.

I heard my shoes hit the scrabble. The unseen fibers vanished back into my body in the blink of an eye. My chest and stomach tingled when I ran my hand over them, a residue of energy hanging over my body like steam on the street after a hot summer rain.

Beyond me in the darkness music called to me.

I had delayed long enough. The trail was wide and the way clear. I began to run through the darkness toward the music.

The music came from a place within a cleft hidden within the folds of the mountain's stone mantle. A boulder the size of a boxcar marked the place the trail slashed back into the mountains. As I came around the rock, I was startled to see a body hanging against a rock wall, its feet ten feet above my head.

I stopped, eyes wide.

It was not actually a body but a carved marble angel like those that grace Renaissance cathedrals. The antique statue was worked in such lovingly realistic style that the folds of its stone robe seemed to float on the air. Broad wings appeared to hold the angel aloft, the divine creature twisting at the waist to look back at me as I approached. The artist had arranged the composition perfectly: head cocked, hair blown back from the serenely smiling face; right knee raised; right hand holding a trumpet; left arm outstretched, palm bent upward at the wrist as if to offer a gift. The angel beckoned me to follow, at the same time pointing the way toward the music.

I *knew* I was close to something wonderful!

On the far side of the ridge was a small canyon with a circular level spot, comprising perhaps the area of ten city blocks, a peaceful area left behind by the primordial forces that thrust up the jagged peaks above. Nestled in the midst of the horizontal space, like something tiny held within the hand of a giant, was what must have once been a thriving town. There were rich silver veins in some Nevada mountains, and I guessed that within the steep cliffs ringing the deserted town on three sides would be the mine shaft that had been the town's reason for being—as well as dying when the silver was tapped out.

The town must have thrived late in the last century, judging from the architecture. The bigger houses were Victorian masterpieces, their elaborate trim intact even though the structures

had all turned that shade of gray the sun bakes wood once the
paint has flaked away. The lack of moisture in the air had preserved the wood, and the buildings were all in surprisingly good
shape, except that they lacked paint.

It was a considerable achievement to have shipped timber so
far into the desert, then to haul it up the mountain over nearly
impassable terrain, an unpaved mine-town road notwithstanding. It must have been a very rich town while the silver lasted.

The cluster of larger structures in the center of the ghost town
indicated where the business district had been. It was from this
direction that the beautiful music continued to pour forth, the
heavenly sound created by someone oblivious of the atmosphere
of broken dreams and lost wealth in the abandoned houses and
shops.

I walked down into the basin that contained the settlement,
following the music.

My footsteps carried me first through the small cemetery,
where perhaps one hundred miners, merchants, and members
of their families were buried. Most of them died prosperous,
judging from the elaborate tombstones. One grave was capped
with the statute of a weeping angel that seemed to be the anti-
thesis of the marble herald who had urged me down into this
lost city.

The main street was preserved to a degree that was eerie. It
was as if the residents had simply packed their bags and left the
day the mine played out, leaving behind the town for whoever
wanted to settle near the top of a mountain in the middle of a
desert, hundreds of miles from civilization.

The half doors to the saloon hung open. I could walk inside,
dust off a chair, and sit down alone at any table in the house.
The curtains hung in the front windows of the Royale Hotel. The sun had long since bleached them white, and they hung
in shreds behind the glass, the fabric rotted away to almost nothing. The shades were neatly pulled at the bank, and the door
was closed and no doubt locked. The building looked prim and
businesslike, even after being deserted for the better part of a
century.

At the end of the main street, occupying the focal point of the
intersection where the street split left and right, was the largest
building in town. The opera house was constructed of brick and
marble and colored tile, imported to the desert at untold ex-
pense. A curious artifact to find in the derelict mining town,
most likely the relic of an eccentric silver baron's attempt to

bring culture to the frontier. Not such an absurd project, I thought, remembering with regret how long it had been since I'd attended the opera.

The theater's center doors were opened to admit the audience—me—for the performance that continued inside. It concluded at the exact moment I passed through the doors. I found myself walking through cobwebs in the dark, brushing them away from my face with my hands. I opened a door that met the center aisle in the abandoned theater and stepped inside.

The decay and filth of a century of abandonment were evident everywhere. But in spite of the mess it was easy to see it had been a showplace in its day. The seats were covered in what was once red velvet. The same material was used in the curtains, now closed, which were fringed with the moldering remains of gold braid.

*Whoosh!*

The kerosene footlights at the edge of the stage came on so fast in the dark, silent room that their brightness temporarily blinded me. I threw up my hands to cover my face, squeezing my eyes shut. When I opened my eyes again, blinking rapidly to adjust to the light, I saw that the opera house had been miraculously restored to its original splendor, a sparkling rococo palace filled with carved wood, fluted columns, and gilded cupids.

"Bravo!" I said, and applauded, although the other vampire was nowhere to be seen. Whether what he'd done to the concert hall was real or illusory, it was an impressive feat.

I took a seat and waited for the performance to begin after an intermission that so neatly coincided with my arrival. After a moment the houselights went down and the curtains parted.

A concert grand piano occupied the space at center stage, supporting two flaming candelabra. Seated at the keyboard, smiling like the Cheshire cat, was the vampire with the red ponytail. He repeated the last few bars of the finale to Piano Concerto no. 21, then stood, faced me, and bowed.

"At last, David Parker," the little German said, standing up straight, "we meet."

# Chapter 22

**P**ARIS, JUNE 25, 1989—I bought a copy of *Le Monde* yesterday and found a brief story about it, three paragraphs buried deep inside the paper.

The article said a young nurse had been found dead in the country. There was no evidence of foul play. Police were investigating the possibility drugs were involved.

Tonight the newspaper devoted two columns at the bottom of page one to a much more sensationalized account.

The woman's death has been labeled *"un mystère medical déroutant"*—a baffling medical mystery. The victim, a twenty-four-year-old emergency room nurse in a private Paris hospital, had been in prime physical condition at her annual physical exam two weeks earlier. Pathologists said she died from massive blood loss, although they were unable to explain how her body had come to be so completely drained, when they were unable to identify either wounds or needle marks during the autopsy.

The part of the story I knew I would find—and dreaded reading—had been saved for the final paragraph:

> One detective muttered something about vampires when asked to speculate on possible explanations for Miss Tranque's death. The official police spokesman discounted the remark as off-color, the result of too many hours without sleep, looking for leads in the case. The spokesman added that any speculation about vampires was simply too absurd to merit reply.

Of course I am responsible for this monumental blunder. *Any speculation about vampires* . . .

I hope the other members of the police force agree that such an idea is too ridiculous to consider.

I cannot blame the Ripper for this, much as I would like to. I was the one who bumbled getting rid of the body. The responsibility is mine.

It would have been easy to dispose of the corpse in a way that left no trace, even if the unfortunate woman's family had been left forever hanging. I should have consigned the body to the flames that incinerated the steamer trunk I used to move the body. God knows she was beyond caring about the disposition of her mortal remains.

I damn myself for lacking the necessary coldhearted pragmatism to have avoided this complication. I can't afford to be anything but ruthless from here on out if I'm to survive, if *my race* is to survive.

One other thing bothers me, nagging at me as I linger over the dregs of a bottle of wine.

The manner in which the nurse was murdered was entirely too neat to be in character with the Ripper's style of crime. His ghastly passion for mutilating victims is too well known. I cannot understand why he would set up a task designed to frighten and revolt me—or get me arrested—yet hold back from furnishing those most appalling flourishes that are his trademark.

Perhaps the body in my hotel room did not seem to have been killed by the Ripper because it was a *second* vampire who drained the nurse of her blood.

Paris—the city has lost its charm for me.

I hurry along the streets, no longer pausing to admire the grace that I used to find in even simple things, such as the Parisian lampposts—cast-iron art nouveau relics of the Belle Epoque. I keep myself pressed close to the buildings, stopping frequently to look over my shoulder, hunted even as I remain the Hunger's hunter.

I move from hotel to hotel, never staying in a place more than one night. I'm like an animal cornered for cruel sport: the survival instinct overrides all other considerations, transforming me from someone who lived for love, music, and poetry into a tormented creature ever ready to strike out at its tormentors.

The David Parker who came down from a desert mountain filled with awe has become a withdrawn, paranoid figure, more wretched than even the weak, self-pitying lawyer who once planned suicide because his overprivileged life was empty of real meaning.

I saw my face reflected in a shop window tonight and stopped to stare. Was it really me? I saw a side of my nature I did not recognize.

Traits are surfacing from the darkest corners of myself, where they had been hidden until the Ripper began to force them out of the shadows. There is an anger inside me that was not there before. I am filled with hatred for my adversary. For the first time in my life I feel capable of violence. I ache for the chance to strike out at *him*, to vent the hostility built up in me, the pressure near bursting, pushing me nearer and nearer the edge.

And if I cannot release my anger upon the Ripper, then perhaps someone else will give me the release. . . .

What am I writing?

That can *never* be.

I do not know the person I have become.

It is more than a week before the Hunger will return to me, yet I have been filled with a craving of a dark nature I am embarrassed to confess.

(This journal must serve as my confessor as well as my confidant now. And in the likely event that I do not survive, it will be my last testament.)

Until now I have fed only to satisfy a need. Though I have tried to make it as satisfying as possible for my host and me, I have never taken blood merely to experience the pleasure, the thrill, the *awesome* rush of power, it brings flooding into my immortal body.

But lately I have struggled against an illicit desire, a deep lust to take a woman and make her my slave for a night, forgetting the tortured present in the erotic abandon of blood.

*Blood!* The word alone sends a thrill through my body. How I yearn to press my lips against a beautiful woman's neck and feel the explosion of ecstasy as the steaming elixir bursts into my ready mouth!

No, that desire does not "fill" me. It *possesses* me completely—body, mind, soul. In moments when I forget the discipline I am fighting to maintain and allow my thoughts to wander, my mind fills with feverish visions of what it would be like to find a woman and take her for the sake of simply doing it.

I imagine having a woman that way, penetrating her body and

blood to delight in dominating her, to experience the forbidden thrill of subjugating someone weaker, someone I could force to gratify any desire I chose to fulfill, no matter how degrading or painful.

I had to pause just now to shake the sick fantasy out of my mind. The same hallucination returns to me again and again and with it a yearning for the blood that is a thousand times more powerful than the addiction that compelled me to buy cocaine when I was mortal.

I have in my mind at this moment the image of a soft body bending beneath mine, yielding to the force of my will, letting me do whatever I want. Our bodies glisten with sweat as we press together in the darkness, limbs intertwined. There is a tingling sensation in my belly as I lower moist lips to her neck. Kissing her there, running my tongue over her skin, feeling the pulse race. Gently sucking, gently biting, love bites. The skin resists the increased pressure when I press down harder. She moans and arches her spine, throwing her head to one side, thrusting her willing neck forcefully against my mouth. I bite harder, harder, harder! Hot blood splashes against my throat. Bliss, wave upon wave of the sweetest bliss, the sweetest imaginable bliss! I am borne away on a great tide of orgasmic pleasure. I drink and drink and drunkenly drink deeper the blood I do not need, more than I should take, exulting in the triumph of my strength as the life ebbs out of the slackening body beneath mine, my sucking mouth fastened to her bruised and punctured neck, drinking great bloody gulps until she is dry and deathly still and at last I am truly and completely satisfied.

*No!*

Who is this monster in my body, guiding me to write these foul words—not my words but a message from Hell expressed through my hand? I stare at the page in this journal with stunned disbelief. I do not even know what I have written! It is like a waking dream, or the automatic writing a medium does during a séance.

I shake off the trance. Thank God I have only been writing!

It was the Ripper *inside my head*. I can feel him now that I've shut him out of my mind, a seething, hostile energy pressing against my consciousness. I will not let him back in. That is the key. Now that I have recognized what he is trying to do, I will lock him out—if I can.

He is appealing to the animal that sleeps inside of me, inside of us all, calling to it, trying to awaken the creature and drive it forward to take control of my being.

I have at least two deadly enemies. One is external: He stalks me through the streets of this city, littering my path with the bodies of his victims. The other is internal: the demonic creature that lives within my own psyche, my dark side, my *other*.

If I am to become like the Ripper, he must succeed in awakening my *other*, in subjugating the angel of my better nature and raising up the sleeping demon within me.

I am not a killer. I repeat it over and over to myself. I am *not* a killer! I am too good to surrender to these base, bloody cravings. I must master these animalistic urges. I must hold out until my ally arrives.

Yet temptation is everywhere! There is a lovely young woman next to the café, visiting the open-air bookstall.

See how her red hair falls across her face, the curling strands filled with golden highlights in the street lamp's soft glow? She's not wearing a bra, and her breasts press against her blouse. Her skirt is short and, with the spike-heel shoes, makes her legs seem even longer than they are. I can imagine those legs wrapped around my back, still wearing those red shoes with ankle straps.

The pulse throbs in her delicious neck each time her heart beats, and my own pulse pounds faster, too, until the blood pumps through our bodies in perfect synchronism.

I do *not* need to feed! The Hunger does not call me. No matter how much I want to taste this beautiful long-legged woman's blood, I do not need it!

I must not get up from this table and go to her. I must not reach into her mind and call her to me. Control. Always, control.

I push the beast within me down. I look into its brutal face and acknowledge it for what it is—*me*!

I must never permit my *other* to get free. If it acts, my *other* will become me, and I will become it, and there will be nothing left but darkness and horror and the unending reek of blood.

# Chapter 23

PARIS, JUNE 26, 1989—The telephone call I received from Ariel Niccolini late this afternoon left me sick with worry.

"It's lovely to hear from you, my darling," I said, "but however did you get this telephone number? I don't recall leaving a forwarding address when I changed hotels."

The fact was that I'd changed hotels nightly, and I'd been careful about *not* telling anybody where I was going each time I moved. There was no logical way to explain how she'd been able to pick up the telephone and reach me.

"You must have inadvertently said something, *tesoro mio*, since the desk gave me this number. But I'm curious to know why you would want to move without leaving word where I could reach you. If I were an insecure woman, I'd suspect you were trying to make it difficult for me to find you."

"I've been changing hotels for another reason entirely. You know that I care about you far too much to treat you in such shabby fashion."

"Yes," she answered without hesitation.

"But you really must tell me who gave you this number, my darling. I've been very careful not to leave forwarding addresses."

"Why?"

"Please do not ask me to explain it now. You'll have to trust me when I say that I have good cause for acting in what I know must seem like a suspicious manner."

"I believe you, *amore mio*."

"However, Ariel," I said sternly, "the fact that you've been able to find me easily gives me great reason for concern. Have you talked to someone who has been following me?"

"I don't know what you're talking about."

"Trust me, Ariel. It's important that you tell me how you got this number. It's a matter of *life and death*. I can't explain why over the telephone, but I must know."

"Then come to Florence tonight, and I'll tell you everything. Your ticket is waiting for you at the airport. It was an impulse I couldn't resist. I simply *have* to see you tonight. I also booked you a return flight that will have you back in Paris before the sun comes up, if your business there is so important, or if you hate me so much that you can't stay with me a single night."

"I don't hate you, Ariel. What have I done to make you speak to me this way? I care about you very, very much. But as I've explained before, I cannot leave Paris."

"Not even to see me for two hours?"

"My love, please . . ."

"Do you know where I am right now? I'm in a room in a hotel five minutes from the airport. I'm lying on the bed, David. I'm not wearing any clothes except for black nylons with seams, and a garter belt. You could fuck me and be back in Paris before the night was finished."

"Ariel!" I was hardly scandalized by her proposition, but the vulgarity with which it was made was completely unlike her.

*"Ti imploro!"* she cried. "I implore you, David. If I don't see you tonight, I don't know what I'll do. I think that I will die."

"You must not say that. What is wrong? This doesn't sound anything like the Ariel Niccolini I know."

There was only silence until I realized Ariel was quietly sobbing at the other end of the line.

"Ariel," I said as gently as I could manage. "My love. *Amore mio*. What is wrong? Are you in some sort of trouble?"

"You remember my patron? The one whose gifts I told you virtually make up my museum's entire budget?"

"Yes," I answered tentatively, the word almost more a question than an answer.

"He wants very much to meet you."

I blinked.

"Why in the world would he want to meet *me*?"

"He said he'd fire me unless you agreed to visit his villa." A sob escaped from her throat. "He may deal with me even more harshly if you don't come. Cesare has been very generous, but he is ruthless. I've heard things whispered about him that make me think he's capable of anything."

"Cesare who?"

"Please, David. Come to Florence. *Ti imploro!*"

"Cesare *who*?" I demanded.

The telephone went dead in my hand.

I did not have an opportunity to repeat the question, although I already knew the answer.

Cesare who?

*Cesare Borgia.*


My immediate reaction was to do something heroic, to get on the plane to Florence and do what I could to rescue Ariel Niccolini from the vampire Borgia, a creature next to whom even Jack the Ripper would seem harmless. Yet the reality of my situation sank in before I got out the door. I did not have the power to defeat so ancient an evil, and if I went to Florence, I would be walking straight into a trap.

If Borgia had Ariel in his custody, halfway across Europe in a Florentine villa no doubt filled to overflowing with stolen art treasures and the dark reek of countless violent deaths, there was nothing I could do to help her. It was hard to admit but true. It would be nothing short of suicide to go to Florence, a case of confusing stupidity with bravery.

Besides, if Borgia and the others want to drive me out of Paris, there must be a very good reason for me to stay. My ally, and perhaps even Tatiana, could be on their way here at this exact moment. Their help might provide just the strength I need to go to Florence and accomplish something more than my own death.

And so I must not leave Paris.

But Ariel!

I feel so helpless! There is nothing I can do but sit and pray I have not condemned her to a terrible fate. The idea that her association with me has put her in such peril fills me with stinging guilt.

Something else occurs to me just now, an observation I would have been more quick to make were it not for this jumble of emotions I have allowed to overwhelm my intellect.

Ariel Niccolini's association with Cesare Borgia clearly began before she met me if it is his money that funds the museum where she is employed.

Did my Italian lover come to Paris with the express purpose of entrapping me?

I could not believe such was the case. I think I would have seen the evil in her mind—unless Borgia had been subtle enough to bury the treachery so deeply within her subconscious that I could not easily recognize it.

The entire situation suddenly seems convoluted, a tangle of plot and counterplot, a Gordian knot not even the mind of a vampire could unravel. And all of this without considering Borgia's other agent in Paris, the Ripper, and perhaps at least one other vampire, an American female with a slight southern accent. They fit into the story somehow, too.

It makes my head whirl. When Mozart arrives, perhaps he can help me sort it out. For the present I will retreat into the past and conclude the story of my life in the desert. In doing so, maybe I will at least for the next hour escape the terrible concerns of the present.


I walked toward the redheaded vampire, filled with caution as well as wonder. Decayed opera house or the splendid gold rush palace—which was real? I climbed the steps to the stage. He extended his hand, and I shook it. The grip was warm and firm. Like so many great pianists, his hands were small, his fingers short, seemingly incapable of the reach one had to have to truly command the keyboard the way he'd so clearly proven he was able.

"How do you do?" I said, bending my head to look down on the little man, feeling foolish at having to do so, because his strengths and talents were so obviously superior to mine.

The vampire released my hand with a flourish and bowed from the waist. His elegant manners, which contained the slightest hint of irony, told me that he, like Tatiana, belonged to a different century. I studied the face with great fascination. It contained the most unusual combination of wisdom and puckish humor. But for his German accent, he might have been Pan—a sylvan creature who cared only for music, wine, and dancing barefoot on the soft grass in moonlit forest clearings. Still, it was impossible to forget that behind this disarming smile burned a knowledge of secrets I had not begun to understand.

"You may call me Herr Wolf for the time being," he said. "It is not my real name."

"I am David Parker, but I'm sure you know that. Is this"—I gestured at the scene around us—"your handiwork?"

"I've always had an attraction for the wild West. Understanding it is, I think, the key to knowing how you Americans think. You are still using your name with mortals?"

"Sometimes. Is that a problem?"

"No, not yet. There are things David Parker must accomplish before he ceases to be David Parker. When you have done all you need to do . . ." He smiled. "It would hardly be appropriate for David Parker to continue living on, his face unaging, while his contemporaries grew old."

"I suppose not."

"A name is a simple thing, until one becomes a vampire. Then it, and everything else, becomes immensely complicated."

"I've found that to be true," I said, sounding a bit too regretful.

"Part of the challenge of being a vampire is thinking one's moves through carefully. Of course rationality is merely the basis for everything else, the jumping-off point for knowledge. I hope you don't find my comments too mystical for your twentieth-century tastes."

"Not at all." I had no idea what he was talking about, but I was anxious to hear anything he had to say.

"A name is of little consequence to a vampire. It is like a suit of clothing. One wears it until it begins to become threadbare—ten, perhaps twenty years, if one is careful—and then it's time to become someone new. I've grown rather to like the process. You tend to discard bad characteristics while retaining good ones when you assume a new identity. After a few such changes, you become an idealized version of yourself."

I nodded, but I doubted it could be that simple.

"How do you think you'll do it?"

"Kill David Parker?" The words sounded strange.

"Yes. Assumed identities are easy to slough off, being artificial from the start. Shedding your true identity is another matter."

I thought for a moment before answering.

"I've always been interested in mountain climbing. I suppose I could fall into a bottomless gorge in the Himalayas, disappearing someplace where my body would be lost beyond hope of recovery. Excuse me for saying it, but I had ample opportunity to do so tonight."

Herr Wolf laughed.

"You have many muscles to strengthen, and the most important one is *here*." He touched a finger to his forehead. "Only through constant practice can you learn to use your powers fully. But I do like the idea about the Himalayas. It's believable, and yet it has an element of romance. Yes, I like the scenario very much. 'David Parker, the brilliant and eccentric attorney-turned-concert-pianist, was killed while attempting to ascend Mt. Everest's treacherous north slope with his Sherpa guide.' Good copy for *The New York Times*.''

Herr Wolf gave me a peculiar smile.

"Incidentially, I have something for you." He reached into a pocket and withdrew a woman's antique French lace handkerchief with the initials *TNR* stitched across one corner.

I accepted the gift and held it as carefully as if it were a delicate ornament that even a breath might shatter. I brought it slowly to my lips, inhaling the magical perfume I so closely associated with the nights I'd spent with my Russian princess.

"You *are* Tatiana's friend."

He bowed his head.

"Where is she?"

"Not here."

"Take me to her."

"That is impossible at this time. I'm sorry."

"Then, when?"

"Come to Paris in six months. There will be a suite of rooms reserved for you at the Ritz Hotel in the Place Vendôme. Tatiana will join you there. If you have learned what you need to know, she and I will take you to Bayreuth. Do you like Wagner?"

The question surprised me.

"Yes, why do you ask?"

"Because we will be attending the Wagner Festival in Bayreuth. That is where the *Illuminati* will gather this year. You must meet them if you are to continue your education as a vampire."

I slipped Tatiana's handkerchief into the inside breast pocket of my jacket so that it would be over my heart. "The *Illuminati*?"

"The guiding lights of our race. They are very old and very wise. They possess what mortals sometimes call enlightenment—which is to say they are in harmony with life as it really is."

"As opposed to the illusion of life as we wish it to be?"

Herr Wolf seemed pleased. "Yes, that is it exactly."

"What do the *Illuminati* do?"

"I'm not sure I understand."

"Are they a sort of high council, the governors of our race?"

Herr Wolf grinned and shook his head. "You Americans are too practical, a character flaw you share with the natives of my own country. They do not govern as such. Their responsibility is more to observe and provide help where help is needed. One of the few deliberative acts they are involved in is deciding who becomes a vampire. The world can support only so many, at least if we are to remain secret. You understand what would happen if we didn't?''

I nodded.

"It would be us or mortals, at least at the current stage of human evolution," he said. "Neither race could survive without the other."

I wanted to ask about this symbiosis between humans and vampires, but he did not pause long enough for my question.

"Vampires come into being rarely, and then usually only after the *Illuminati* have carefully weighed the circumstances of each case. It is not easy to be a vampire. Few have the strength it takes to survive—and resist power's tendency to corrupt.''

"Then the *Illuminati* approved my transformation?"

"No. There was no time, Tatiana felt, and she acted on her own. Not the most conservative course of action, but sometimes even a vampire must listen first to the heart's counsel. Your case has been closely monitored."

The implication seemed clear.

"And if, for the sake of argument, I proved incapable of controlling myself, the *Illuminati* would terminate me?"

"That's putting it rather bluntly. A vampire has great powers, Herr Parker, and also great responsibilities. But do not become unduly concerned. Tatiana made sure most of the main criteria were met. Your musical talent, for example, which is quite extraordinary despite the fact that it was improperly nurtured. The fact that you were planning a suicide, although when we step in to prevent special talent from being prematurely stifled—the most common reason for transforming a mortal into a vampire— the threatening factor usually is medical or even political, but rarely psychological.

"Frankly, my young friend, your predisposition to depression indicates a serious weakness, though not a surprising one: In dominant, highly creative individuals, self-pity and an overblown sense of injustice tend to be the natural consequences when creative outlets are blocked. Don't look so insulted. There's no need to act as if your feelings have been hurt. I'm speaking strictly of matters of fact."

"My feelings aren't hurt," I lied, almost squirming at the

thought of my inadequacies being discussed by Tatiana and the *Illuminati*.

"The reasons for your depression were, as I said, understandable," Herr Wolf resumed, politely ignoring my distress. "The key for you then was, and is now, to channel your ego into your music. In fact, the more you forget your ego, the better off you'll be. The ego, with its lust for power, is your greatest enemy. Conversely, music and love will give you the strength you need to keep from becoming too much attracted to the dark forces."

"The dark forces?"

The vampire ignored my remark.

"Frankly, *mein Herr*, few of the *Illuminati* thought you'd make it this far without proper guidance. Because of the circumstances surrounding your transformation—which no one, not even the *Illuminati*, had any control over—there was no one available to serve as your mentor. However, I have been convinced from the first that Tatiana made the correct choice. That is why I have agreed to become your teacher. It is my duty to help you come into full possession of your powers and to teach you to use them in a moral manner."

"I'm honored," I said, not knowing how else to thank him.

"I see something of myself in you. I, too, was once a young composer at the edge of the abyss. A kind and merciful vampiress gave me a reprieve, enabling me to make my full contribution to the art."

"Are you one of them?"

"The *Illuminati*?" Herr Wolf smiled serenely. "You will learn all you wish to know about the *Illuminati* once you have proven yourself worthy of the gift that has been bestowed upon you."

"Are there many others like me?"

"There are a few novices, but our race's population remains relatively static. There are vampires enough in the world, for we seldom die. Besides, it almost always is a mistake to create new vampires. Ours is a difficult existence. Few have the inner strength. There was a time many hundreds of years ago when our race was not particularly careful about creating new vampires. The result was quite often tragic, both for the human population and the individual trying to manage such tremendous power without sufficient spiritual resources. In the end most destroyed themselves, although many had to be destroyed."

"By mortals or other vampires?"

"Sometimes by mortals but usually not."

That took a moment to sink in.

"There's one thing I don't understand."

Herr Wolf raised his eyebrows. "Only one thing, Herr Parker?"

"It seems to me that given the choice between good and evil, a vampire's superior intellect invariably would lead him to choose good. There are people who say there is no good or bad, only good or bad choices. Bad choices are by definition bad only because they have negative consequences. How is it possible for a creature as intelligent as a vampire to choose evil?"

"You have come to the heart of a very perplexing problem. I'm afraid there is no answer. Some individuals simply are predisposed to destruction. That is why it is important, in repopulating our race, to choose individuals inclined the one way and not the other. Make no mistake: some vampires are evil, *extremely* evil. I think you already know that one of these dark creatures is obsessed with Tatiana."

"Chicago?"

Herr Wolf nodded.

"Yes, I know of his existence, I even felt it myself as a mortal. Who is he?"

"You do not need to know that now. It would only frighten you, and that would slow your progress. You must grow stronger if you are to defeat him. We need you, Herr Parker. We need all the help we can get to stop him and the others."

"What others?"

"The disciples of darkness."

A cold breeze seemed to brush against the back of my neck.

"What are they? An *anti-Illuminati*?"

"Exactly. You are familiar with the house of Borgia?"

"You mean the Italians who were supposed to be poisoners during the Renaissance?"

"The same family."

I don't know why, but at that moment I had a vivid recollection of the dream I'd had while delirious during my transformation—the nightmare about the man dressed in a cardinal's robes, wearing an enormous gold signet ring decorated with the initial *B*. Was my dream a vision of one of the Borgias? I looked at the other vampire; he was smiling to himself, giving me the impression that he was following my thoughts word for word.

"Was one pope?"

"Rodrigo Borgia was Pope Alexander VI. He was one of the so-called 'bad popes,' men who headed the church during a period of extreme moral darkness. He bought his election with gold and did everything he could to keep the papal treasury empty. Pope Alexander VI began his reign with the most magnificent coronation Rome had ever seen. An army of naked youths painted gold acted as living statues throughout the city. The Borgia coat of arms includes the image of a bull; outside the Palace of St. Mark a giant bull was built, with an unending stream of wine cascading out of its forehead, which delighted the mob and turned the sacred ceremony into a drunken bacchanal.''

"You sound as if you were there."

"No, it was before even my time," the redheaded vampire said with a thin smile. "It's all in the history books. Or are you one of these twentieth century know-nothings who refuses to read?"

"You know that I read."

"Well, yes, poetry, but there is so much more. You might consider beginning with history. The theory behind modern education is radically unsound. You must educate yourself."

Herr Wolf seemed to catch himself on the verge of launching into a familiar argument. With a small shake of his head that made his red ponytail snap, he returned to the subject at hand.

"Pope Alexander had two illegitimate sons. One, Cesare Borgia, is of special interest to us. Do you know his story?"

I said that I didn't.

"Cesare was born in Rome in 1475, and his father helped him establish what would have been a successful career in the church were he not too amoral for even fifteenth century Italy. His incestuous relationship with his sister, Lucrezia, was a scandal throughout Europe. Cesare quarreled with his brother, Giovanni, over her affections, and had him murdered. Cesare fled to France and returned to Italy as a traitor in the service of Louis XII. Louis's invasion failed. Cesare, however, was light on his feet, and instead of landing in prison, as he so richly deserved, he managed to have his father proclaim him duke of Romagna.

"Alexander loved his son, you see. They were cut from the same cloth, and not even Giovanni's murder could come between the criminal pair.

"Pope Alexander reigned eleven years. During that time, Cesare orchestrated corruption on a level that was gross, even by Italian standards. Poison was the Borgias' political weapon. They'd invite a wealthy cardinal to a banquet, and Lucrezia, a master poisoner, would minister to him with her powders and potions. The man would die, his estate would be stripped of its gold, and his office sold to the highest bidder. When the new cardinal amassed enough wealth, he in turn would be invited to supper. In this way, rich benefices were sold and resold to keep Alexander's coffers filled with the gold required to maintain a life of unparalleled hedonism.

"There was only one problem with this arrangement for Cesare: his power depended entirely on his father. Cesare's best hope was to become a secular power with enough might to withstand the inevitable backlash, but he never succeeded. He was his own worst enemy. Intrigue was like a drug to Cesare Borgia. He could not keep himself from playing both ends against the political middle, and his enemies always outnumbered his friends because he made it his policy to have no friends. Niccolo Machiavelli's *Il principe* was modeled after Cesare, you may know."

Taking a lesson from my own father, I remained silent, thinking it might make me appear less ignorant.

"When the pope died, the source of Cesare's power ended. Cardinal Giuliano della Rovere, one of the Borgias' countless enemies, was elected Pope Julius II and ordered Cesare's arrest. Cesare escaped to Naples, where his endless plotting got him locked up in the castle of Medina del Campo. He spent two years imprisoned there before escaping to Navarre. He joined the Navarrese king in an expedition against Castile. They say he was killed in battle at Viana in 1507. But that is not what really happened."

The night, still as it was, sank into an even deeper silence.

"In Navarre, Cesare Borgia ceased to be mortal. The name of the vampire or vampiress who transformed him has been lost to time, but cursed be the night that saw so vile a creature delivered the power and immortality to work his own revenge against the world over the centuries.

"The vampire Borgia disappeared to his family's native Spain, where he adopted the identities of a series of noblemen of intermediate rank who lived on remote estates and were notorious for their sadism. But finally the Inquisition made even backward Spain unsafe for Borgia, and he fled to South America, where there were no constraints on his wickedness.

"Bit by bit, he has built a new power base for himself, one in which the foot soldiers are vampires of a very different sort than you and I, Herr Parker. Tonight Cesare Borgia is back in Italy. He controls a small army whose inclinations are as dark as his own, including the one who considers himself your rival suitor for Tatiana's affections. They must be stopped, of course.''

"What do they want?''

"The world, my dear boy. They want the world.''

I did not know what to say.

"We are not that much different, you know, mortal and vampire. Cesare Borgia the man was as evil as Cesare Borgia the vampire, but he was less powerful. Consciously or unconsciously, mortal or vampire, we choose the force to which we pay our allegiance.''

The vampire's eyes looked at me very sharply for a moment, dissecting me with all the precision and perception that the mind behind his eyes possessed.

"Your first choice is light, not dark, Herr Parker. Tatiana correctly saw that in you, or she would never have allowed you to undergo the metamorphosis. But you must remember that even one's best intentions can be undermined. Evil is seductive and subtle. Be aware of it. Confront it. Evil works best when ignored and left to work unnoticed. It will try to dazzle, charm, trick, impress, seduce, or frighten you—anything to get you under its spell. Evil is your enemy, my young friend. You must learn to understand it, if you are to become one of us. I can point you in the right direction, but you will have to learn the lessons for yourself. There will be many opportunities for you to learn. Our enemies will make sure of that.''

"But I know the difference between right and wrong, between good and evil.''

"Of course you do, but that is not enough to protect you. Your special powers make you a rich prize. You have the seed of evil within you. You were born with it. We all were. Guard against the shadow, Herr Parker. You must never allow the shadow to take control. Otherwise the Hunger will force you to the outermost limits of criminality.''

"The Hunger . . .'' I echoed, my voice trailing off.

"You speak of it with horror, yet I know for a fact that you have mastered it.''

"But not easily. I have something to confess, Herr Wolf.''

"You think that you killed someone.''

"But how did you know?''

"The guilt is in your eyes. Did this happen intentionally?''

"No.''

"Do you regret your actions?''

"God, yes!''

"Then what you did was unfortunate, but I would not say you were responsible. You were—what is the phrase?—temporarily insane. The Hunger is difficult to control, especially when it is unfamiliar. That was why it was so dangerous for Tatiana to leave you alone in Chicago. Now, more than ever, you have a responsibility to make sure the sum of your good deeds exceeds the sum of your mistakes. That is how our lives are judged, not by one remarkably saintly act or a single moment of weakness."

"Even though I can control the Hunger, I can't escape the feeling that I'm a predator, no matter how refined I am about it. You know how a mortal would react if I tried to explain my need."

"Do not concern yourself with what mortals would think about your actions. It is not for them to judge you or you them. We simply are what we are. You need fresh human blood in order to live. How can it be a sin or a crime to take only what you need to survive, as long as you cause no permanent injury in doing it?"

I did not answer.

"I understand your inner torment. The Hunger is the serpent in our garden. Those of us raised in the eighteenth-century German church would explain it as a matter of free will: God gave us the Hunger so that we would have the opportunity to choose between good and evil."

"Religion was little help to me as a mortal. I can't see what questions it answers now that I'm a vampire."

"You moderns are quite incapable of elegant discourse!" the vampire exclaimed, more amused than irritated with me. "What you're really wondering, although you won't admit it even to yourself in such unfashionable terms, is whether becoming a vampire relegated you to a race of the damned."

"Well, yes, I suppose . . ."

"You say you put no stock in religion, and yet your real concern is whether your soul is going to Hell!" Herr Wolf's laughter filled the empty opera house. "It is you, my friend, who are the superstitious one."

"But is it only a way of thinking, or is it *the* way of thinking? You have lived for centuries. You must know."

"I have perceived the dim outlines to a few truths."

"Then, tell me," I blurted out, suddenly aching to know answers that can never be known. "Is God real?"

"Yes."

"How do you know?"

"I see signs of perfection everywhere."

"Is there life after death?"

"I do not know. Nobody who is alive does."

"Why are we here?"

Herr Wolf threw back his head and laughed.

"At last a question I can answer with certainty," he said. "*Streben nach dem Undendlichen.* Do you have any German?"

I shook my head.

"*Streben nach dem Undendlichen:* To strive for the infinite."

"What does that mean?"

"How could it be more plain than that? Oh, do not look so discouraged. Think about it. Some things are so obvious to see that they're practically invisible. If you put your hand in front of your eyes, you can make it impossible to see even the largest mountain. Take the hand away from your eyes."

I felt like a complete idiot. I did not understand.

"It will come to you," the vampire said, patting me on the arm. "Do you have other questions? Go ahead and ask. Don't be afraid, no matter how ridiculous."

"Can a vampire be killed?"

"Except by a stake through the heart?" Herr Wolf's mocking grin made me blush.

"It's not so absurd a question," I said. "Once, very early on, I made the mistake of going out into the sun. The pain is still sharp in my memory. I thought I would die, even though my body quickly healed itself. If I could recover from that, is there anything that can hurt me?"

"Of course. But do forget the Hollywood nonsense about the so-called living dead. We can be injured and killed like any other living creature, but our unusual strength and the speed with which our bodies heal themselves mean that massive trauma is required to cause death."

"But how massive? My burns—the skin was charred black."

"A wooden stake through the heart would do you in if your assailant wanted to be theatrical, but a knife would do just as well. Decapitation, dismemberment, total incineration—all these would prove fatal. So would electrocution, although a massive amount of voltage would be required. I can't tell you precisely how much. It's a macabre subject, and I've given it little thought. I have witnessed vampires recover within hours from serious gunshot wounds that would have been instantaneously fatal to a mortal."

Herr Wolf's eyes seemed to change their focus, and I couldn't help but get the impression he was recounting something that had happened to him.

"It's a curious process. It works from the inside out, concluding when the body expels the slug just before the wound closes upon itself, rather like a pair of lips squeezing out a cherry pit."

"Yet our bodies cannot tolerate sunlight."

"Your experience would tend to confirm that hypothesis."

"I'm glad you are able to laugh about it."

"There's no need to take offense," Herr Wolf said, removing from his vest pocket a gold watch at the end of a chain. He opened it, checked the time, then returned it. "We haven't much time left." He indicated the piano. "Would you do me the very great favor of playing?"

"I'd much prefer to hear you again." What I'd heard from a distance had been performed with a sensitivity I knew I was unable to match.

"No, please. I'd consider it a favor."

"How can I refuse you?"

He smiled and nodded at the piano.

"Is there anything in particular you would like to hear?" I slid the bench a few inches closer to the piano. "Tatiana always liked—likes—Rachmaninoff."

"He's a bit noisy for me. I think Mozart would be closer to our tastes, yours and mine."

I lifted my wrists until the tops of my hands were parallel to the keys, my fingers straight but not stiff. I thought for a moment, then began to play my arrangement for piano of Mozart's orchestral "Eine kleine Nachtmusik." I thought my arrangement of "A Little Night Music" did, in all modesty, an excellent job of translating the dynamics of the string lines to the piano. I was surprised to finish and look up to see the vampire frowning.

"That's not at all bad," he began diplomatically. "You have an undeniable gift, and your interpretation is insightful. But you've made a mistake with the phrasing that has become common in the present century. It is slightly wrong in the opening figure, and that throws the piece off mark. May I illustrate?"

"Please do," I said a little coldly, getting up to let him have the piano. His playing had impressed me, but I was far from convinced that he was correct in his criticism.

"I think if you tried to get through this part with a bit more definition," he said. "Like this."

He knew the piece perfectly—I do not mean "Eine kleine Nachtmusik," but *my* arrangement of it. He played it back, note for note, a daunting feat of total recall. His interpretation transformed my arrangement into something unquestionably improved. His fingers danced through the music with an intimacy that made my understanding of the composition seem superficial.

Instead of stopping at the end of "Nachtmusik," the vampire played on, improvising an entirely new movement. His eyes had fallen closed, and he made no effort to conceal a smile. There was a smile on my face, too. The music was perfect, a miracle that transformed mere listening into a mystical experience. (Even remembering it tonight makes me feel as if I have been touched by a special grace.)

I was unable to speak when he finished. I stared into that grinning, impish face, with its thick red hair drawn back straight from the forehead and sides, and a realization crept over me.

"My God! You're him!"

"I thought you'd never guess."

"You are . . . Mozart!"

The red ponytail, the cackling laugh, the short stature, the outstanding command of the piano—I felt like a fool for not having known. But I *had* known, except he'd obviously used his mental powers to block my mind.

Of all the amazing things that had happened to me since I followed Tatiana home that night, this was the most astonishing. And yet it made perfect sense that Wolfgang Amadeus Mozart should be a vampire. If I were to go looking for geniuses to save from the grave in order to preserve their gifts, there could hardly be a better choice for transformation than the greatest musical prodigy the world had ever known.

And I, who had been as much a worshiper of Mozart's talent as any, now stood three feet from the immortal giant—immortal in body as well as in art. What a secret to possess! Mozart alive, not turned to dust in a mass grave, as the world mistakenly believed. It was the greatest miracle of all. Mozart, Tatiana Nicolaievna Romanov, Cesare Borgia—which other of history's most illustrious, and notorious, figures lived on as members of our hidden race?

(There was the vampire whose presence I sensed in Chicago, who now haunts me here in Paris, the infamous Jack the Ripper. Mozart had been right: Knowing about him at that time *would* have frightened me into inaction. Yet I feel betrayed. With so formidable an enemy, I would have thought my friends would want me to know whom I was up against. But it was a judgment call, and Mozart thought differently. I suppose his faith in my ability to deal with the Ripper should give me confidence.)

"I almost can't believe it," I said, still dumbstruck, "and yet I know it's true! You are Mozart."

"But only in the company of other vampires, Herr Parker. Please remember that among mortals, I am Sebastian Wolf, at least for another ten years. Mozart the man died many, many years ago, even though Mozart the vampire lives on."

He stood up from the piano.

"Now that I've established my credentials, would you do me the favor of playing one of your own compositions? If I am to be your teacher, I must help you develop *all* of your potentials, including those that are musical. And after all, we vampires live for art."

"Please, no," I pleaded. The prospect of playing my own music for Mozart terrified me even more than having to leap across the crevasse on my way up the mountainside. "They are not fit even to be called compositions. They are only sketches, really, skeletons of ideas."

"Very well," he said finally. "But I will expect you to have something completed for me by the time you come to Paris. I cannot teach you unless you're willing to take criticism."

"No, of course not."

Mozart, my teacher! I'm sure I was grinning like a fool.

"The sorry state of today's music—if you can call such undisciplined noise music—is overdue for a breath of fresh air to blow away the stagnant ideas. Perhaps you are the person to set things right."

"Why don't you do it yourself? Imagine the world twice blessed with Mozart. Who would guess the truth?"

"An intriguing idea, but I've had my opportunity. Besides, the music I write comes from an eighteenth-century heart; to have the revolutionary impact that serious music needs to save it from itself requires a perception of the world I do not possess. Music is bound up with too many antique ideas as it is. It's time for something new, something contemporary, something brilliant. Something, perhaps, that David Parker will write."

"Are you still composing?"

"Upon occasion. I spend several hours a day playing, but mostly to relax. Time changes you. Over the years my passion has turned from music to higher mathematics. Mathematics and music are closely related, as you'll realize if you think about it. I have given the world my best music, but your day as a composer is ahead of you. There are great things inside of you, Herr Parker. Trust me, I know. I'm never wrong about music. And Tatiana is never wrong about an individual's character.''

I followed his glance upward. The underside of the domed ceiling had been painted as a trompe l'oeil mural. It was in the style of Raphael—if not *by* Raphael, for all I knew. The dome was painted to look as if the ceiling were open to the night sky. Cupids sat on the edge, dangling their legs—one of them bearing an unmistakable resemblance to Mozart's impish face. The central figures, pictured ascending into the sky together, were Tatiana and me. She was dressed in a white dress, a rose held lightly in her left hand, her long hair flowing loose past her shoulders. I wore a toga, which did not look as absurd as it must sound reading about it in this journal. We were being born upward by angels. The symbolic message seemed to be that, together, Tatiana and I would achieve a higher plane of being than either of us could know alone.

"Beautiful."

"She is a vision of loveliness," Mozart said, meaning Tatiana. "I love her very much."

I looked at him closely.

"As a friend and pupil," he added. "I could have loved her in another way, but it was not meant to be. Do you believe in true love, Herr Parker?"

"Yes, I think I do."

"Tatiana Nicolaievna Romanov has waited a long time to find true love. She waited through her mortal life, brief as it was, and, until now, through nearly a century of life as a vampire. You were fortunate to find each other when it was getting so near the end for you both. Tatiana was alone despite her many good friends. But that has changed. She is so radiant now, in a way I haven't seen since before her family died."

"You knew her before the revolution?"

The vampire nodded.

"Was it you who . . . ?"

The question seemed too impertinent to complete, but Mozart knew what I meant, and he shook his head. He had not been the one to transform her from mortal to vampire.

"She was a lovely child and a lovely young woman. Unfortunately the machinery of history pays no attention to individuals; it has a way of catching them up in its gears.''

''Tell me about her.''

Mozart looked at his pocket watch a second time.

''Stories best left for another night, my young friend. The sun will be coming up soon.''

I glanced at my wristwatch and felt a pang of anxiety. The night had flown past. It would be a race to make the safety of my house before daybreak.

''We've got to get back.''

''Don't worry about me. I've made the necessary arrangements. But you must go now.''

''Are you sure?''

''Quite. Good-bye.''

He held out his hand.

''Thank you for everything,'' I said. ''I wish we had more time.''

''Be patient, my friend. Time is one thing you now have in abundance. Spend the next few months becoming strong and becoming good. We need all the help we can get against the Borgias. Enjoy the peaceful nights in the desert, for there are temptations and troubles enough ahead as we continue your education as a vampire. And be brave.''

It made me think of Tatiana's final words to me: *''Many trials lie ahead of you David Parker. Through all that happens, my beloved, remember this: Wherever you go, I go before you. Remember our love and be brave.''*

I nodded.

''And don't forget,'' Herr Wolf added, ''I'll expect you to have a composition ready for me to critique in Paris.''

''I won't see you again until then?''

''I do not believe so.''

It seemed unfair to have so many wonders dangled before my eyes, only to have them snatched away for another six months. But it hardly mattered, I reminded myself; there were centuries ahead of me.

Mozart made a stiff little bow that reminded me that he was, indeed, a man of the eighteenth century. The air seemed to shift the way it does when you see the heat rising in currents off hot concrete in summer. Mozart, the opera house, the town—all of it vanished in the blink of an eye. I found myself standing alone on the barren mountainside. The *entire* ghost town had been an illusion!

I touched my pocket. It was still there. I pulled out Tatiana's lace handkerchief and kissed it once more, breathing in its rich perfume.

Then I turned and began to make my way back down the mountain and toward the city that never slept.

# PART III

✧

# The Nemesis

# Chapter 24

PARIS, JUNE 28, 1989—Much has happened, so much so that this is my first opportunity in two nights to make a journal entry.

Frankly this is a bit of a chore tonight. I'd rather put my pen aside and sit reflecting on how good it feels to be happy and secure. It's been a long time since I've enjoyed such peace. I know it cannot last, yet while it does . . .

It is early evening. Venus, rising first and shining best, occupies the exact center of one of the rectangular panes of glass in the window in front of this desk, its light just above the topmost boughs of the chestnut tree. The planet seems to be an ornament on the tree, or perhaps a fairy pausing there to rest. The glass is antique, as old as this palace, which Napoleon built; there are bubbles and other tiny imperfections in it, and a slight waviness to its surface, so that when I move my head, the light moves and twinkles.

The way to tell the difference between stars and planets is that stars twinkle and planets don't, somebody told me once. Or was it the other way around?

Before I lose myself completely in reverie, or even more enjoyable diversions, I must finish the work at hand and bring this journal up to date.

June 26 was a turning point, a moment of crisis of the sort that tests strengths, finds weaknesses, and defines who and what, we are.

I let a great opportunity go by. I must prepare myself mentally so that I do not hesitate again the next time I have a chance to strike down the Ripper.

Sometimes we control events; sometimes they control us. Last night was an example of the latter. I'd planned another evening of waiting—a visit to a café, dinner in a good restaurant, a few hours with this journal in another café, then off to find a new hotel before dawn. However, things began to happen even before I got out of my hotel.

When I went to the desk to check out, the clerk handed me an express mail letter. The stamp was postmarked Florence, Italy. How had she found me again? My enemy—or enemies—had to be following me, but I had been so careful that it astounded me they could watch me so closely without my knowing it.

Pretending to have forgotten something upstairs, I returned to the privacy of my room and tore open the envelope.

I expected a note from Ariel Niccolini, an embittered follow-up to her telephone call, a plea to come to Florence and meet with Cesare Borgia. The letter and enclosure mailed with it turned out to be something even more sinister:

From Hell

Dear David,
    If you're moving from hotel to hotel for my benefit, you'd might as well stop. There is no place in Paris you can hide from me. What's the point of running?
    Join us. Have a part in ruling New Europe.
    Enclosed is a rather good critical review of my performance on the whore several nights back, now that the press has finally gotten hold of the story. I was a bit careless and didn't go back to clean up after myself, and they found her just where *you* left her. Having your work appreciated is half the fun. Alas, I'm required to be more circumspect most of the time.
    Incidentally, what I read about your taking my nurse for a ride in the country indicated a rather pale imagination on your part, although I liked the effect you achieved by dumping the corpse in the country. Sometimes one can obtain a spectacular response simply by depositing a dead body in an unexpected place—as you well know!
    Best regards,
    Jack
P.S. Ariel sends her love.

The letter was written in black ink except for the signature, which was a faded reddish brown. I smelled the paper. He'd signed it in blood. Closing my eyes with horror, I touched the tip of my tongue to the paper. At least it was not Ariel Niccolini's blood.

I read the clipping, from one of the city's more sensationalist tabloids, then threw it down with disgust. The story quoted an unnamed policeman, who compared the "maniac" responsible for the mutilation and murder of a prostitute in her squalid apartment to the handiwork of Jack the Ripper. Of course there was no way for the police to know, as did I, that the individual responsible for the Paris murder and the mad Victorian killer from one hundred years past were one and the same.

The mention of a New Europe in the Ripper's letter disturbed me. United under the leadership of Cesare Borgia, the criminal members of our race were seeking to rule the world, Mozart had said. Perhaps they planned a modest beginning—Europe.

And poor Ariel. Sending the letter from Florence was a vile touch, but at least it confirmed that the Ripper and Borgia were working together, that what had been happening to me in Paris somehow fitted into their dark designs. I could only hope that since they hadn't hurt Ariel so far, they would not do so in the future, in order to have the opportunity to use her against me again.

I scanned the room as I was shown to my table. Too many people, too many distractions to make it easy for me to sit and puzzle over the Ripper's latest communication. Maybe it didn't matter, I told myself. Diversion might be exactly what I needed.

A blonde in a black velvet dress looked up at me long enough for our eyes to meet. She wore a gold necklace with a turquoise scarab that looked as if it might actually have been stolen from an Egyptian tomb. For a moment I considered inviting her to spend the evening with me, but I did not especially trust myself with casual temptation after the powerful urges I had been experiencing. I also did not want to expose any more mortals to danger by my association with them. I gave her a cold smile. She looked away fast.

Instead of companionship I would lose myself in the enjoyment of an excellent meal. I would not be in the French capital much longer, with any luck at all, and I'd decided to at least sample some of the better places to eat. Being in Paris had given me the opportunity to gradually accustom myself to some of the

richer foods and drinks I'd been forced to give up after making
the transition.

Michel's is a restaurant in the best *grand bourgeois* tradition:
The cooking is old-fashioned and very good. It is one of those
places that, in a city filled with foreigners, remains an unofficial
refuge for the French. Americans never seem to be able to get
reservations at Michel's, so I made mine in French. As far as
the staff knew, I was Monsieur Picard from Nice.

The restaurant is a rectangle three times longer than it is wide,
with forty tables in three rows, one along each wall and one
down the center. The tables along the left sit on a platform, and
are separated by beaux arts leaded-glass dividers. On the main
floor, the tables are ingeniously situated among a series of half-
wall partitions and potted palms, which patrons virtually disappear behind once they take their seats. There is not a less
public place in all of public Paris or a better restaurant to have
a private dinner.

My table was on the dais near the rear of the restaurant, one
of the few places in the house that afforded a view of the entire
room. Sliding my chair backward and a bit to one side put my
face in shadow, and I could discreetly watch the people come
and go.

A waiter brought a menu. The *spécialités de la maison* were
hand-lettered on a parchment sheet inside the red folder: trout
cooked in Arbois wine, veal cutlet *en papillote*, iced raspberry
soufflé.

The murmur of voices swirled around me as I studied the
menu. I heard the words without focusing enough attention on
them to pick up more than the soothing hush. It was like sitting
on the beach at night, listening to light waves steal up on the
sandy carpet and then retreat, the cycle repeating endlessly.

The wine list—open before me on the table—presented as
many interesting choices as the menu. I wished I'd thought to
telephone a few hours ahead to ask them to uncork a bottle of
Château d'Yquem 1869 to breathe. No, on second thought, it
was a good thing I hadn't. Such an experience would have overwhelmed my sensitive palate completely and made it impossible
to enjoy the food.

I looked up.

The restaurant had become completely silent, and the change
had come with a suddenness that was startling. In place of the
murmuring talk, ringing of silver against china, and indistinct
background noise was an unnatural quiet. Even the house sound

system, which had been softly playing a recording of Vivaldi, had switched off as if in response to a hidden signal.

My eyes moved from table to table. The people stared into space, their eyes containing only the glassy blankness of a hypnotic trance.

I had a sinking feeling. Something very bad was about to happen.

What dim lighting there was in the restaurant flickered off, leaving the room in darkness except for the candles that burned on each table. Reflected upward, the tiny flames illuminated only faces, the weak yellow light touching foreheads, cheekbones, and chins; eye sockets and hollow cheeks were painted in deep shadow, making it appear that the restaurant was filled with disembodied skulls hovering in groups of two and four around the candles.

I heard the scrape of wood against carpet. A patron got up from his table. One by one, the others followed suit and stood. They shuffled toward the door like zombies, bumping into chairs and tables as if unconscious of what they saw.

There was a crash. A plate had fallen to the floor and shattered.

I did not move. The Ripper's presence was suddenly strong and near. I felt a surge of energy flow through my body. Once again I was ready for the confrontation. Let tonight finally finish it, I thought. And to the long score I had to settle with the monster, I had added another item: Ariel Niccolini.

The last man filed through the door, which closed behind him with a bang. I heard the metallic sound of tumblers turning in the lock. That made me smile bitterly. As if a door, even a stout oak door like the one guarding the entrance to Michel's, could hold *me*.

The candles on the tables began to blink off, starting at the tables closest to the exit, until I was left alone in a darkness interrupted only by the light at my table.

I kept my eyes on the flame, meditating on it as I gathered my powers. It was orange-yellow except for a thin blue line that formed its crown. I breathed slowly, experiencing each breath fully, focusing my attention, and my anger, on the flame until both burned with the same sharp intensity.

A thin hand with long fingernails that were almost like claws thrust itself into the circle of light around my table. It hovered in the air a moment, then withdrew.

"Does this mean we aren't going to be friends?" The sarcasm

was in his upper-class English voice. "I did so hope that we would be pals."

The vampire stepped into the light, narrowing his cold eyes against the brightness of the single candle.

He wore a black, double-breasted suit cut to accentuate his thinness. The tie and the handkerchief in the jacket breast pocket were bloodred and matched the tea rose fixed on the right lapel with a golden pin. When he removed his black fedora, I saw that his hair was longer than I remembered it, brushed straight back to fall to his shoulders. His chin was a little weak, I noticed, for the first time, an outward sign of the deficiencies in his character. He wore a diamond earring that contributed to his overall appearance as a fashionable, wealthy—and altogether evil—individual. He was exactly what I would have expected Satan to look like, were Satan standing at my table, smiling down at me. For all I knew, he *was* Satan.

"You don't mind if I join you, old boy?" He pulled out the chair and sat down, putting his hat on the table.

"What makes you think I'd agree to share my table with Death?"

"Death? You do flatter me, Mr. Parker. The Reaper is not what they call me, though it's close enough that I can understand how you confused the two."

"Perhaps the Reaper is just as appropriate a name."

"You give me too much credit. I have my fun, but I'm simply a vampire, the same as yourself. Better born than you, older than you, more powerful than you. But still"—he held up his opened hands with their long, vaguely effeminate nails—"just a vampire."

When he smiled, his teeth all looked unnaturally sharp and pointed. He indicated the empty restaurant with a tilt of the head.

"You're impressed with my abilities, aren't you? I could teach you. Seventy-two minds to control, counting the staff. I'd be glad to help you expand your powers. My royal blood does not prohibit me from uplifting inferiors. Noblesse oblige, as they say. You could serve as my faithful squire."

"What could you teach me? To take pleasure in killing?"

My anger amused him.

"Would you shrink from stepping on a cockroach? Then, why such a quaint attitude about mortals? They are an inferior life-form, infesting as much as inhabiting the world. It is hardly a crime to step on one now and then.''

"It has nothing to do with dubious claims to superiority. Mortals think and feel and suffer. It is wrong for us, as beings who also think and feel and suffer, to injure them. You have no more right to interfere in a mortal's life than''—I banged my fist on the table—''to interfere in mine!''

"Temper, Mr. Parker,'' the vampire said. "And do spare me your liberal ideals. It is others like you who have upset the natural order of things, who have taken power from the strong and turned it over to the weak. Quite perverse. Not at all the way of the world.''

His smile vanished, and his mouth set in a grim line. His eyes looked especially insane now that they were full of anger.

"We once ruled the world's greatest empire. My uncles and cousins sat on thrones throughout Europe. But the idealists of my class turned their power over to the commoners. Now, the luckiest of them live in genteel poverty, letting bus drivers and barmaids traipse through their ancestral estates at one pound per head. No, do not preach to me about rights. What of my rights?''

He smiled coldly.

"But why talk of rights? Power is the only reality. It determines what is right.''

"Your power does not give you the privilege to torture and murder innocent women. You must be stopped.''

The vampire looked at me very closely, a tight, cruel grin on his face. I leaned backward in my chair, half expecting him to lunge across the table at me.

"And who is going to stop me?'' he asked in a low voice. "You?''

I returned his stare as long as I could.

"I'm disappointed in you, Mr. Parker. Either you are very naive, or you've made the mistake of listening to the doddering old fools among our race who remain saddled with outdated and irrelevant conceptions of morality. You would be well advised to ignore what Mozart has told you and become my apprentice. That is the only way you will learn the secrets of true power.''

"You know Mozart?''

"A weak old man haunted by antique ideas.''

"I wouldn't agree that he is weak.''

"Ha! Compared to Borgia . . .'' He stopped himself and looked at me suspiciously, as if wondering if I'd tricked him into saying more than he should.

"Who is Borgia?"

"Never mind."

"Evidently he is a powerful vampire," I continued. He *had* said too much. I decided to taunt my enemy. "Is he any relation to the inept Borgia family who caused minor trouble in Italy before a reform-minded pope kicked him out of the country?"

"Enough!"

His roar pushed me against my chair.

The vampire took out his red silk handkerchief and patted his brow. He seemed to be trying to keep his composure, although I couldn't imagine why an undisciplined creature like the Ripper would be the least worried about controlling his behavior, unless he was acting on his master's explicit instructions.

"There is a group of us, Mr. Parker, led by a brilliant intellect. We are gathering power, building it to a level neither mortal nor vampire will be able to challenge. We are going to remake the world. Join us. All you need is the will to greatness."

"Join you and follow Borgia?"

He stared at me a long time before answering with a monosyllable: "Yes."

"But how, exactly, do you plan to change the world?"

"As we bloody well see fit," he snapped, his temper getting the better of him. "Quit playing for time, and tell me your decision. Which would you rather be, Mr. Parker, master or slave? Between those two every man—every vampire—must choose. Join with us and rule the world. Even though your blood is not royal, there is a role for you."

"It is you who should join *us*," I said. I could see that it surprised him. "There is no way you can atone for the senseless crimes you've committed, but it's obvious that you're deeply disturbed. Perhaps we can get you help. Think of what it would be like finally to have some peace. Your life must be an endless torment, ever since you started killing so many, many years ago."

"Then you have figured it out, have you?" the vampire said, pleased. "I rather thought that you had."

He took a scalpel from an inside jacket pocket and held it lightly in front of his face between thumb and forefinger.

"I know that you are the one they called Jack the Ripper. But Jack is not your real identity. Tell me, *who* is Jack?" I strained to penetrate his psychic defenses, but they seemed impregnable.

"I've fooled them all," he grinned. His smile suddenly turned into a fierce grimace. "Nearly all of them," he hissed, and stabbed the scalpel's blade into the table.

"For your own sake, and the sake of the mortals you've killed in the past and will kill in the future, turn for help to the *Illuminati*. If anybody can help you, they can."

The vampire's terrible laughter shook the restaurant until the windows rattled.

"Submit to you and the *Illuminati*? You arrogant little worm! Would a lion yield to a cur? Would an eagle yield to a sparrow? I am a prince, sir, and I would have been a king, if it hadn't been for the meddling of commoners like you, with blood in your veins no more noble than the sewage that used to run through the open gutters of Whitechapel."

His eyes flashed from me to the scalpel and back.

"I shall be king yet, do you know. Borgia has promised it."

"You're raving mad."

A murderous fury filled the vampire. Veins stood out in his temples, and the gleaming points of his blood teeth jutted grotesquely from beneath his upper lip.

"That's what my grandmother's ministers said! Queen Victoria, that waddling old bitch, couldn't possibly live forever, and once she was out of the way, my father would become king, and I after him. Who were they to presume to judge Prince Albert Victor, the Duke of Clarence, second in line to the crown? I came so *close*! My father, Edward the Seventh, lived just nine years on the throne. Nine bloody years, and I would have been king! But the scheming bastards put me out of the way. My younger brother, George, got the crown that by rights was mine!"

I sat and stared at him, frozen with a combination of fascination and horror as he raved, white spittle flecking the corners of his mouth.

"History would have taken a different turn had Albert Victor worn the crown that was his by right and providence. Europe was sick with a rotting disease that ate away at royalty, while the commoners fattened off our corpses, like worms gorging themselves inside a coffin. Goethe was right: 'Had the kings been kings, they would still stand today.' I would have shown them all their rightful places, by God!

"Yes, I killed a few whores in Whitechapel. I'm not ashamed. I reveled in it! It was medical research. I needed to dissect their bodies to confirm certain theories. And where was the crime in it? By the right of kings, I had absolute power of life or death over any commoner, even to kill one if I chose to do so to satisfy a whim.''

He began to laugh, a scratching giggle that turned into the horrifying bray of someone totally beyond the bounds of rationality. It took all my courage to look into the vampire's mad eyes, which glowed from within with a terrible red light.

''The newspapers called me Jack the Ripper. The name was based on a letter that was sent in as a hoax, but the name stuck. I had no complaint. Jack the Ripper was a good name that inspired terror. Jack taught them all to cower in fear, to feel their true weakness when the might and majesty of royal blood walked through their midst, whether armed with a scepter or a scalpel.

''The Home Office was afraid of the political implications. The House of Commons was busy then trying to eviscerate the House of Lords, when along comes the most brilliant of killers, Jackie Boy, doing his best work in London's poorest quarters. The mob got quite worked up over my handiwork, doing to them what they were doing to us.

''One of them gave me, a prince, syphilis. She was the first, the bloody bitch. Political acts? Yes, the murders were political. But don't think I didn't enjoy every bloody second of doing those whores to death! Besides, I had to gather my research!''

The vicious leer disappeared from his face.

''Careful and nimble as Jack was in his fun with the lassies, he made one or two small mistakes that put Scotland Yard onto him. Revolution—that is what the cabinet told my grandmother would happen if the mob learned Prince Albert Victor liked to take his doctor's bag and go out ripping in Whitechapel.''

The vampire's attitude changed from manic to depressed.

''They sentenced poor Albert Victor to death by secret imperial decree. There was to be no trial, no jury of men tried and true, no written record to fall conveniently into the wrong hands.''

I nodded to keep him talking. Damn me for my interest, but I had to hear the rest of his tale.

''They were going to poison me, get me out of the way quietly, whisper the syphilis did me in. But fate intervened. The last whore I picked up in Whitechapel—a saucy little wench painted cheap and tawdry the way I like them best—was Lucrezia Borgia, Cesare Borgia's sister.''

''Yes, I understand,'' I said with quiet horror.

''Her brother had heard of my brilliant work and decided Jackie was the sort of chap who deserved to live forever—

especially when he learned that the blood of kings ran through my veins.

"What they used to poison poor Prince Albert Victor was utterly incapable of harming a vampire. I had to leave England, of course, but the world is a very big place even for a prince, and I had no trouble thriving outside the British Isles. I was the head of the state police in a South American country I needn't name. I had my own prison, an inexhaustible number of suspects to lock up—my agents would pick them up off the streets at random when the supply got low—and the authority to have all the fun I wanted. A sweet arrangement!

"But I'm skipping ahead in my story. Before I left London, I got even with the swine who conspired against me. One by one they paid the full price. I got them all, except for my grandmother."

His face became very red, and he began to tremble until I thought he was having a seizure.

"No commoner will ever put a hand on me again," he said, his voice shaking.

I leaned backward as he jerked the scalpel out of the table and waved it in the air.

"They denied me the crown, but I"—swoosh!—"showed them. I"—swoosh!—"showed the common bloody bastards!"

He sat staring at me—or through me, rather—as the fury drained from his lunatic eyes. Jack the Ripper as king of England: The prospect of the crimes he could have committed with the apparatus of the British Empire behind him was appalling.

"I have, you no doubt have perceived, rather old-fashioned ideas about the differences between royalty and commoners," he finally began again, demonstrating a lunatic's characteristic ability to skip from subject to subject as easily as from emotion to emotion. "That is why I shall never consider you my equal, Mr. Parker, even though you are a vampire."

I did not respond. He regarded me through narrowed eyes.

"That is also why you must abandon any impossible designs you have on Princess Tatiana. I know she has charmed you. She has that effect on men. Nevertheless, it will not be permitted. If I ever learn that you have as much as touched her . . ."

The red glow flickered again in his pupils.

"As you know, our race is small. There are few among us whose breeding is good enough to make them worthy of being my mate. Lord Borgia has promised me Tatiana's hand."

"What does Tatiana say about this?" I said tightly.

"That is irrelevant. She is betrothed. She belongs to me, and when I find her, I will take her."

"I don't think so."

"What did you say?"

"I said I do not think that you will."

"We shall see," the Ripper spat at me. The silver scalpel flashed in his hand. "If it were not for my fealty to Lord Borgia, I would kill you now."

"Why should Borgia protect me?"

"It is the game he plays. If you prove intelligent enough to join us, it again proves our superiority over the *Illuminati*. If you don't, I kill you and prove our power all the same."

"Then you'd might as well kill me—or try to kill me—now."

"What are those words in your mind?" the Ripper hissed. "Some incantation?"

"No."

"It's—" A scowl spread across his face. "You waste your time on that? Music *and* poetry? Two pursuits fit only for weaklings."

"And those strong enough not to have to worry about appearing weak."

"Touché, Mr. Parker." The vampire looked at me with great curiosity, but there was no warmth in his stare. It was as if I were a familiar insect with an interesting anomaly, a fly with an extra eye or set of wings.

He pursed his lips, his expression halfway between amusement and disgust. I could feel him inside my head, reading my thoughts. It was an entirely disagreeable sensation. I blocked him out, but not before he got part of a stanza from me, which he recited mockingly.

*"Tyger! Tyger! burning bright*
*In the forests of the night,*
*What immortal hand or eye*
*Could frame thy fearful symmetry?"*

I kept my face completely blank.

"Why are the words spelled so queerly?"

"It's from the eighteenth century. William Blake."

"Ah, Blake. Of course. I read him at Oxford. Recite the rest of it for me. Go ahead. Indulge yourself."

I sat absolutely still, not even breathing, and looked back into the bottomless dead wells that were his eyes. I felt as if I were sitting across from the tyger itself. My throat felt dry and tight. I took a sip of wine—careful not to let the glass shake in my hand—and complied with the creature's request.

> *"In what distant deeps or skies*
> *Burnt the fire of thine eyes?*
> *On what wings, dare he aspire?*
> *What the hand, dare steal the fire?*
>
> *And what shoulder, & what art,*
> *Could twist the sinews of thy heart?*
> *And when thy heart began to beat,*
> *What dread hand? & what dread feet?*
>
> *What the hammer? what the chain?*
> *In what furnace was thy brain?*
> *What the anvil? what dread grasp*
> *Dare its deadly terrors clasp?*
>
> *When the stars threw down their spears,*
> *And water'd heaven with their tears,*
> *Did he smile his work to see?*
> *Did he who made the Lamb make thee?"*

A sardonic smile twisted the corners of his mouth upward.

"I see why you are charmed with these rhymes, trivial though they are. It's the power that attracts you, the daring to 'steal the fire.' It's very Promethian."

"Satanic is the word I would use."

The vampire threw back his head and roared with lunatic laughter. Prince Albert Victor, the Duke of Clarence, better known to the world as Jack the Ripper—my God, what had Lucrezia Borgia and her brother loosed upon eternity?

"Listening to you play the bard has given me rather an appetite," the Ripper said. "Do you mind if I join you for a bite? Garçon!"

The double kitchen doors swung open for the waiter. He shuffled to our table in a trance and turned to stand next to the Ripper.

"On your knees, varlet!"

The man wore a traditional French waiter's apron, white and stiff with starch, that fell nearly to his feet; it bunched at his knees as he stiffly knelt and, facing the vampire, lowered his head like a serf bowing to his lord.

My attention was on the waiter, and I missed the start of the ghastly transformation at work in the Ripper's face. His skull became plastic and began to change shape. The nose stretched and flattened until it was no nose at all but two gashes of the sort one sees on a decomposing corpse. The eye sockets grew almond shaped and rearranged themselves from the front to the sides of the head. The eyes themselves became reptilian, with pupils that were vertical diamonds, like a snake's; when the thing blinked, a translucent film coated with mucus slowly covered and uncovered the eyes without completely hiding them. The effect was altogether unnerving.

At the same time the eyes were changing, the upper and lower jaws grew out from the head until it was no longer a humanoid face but the muzzle of a predatory beast. A row of gleaming teeth from the bottom jaw overlapped the upper gum, which had the blue-black tattooed color of a dog's lip. When the abomination opened its mouth to make a sound that was something between a snarl and a laugh, it exposed a row of smaller but equally razorlike teeth in the upper jaw.

I tried to lock my mind against his attempt to confuse me with illusions, but this was no illusion. The transformation was real.

The creature the Ripper had become leaned forward in his chair and took hold of the waiter's bowed head with both hands.

"No!" I shouted, realizing too late what was about to happen.

The psychic energy in my projected command forced the monster to pause for a moment and look back at me with something that even in the inhuman face resembled surprise. Then, before I could do anything else, it turned away from me and bit a huge chunk out of the top of the waiter's skull.

There was the wet splintering sound of bone shattering under torn flesh as it chewed, lifting its head toward the ceiling, ravenous as a hyena feeding upon fresh carrion. The beast lowered its mouth to the gaping wound. A long, lizardlike tongue darted into the cranial cavity. With a loud sucking it drew the remains of the man's brain out of the skull in big bloody chunks, gulping them the way a starving dog would wolf down a meal of discarded entrails.

"You son of a bitch!" I shouted, kicking my chair backward and grabbing a knife off the table.

I almost did not see the back of the beast's hand coming toward my face. It was like being hit in the side of the head with a cement block. The creature dropped the waiter and came at me, but I projected a wall of energy powerful enough to force it to stop while I scrambled to my feet.

"So you have some power after all," the beast said, the words indistinct because of the shape of its mouth and the remnants of flesh that filled it.

I stood panting, the adrenaline surging through my body, ready to kill or be killed.

"Do not"—the disgusting tongue came out of its mouth to lick bits of stray gray matter from its lips—"flatter yourself into thinking you are strong enough to do anything but annoy me," it said with great contempt. "Were it not for Lord Borgia's orders . . ."

He stepped to the nearest table and picked up a glass of wine the departed occupants had left untouched. I had a chance to fall on him when he turned away to drink, but I hesitated. The opportunity lasted only a moment—and for that moment I remained frozen, unable to make myself react.

The Ripper was wearing his human face again when he turned back to me.

"Do not feel too much the coward for neglecting to press your advantage," he said, carefully wiping his lips with a white table napkin. "Lift so much as a finger against me, and I'll have *your* brain for dessert."

I was unable to suppress a shudder. Prince Albert Victor laughed and blotted up the last remaining bits of pink flesh from his face with the table napkin, which he then slipped into his jacket pocket, along with the scalpel from the table.

"I return to my earlier question and the issue that brought me here tonight to share this lovely meal with you. Will you join the master race, or will you remain, for however briefly, among the slaves? You must choose."

I shook my head slowly, gripping the knife that was still in my right hand. I raised the knife, thinking to plunge it into his heart if he came at me.

"The world no longer needs masters and slaves," I said. "I choose to oppose you and others like you and everything you stand for. Alone or with the *Illuminati*, I will fight you."

"Then I will see you in Hell," he hissed.

"You already have—the Hell of your own making."

"You have twenty-four hours to come to your senses," he said. "If it were up to me, I'd kill you where you stand."

"Try it," I said.

"Remember: twenty-four hours."

He snapped his fingers and the corpse scrambled to its feet.

Prince Albert Victor picked up his hat from the table and used it to cover the gaping wound in the dead waiter's head. Without speaking, he turned and stalked out of the restaurant, the reanimated body following him at a respectable distance, a servant from beyond the land of the living.

I picked up my chair and sat down, feeling a weariness that went to the core of my being. I looked down at my hand. It was shaking. I dropped the knife.

The door opened again, and I looked up, startled, expecting to see the Ripper's insane face again. Standing in the doorway, his figure backlighted by the streetlight outside, was Mozart.

"I see I am too late," he said. "I am sorry. *They* delayed me. But come, my friend, let us leave this unhappy place at once."

*I must stop for tonight. More tomorrow . . .*

# Chapter 25

PARIS, JUNE 29, 1989—Mozart and I rushed along the street, his hand on my arm in a manner that seemed to be partly protective and partly a means to hurry me.

"I'd started to doubt you were coming."

"I've been quite busy," Mozart answered, pushing me faster along the sidewalk. "Much has happened in the past few months. It's difficult to appreciate the true meaning of misery until you've been in Africa."

"Africa? What were you doing in Africa?"

"Undoing Borgia's work. I gather the past few weeks have been interesting for you."

"Interesting is hardly the word. Did you know that Prince Albert Victor—better known to most by his *nom de guerre*, Jack the Ripper—was one of us?"

"Not one of *us*," Mozart corrected with emphasis, "He is one of *them*."

"Yes, he's in with Borgia. And he is also after Tatiana, with some crazy idea that he is going to make her his vampire queen."

"He's utterly mad."

"They've also got their hands on a woman named Ariel Niccolini. A mortal. They're holding her in Florence, in Borgia's villa, I think. I'm afraid for her life."

"Yes, I know all about Ariel Niccolini. You were rather easily taken in by her, weren't you?"

"I don't even think she knew what she was doing."

"No, not consciously, but you've got to be more careful. There is indeed certain safety in the random way you feed, but as you have learned, there's also room for disaster."

"Can't we help her?"

"The one thing I want you to do is put Ariel Niccolini completely out of your mind. I'll attend to her. So, Albert has been up to his usual?''

"He's been killing ever since I got to Paris. Just before you arrived at the restaurant he—it makes me sick to think about it.''

"Albert did not actually attack you?'' Mozart asked, glancing at me out of the corner of his eye.

"He struck me and came at me, but I was able to hold him off using the force of my mind. It apparently was long enough to show him I'm capable of more than he'd expected.''

"Albert is a coward,'' Mozart said. "He's quite the dread menace when he's dealing with weaklings, but he shrinks the moment anybody dares stand up to him.''

"He transformed himself into this thing.''

"Physioplasty is a parlor trick.''

"It scared the hell out of me!''

"That was exactly the point. A trick to influence your emotions, to frighten you into submission. Keep yourself in control, *mein Herr*. Do not be so easily impressed. Prince Albert Victor already suspects he lacks the power to destroy you, although he probably would have tried harder had he not sensed my approach.''

"I wish you could have got there a few minutes sooner. I've seen him kill quite enough.''

"I'm sorry that I didn't. You must understand that innocents sometimes get hurt, Herr Parker. It is an unavoidable reality.''

"We must stop them.''

"I agree completely, but it won't be easy. Albert Victor's master is a creature of almost infinite resourcefulness, who could teach even Jack the Ripper many things about cruelty. Borgia is the true source of evil in all of this. Imagine a fiend so bereft of good that he would give a homicidal lunatic like Albert Victor the power and immortality of the vampire.''

"It actually was Lucrezia Borgia who transformed him.''

"Acting on her brother's direction. She is his slave. They all are his slaves.''

"What prevents us from stopping the Ripper before he kills again? Are his powers greater than yours?''

"Do not be absurd.''

"Then why not do something? You had the chance when he left the restaurant, leading his freshest corpse off for God knows what purpose.''

Mozart gave a quick glance over his shoulder.

"I did not move against Albert tonight because he was not alone."

I looked backward, too. There was no one on the street behind us—at least, no one I could see or sense.

"Other vampires?"

Mozart nodded curtly. "*Many* others. Albert lacks the courage to do anything alone. His allies were nearby, including three you know personally."

"Three? Who are they?"

"You'll find out soon enough."

"No, please, who?"

"Do not concern yourself about it now. The real problem is Borgia. His current plan must be defused, or millions of mortals will suffer. But we must proceed with caution. Borgia is cunning. Otherwise we would have eliminated his threat long ago."

"Can the *Illuminati* defeat him?"

"Eventually we will, but that day remains far in the future. Borgia has been working more than twenty years on his latest scheme. One at a time he has installed his agents in sensitive posts throughout Europe. Albert, for example, has taken over one of England's largest banking houses. He is to play a central role when events reach critical mass. The *Illuminati* want you to take Albert and several others out of the picture before he can act."

"Me?" In my mind I again saw the Ripper transform himself into the monster he had become in the restaurant. "What could I possibly do to stop *him*?"

"Your inherent powers are much greater than his, although you seem to be having trouble realizing that for yourself."

Mozart looked over his shoulder again.

"We're being followed closely," he said. "Can you feel it now?"

I again tried to pick up the presence of another vampire somewhere behind us, but there seemed to be nothing there besides the usual benign mortal life-forms one would expect on the street. I shook my head.

"It's von Baden. He's a crafty devil."

"Who is von Baden?"

"Later!" Mozart whispered harshly and pulled me into a darkened doorway. "Now I want you to clear your mind. Think of absolutely nothing. I will take care of the rest. Unless your thoughts give us away, we will be safe."

I blanked my mind, trusting Mozart knew what he was talking

about. After five minutes he stepped out on the sidewalk and lifted his chin as if to sniff the air, looking up and down the street.

"It's safe now," he said finally, "although they're bound to pick up your presence again if we remain in Paris. You must improve your ability to conceal yourself if you are to succeed against Prince Albert Victor. We will have to work on that before it is time to take action. You have a more inviting engagement this evening, so I hope you can pull yourself together after your earlier shock."

"Tatiana is in Paris?"

Mozart's eyes glittered. He held up his hand, and a taxi came around the corner as if on command and stopped at our feet. The tiny German held the door, then climbed into the back seat beside me.

"No. 17 rue des Fleurs," he told the driver. The car lurched forward and we headed off for the rendezvous I had been looking forward to for nearly a year.


"The Ripper was in Chicago," I said as the cab turned a corner. "It was him. I *felt* him there."

"Driver: You will hear nothing that we say." The man behind the wheel did not respond. It was as if Mozart had never spoken. "Yes, I know. Tatiana left Chicago to draw him away from you."

"But how did he find me here?"

"Oh," Mozart said with great casualness, "I arranged for him to know you were coming to Paris."

"You what!"

"For two very good reasons. Good steel must be tempered in fire if the impurities are to be hammered out. The only way for you to develop a true sense of what you are is through facing adversity. That is how you learn to get past the petty, inconsequential concerns that dogged you during your life as a mortal."

"That's one," I said, dubious and more than a little angry. "What's the other reason?"

"Think of it as deep chess. Bringing you to Paris helped us maneuver Albert Victor and von Baden toward a vulnerable position. If all goes well, you soon will sweep their pieces from the board. That will put us a series of moves closer to checkmating Borgia."

"That's the second time you've mentioned von Baden. When are you going to tell me about him?"

"A loathsome creature," Mozart said. "Von Baden was born into the last generation of German royalty. They led the nation into defeat in World War I. After the war, impoverished, decaying German society nurtured the worst elements in the Teutonic soul. Von Baden, no longer mortal, was there to help Germany stumble once more into the abyss. It was a time when Borgia was trying to further his aim by setting up totalitarian governments. He had von Baden help establish the Nazi Party."

"When von Baden was a vampire?"

"Yes. Von Baden was the one who found a paranoid, failed artist named Adolf Hitler and set him on a course that nearly destroyed Europe. Prince Albert Victor is capable of horrific crimes, but only on a small scale. Where Albert kills women, von Baden likes to wipe out entire populations. Von Baden is like his master, Cesare Borgia: They both think in global terms."

"They are planning something to do with Europe."

"Yes, they entertain the delusion they can take over Western Europe." Mozart smiled sadly and shook his head.

"Could they succeed?"

"Borgia's plans have partially worked in the past. Witness World War II. The problem for him has always been that it takes one set of skills to conquer, and an entirely different set to rule. This was his weakness even when he was mortal. But yes, Herr Parker, Borgia's plans do have a chance to succeed in the short term. And even if they fail, they will cause untold misery if the conspirators get far enough. That's where you come in. You must stop Prince Albert Victor and General von Baden. The *Illuminati* have sanctioned it."

"But for the sake of God, how can I . . ."

"Please, Herr Parker, before you ask me how again, I must remind you to be patient. We have only a few minutes now. There will be ample opportunity to go over it all. Kindly leave it for the proper time."

"The Ripper told me Borgia had promised him Tatiana."

"That does not surprise me. Tatiana was unhappy for a long time before she met you. It made her vulnerable. Borgia hoped to capitalize on that vulnerability. Creatures like him live to corrupt the sort of purity Tatiana represents, and he no doubt fed Prince Albert Victor's twisted fantasies."

"I suppose there must be some consolation in knowing even a butcher like the Ripper is capable of love."

"I wouldn't say he loves her. I do not believe that madman is capable of love. He wants to possess Tatiana to complete a twisted ideal. Albert is quite arrogant about his bloodline—which is ironic, since inbreeding was probably responsible for his mental infirmity. Albert is convinced Princess Tatiana Nicolaievna Romanov is the only woman worthy of becoming his consort. He fancies the two of them one day reigning over our race, king and queen of the vampires. Which is absurd. Borgia is the real power in the dark faction, and there are many more under him, including von Baden, who would crush the degenerate Albert like the noxious insect that he is if he tried to take on more than his small share of authority.''

"The Ripper said Borgia wants me to join them, too. He said I had until tomorrow to agree or die.''

Mozart laughed. "He cannot harm you. His strength is no match for yours.''

"You keep saying that, but I find it hard to believe.''

"Albert's abilities are superficial. True power comes from a quiet place deep within, a place a vampire like him has no chance of reaching. His brutal little exhibitions have been nine-tenths style and one-tenth substance. Someday, my friend, you will awaken the source of your inner strength. Then you will understand that Prince Albert Victor and vampires like him pose little threat to you.''

"He's tried to manipulate my mind. Maybe he was more successful at it than I've admitted even to myself. I have had urges I'm loath to repeat.''

"He's only trying to corrupt you. He wants to get you into Borgia's camp. And mad as he is, Albert realizes that his chances with Tatiana, however slight, will only improve if he turns you into something she could love no more easily than she could love him. And as far as Borgia is concerned, if he can get to Tatiana through you, he stands to gain two slaves instead of one. It would truly be a coup for him.''

"Still, since I've been in Paris, I've felt the Hunger pull at me in a way I've never known before.''

"Do not feel such guilt,'' Mozart said, and patted my arm. "You have not lost your innocence so much as awakened the understanding that all of us have impulses which must be resisted. Use this knowledge to your own advantage. Use it to propel yourself toward goodness.''

Rue des Fleurs is a street of expensive houses in the city's diplomatic quarter. Ambassadors and their families and staffs live in the mansions; some of the houses are large enough to serve as embassies.

A walk down the street in early evening, I learned later, is like going around the world in five minutes. Traces of curry and plum brandy and lamb linger in the air as families from a hundred different nations sit down to supper.

It was late when I drove down the street in the taxi with Mozart, and we were the only automobile traffic on the wide, smooth boulevard. Security was tight, regardless of the hour. Guards and plainclothes policemen sat in cars, loitered in doorways, and strolled back and forth along the sidewalks, conspicuous in their attempts to appear inconspicuous. No one seemed overly interested in us. The big threat in Paris that summer was car bombs, and until we stopped, we were perceived as harmless.

Most of the houses were surrounded by walls, with gates blocking their driveways. In some compounds TV cameras were hidden in the trees; in others, where the occupants were less concerned about presenting an authoritarian face to the world, rotating surveillance units perched on tall poles in the lawns. One residence had a guardhouse beside the gate to the street. Inside, a soldier in a khaki uniform and a turban stood at attention, an AK-47 slung over his shoulder.

The cab pulled over to the curb in front of a palace ablaze with light.

"Napoleon built this house for a mistress," Mozart said, reaching across me to open my door. "I did not approve of Bonaparte, but I must give him credit for knowing how to live in grand style."

"You knew . . ."

"I wish you a very good night, Herr Parker," he said. There seemed to be no end to my German friend's surprises. I smiled and nodded. There would be plenty of time to ask him about Bonaparte. Tatiana awaited.

As I shook Mozart's hand, the strangeness of the past year came upon me in a rush. I had the sensation that I was watching myself climb out of the taxi, nodding good-bye to Wolfgang Amadeus Mozart, turning slowly toward the mansion where I would be reunited with my lover, Princess Tatiana Nicolaievna Romanov. At the same time it was impossible to forget that somewhere out in the night waited Jack the Ripper, the Nazi von Baden, Cesare Borgia, scion of a corrupt Renaissance pope, and their allies, biding their time until they could spring a plot intended to topple governments throughout Europe and replace them with rulers controlled by an ancient vampire who lived in Florence. That is, unless I, David Parker, former Chicago lawyer and neophyte vampire and composer, could stop them.

It was a lot to hold inside my mind and still remain sane.

I stood on the sidewalk and tried to compose myself, confronted with the most momentous thing of all: Tatiana. I had lived for this moment ever since we parted. Now that the time had come to rejoin her, I found myself feeling curiously anxious. The previous months had seen me much changed. Was I so altered, in body and mind, that Tatiana would no longer love me?

The doors to the house swung open, and a servant came down the walk to open the gate for me. There was something very familiar in the air—Jasmin de Corse perfume—that made my hesitation dissolve like sugar in hot tea.

An orchestra somewhere within the palace began to play as I ran up the front steps and inside without acknowledging the two liveried doormen standing at attention. A broad marble staircase occupied the center of the entry hall, splitting into two sections that went right and left at the first landing. I took the steps two at a time, following the music.

The stairs led to a fourth-floor ballroom. The room was ablaze with candles burning in cut-glass chandeliers. A chamber orchestra, its members dressed in powdered wigs and gold brocade coats, was set up in the balcony and was playing Strauss's "Blue Danube" waltz.

Standing alone in the center of the room, dressed in a white gown and diamonds that glittered with the captured light of a thousand flames, stood Tatiana. She was like an antique doll with exquisitely formed porcelain features. There was a fragility about her despite the pride in her erect bearing and the unmistakable strength in her green eyes. She needed to be protected, if not from the world then from the loneliness that comes from being alive so long without someone to love.

I felt Tatiana's smile in my heart before it came to her lips. She curtsied, and I, feeling more like a character in *Doctor Zhivago* than a former lawyer from Chicago, bowed from the waist.

I took her in my arms. Looking deeply into the inexpressible beauty of her emerald-green eyes, I held her close, and we began to whirl through the room as the orchestra played Strauss's slow, elegant waltz.

# Chapter 26

**P**ARIS, JULY 2, 1989—Tatiana and I have spent four bliss-ful nights together, not once leaving No. 17 rue des Fleurs. I've never before experienced such a feeling of completion. Tatiana is my ideal complement in love, in conversation, in every way. She's right to my left, up to my down, light to my dark. Together we are a perfect whole. She understands my needs almost before I recognize them, and I hers. We are so close that even writing the words *my* and *hers* seems redundant.

And Tatiana's stories! How I have loved to sit beside her in the darkness, listening to her spin fantastic tales about a princess who lived once upon a time in a faraway land of castles, war-riors, and forests where timber wolves howled at the moon . . .

Yet my Scheherazade's stories are true. Born to Czar Nicholas and Czarina Alexandra, raised a grand duchess in the imperial household, transformed into a vampire by a mysterious bene-factor, the sole survivor of a bloodbath that obliterated the royal family—Tatiana's adventures and tragedies were not the subjects of fiction but real.

And after the dream of her early life ended with her family's massacre, Tatiana escaped to Paris, where she filled the time studying ballet, a childhood passion. She has spent the interced-ing decades dancing anonymous parts, waiting for the last of the White Russians who might recognize her to die. Only then, when there is no chance that someone will guess the truth, will she begin her career and make her contribution to the vampire's greatest passion outside the heart: the arts.

We have shared almost everything with each other during these deliciously intimate nights together. Only the details of the final year of her mortal life and the first few months of her existence as a vampire remain obscure to me. Pain fills her eyes whenever her stories touch upon this period or I ask about some detail concerning it. It hurts me to see her suffer, but there seems to be nothing I can do to free her from this part of her past. There are some tragedies not even time can erase.

I still do not know the identity of the vampire who made her a member of our race during those final desperate days before the collapse of the empire.

"He made me what I am out of a desire to protect my family, yet I was bitter about it for a long time," Tatiana told me two nights ago. "I will always think I should have died with my family. It was all very difficult for me to understand when it was happening. In a way I blamed him, even hated him, although that is all behind me now. You may ask him about it yourself."

"He's still alive?"

"He's one of the *Illuminati*."

"But why won't you give him a name?"

"You'll meet him soon enough. I don't want to prejudice you, *liubov' moya*. The personal details of a vampire's mortal life are unimportant. If I told you who he was, you would draw the wrong conclusion."

Only one thing threatened the happiness Tatiana and I have shared: the truth about my own past—the past I've lived since parting from my Russian lover in Chicago a year ago.

Tonight the truth finally came into the lights. It was a moment I dreaded, concerned that it might severely wound our love. It happened as we finished dinner, an excellent meal that satisfied the hunger in my stomach but not the one that had begun to burn at the very center of my being.

"I don't want to do anything to interrupt the magical time we've shared here, Tatiana, but I must leave you for a few hours tonight."

"Why must you go, *moi dorogoi*?" Tatiana asked, putting down her wineglass.

"I have a need that I must attend to."

"The Hunger?"

I nodded.

"You do not have to leave here for that *liubov' moya*."

"No? I've become accustomed to a routine."

"Routines can be changed."

"Yes, but I do not trust the Hunger. I am wary of letting it escape my control."

"I will help you."

I nodded but said nothing. I'd kept my secrets for too long, but I didn't know how to tell her about them.

"Dah-veed," she said in her characteristic way. "Something is bothering you. What is it?"

"I have a confession," I began.

I told her everything: the bad experience with the prostitute in Chicago; my cowardly loss of nerve when I thought I'd killed the woman; how I had been determined to turn taking blood from an act of violence into an act of passion.

Without looking at my lover, I admitted each infidelity. I admitted the complications. How my relationships with the poetess Anna Montoya and with Ariel Niccolini became something more than I'd intended. I told her how my affair with Ariel had taken a disastrous turn, that in the end she turned out to be one of Borgia's unwitting pawns.

When I finally ran out of things to confess, I sat staring at the floor not daring to look up and see my lover's reaction. Rage, hatred, bitter expressions of betrayal—hearing any of these things from Tatiana's lips would not have surprised me. Yet, when I raised my eyes, there was only compassion in my lover's face. She understood what I'd gone through, the horror and the guilt and the struggle to control the monster that lived inside of me, inside of us all.

"Did you think I would be angry?"

I nodded.

"I know you would never do anything to hurt me or anyone else. Remember, wherever you go, I have gone before."

I went to Tatiana and embraced her, kneeling beside her chair, laying my head in her lap. She stroked my hair, soothing away the last of my fears.

"There are other ways," she said finally, "simpler ways."

I opened my eyes and looked up at her.

"The solution I prefer perhaps occurred to me because I grew up surrounded by devoted servants."

I stood when Tatiana rang the china dinner bell to summon a servant to clear the dishes. The maid who came into the dining room was a lovely young French girl with a face that reminded me of Brigitte Bardot when she was young.

*Colette will give you everything you need,* Tatiana said, speaking inside my mind. *She will not object. She is a good girl and entirely willing. I may even feed from her myself before we leave Paris.*

*But does she know about us?* I asked.

*I've blocked it from her mind. When we leave, she will receive generous compensation commensurate for her service. This way is not as romantic as yours, but there are fewer complications. We could continue this convenient relationship for years if we were to remain in Paris. She's young and strong and healthy.*

Tatiana caught Colette's eye and nodded.

The girl came toward me, unbuttoning her blouse. When she stood so close to me that our bodies nearly touched, she pulled her shirt down until it hung suspended by her elbows. Her breathing had quickened, and a light sweat glistened on her breasts. She looked up at me and licked her dry lips, then dropped her head against her shoulder, rolling it to the side.

Her strong pulse beat in her jugular, a throbbing rhythm that would have instantly mesmerized me, if I hadn't resisted. I was embarrassed to feed in front of Tatiana, yet the Hunger was almost too strong for me to resist this ready invitation. My teeth were slipping down from my upper jaw, hard and sharp, and ready. The smell of blood was so heavy in the air that I seemed already to taste it.

Feeling like an exhibitionist—and strangely enjoying the sensation—I took the young woman in my arms, breathing in the intoxicating aroma of blood, mingled with fresh perspiration on powdered skin.

I held Colette tight and bent to gently kiss her neck. Her body went slack in my arms, assuming an attitude of absolute submission. The Hunger was rising fast in me now, coming up like a huge wave that would pick us both up and carry us out to sea.

As I pricked Colette's soft flesh with my teeth, I happened to glance up and notice a strange look of pleasure on Tatiana's face. It excited her to watch me take the other woman.

I closed my eyes and bit into Colette's neck.

I may have been mistaken, but I'm almost certain I heard Tatiana moan with vicarious pleasure.

The happiness Tatiana and I have shared during this Parisian interlude has occupied my mind to the degree that I have scarcely thought about the Ripper and the others, who, I suspect, have spent their time combing Paris for me. Trouble cannot touch us here, secure behind palace doors guarded by an impenetrable matrix of our combined power, which Tatiana said makes us invisible to the evil ones.

I wonder what crimes the insane Prince Albert Victor has committed in my absence? Perhaps without me to torment, he has become bored with murder and gone on to less lethal diversions.

Tatiana has shown little interest in discussing the Ripper, beyond saying the monster must be stopped. I did not bring up his fantasy about making her his vampire queen. If she knows about it, the subject must be too disgusting for her to mention; and if not, I see no reason to distress her with it.

Mozart also has remained absent. I know I need not worry about him. He is far too old and clever for the others.

I should, however, be concerned about the mission Mozart has for me—to kill the Ripper *and* von Baden—but for now I am content to lie in Tatiana's arms and remain lost in an enchanted dream that makes it impossible to think seriously about anything.

And still, outside the haven Tatiana and I share, life goes on, an endless cycle of creation, struggle, and oblivion that is the fate of man and vampire. Soon I must rejoin the world and face my own fate.

# Chapter 27

**P**ARIS, JULY 3, 1989—In the time it takes to close a door. Or sigh. Or watch a cloud move across the moon, extinguishing its light. . . .

In the time it takes to buy a newspaper. Or say good-bye. Or feel the sinking in your heart when something you wanted to last is too soon finished.

That is how quickly happiness can end.

I know.

I should look to the future, anticipating the chance to regain my reason for living, to strike a killing blow against the monolithic evil that has caused me this sorrow.

But I am too distraught for that. Tonight the only thing I can do is grieve. Let this cold, numbing darkness of spirit bleed out of me through my pen, its golden tip scratching black lines across the blue-ruled pages of this journal.

> To whom shall I hire myself out? What beast should I adore? What holy image is attacked? What hearts shall I break? What lies should I uphold? In what blood treat?

Oh, Rimbaud—you know the hopelessness I keep hidden in the most secret corner of my soul. A few hours ago your bleak verses did not interest me, but now they burn through me like X rays, exposing the emotional cracks, the tumor strangling my heart—making my spiritual sickness as plain to see as a fracture or an embolism on a plate of photographic film.

Instead of love all I have are your bitter lines, echoing inside me like the receding footsteps of the last mourner departing an empty room after a wake.

I am alone.

In the next room Mozart and a stranger he treats as a friend speak in hushed voices. The others will not find us here, they said. They wouldn't have found No. 17 rue des Fleurs, either, if I'd been more careful.

Tonight, dear diary—my friend, my confidant, my confessor, my judge, and my jury—my brief idyll in Paris with Tatiana came to a crashing finale, punctuated at the very last by death.

We had decided to spend the evening at a concert or the opera. I went to the newsstand to buy a copy of *Le Monde* to learn what music the city had to offer. Tatiana was soaking in the bath when I left. She was alone. The servants, including the night staff, had been sent home for an unscheduled holiday, one of those spontaneous expressions of generosity Tatiana was in the habit of making.

The newsstand was run by a blind youth who might have had a role in *Les Misérables* for the asking. The Dickensesque boy was thin and pale, with longish blond hair that swept down across his forehead from the side, partly obscuring his sightless gray eyes. He got around the stall without the aid of the white cane, which remained in one corner.

I picked up that day's edition of *Le Monde*. Feeling suddenly out of touch, I also got copies of *The New York Times* and the London *Times* off the rack. It was time to reacquaint myself with the world, to begin preparing myself for the task the *Illuminati* had set out for me.

As the blind newsboy counted the change into my outstretched hand, a feeling of foreboding came over me. It was a familiar sensation. Evil was nearby. There was no mistaking it.

I looked around me, unable to identify the source. It was not like the Ripper to declare himself in this manner. A variation on his usual theme? Perhaps it was von Baden or one of the other conspirators.

At first I was not sure what to do. My immediate impulse was to rush back to Tatiana, yet I certainly didn't want to lead them to her. On the other hand, I'd left on my errand with my head filled with thoughts about my lover and the evening ahead of us; I hadn't been particularly careful about hiding my presence while strolling the four blocks to the newsstand. I might have left enough of a trace in the air for my enemies to find their way to No. 17 rue des Fleurs, even if I didn't return there.

Then, in the flash of an instant, I *knew* I had to get back. My sixth sense told me Tatiana was in danger.

I was at the end of the block, just breaking into a run, when some invisible sign commanded me to stop. I stood at the edge of the intersection, with the evil presence—a low, inaudible hum making me sick in the pit of my stomach—growing stronger somewhere behind me.

Holding my breath, I looked over my shoulder. I saw the blind boy stumble past the bundles of papers and magazines that surrounded his stand and head toward the busy street. The white cane was not in his hand. He walked with the oblivious certainty of a sleepwalker, only narrowly missing being struck by a car that swerved out of its lane, the driver cursing in French at the unhearing youth.

I reached out to the boy with my mind, but it was too late.

The door to a black Mercedes parked on the opposite curb swung open, and the unmistakable presence of a vampire—and *evil*—filled the still night air. The boy climbed quickly into the car, ducking his head as if he could see.

"Wait!" I cried, but the car pulled into the traffic and began to head up the avenue.

The awful horror of the dilemma made my throat tighten. Which to do: Rush back to Tatiana, or try to save the newsboy? Tatiana's powers would give her some defense against the evil faction, but the blind boy would be helpless to resist the web that had caught him.

A courier was climbing off his BMW motorcycle with a large envelope sealed in glossy blue plastic. I wordlessly commandeered the cycle, refusing the courier's offer of his helmet, and gave chase.

There was a strong likelihood that I was being lured into a trap, but I could hardly leave the blind boy at the mercy of the creature who had abducted him. I told myself there was a chance—a very small chance—that the vampire I was following had nothing to do with Prince Albert Victor and the other conspirators, but I knew that was a lot to hope for.

It was easy to follow the Mercedes through the heavy traffic on the motorcycle. However, after turning a corner I lost sight of the automobile for about half a minute. When I found it, it had pulled into an alley between two buildings. Both front doors had been left open, and the keys were still swinging in the ignition. Its occupants had left in a great hurry.

The boy wouldn't have much time left, I knew, assuming it wasn't too late already.

It was no great feat to stay with their trail. There was a lingering presence in the air—a combination of blood, fear, vampire, and crackling malevolence—the abductor had made no effort to disguise. She—I could tell by then that it was a *she*—either didn't realize I was following or didn't care.

There was something vaguely familiar about the vibration in the air, but I was unable to discern whether it was because I'd known the vampire from somewhere else, or because of the newsboy whom I'd just met. I told myself I'd have to get better at reading such mixed clues in the future, if indeed I had a future in front of me.

I followed their trail to a metal fire door adjoining the alley. It was locked. I tore it off its hinges, threw it aside and entered.

The building was at least a century old and beginning to show it. I followed the trail down several flights of stairs to the basement, which was dark and damp and had low ceilings that pushed oppressively down on me as I hurried along, hoping to prevent murder.

The basement would have been silent to mortal ears, but to mine it held a concert of hushed sounds that transposed themselves to mental snapshots: A rat scuttled in the darkness; beetles burrowed in the flaking masonry; the low-banked flames in the furnace burned with a muted roar. And most significant of all: Two heartbeats, one mortal, beating with an irregular rhythm that suggested a congenital defect, and one a vampire's, strong, loud, immortal.

Somewhere farther on in the darkness, I heard the vampire laugh—a low, throaty laugh that sounded as if it could take pleasure in administering pain. There was something familiar about that laugh, but I could not pinpoint the identity of its owner.

Trying to shield my life force as much as possible, I slipped through an open doorway, knowing they were very close. I found myself standing on a steel scaffold that surrounded the upper portion of a two-story boiler room. Below me was the massive old furnace and, on the lower level, the pair I'd been chasing.

The boy was on his back on a worktable, the vampire bending over his trembling body. She wore a long, capelike coat; all I could see of her body was the head of blonde curls. She kissed his face, then moved her lips lower, toward the bend in his neck.

"Let him alone!"

The vampire hissed and spun around, her red fingernails coming up like claws.

"You!"

"That's right, mother-fucker."

I finally was able to put the voice into context, now that I could pair it with a face. I'd only heard it twice: once, a year ago in Chicago, the second time in the brief, hate-filled telephone call to my hotel on the Place Vendôme. The smooth café au lait skin, the absurd bleached-blonde hair, the hint of an early childhood in Virginia or North Carolina in her voice—the pieces of the puzzle suddenly fell together.

She wasn't dead. The prostitute I'd left in the parking lot outside the Half Moon Grill was still alive—and changed.

"You remember what you did to me?"

I didn't answer. I couldn't. It was such a shock to find her alive. In Paris. A vampire.

"I'm talking to you, white trash!"

I'd thought I'd killed her, but an infinitely worse fate had befallen her. I hardly needed to see the sadistic leer on her face to know she was someone who should not ever, under any circumstances, have been granted the extraordinary powers of the vampire.

"I asked if you remembered what you did to me?"

"I didn't do this to you," I said finally.

"No, but you started it," she spat back. "Then I met someone special. Someone who knows how to love Regena. He finished the job you weren't man enough to finish. You're just a spoiled rich boy, but he's a prince. A real prince. And one day he's going to be a king, and when he is, he's going to make me his queen!"

The Ripper! He was responsible for this abomination, this—there really was no other word—*monster*. I wondered if I should tell her Prince Albert Victor had plans to make someone entirely different than Regena his vampire queen.

"I'm going to fix you right. But first . . ." She spun to face the blind boy.

"Let him go."

"You know I can't do that," she said almost tenderly, stroking his face. Then, her voice defiant, she added, "And you can't stop me!"

"If you are truly strong, Regena, prove it to me by taking only the blood you need. Let him walk out of here alive."

Her cackling laughter reverberated off the boiler room's crumbling brick walls.

"Walk out of here alive? When I will get such a rush out of

feeling him die beneath me?'' She looked up at me with burning eyes. ''Heroin was no kick at all compared with this!''

I jumped over the edge of the catwalk and grabbed her by the shoulder. Not a moment too soon, either. As I dragged her off the boy, her teeth scraped against his neck, drawing two red lines in his pale skin, where blood quickly bubbled up, making my own Hunger growl within me. I ignored the temptation and shoved her away.

Regena snarled at me, her blood teeth obscenely distended, her upper lip drawn back, like a wild dog ready to attack.

''I'm going to get you for what you did to me. I'm going to cut out your heart and then do the boy just the way I want.''

There was a scalpel in her right hand. She held it up in front of her eyes, jabbing the point in my direction as she came toward me.

''Put the knife away, Regena. You can't hurt me with that.''

''Prince Albert Victor has been teaching me to use this in the most interesting ways. I think I'm going to do something special with the boy once I finish with you.''

''Give me the knife. I can help you, Regena. I swear I can. Just give me the knife.''

''I am going to kill you, fucker.''

There was malice in her words but no *power*. She was an example of what Mozart had said about vampires who are attracted to evil never gaining full possession of their abilities. She could threaten me with nothing but physical attack, counting on her reflexes to be quicker than mine. But reflexes were irrelevant, I had no intention of indulging in a physical confrontation. Still, there was no escaping the murderous intent in her eyes. She was ready to kill the blind boy and kill him slowly and horribly, and if not him, then someone else.

''Come on,'' she taunted. ''Make your best move.''

''I'm sorry you were dragged into this,'' I said quietly. ''I know it's partly my fault. I involved you. You're too weak to handle your strength, to come to terms with your pain. You couldn't resist the temptation to shoot heroin into your veins when you were mortal; how could you possibly maintain control of an infinitely more powerful intoxicant?''

My words only inflamed her. With an animal scream, she started to throw herself at me, but I stared at her—hard!—and she froze in midstep.

I saw it in her eyes then: the horror she felt, realizing she'd made a fatal miscalculation, that she'd come up against someone she could not begin to handle, that it was going to cost her the supreme penalty.

"I would save you, if I could, but you are beyond help," I said, feeling my eyes burn, fighting to keep control of my own emotions long enough to do the thing that had to be done. "If only you had the smallest degree of self-discipline."

"Fuck you!" she screeched and spat in my face.

I waved a hand, and the door to the furnace behind her banged open.

"The only humane thing to do is to put you down, like a dog with rabies or a horse with a broken leg. Focus your attention on me. I can make it so you don't notice the end, or feel any pain."

She refused to allow me to give her even this small bit of relief. She stared back at me, her face filled with the eternal hatred I knew would rule her sad life until the moment it ended.

"So be it," I said. "I'm sorry, Regena. Good-bye."

I waved my hand again, and she flew backward toward the open furnace door. The sound of the flames roared louder in my head. She managed to stop herself with her hands and feet, desperately gripping the edge of the door that was the last thing between her and incineration. The sickening smell of burned flesh assaulted my senses. I focused a stronger burst of energy in her direction. She flew through the door and into the fire that would bring her death and, with it, purification and peace.

Her screams lasted only a few seconds, but they seemed to go on forever. Then, suddenly, there was only the low roar of the flames. I nudged the door shut with my mind and turned my attention to the newsboy.

"I'm afraid that you fell down and bumped your head. I found you wandering several blocks from your newsstand. If I put you in a taxi, do you think you could remember your address and explain what happened to your family?"

The boy nodded.

"Good. You were never in this building, and you remember nothing except falling down and bumping your head outside your newsstand. Do you understand?"

He nodded again.

"Please come with me."

I put the boy in a cab, then turned and ran toward Tatiana's.

I had not recognized Regena's presence earlier because some-one much stronger than her had blocked my mind. She had been a tool, a pawn, for a stronger player in the game. The Ripper had played her against me as a diversion, not caring what fate she met at my hands.

The logical explanation for such a maneuver was to delay my return to Tatiana's residence. As I turned onto the rue des Fleurs, I was filled with horrible foreboding: Something terrible had happened to Tatiana.

It wasn't until much later—when I sat down alone in this room above a bicycle shop in a neighborhood where many Soviet émigrés live—that I realized the terrible premonition I'd had while getting rid of the nurse's body had come to pass.

The Ripper had done it almost effortlessly: He'd steered me into a position where he was able to force *me* to kill.

# Chapter 28

**PARIS, JULY 4, 1989**—It's the Fourth of July. Strange how completely I've become caught up in my new life. Independence Day—it seems like something that belongs to another life.

This will be my last entry from Paris. We leave at sunset tomorrow.

Continuing my notes on the events of two nights past . . .

The front doors to No. 17 rue des Fleurs had been left open. I ran up the steps two at a time and stopped. They might still be inside, I knew—whoever *they* were.

I stood in the entryway, my chin held high, breathing in the atmosphere. I detected no other living beings, but I did perceive something that alarmed me. There was an unusual substance in the air, something close to blood but infinitely richer. The complex aroma was as heady as good cognac aged to mellow, golden perfection in a deep, lightless wine cellar. There was a slightly flowery bouquet about it, like rose petals slowly wilting in a silver bowl.

It *was* blood, I realized, the truth sinking in—*vampire's* blood!

I flew up the staircase so fast that I found myself standing, not more than a second later, amid the splintered remains of the fourteen-foot-high carved walnut door that formerly had barred the way to Tatiana's bedroom. I pushed a piece of shattered wood out of my way and stepped into the room, fighting back a rising panic.

In the center of the bed, arranged neatly with legs straight and arms folded over the breast, was a female body. The embroidered comforter had been pulled up to cover the body and head. No life force emanated from the figure, no breath or heart-

beat, or any of the more subtle signs of life. Even its aura had
darkened to a blackish purple that hovered no more than an inch
above the covered form, the funereal color growing more dim
even as I stood looking on in grief and disbelief.

The smell of vampire blood was strong—so strong that I had
to put a hand against the door to keep from losing my balance.
A red stain had soaked through the comforter over the face, a
horrible wet blotch that seemed to be spreading slowly larger.

"Tatiana!" My lover's name broke from my lips in a great
anguished cry.

"No."

The voice was Mozart's. He was standing in the shadows
beside the armoire. As strong as my powers had become, they
still were insignificant next to his; he had masked his presence
perfectly. He was not alone. At his side stood a man I had never
seen before, an enormous figure dressed entirely in black. He
had a full beard and long black hair brushed straight back. His
hypnotic eyes made my stomach tingle when they caught me in
their direct stare. He had to be at least seven feet tall.

"It is not Tatiana," Mozart said, coming over and putting his
hand on my shoulder.

"Thank God!" I sagged, as if the air had been let out of me,
and looked slowly around the room. It was a wreck. The curtains had been torn down. Furniture was overturned, some of it
smashed to pieces. A furious struggle had taken place not long
before my arrival. With all that had happened, I'd been gone
less than a half hour.

"Where is she?"

"Tatiana is all right," Mozart said a little tentatively.

"Prince Albert Victor has her," the bearded man said, his
voice a bass rumble that seemed to come from the bottom of a
steel drum. Like Tatiana he spoke with a Russian accent, although his was harsh and much thicker; I guessed it betrayed a
peasant origin, looking at his plain, almost coarse features.

"Do not worry," Mozart told me. "They will not harm her."

"How can you say that?"

"Because they cannot," the bearded Russian said. "The
princess is very powerful."

"Apparently not powerful enough to save herself from being
abducted."

"The princess *is* very powerful," Mozart interjected diplomatically. "Let us say simply that we know it is not in their best
interest to harm her at this time. You realize you were seen on

the street when you left her, Herr Parker. They followed your trail back here. They have been waiting for an opportunity like this. They did not hesitate once they saw their opening.''

I blushed with shame, already knowing that I had stupidly betrayed Tatiana. "Who exactly are *they*?" I asked.

"Albert Victor, with the help of General von Baden and his henchmen," the Russian said. "Or perhaps I should say 'henchwomen.' "

"Yes, I know about them. I had to kill one of them to stop her from murdering a blind newsboy. Who is it?" I asked, indicating the body.

"I'm sure you did what you had to," Mozart said, ignoring my question. "Did you know the woman who attacked the newsboy?"

"She was someone I knew from Chicago."

Mozart and the Russian looked at each other significantly.

"The Ripper transformed her," I said quickly. "It wasn't me."

"We know that," Mozart said. "He did it as a way to shock you, to get you off your guard."

"It worked. It probably gave them time to kidnap Tatiana. I never should have left her alone."

"Do not blame yourself," Mozart said. "Tatiana was quite prepared for something like this to happen."

"If anything happens to her . . ."

"Look at this room!" the Russian said. "The heavy-handed oxen. Still, surprisingly fast work for individuals who are so inept."

"Do I know you?" I asked. Something—perhaps his hypnotic eyes—seemed familiar.

"He is a friend," Mozart said simply, dismissing any question of a fuller introduction.

"Where did the four abductors take her?" I asked, looking at the body on the bed.

"How did you know there were four others?" Mozart's associate asked, an inscrutable smile nearly hidden beneath his beard.

"I just *know*," I said, feeling a little confused.

"Your powers are continuing to develop," Mozart said.

"We'll make a vampire out of you yet," the Russian said. "Tatiana handled herself very well, considering the odds." He nudged a broken chair with the toe of his shoe.

"You realize she was acting completely in self-defense?" Mozart asked.

I continued to look at the still figure on the bed. "Absolutely."

"You also must remember that evil is seductive, Herr Parker. You must continue to remain strong. Even a saint can be corrupted if he or she opens the door to temptation. Do you understand why I'm telling you this?"

I shook my head. He seemed to have gone off on a tangent.

"I thought not. There is something you must know. It's going to be a shock."

"You said Tatiana was all right?"

"Yes."

"Then, what?"

"You do not recognize her essence, do you?" the Russian said, looking toward the body. "I'm not surprised. She is much changed."

I followed Mozart to the still figure and, biting the inside of my lower lip, watched him draw back the comforter, which had become heavy with blood.

In those last few moments, I expected to see Ariel Niccolini's body lying there, killed in a struggle with Tatiana.

It was not Ariel.

The body on the bed belonged to Anna Montoya, the poetess who had been living in my Chicago town house. The two blood teeth that extended beneath her upper lip told me in short fashion what had happened after I left her unprotected. Tatiana had warned me our enemy might return to Chicago looking for me. But instead of me, he found Anna and the woman I had known an even shorter time, the prostitute Regena.

"My beautiful girl," I said and touched her cooling cheek. "What did he do to you?"

Blood seeped from Anna Montoya's ears, nose, and mouth. Across her forehead and around the temples were discolored lines where the bones beneath the skin had broken. Her skull had been crushed from the inside out.

No trace of poetry remained in my Gypsy lover's staring eyes. I will always remember her eyes in death—depraved eyes that had once burned brightly with a different sort of passion.

Beneath the welter of blood her face was still young and lovely, but no hint of its former innocence remained. Her simple beauty could not mask the brutal creature she had become. The story of Anna Montoya's corrupted soul was forever frozen in the subtle, almost invisible changes in her face.

Prince Albert Victor, who had chased Tatiana out of Chicago and tormented me in Paris, had transformed this precious young girl into a vampire—the *worst* kind of vampire. More frightening than the deed was the question it raised: If someone as good of heart as Anna Montoya was not immune to the fiend's whispered lies and promises, who was safe?

"She was one of the purest, most innocent young women I've ever known," I said softly, eulogizing her.

"Which is why Albert Victor had to have her," Mozart said.

"I'm surprised he didn't just rip her," I said. "That's what he likes most to do to women, isn't it?"

"She's not the type he usually likes to hurt," the Russian said. "Think of his psychology. His rage is directed at an altogether different sort of woman."

"Then why didn't he kill the prostitute he sent after me earlier tonight?"

"Because it didn't suit his master. He transformed her for the same reason he changed this one," the Russian continued, nodding toward Anna's body. "They don't matter, and neither do you, as far as Borgia is concerned. It is Tatiana he is trying to maneuver into a corner. If they hook you, too, then all the better."

"Why does Borgia care so much about Tatiana?"

"Partly as a way of keeping Albert Victor in line," Mozart said, "but mostly because it would be a great coup to get her to join him. Tatiana Nicolaievna Romanov, like the Anna Montoya you once knew, possesses an unmistakable purity about her spirit. Destroying her sort of goodness is the thing that propels Borgia and the rest of them. That and a lust for revenge."

"Revenge against whom?"

"Against you, against me, against the world," the Russian said. "Those who are drawn into the dark side of vampirey, like their mortal counterparts, are egocentric personalities at war with the world for failing to recognize their importance, their talent, their genius. You start with a monstrous ego and end with simply a monster.

"And like Prince Albert Victor and von Baden, Cesare Borgia is a royalist," the Russian continued. "It's nearly incomprehensible to a modern mind, but to those of us born under a monarchy, it's easy to understand how such prejudices can endure in the souls of arrogant noblemen transformed into beings who can live for many centuries.''

"If Borgia succeeds, he will reestablish an aristocratic order, with the rulers at the pinnacle vampires of royal birth. Prince Albert Victor and his intended consort, Princess Tatiana, will lord over a significant portion of the empire—if the Ripper doesn't overstep his bounds and get himself crushed for his trouble,'' Mozart said.

"But first they must succeed,'' the Russian said.

"Which is exactly what you are going to prevent them from doing,'' Mozart added.

There was a moment of silence. I started to cover poor Anna's face. "Why are her blood teeth out?"

"Albert Victor assumed the shock of sending this young one against you would have confused you long enough for them to overwhelm you when you returned,'' Mozart said. "She would have tried to kill you."

"And she would have succeeded, with the help of the others, if you hadn't been able to kill her first,'' the Russian said. "Would you have been able to do *that*?"

I did not answer.

"I thought not,'' the Russian said. "Then it is better that Tatiana was here alone. They've apparently decided things will be less complicated with you out of the way."

"You know Tatiana acted only in self-defense,'' Mozart repeated. "When she learns of your connection with the girl, she will be very sad indeed!"

"She need never know,'' I said softly, looking down at my dead lover's face. She would know only peace now. But for the living the struggle would continue.

"I will burn the body,'' the Russian rumbled in what was intended to pass as a quiet, respectful voice.

"I'm so sorry, my darling,'' I murmured, wiping the blood away from Anna's face with a corner of the sheet. "I only wanted to be your benefactor."

I bent low and kissed her lips one last time.

"David.'' Mozart spoke my name with the utmost kindness. "We must leave."

I covered Anna Montoya's face and slowly turned away. "Those animals,'' I said, my voice somewhere between grief and anger.

"They are not animals,'' the Russian said. "Animals kill only when they must to survive. These creatures kill to gain power, or for the pleasure of dominating others. They are not animals; they are much worse than that.''

"How much danger is Tatiana in?''

"Some,'' the Russian said, seemingly showing concern beneath his heavy beard, which hid most details of his expression. "We all are in some danger. You much more than we, Herr Parker.''

"It doesn't matter. The only thing I care about is freeing Tatiana from the Ripper.''

"If you want to save her from Prince Albert Victor, the thing you must do is help us stop them from executing their current plot,'' the Russian said. "Nobody is safe as long as Borgia's lackeys are loose to work his insane schemes.''

"You, Herr Parker,'' Mozart said with a tight smile, "are the one who is going to bring this current madness to an end.''

I was ready to do anything it took to get Tatiana back, anything that would make the Ripper pay for what he'd done to Anna Montoya, anything to stop the maniacs who had butchered so many innocent mortals.

"Just tell me what you want me to do,'' I said, staring furiously at the covered body on the bed.

Mozart nodded to his associate, who reached inside his coat and pulled out an enormous pistol. He held it out to me.

"Is this a joke?''

"No,'' the Russian replied laconically, "this is a Browning 9 mm semiautomatic pistol with a nonreflecting black combat finish. Get close enough to Albert Victor and von Baden, and you can blow them in half with this weapon.''

"It's true,'' Mozart said. "Not a very elegant way to dispatch a vampire but quite effective nonetheless.''

"My advice is to blow their heads off,'' the Russian said. "Even Jack the Ripper can't live without a head.''

I accepted the weapon doubtfully, bouncing its weight in my hand. It had a hefty, solid feel.

"What does it shoot, silver bullets?''

"Armor-piercing exploding rounds,'' the Russian said dryly. "I got them from a man in the CIA. You can drop a bull elephant at full charge with that gun. It will do the job.''

"And you think I can simply walk up to the Ripper and blow him away?''

"Of course not,'' Mozart said. "He's not going to let you shoot him. You're going to have to be strong mentally. You will have to resist his attempts to control you, to frighten you, to tempt you. And beyond that, you will have to control *his* mind. Don't let him see the gun. Block his senses. Make it so that he sees neither you nor the gun—until it is too late."

"How am I supposed to do that?"

"I'll teach you," the Russian said, his beard rearranging itself in a smile. "I know a thing or two about mind control."

"Wouldn't it be simpler—and more certain—for one of you to do it? Both of you obviously are much more powerful than I."

"In medieval times, before even I was around," Mozart said, and smiled, "a squire accepted a quest before he became a knight. It was a way to earn his spurs, something he did to prove his worthiness to his peers and to himself. Accept this quest, David Parker. Slay these monsters, and prove to yourself and to the *Illuminati* that you are worthy of the gift of eternal life and boundless mind that Princess Tatiana has bestowed upon you."

The two vampires looked at me closely as I considered the challenge. The decision was surprisingly easy to make.

"I'll do it for Tatiana," I said.

"And for yourself," Mozart added.

"And for the world," the Russian said, fixing me with his penetrating eyes.

# Chapter 29

**S**OMEWHERE IN FRANCE, JULY 5, 1989—The train rocks gently from side to side. I listen to the rush of air; the deep, faraway rumble of the engine; the rhythmic click of wheels against steel track. It is difficult to keep my eyes open. I am in the arms of a great mechanical mother who wants to lull me to sleep. I cannot sleep. I must practice zazen and return to the others within the hour, which leaves little time to make a few quick notes in my journal.

I'm working at a small, fold-down writing table in the private sleeping car. My companions are in the salon, where we spent several hours this evening, sipping brandy and talking over many incredible subjects.

We boarded in Paris. The train will carry us to Zurich and Innsbruck, where we transfer to a spur line and travel north into the Federal Republic of West Germany. Our destination is a tiny Bavarian town called Jachenau. From there I go by car to my ultimate destination: Burg Wolfsschanze—Wolf's Lair Fortress—a twelfth-century castle in the mountainous southern part of the country.

Mozart showed me Burg Wolfsschanze on a map tonight. With a pencil he drew a line through Nuremberg, Munich, and Innsbruck: the line touched the castle midway between Munich and Innsbruck. "And after Wolfsschanze . . ." Mozart pushed the pencil farther, curving his line slightly to the west to Bayreuth, which he circled.

"The *Illuminati* already are congregating there."

I welcomed the implication that I would be with them in Bayreuth. I wish I were as certain as he that I will survive my ordeal and join the others. The *Illuminati* and Princess Tatiana seem

256

as far away as ever, while Burg Wolfsschanze looms ahead, a barrier I cannot go around but must somehow pass through.

Burg Wolfsschanze . . .

Even the name sounds sinister, like the setting of a Gothic horror story. However, there is nothing fictional about the force that awaits me within the dank walls of the Bavarian castle, a setting poisoned by centuries of violence, treachery, and an impenetrable darkness of spirit.

I banish my fear with the remembrance that within those stone battlements is Tatiana, hostage to Borgia's agents. If she is to be freed, I must face my fears and meet whatever fate has in store for me there.

Mozart expects me to destroy Prince Albert Victor and General von Baden, late of an S.S. *Totenkampf*, Death's-Head regiment. The Ripper I know only too well. I have yet to meet the general, but I cannot say I look forward to the experience with any great enthusiasm.

Mozart described Bavaria as a place of transcendental beauty. Despite his obvious prejudice for all things German, the district Burg Wolfsschanze rules over did indeed sound like something out of a Brothers Grimm fairy tale. The castle sits high above the valley floor atop the centermost of three mountains to the south of the tallest peak in the area, Benediktenwand. The castle looks down on a lake with a musical name: Sylvenstein Stausee.

"Wolfsschanze Mountain has steep slopes and a flattened summit, which is completely occupied by the castle and its battlements," Mozart said. "You can sit in a beer garden in Jachenau and look across the valley and see Burg Wolfsschanze thrust up into the sky, tall and erect as a Prussian officer, its upper spires reaching toward the clouds. The mountainside is covered with a thick forest of oak and beech trees that gradually gives way to pines and firs. The incline sharpens into a vertical cliff for the final five hundred feet to the summit. The castle is accessible across a single drawbridge that spans a deep gorge. It is an ideal place for a citadel—or at least it was during a time when armored men on horseback were the ultimate weapon."

Burg Wolfsschanze was the ancestral home of the von Baden family, Mozart said. Its resident master was the Count General Dedrich von Baden. Von Baden was one of Cesare Borgia's top lieutenants; he also was a second cousin to Prince Albert Victor, English and German royalty having intermarried extensively during the nineteenth century.

Von Baden, Albert Victor, and Tatiana were at Burg Wolfsschanze, the Russian said, along with an unknown number of associates.

"The von Baden you will meet is not the first of his family to earn a reputation for evil," Mozart said. "The von Baden bloodline has been polluted with madness and criminality for centuries. Even during my mortal lifetime they were dissolute swine. Aristocrats like the von Badens made revolution against their class an inevitability."

Dedrich von Baden allegedly did not survive the war, although a body that conveniently resembled his was recovered and buried in the family crypt. After Hitler's "Thousand-Year Reich" collapsed in a heap of bombed-out rubble, von Baden and the other vampires in the Nazi hierarchy faded from mortal view. Lately, however, von Baden has come out of deep cover to help his Italian master arrange what they intend to be a rather spectacular surprise for Western Europe, as Mozart puts it.

"Von Baden has rather foolishly insisted on taking up his old place of residence, but first he had to get the mortal Count of Wolfsschanze out of the way. When the general learned his descendant had an interest in illicit substances, he arranged to help the young man develop an addiction to heroin. The German authorities are rather straitlaced about that sort of thing, especially in Bavaria. Consequently the general's friends set the youth up in an apartment in Amsterdam, where he is kept steadily supplied with high-grade Golden Triangle junk."

"Junk?" the Russian asked.

"American slang for heroin," Mozart said.

"Ah."

"Von Baden must be taking quite a risk in returning to his mortal residence after so few years," I said.

"Especially when you consider that he looks exactly as he did in 1945. Even today there are people prowling the globe in search of war criminals. This is typical of von Baden's arrogance, of his attitude that neither rule of law nor reason can govern his actions. Returning to Burg Wolfsschanze was his way of defying authority, mortal and vampire. That is why he has taken not only an enormous risk to himself and to mortals, but also to the entire vampire race."

I turned my attention to the Russian, who looked away from me to stare out the window with an impassive expression. He exuded an air of mystery that made me nervous, but it seemed that whenever it began to bother me too much, a glint would come into his deep-set, hypnotic eyes, and my discomfort would vanish. He was manipulating my mind, I knew, and although he was extremely subtle about it, I didn't like it. It was an invasion of my privacy.

"If I am going to kill von Baden and the Ripper—" I saw no need to equivocate—"how will I get into Burg Wolfsschanze without attracting their attention? How am I supposed to find them before they find me in a castle that von Baden is intimately familiar with, that I have never visited?"

"Neither Albert Victor nor von Baden is as powerful as you assume," the Russian said.

"So Mozart has told me, but perhaps I'm not as powerful as you both assume," I countered. "Frankly the Ripper ran circles around me in Paris. As far as I can tell, going into Burg Wolfsschanze will be little more than heroic suicide."

The Russian shook his head to dismiss my concerns. "He hasn't shown you anything except tricks that amount to child's play. You can learn to do anything he can—and much more."

"If it's all so simple, why haven't I learned it on my own?"

"Because you have a noisy, undisciplined mind," the Russian said. "People train themselves to speak a foreign language or, in your case, to perform a complicated task like playing the piano, but when it comes to learning to control the mind in order to awaken its latent powers, most do not even know where to start."

I listened carefully. I had to. If the Russian couldn't help me, no one could.

"To be able to accomplish anything with your head—even something as inconsequential as Albert Victor's parlor magic—you must truly know how to concentrate. But before you can do that, you need a quiet and unified mind. The quickest way to quiet your mind is through meditation."

"Do you mean like Transcendental Meditation?"

"You should not smirk. Mortal or vampire, the same principles apply. Did you learn to meditate? It will make things easier now."

"I didn't go beyond the free lecture in college. It seemed like a con game."

The Russian smiled under his beard.

"Oh, come on," I protested. "They said I could learn to levitate if I was willing to part with the money."

The Russian continued to smile at me.

"Are you telling me they could have taught me to levitate?"

"I don't know whether they could have taught you. I would tend to doubt it. However, for a vampire who truly can control his mind, anything is possible."

The sparkle in his eyes made it impossible to tell if he was putting me on. "*I* could teach you to levitate. And the price would be the best part. It wouldn't cost you a ruble."

"I'm ready to try anything if it will help me walk out of Burg Wolfsschanze alive with Tatiana. So what do I do? How do I achieve this quiet and unified mind?"

"You begin with a few simple exercises. As you become more advanced, so do the exercises. The techniques are thousands of years old. They were perfected by early Zen masters in China and Japan. The basic techniques are not, I suspect, substantially different from the ones you would have learned from a TM instructor."

"They were all members of our race," Mozart said. "The Zen masters, not the TM instructors."

"The roots of our race run all the way back to northern India, Tibet, or China ten thousand years ago. But that is a matter for discussion at a later date. You must not clutter your mind now with superfluous information. It would only get in the way. We will start simply. If you make an honest effort, you will see results almost immediately. The key, however, is to expect nothing. You simply do the exercises without desiring any particular results. You will learn that the best way to try is through not trying."

"One of the benefits of having a vampire's mind is that we are quick studies," Mozart said. "There is no staring at a stone wall for five years, waiting for your first clue to enlightenment. Even for the dullest of us."

"What you need to know to best Prince Albert Victor and von Baden isn't much." The Russian flipped a hand in the air dismissively. "But first you must master the basic principles."

"Never underestimate the strength of goodness, and the relative weakness of evil," Mozart said. "It may sound moralistic, but it's a matter of fact that evil is inherently weak. For both the prince and the general the inability to control their overblown egos has prevented them from learning anything important about the art of vampirey, which, as you already know, requires a certain degree of sensitivity. They have only developed the negative side of themselves, in the process neglecting the infinitely stronger positive side. Narcissism has cost them the chance to tap their greatest talents. They are consumed with the darkness. And the darkness will be their downfall.''

"The light will be the source of your triumph," the Russian said. "You think I am speaking metaphorically. I'm not. I mean it literally: The *light* will be the source of your triumph. You will go to Burg Wolfsschanze by day, and you will find it unprotected. The element of surprise will give you the advantage you need to ensure victory.''

"By *day*?"

"At the very height of noon!" the Russian said dramatically. "You will go to the castle and march in unmolested while your enemies cower from the sun, asleep deep in the castle's bowels, dreaming their malignant dreams.''

"But how am *I* supposed to survive the sunlight?"

"The way all enlightened vampires do," Mozart said. He nodded at the Russian. "He will teach you."

"Did you think we were incapable of going out in the daylight?" the Russian asked. "The weaker members of our race must hide in night's shadows, but those of us who are in touch with our inner resources think nothing of joining mad dogs and Englishmen by going out in the noonday sun.''

"It's the reason we call ourselves the *Illuminati*," Mozart said. "It's a *pun*."

"But how can you possibly do it?"

The Russian touched his forefinger to his head. "It's all up here.''

"Who are you anyway? If you're going to ask me to immolate myself, I want at least to know your name."

"If the sun couldn't destroy you before, David Parker, what makes you think it could harm you now that your strength has begun to flower?" the Russian asked. "Please have a little more faith in your new teacher.''

The Russian extended a bear-paw–sized hand.

"Permit me to introduce myself. My name is Grigori Efimovich Novykh. Or, as I am better known in popular accounts, Rasputin.''

And why not?

If I was to sit sipping brandy with Wolfgang Amadeus Mozart, why not be joined by Rasputin, the Mad Monk, one of the most famous figures from the final days before the collapse of the Russian Empire? Perhaps Napoleon would walk into the salon car next, and we could discuss the strategic failings of his late-season march on Moscow.

The overpowering giddiness went out of my head the instant Rasputin looked at me and frowned. I must have turned red as an apple, because Mozart chuckled and shook his head.

"I know this is all a bit much to absorb, *mein Herr*, but try not to let the quick tempo get the better of you."

I looked back to Rasputin. The frown was gone, and in its place was an inscrutable blank expression—and his eyes, his penetrating eyes.

*I will thank you not to think of me as "one of the most infamous figures from the final days before the collapse of the Russian Empire,"* he said telepathically.

I began to stammer an apology, but he and Mozart burst into laughter, and I gave up the attempt.

What I knew about the Russian were bits and pieces of things I'd heard, read, and even seen in movies. He was a Siberian peasant with a brilliant mind and a strong appetite for women, drink—and power. He was an exceptionally talented mesmerist; he'd used his hypnotic powers to insinuate himself with the Russian royal family, preying on the empress, who was especially vulnerable to charlatans because of her anxiety about her hemophiliac son. Rasputin had involved himself with palace intrigues, which resulted in disastrous policy decisions for the czar and helped speed the revolution.

I remembered the icon, the delicate enameled painting of Saint Sebastian I had seen at Tatiana's mansion in Chicago. A gift from Rasputin, she had said.

The Russian seated across from me looked different from the photographs I'd seen, although the resemblance was definitely there. He wore his hair shorter now, and his beard had been neatly shaped, instead of the ragged Edwardian "chest-warmer" he'd had when Czar Nicholas and his family were still alive.

In photographs Rasputin's eyes were pale, shining orbs. In life they were electrifyingly powerful when he chose to make them so, and they seemed capable of boring straight to the core of whatever—of whomever—they were trained on.

If Rasputin still considered himself a member of a religious order, you couldn't tell it from his dress. In place of a black caftan, he wore a black double-breasted suit that was plain but exquisitely tailored.

Was Rasputin the one who transformed Tatiana from mortal to vampire? It was not the first time such a possibility had occurred to me. Even his old photographs possessed a strange presence that seemed to go beyond anything the camera captured from an ordinary mortal.

"The stories you have heard about me are mostly lies strung together with just enough truth to keep the oleaginous mass from falling apart."

"It's true," Mozart said. "My good friend Grigori has been the recipient of some of the worst press in history."

"Not that I didn't deserve some of it." He smiled. "I made my share of mistakes. After all, I was only human."

"Was it you who transformed Tatiana?"

"Now that we're acquainted," Rasputin said, pointedly choosing to ignore my question, "you may call me Rasputin, at least when we are in the company of mutual friends. Rasputin originally was intended as a derogatory nickname, but I long ago got used to it. In fact, I even like it. Rasputin is Russian for *debauchee*, which I certainly was many years ago." He shrugged. "What was your father's name?"

"Michael."

"Then your patronymic is Michaelovich. I will call you David Michaelovich. When we reach Jachenau, it will be David against Goliath. But do not worry. The outcome will be the same as in the Bible story."

"Rasputin is *the* expert on mind control," Mozart said. "He was even as a mortal."

"I've been interested in how the mind works since before the science was even called psychology. The interior of the human brain—now, there's a jungle worthy of exploring. It's a wilderness of mirrors, as your T. S. Eliot would say."

I blinked. Rasputin knew of my interest in poetry. (Poor Anna Montoya!) No doubt he knew many things about me. I shifted nervously in my seat. Being in the presence of so powerful a mind—or minds, because I certainly had to include Mozart—was like being naked.

"All vampires worthy of their gift become involved in some form of art," Mozart said. "For Rasputin it has been psychology—which is certainly more of an art than a science."

Rasputin roared with laughter.

"An old argument between the piano player and myself," the Russian explained. "He's been a skeptic about some of my more advanced theories."

"Nonsense. We all know the human race is as filled with inner turmoil as it is with external strife. Rasputin has done quite a bit to steer mortals toward relative mental enlightenment.'' He swirled the brandy in his snifter. ''Rasputin was the one who told Freud his seduction theory was off track. And it was he who got Jung thinking about the collective unconscious.''

''I've made my small contributions,'' Rasputin said. ''As have you, Wolfgang.''

''Yes, to music,'' I said enthusiastically.

''And mathematics,'' Mozart added with only the slightest hint of vanity.

''He gives piano lessons to a girl whose father is a theoretical physicist at Oxford,'' Rasputin said. ''The father likes to lie on the couch, meditating on his work in superconductivity while he listens to the two of them play for an hour every Tuesday afternoon. He gets some of the most remarkable insights about quantum mechanics listening to those lessons.''

''The ideas just come to him out of thin air when his daughter plays Mozart,'' Mozart said.

''Do you suppose it is the music that inspires him?'' Rasputin asked jokingly.

''It isn't his daughter's playing!''

There was a blast of noise outside the window. The train was entering a tunnel. The conversation paused until we came out the other side.

''You knew Tatiana when she was mortal,'' I said to Rasputin, thinking it a polite way to indirectly restate my earlier question, which he had refused to acknowledge.

The Russian nodded solemnly and put down his brandy. I could almost see the memories rising up around him like sad mists.

''What was she like then? What really happened when the revolution came?''

Rasputin settled into his seat, folding his massive hands one over the other in his lap. He looked out the window at the darkness for a moment, already lost in the past.

Mozart and I sat back in our own chairs and quietly waited for Rasputin to begin his story.

# PART IV

✧

# Rasputin's Tale

# Chapter 30

JACHENAU, JULY 6, 1989—The bright smell of pine fills the air, mixed with smoke from the blaze in the fireplace. Even in summer, nights are cool in the mountains.

We are staying in the sort of picturesque Bavarian inn that might be featured in a travel brochure. The hotel has a steeply peaked roof to slough off heavy snows, and the eaves are decorated with elaborate gingerbread trim that must have kept a German craftsman busy at his carving bench many winter nights. There are exposed beams in all the exterior walls, and also in the ceilings, and many are decorated with painted designs and German phrases.

I gradually am learning to relax in this place. It isn't easy, considering that we are so close to a concentration of evil stronger than anything I have ever felt before.

Earlier I stood in front of the window and stared through the diamond-shaped panes, looking up at the silhouette of the castle against the rising moon. I almost expected to see Jack the Ripper come down the narrow cobblestone street searching for me. I suppose it is General von Baden I should expect, although I have no idea what he looks like. One is as bad as the other, and both are nearby.

It seems insane for us to stay in Jachenau with Burg Wolfsschanze such a short distance away. Nevertheless this is where Mozart and Rasputin say we will wait. My two teachers insist the others will not know we are here. That seems incredible, when even *I* can feel the evil emanating from Burg Wolfsschanze.

Rasputin has taught me to shrink my presence to the dimmest hint of a glimmer. Perhaps that will be sufficient to shield us, but I think it more likely that it is the power of Rasputin and Mozart that protect us here.

As usual I remained in my room today while the sun was in the sky. I do not know whether my traveling companions did the same. For all I know, they could have gone for a stroll through the town this afternoon to admire the flowers and the quaint Bavarian architecture. Jachenau must be lovely in the summer sunlight, which I remember as being particularly sharp in the thin mountain atmosphere.

I can imagine Mozart dropping a coin in the telescope in the park in the center of town, then stepping back to invite Rasputin to take the first turn viewing the castle atop the centermost of the three mountains grouped together in the blue distance. A pleasant fantasy: vampires in the park at noon.

Perhaps in a short time I no longer will have to hide myself away at dawn, lurking like a spider in the shadows until the edge of darkness once more creeps across the sky.

I would *love* to see the sun again. I miss seeing motes of dust rising in a shaft of sunlight. I miss sitting in the sun with my eyes closed, feeling its warmth on my face. I wish I could get up tomorrow morning, throw open the curtains and see the brilliant light glittering like diamonds on the waters of the Sylvenstein Stausee.

For now, however, I must stay in my room no matter what the hour, doing my best to obey my teachers' instructions to allow no hint of my presence to escape these four walls.

The Black Forest cuckoo clock above the fireplace continues to mark the alternating seconds with loud ticktocks. I fill another page with script, quietly biding my time until I go to Burg Wolfsschanze to meet my salvation or my death.

I've been practicing the new technique Rasputin gave me to learn.

"Simply count your breaths," he said. "Inhale, and when you exhale, count one. Inhale again, and when you exhale, count two, and so on, all the way to ten. Then start over. If you lose your place, begin again at one. Thoughts will come into your mind as you meditate: Do not let them interfere with your concentration. Gently and effortlessly push them aside and keep your attention centered on counting your breaths. Imagine yourself growing lighter and lighter until your body has no more substance than a feather."

"And what will this do?"

"Quiet and unify your noisy, disordered mind and increase your concentration. Counting your breaths will teach you tranquility and give you the mental focus you'll need to go outdoors in sunlight."

My skepticism, which I thought I'd kept well disguised, must have shown on my face, because Rasputin was on me in an instant, rebuking me to reserve judgment about whether he was wasting my time.

"A little faith is sometimes required, David Michaelovich."

"I'm sorry, Rasputin."

"What is that you're thinking?"

"It's from a William Blake poem."

"Say it out loud."

*"If the sun and moon should doubt*
*Certainly, they would go out."*

"That is my point exactly. The sun and moon do not question. They simply *are*. The sooner you simply are, David Michaelovich, the sooner you will fully master your sleeping powers.

"Like most modern mortals," Rasputin continued, warming to his subject, "you view your attitude of ready skepticism as evidence you have a free and open mind. The truth is, you are not thinking at all. Any fool can disbelieve, but it requires mental effort to work out what it is you believe, and maintain your faith in it. You must ask yourself what is the meaning of life. The answer may be impossible to know, even for a vampire, but you *must* ask. The fact that some things cannot be understood objectively only means you eventually reach the point where you must develop faith to trust in a power greater than your own hungry ego and your grasping, empirical mind. We can yearn to know everything, David Michaelovich, but only God has that privilege."

Rasputin waved his hand as if to clear his argument from the air.

"But do not become overly concerned with my epistemology and theology. I am only asking you to have faith that I can teach you to use the powers given you. Can you have that much faith, David Michaelovich?"

I said that I would try my hardest.

As Mozart had promised, Rasputin's exercises brought quick results.

Last night I sat on the floor in my sleeper car on the train and counted my breath for the first time.

After about ten minutes a feeling of complete peace came over me. With each new breath, I felt as if I were actually becoming lighter, losing weight and physical substance as I became pure, radiant energy. I became so engrossed in following my breath that I floated several inches off the floor for some minutes before I realized I was levitating.

The moment I noticed I was actually floating, I became excited and—*bang!*—I was back on the floor in an instant.

I'd allowed my mind to become distracted. The next time, I kept my mind quiet and clear and felt myself rise higher and higher until my hair brushed gently against the ceiling. This jogged my conscious mind into action again. I barely got my legs unfolded enough to absorb some of the shock of the fall as I sprawled to the floor in a heap.

Now I know that vampires *can* fly—but not by turning themselves into bats!

Rasputin says I must not become overly concerned with levitation—one of the phenomena he refers to as "parlor magic"— or it will inhibit my progress. Instead of my becoming light as a feather, he now wants me to concentrate on the area just below my navel while counting my breaths. He refers to that part of my body as my "hora" and says I must learn to breathe through my hora. I have no idea what he means, but I am trying to do as instructed.

I look up from this desk at my profile drawn on the wall in shadow. It seems to belong to someone I am just beginning to know. Almost nothing remains of David Parker the mortal but memories.

Blood, breath, bone, and soul, I am a vampire.

"Russia before the revolution . . ."

It took Rasputin a long time to begin telling us his story during the train ride to Jachenau, and after the first four words, he lapsed again into a haunted silence and stared out the window, absently stroking his beard with the fingers of his right hand.

The French countryside moved quickly past, a fleeting procession of shadows as dark as the memories racing through the vampire's great mind.

"To imagine life in Russia before the revolution, forget everything you know about the Soviet Union. We are talking about two completely different countries. Russia did not become the

Soviet Union. Russia died seventy-one years ago. Taking its place—as if called into being by the sudden void—was an entirely different nation. The party apparatchiks, the gigantic murals of Lenin in Moscow, the lines that stretch for miles outside of the shoe stores, the KGB, with its endless capacity for brutality and murder, the deadening gray monotony that kills the mortal soul as surely as a pistol shot behind the ear—those are as foreign to me as they are to you, David Michaelovich.''

There was another long silence, and I waited patiently for him to continue, as I knew he would when he was ready. Poor Rasputin. He'd lived through one of the most interesting—and tragic—periods of history, and now he was doomed to live on from generation to generation, repeating his tale like Coleridge's ghostly Ancient Mariner.

''You also must forget the other European countries at the turn of the century,'' Rasputin resumed. ''Go back farther, another one hundred, two hundred, three hundred years, back to a time when the West was still trying to claw its way out of the Dark Ages. Think of a place where a few members of an aristocracy had all the wealth; where life for the masses was brutal, wretched, and short; where there was no justice except for the privileged few; where ignorance and misery were the conditions of the typical person's brief life.

''But at the same time imagine a place rich in tradition and land as romantic as the setting of a fairy tale, with a people who shared a great soul because of the suffering they had seen.

''This,'' he said, fixing me with his burning eyes, ''was Rasputin's Russia. A nation that desperately needed reform. A nation mired in corruption and injustice. A nation I, Grigori Efimovich Novykh, desperately fought to protect in all its imperfection.

''Some would say I earned damnation for helping Czar Nicholas. A woman who tried to stab me to death a long time ago, the mother of a girl the czar's secret police tortured to death for some imagined crime against the crown, told me so to my face as she plunged a dagger into my chest. Many others agreed. Sometimes even I agree. . . .''

The train shot through a town without slowing. The irregularly spaced street lamps made light flicker on and off in the dimly lit railway car, alternately turning the Russian's face into a stark mask with sharply highlighted features, and draping it in shadow so that only the eyes remained luminous. The surrounding buildings reflected the train's sound back at us, making the background noise double in volume. The engineer repeatedly blew the air horn. Outside, bells clanged, and there was the harsh sound of metal screeching against metal as we passed street crossings where the tracks were poorly aligned.

"Perhaps I was wrong to have tried to save the Romanov dynasty," the Russian resumed, the town suddenly behind us. "The time for kings was long past even then. Power and wealth had become concentrated in the hands of an increasingly corrupt and inept few. The aristocrats had intermarried until their bloodlines became so polluted that the entire structure of society began to crack from the infirmity of its own inbreeding.

"The czar, God rest his soul, on balance was a good man. He loved his wife and family and was, in most cases, gentle, compassionate, and charming—and completely unlike his autocratic father. Contrary to what you might have expected from the mentally deficient uncles and cousins who surrounded him, he was quite intelligent. But one man—even with the help of a vampire—cannot hold back the tide when the earth turns round and the vast oceans begin to move. Modest reforms might have slowed the inevitable. Truly inspired visionary changes in the system might have prevented the revolution, might have made it possible to ease the country into the sort of constitutional monarchy there is in England."

Rasputin's massive chest rose and fell with a deep sigh.

"Unfortunately I could not bring it off, and all the misery that had been accumulating during years of ineffectual rule brought doom crashing down on my motherland."

"The opposition was strong," Mozart offered.

"Strong? It was overwhelming. The whole country was against me, including the entire class who had the most to lose if the government collapsed. Everywhere I turned in those days, I found people trying to extinguish the early sparks of revolt by dousing them with gasoline. The incompetent generals sent Russia's sons to be slaughtered by the Germans. The grain speculators orchestrated famine in the countryside and breadlines in the city for the sake of gouging additional profit out of the populace. The superstitious peasants couldn't make up their minds whether the czar should be worshiped or beheaded. And the decadent aristocracy, with its boundless wealth and property, gaily danced nearer and nearer the precipice, unable to believe it was possible that they might tumble over the edge.

"And I must not forget the church," Rasputin said, openly angry. "The church did not waste its time with anything as inconsequential as the poor, the weak, the powerless, and the hungry. Its preoccupation was in helping the nobility hang onto power—but only after maintaining its own influence and wealth.''

"A human institution has human failings,'' Mozart interjected.

"It is a human institution that you have more faith in than I,'' Rasputin replied. "In another land, in another time—what does it matter? It's always the same: self-proclaimed spiritual leaders using public sanctimony to mask profane appetites. Which is the worse: undisguised lust for money, power, and sex, or the same urges hidden beneath a veneer of hypocritical piety? I'll take the aristocracy over the clergy any day—and I thought the same even when I was a monk!''

"You go too far,'' Mozart said, more weary than irritated. It was, apparently, an old point of contention between the two vampires.

"Gentlemen, please,'' I interrupted.

"My apologies. Please, Rasputin, continue.''

"History books are written by the winners, who are under no obligation to tell the story fairly and seldom do. The czar was a good man and a better-than-average ruler. Nevertheless he was neither brilliant enough nor lucky enough to stop the deluge we all knew would come to Russia, as it had to other European nations when the common people decided they had suffered enough. And like so many cases, one oppressive government replaced another, but that is a familiar story.

"When an animal becomes old and weak and sick, all kinds of opportunistic parasites will affix themselves, sucking the last bits of life out of the dying carcass. Czar Nicholas once told me, 'I do not rule Russia; ten-thousand bureaucrats do.' And he was right. The vast apparatus of government, controlled at the top by the corrupt aristocracy, was completely bogged down by its own enormous size.

"However, not all of the terminal-stage leeches afflicting Russia were mortal. A cadre of vampires had deeply penetrated the upper nobility and used their position to bleed the country, both literally and financially, at the behest of their master in Italy.

"Russia before the revolution was a perfect place to be a vampire, at least one bearing Borgia's brand. The country continued to stumble through the shadows of the Middle Ages. Horrible roads, impassable in winter. Poor communication. A police force suited best for battling criminals of the political sort. A superstitious peasantry too cowed to question the activities of the sinister new nobleman who invariably moved into a district just before a series of violent murders began. Creatures of this sort were able to function freely in my backward land. Meanwhile, behind the walls of the Kremlin and the Winter Palace, playing a game of chess in which the stake was Russia's future, two vampires faced each other, one good, one evil.''

Rasputin clasped his hands together. The knuckles stood out bold and white as he represented the conflict of two opposing powers locked in a death struggle.

''You would not know it from the version of the story that has come to be accepted as historical fact, but I was, at least in relative terms, the good vampire. It was my job to prop up the decrepit Romanov regime in order to save Russia from the even greater disaster of the one that would follow. My foe early on was a vampire named von Plehve, who was in charge of the czar's police. He succeeded in removing my pieces from the chessboard one by one, even after I atomized him.''

''Excuse me?'' I interrupted. ''Atomized?''

''Yes, I atomized him,'' Rasputin repeated. ''He was a beast! When Alexander the Second, Nicholas' father, was assassinated, von Plehve organized the mass execution of thousands, most of whom he knew were completely innocent. With the exceptions of Prince Albert Victor and General von Baden, I have never personally known another vampire who took so much pleasure in murder, although Borgia and his sister are said to be infinitely worse. It got to be so bad that I decided I had no choice but to eliminate him. I arranged for a cell of anarchists to blow him up. The bomb they threw beneath his carriage was so powerful that he was atomized—literally blown to atoms.

''Unfortunately, killing von Plehve wasn't enough to reverse the damage or even slow its advance. Von Plehve's lieutenants had infiltrated the power structure to the degree that it was utterly rotten, like a house with a flame that has been all but consumed by termites, ready to collapse at the first strong wind.

''The irony was that von Plehve and Borgia's other agents would have been better off if they had allowed me to be modestly successful. With moderate reforms, Russia might have continued on as it was for who knows how long. Instead the revolution brought about a police state in which it became impossible to circulate with the freedom that the vampire requires.''

''As a rule, we never involve ourselves directly in mortal

affairs," Mozart said. "When we do, it is usually because the *Illuminati* are trying to counter Borgia. If Borgia and his allies had their way, men and women would become nothing more than cattle, to be fattened for the slaughter. The question is no less than who will rule the world. On the one side are the mortals, who despite their muddled, volatile minds, are slowly progressing toward the dawn of an age of peace and harmony. Helping them, but only when strictly necessary, are the *Illuminati*. And on the other side of the struggle are our vampire rivals, egotistical and haughty beings, who would turn the Earth into a very dark place indeed."

"The odds are by no means in Borgia's favor," Rasputin said. "Russia is a prime example. They ruined Russia for vampires, and for mortals, too, if you ask me."

"But they will never again make the mistakes they made in Russia," Mozart said.

"No. They have abandoned the monarchy model, at least in terms of mortal government, as outmoded for the modern world. They've adopted a totalitarian strategy that is much more efficient, even if they couldn't make it work in the forties."

"With a little better luck they'd have succeeded in Nazi Germany," Mozart said.

"Yes, especially if General von Baden had turned Hitler into a vampire earlier in the war."

"What did you say?" I asked incredulously.

"Surely you have read about how Hitler slept all day and held court over his weary factotums all night?" Rasputin asked, evidently enjoying my amazement.

"Well, yes."

"Did you think it was a simple matter of his liking the night better than the day? He was a *vampire* I'll tell you another secret: The pictures you see of Hitler toward the end of the war? I am thinking in particular of the one of him outdoors in the daylight, pinning medals on the children he put in uniform for the final defense of Berlin."

I nodded.

"That was not Hitler."

"Then, who?"

"His double," Rasputin explained. "After his generals tried to blow him up, his friend von Baden found a man who closely resembled Hitler. General von Baden's plastic surgeon—the same individual who was known to an earlier generation as

Prince Albert Victor by day and Jack the Ripper by night—
turned him into the führer's double.''

"Accurate down to the bridgework in his mouth," Mozart
said.

"Then you mean . . ."

"Exactly. The body carried out of the Berlin bunker and
burned with Eva Braun's was not Hitler."

"And the real Hitler?"

Rasputin sat back in his chair and fixed me with his steely
eyes.

"I killed him with my bare hands in a jungle in Paraguay."

"Hitler received his orders from the same vampire as General
von Baden and Prince Albert Victor," Mozart said.

"Borgia," I said out loud and shuddered to think of the mortal world threatened by a dark force human beings could not,
with their limited understanding, imagine, much less defeat.

Rasputin and Mozart simultaneously nodded.

"And Cesare Borgia," Rasputin said with great bitterness,
"was responsible for bringing down the czar's government and
igniting the revolution that led to the murder of the Romanovs.
It was because of him that I was forced to act against my better
judgment and transform Tatiana into a vampire."

# Chapter 31

JACHENAU, JULY 7, 1989—Rasputin is displeased with me, or so he wants me to believe.

He came into my room at nine o'clock and threw a brass skeleton key on a large metal ring onto my desk.

"Tonight we will see how good your concentration really is. That pass key will get you into any room in the inn. Choose one. It does not matter whether it has an occupant, as long as you do not disturb him or her. I will leave the inn at a quarter after nine and return at half past the hour. When I come back, we shall see how long it takes me to find you."

"A game of hide-and-seek?"

"There is a time for levity and a time for seriousness, David Michaelovich," he said, sounding very much like my father. "With so much depending on your performance, I am surprised I must remind you that this is hardly an appropriate occasion for humor."

"I'm sorry," I offered, but he ignored my apology. Rasputin's attitudes about authority are extremely rigid.

"I know you can conceal yourself from mortals, and you have done well enough masking your presence from our enemies, even though we have helped you. However, you are going to have to do a flawless job if you are to get inside the castle and accomplish your mission."

His eyes drilled into me. I don't think I could have looked away if I had wanted to.

"I want you to use your sharpest concentration to wrap your life force tight around you. Imagine yourself winding a cloak around your body to stay warm in a blizzard. Remember: As *tight* as possible. Let no more of your essence escape than is absolutely unavoidable. Wear your vibration like a second skin, and certainly let it extend no farther than your skin. If they bump into you, they will know you are there, but otherwise you will remain invisible.''

Rasputin gave me a disparaging frown I assumed was meant to embarrass me into performing well during the exercise.

"I will not have any trouble finding you, of course, but I want to see how much additional training you need before Burg Wolfsschanze."

Exactly thirty minutes later Rasputin walked into the room where I was hiding—which happened to be my room, a ploy I thought was rather clever.

"I knew where you were the minute I stepped off the street," he said angrily. "You are going to have to concentrate better than that, my young friend, or your fear that you will be committing suicide by walking into von Baden's lair will prove only too accurate."

"I think I can do better."

"I *know* you can do better," Rasputin said hotly. "You moderns are such weaklings! Force yourself to concentrate with every atom of your being. Kick your intellect in its ass if that is what it needs—or I will kick it for you!"

"You can't speak to me that way!" I said. "I won't be threatened."

"Shut up!" Rasputin yelled.

He moved so quickly that I barely saw him grab my left arm in his massive hand. I tried to pull away, but I could not free myself from the iron grip.

"In my day a student treated his teacher with respect. You are weak, David Michaelovich, but I am going to teach you to be strong. I am not one of your simpering liberal American schoolmasters. You *will* do your lessons *exactly* as I say, and you *will* give me *one-hundred-percent* effort! Mozart and I have gone to a great deal of trouble to orchestrate your education as a vampire. Before the next full moon the criminals Prince Albert Victor and General Von Baden will be dead, and you will have proven your worthiness to the *Illuminati* and to yourself—or else!''

He shoved me toward the door.

"Now get out and see if you can do any better on the streets. I hope to heaven you can, because otherwise our enemies in Burg Wolfsschanze will smell you the moment you're outside the umbrella of protection Mozart and I have put over this inn. Then we all will be in jeopardy, including Tatiana.''

"Perhaps I shouldn't go," I said, suddenly lacking the confidence to take such a risk after being proven inadequate. "Maybe I should spend tonight meditating, and we could try again tomorrow evening."

"Go!" Rasputin roared, and pointed toward the door.

I was more successful in our subsequent exercises. I could not evade Rasputin for long, but at least I was able to keep him from finding me immediately. He finally sent me back to my room an hour ago, pretending he was still angry. I think he was secretly pleased, however, since he actually walked past the alley where I was concealed three times before finding me during our final exercise.

Rasputin is a stern teacher, and not a very pleasant one by my standards, but I am grateful for his effort and sympathize with his unwillingness to accept anything short of maximum effort from me. I have much to learn, and my time is frighteningly short.

*Resuming Rasputin's tale on the train trip to Jachenau . . .*

"To tell you my story correctly, I must start again and begin, as all stories should, at the beginning.

"I was born in a tiny Siberian village called Pokrovskoe, where I lived until I was twenty-three. My mother nearly died delivering me. I nearly died, too. The umbilicus became wrapped around my neck, and when I came out of my mother, big and blue and glistening with blood and afterbirth, the midwife could not get me to breathe. Born dead, she said I was.

"My father knocked the midwife aside and snatched my lifeless body. He threw a blanket around me and, with an ax in one hand, burst through the door and dashed down the narrow streets of our village until he reached the river. He put me down on a snowdrift long enough to chop a hole in the ice. Then, holding me by one leg, he dipped me, head first, into the frigid waters up to his elbow. When he pulled me out, I sputtered and began to wail.

"And so I was born. A dramatic, larger-than-life way to enter this world, and it set a precedent to follow.

"My father named me Grigori Efimovich Novykh. Grigori Efimovich Novykh . . ."

Rasputin cocked his head, listening to the sound his own name made against the background noise of train wheels clicking against the rails.

"A good peasant name. A baby introduced to life with a dunk

in a frozen Siberian river would be strong enough for anything, my father used to say. And he was right. Unlike most of the infants born in my village, I survived childhood and eventually joined my family toiling in the fields on the local lord's estate. Not much of a life, but the only life there was for a child born in a peasant's cottage in Pokrovskoe.

"But I was not like the other peasant children. I always sensed that there was something more.

"One day, when I was fifteen, I saw the local baron carried through the muddy streets of our village in a gilded sedan chair. I spent a great amount of time after that wondering how an accident of birth made my lord's life so much better than my wretched one. There was no answer, of course, though the inequity of the situation began to eat at me until it became an ulcerated sore in my heart, and I found myself dreaming of killing the baron with these two hands. If I'd ever met him alone on the street after dark, I certainly would have done just that and ended up swinging from a gibbet.

"I quelled my youthful anger with the two usual escapes: women and vodka. As it turned out, I had an aptitude for both. I could go glass for glass with any man in the village when I was sixteen, and the wenches in Pokrovskoe all knew that my arms and legs weren't the only unusually large parts of my anatomy. By the time I was eighteen, my prodigious drinking and whoring were legendary throughout the district.

"I was staggering home drunk one night when I ran— literally—into our priest. It hit me like a thunderbolt! It was not rare for men of humble origin to join the priesthood. Our priest— a fat, effeminate fellow who had never put in a day in the beet fields—had an easy life. Had he been less stupid, he might even have won an appointment to church in an actual town.

"I stayed out of the priest's way for a week before going to him to discuss the miraculous spiritual experience that had called me to devote my life to the church. I expected him to be filled with joy at my salvation and the prospect of helping transform the province's biggest sinner into its youngest saint. I was the brightest young man in my district, renowned for my wit, and I thought the church would be glad to have me. I was unschooled but not unschoolable, unlike many better born than I, and easily superior to the usual hysterics and witless younger sons who came to the church looking for a way to continue living in their accustomed fashion after their fathers' inheritances passed on to the eldest brothers.

"I would have made a good priest. I probably would have gone on to become a bishop, even without family or fortune behind me." Rasputin sighed. "It was not meant to be.

"The village priest scoffed at my alleged spiritual rebirth, to my astonishment. I prayed and fasted outside his door for two weeks to demonstrate my faith and determination, but it went for nothing. I appealed to the bishop. He also refused me. I flogged myself with a knotted rope and crawled one hundred times around his cathedral on my knees, until my hands and knees were masses of raw, bleeding flesh.

" 'Suffering is good for the soul,' the good bishop told me. 'Keep this up for a few years, and you may yet get to Heaven.'

"Heaven? My needs were much more practical than that. The sanctimonious faker! Who was he to deny me? He was one of the biggest thieves in the province, with a fifteen-year-old mistress in the village and two bastard children by his so-called housekeeper, who lived with him as openly as a wife. Yet that didn't stop him from holding Grigori Efimovich Novykh up to judgment and finding him wanting."

Rasputin leaned toward me and spoke in a harsh whisper.

"I cursed him. I cursed myself. I even cursed God in my despair. But God did not intend for me to become a priest."

The darkness seemed to grow thicker in the salon car, until there were only Rasputin's eyes and the sound of his voice.

"I bided my time, knowing the opportunity to escape Pokrovskoe would come if I waited long enough.

"One day, a starets came to our village. A starets—there is no exact translation in English or even German—was a wandering holy man indigenous to the Russian steppes. Most belonged to religious orders that existed outside control of the church. These Gypsy monks traveled from village to village, either alone or in small groups, as the spirit moved them. Invested with an apparent unworldliness the general population mistook for holiness, they were the only people in Russia outside the aristocracy who went where they wanted and did what they chose.

"Russia was a superstitious land, a place where even the educated were forever on their guard against the evil eye. A starets—with his long hair, fierce, staring eyes, and unpredictable behavior—was feared as well as revered for the extreme piety evidenced by his unceasing pilgrimage. Neither the church nor the civil authorities would dare lay a hand on a starets."

Rasputin smiled to himself.

"Dostoyevsky understood well what it means to be a starets.

He said in *The Brothers Karamazov*: 'The *starets* is he who takes your soul and will and makes them his. When you select your *starets*, you surrender your will. You give it to him in utter submission, in full renunciation.'

"When the starets left Pokrovskoe, traveling with him was a novice brother: Me.

"I will not strain my credibility by telling you religious conviction had anything to do with my becoming a monk. I wanted to escape village life. My secondary motivation was to make as good a life for myself as I could. I am not ashamed to admit it. Who is any different? In my place and time becoming a monk was the only way to escape a hard life in the fields and an early death. I also hoped to obtain a few luxuries for myself. What man does not?"

Rasputin looked at me, but I said nothing. I was born with every privilege. Who was I to question someone born into abject poverty?

"The starets I first traveled with, Gregor, was mad as the Hatter. He'd once been a blacksmith and had a wife and family somewhere. One day, while shoeing a neighbor's horse, he was kicked in the head. After that he saw visions and heard voices. One of his voices told him to become a starets. Gregor was convinced that all horses were possessed with demons. He traveled aimlessly around the countryside, performing equine exorcisms. And he did quite well for himself. Upon learning their animals were possessed, the frightened owners were usually so delighted to have the devils driven out they would force what little money they had on poor Gregor."

Rasputin laughed deeply in his belly.

"Gregor thought money was Satan's tool. No doubt he was correct. He promptly turned his earnings over to Rasputin to free his soul from the pollution. I, in turn, gave the money away—to saloon keepers and women of the night!

"Gregor and I eventually parted, and I fell in with the Khlysty, a mystical sect that purported to believe sin and subsequent repentance were the only means of achieving salvation. It seemed especially apt that I should help others sin so that they could likewise be redeemed. Our teaching—sin first in order that you may obtain forgiveness—had a certain resonance with the wealthy, debauched merchants who were our principal supporters, along with lonely spinsters anxious for a well-endowed young monk to help them with both halves of the Khlysty prescription for redemption.

"My life was not, however, the endless bacchanal my detractors made it out to be. I actually spent a fair part of my time cloistered in various sects' monasteries. I must emphasize that their libraries, not their sanctuaries, were what attracted me. The libraries in these fortified abbeys were the sole repositories of learning in many parts of the backward country, each a treasure trove for a young man hungry for knowledge after too many years in an almost bookless village. Aristotle, Livy, Heroditus, the mystical Persian poets—all of these wonders became known to me during this period of my life.

"Think, David Michaelovich, of the miracles you found when you were introduced to the world of vampirism. It was no less incredible for me, an intellectually starved child of the steppes, to discover, as if by accident, the greatest minds the world had ever known.

"I was no saint. I am not trying to mislead you. When I became tired of musty manuscripts and the endless echo of monks chanting at all hours of the day and night, I would go on 'pilgrimages' seeking pleasures of an entirely earthly sort. Sometimes alone, sometimes with other Khlysty brothers, I visited the homes of the wealthy and the wellborn, where the vodka flowed freely and my impassioned preaching that sin was the first step on the road to redemption preceded every orgy."

"Chance has always played an important role in my life," Rasputin said.

"It was sheer chance that I saw our baron being carried through the muddy streets in a gilded sedan chair, which, in turn, made me decide to get out of my village at any cost. It was chance that brought Gregor to my village. And it was chance that brought me to the parlor of a wealthy butcher, where I met a mesmerist. The brief experience changed my life.

"In those days the mind's powers were only beginning to be understood. We take it for granted today that the mind can influence one's health. Back then, to propose such an idea was to risk being labeled a witch. Nevertheless this was the notion the mesmerist planted in my head. He had promised the butcher he could cure his insomnia through hypnotism. The promise was fulfilled. Fate intervening, I was invited back to the butcher's for a second party that the mesmerist also attended. Before the evening ended, I'd convinced the mesmerist to teach me his few crude skills.

"I quickly discovered that I had an unusual faculty for hypnotism. And as suspected, I found mesmerism helped me even more easily to take advantage of the rich and gullible.

"News of the starets Rasputin's amazing powers began to circulate throughout the province. Instead of seeking out the best patrons, as had been my habit as a faith healer, the best patrons began to seek out me.

"It was inevitable that I was attracted to Petrograd, where the empire's money and power and the most bewitching beauties congregated, drawn, like bees to pollen, to the royal court of the Romanovs."

"Mysticism was all the rage when I arrived in Petrograd. The close of the nineteenth century saw the blossoming of the great spiritualist movement. Everywhere mediums and occultists sought to bring their patrons into contact with the spirit world. It was, in short, the golden age of the con artist.

"It also was the twilight time for the *ancien régime*. These were the glorious last days of the empire, the final cotillion before the deluge. Petrograd was ripe for Rasputin, and Rasputin, I can assure you, was ready for the decadent pleasures the capital had to offer.

"I had worn many of the rough edges off myself by the time I arrived in Petrograd in 1903. I knew exactly how to go about obtaining the things I coveted most—power, wealth, and beautiful lovers.

"I made it my first order of business to ingratiate myself with a high-ranking Orthodox prelate. I used hypnotism to help him overcome a chronic case of venereal disease, earning his eternal gratitude. He provided me with my introduction to aristocratic society. That was all I needed. I used my powers and charms to the extent that, after only a month in the city, I had made myself all but indispensable to many of the upper bureaucrats, church functionaries, and nobility who hovered around the fringes of the Romanov court, scrambling for what diamond-encrusted crumbs they could find.

"With time the unending banquet Petrograd provided began to stale. A life of constant indulgence is attractive—until you've lived it for very long. Take it from one who knows: Eventually even the most dedicated profligate begins to tire of the game. So it was for me. In short I began to become bored, and boredom frightened me more than anything else. To have attained my highest expectations of my life only to tire of them after a short time smacked of mortality to me—for what was life, I thought, once pleasure had died?

"I decided I had been too long in the capital. What I needed was a pilgrimage to cleanse my spirit and renew my appetites. A month in a monastery library reading Ovid would reawaken my passion.

"However, I did not go to a monastery. One of my mistresses convinced me instead to travel south to Privetnoje, a charming resort town on a strip of land hemmed in between the Black Sea and the Krymskije Gory mountains.

"I still do not know exactly why I decided to go there alone. It was out of character. The only explanation I have is that fate drew me to that town. I stayed alone in a quiet spa where most of the other guests were old enough to be my grandparents. I kept to myself in Privetnoje, sitting up all night to devour the trunk of books I had brought with me.

"The most interesting material I read was by a Jewish doctor in Vienna named Freud. My involvement in hypnotism gave me a natural interest in the mind, and Dr. Freud had proposed a number of startling theories about the subconscious. I would have liked to go to Vienna to study with Freud, and I, in fact, seriously considered doing so. I had the brains, and I had enough gems and gold hidden away that I could have lived comfortably in Vienna for as long as I cared to stay. But I knew the distinguished doctor would want little to do with me, a debauched monk and quack healer who probably was notorious even in Vienna.

"My thinking about Freud started me brooding about my life. I had exceeded even the wildest goals I had set for myself before leaving the Siberian village where I was born, yet I felt as if I were hardly any farther than where I started. I wanted more than anything else to devote my life to the serious scientific study of the human mind, and yet my reputation closed off that avenue to me unless I emigrated to America or some other place with even lower medical standards than Russia. I felt like an explorer who has exhausted his supplies, knowing without doubt that he is halfway to the place where a truly great discovery is to be made.

"I found it all very depressing, and yet, what could I do?

"Early one evening during my second week in Privetnoje I was sitting on the terrace outside the inn, sipping tea and reading a book by William James, when a servant from a nearby estate arrived with a letter from his mistress. It seemed the reputation of Rasputin, the famous mesmerist from Petrograd, was known even in the shadow of the Krymskije Gory.

"It was quite a solicitous letter, and ordinarily it would have pleased my hungry ego. Yet it only served to remind me that I was trapped in the role I'd invented for myself. I had worn the mask of the debauched mystic too long to take it off; its distorted face had become a part of my permanent physiognomy.

"The letter was an invitation to visit a villa halfway up Gora Roman-Kos mountain. The estate was home to a young countess widowed after only three years of marriage. She suffered, the note said, from certain uncontrollable urges. She prayed the starets, with his holy powers, would be able to exorcise the demon that burned within her.

"The innkeeper confided that the countess was a woman of rare beauty whose husband was killed when he fell from his horse while hunting wild boar. After a period of deep mourning she took a lover—then another, and another, and another. The young widow quickly became a figure of high scandal in the district. Then, about six months before my arrival in Privetnoje, she mysteriously retired from society to live as a virtual recluse in her villa. She was scarcely ever seen, and then only at night. Certain things were whispered about the countess, but the innkeeper of course knew none of the details."

"I confess I began to feel familiar perverse desires. I had been away from Petrograd two weeks—meaning I'd gone two weeks without a woman. Besides, there is nothing that tempts a rake as much as a woman of virtue, unless it is a fallen woman returned to virtue.

"The next day I hired a coach and four and set off down the coast to where the Gora Roman-Kos thrusts its stony ramparts up above the other peaks. The thought of what lay ahead made me hungry, and we stopped for a midday meal at a tavern in the village of Alusta. As the tavern keeper served me, I inquired about the Countess Katerina Trifonov, not bothering to mention I was on my way to her villa. The man's first response was to hastily put down the plate of mutton and flagon of wine he was holding and make a sign to protect himself against the evil eye.

" 'She has brought nothing but trouble to Alusta, holy father,' he said.

" 'Whatever do you mean?'

" 'I'd rather not say, holy father. They would not be fitting words for a man such as yourself to hear.'

" 'Do not worry about offending me,' I told him. 'There is no sin I have not seen. And I do have a reason for asking. It's not an official inquiry, however. At least not yet.'

The tavern keeper leaned near.

" 'She has loved many men to death,' he said in a low voice."

" 'Which men?'

" 'It started with her husband. He fell from a horse and was killed. I don't suppose she can be said to have had anything to do with that, except that she brought the poor man bad luck. He was a captain in the dragoons. If any man could ride a horse, it was the count, God rest him.

" 'She was as grief-stricken as any young woman is when her husband dies, but she shocked the district by taking a young officer from her husband's regiment to bed before her period of mourning was even half over. She brought disgrace on her house, and people said it was divine justice when her lover developed a mysterious wasting illness and died after several weeks of enjoying her charms.

" 'I know his story only too well,' the tavern keeper said. 'He had rooms upstairs. This is where he died. I've never seen a strong man fade so fast, holy father. The countess burned him up with her passion, like a paper soldier in the fire.'

" 'Be careful about loose accusations,' I warned. 'You could have your tongue branded for slandering a noblewoman.'

" 'I do no more than speak the truth,' he answered boldly. Like many people of common birth, he had grown tired of indulging the aristocracy and was ready for the confrontation that was beginning to brew throughout the country.

" 'The lieutenant wasn't the last to expire from an excess of her affections, but the first of an even half dozen, by my count,' the tavern keeper continued. 'Do you know what they call her? The Black Widow.'

" 'Tell me about the others,' I asked, fascinated.

" 'Her next lover worked in the fields.'

" 'A peasant?'

" 'Yes. And a friend, so I'll thank you not to make the usual rude remarks. I warned him, but he wouldn't listen. What plain man could ignore the attentions of a beautiful woman of noble birth? It's not often the likes of us gets to make love to a lady.'

"I understood perfectly.

" 'Uri used to come here and play chess with me. Strong as a horse. One night, after they had been together, he was found crawling along the road, pale and weak. He died the next day.

The rest were the same. Found after dawn, and if they weren't already dead, they didn't live to see the noon.'

" 'She loved them to death?'

" 'As surely as the sun comes up in the east. There haven't been others from the village in several months. I don't think there's another man in this town who would dare bed the Black Widow. I understand she preys mostly on travelers now, although I do not know. We used to see her quite a bit, but she almost never leaves her villa now during the day. I warn you to stay away from her, even though you are obviously beyond the temptations of the flesh.'

"I said nothing to make him think otherwise. The tavern keeper slowly wiped his hands on his apron and bent nearer.

" 'They say she is a witch.'

" 'Do you believe that?'

" 'No,' he said, looking at me straight. 'I think that she's something much worse. She stays up on the mountain and almost never comes down, not even for church or to visit her husband's grave. When she's seen at all, it's riding along the road in the night at breakneck speed in her coach. Some say they've seen it, moving to beat the devil, without a driver sitting up top to hold the reins.'

"The tavern keeper crossed himself and repeated the ritual of spitting three times to protect himself against the evil eye.

"I did not—and do not—believe in witches. The tavern keeper's warning only made me more impatient to meet the beautiful Black Widow. She sounded like an intriguing conquest, someone whose reputation was as tarnished as my own. The wine I drank with my mutton made me lusty, and if the innkeeper had had a wench working in his back room, I think I would have had her before leaving to visit the countess. *That* would have given the busybody something to gossip about.

"It was dark by the time we reached Countess Katerina Trifonov's villa. The full moon was rising. I can see it perfectly in my memory, as yellow as butter, illuminating everything in shimmering silver light. I remember laughing to myself about the foolish peasant superstitions linked to the full moon. Witches, hobgoblins, and monsters—all imaginary products of the mythic unconscious, I thought.

"The villa was halfway up the mountainside. It was one of those magnificent country palaces the Red commissars rushed to claim as their summer dachas after the revolution. Despite its expansive luxury there was an unmistakable air of neglect about the place. It was as if the estate's masters had gone to the capital for the season, leaving the property in the hands of an unfaithful caretaker who had gone on a drunk, dismissed the staff, and completely ignored the considerable daily work needed to keep such a residence in good repair.

"The front lawn was a sweeping vista that flowed down from the white limestone great house to a distant cliff overlook. I looked out the carriage window as we drove up the long private lane to the formal entry and saw that the grass was knee-high; the tops of the stalks were heavy with seed as they waved in the gentle night breeze.

"Weeds competed with flowers in the gardens nearer the villa and grew up amid the spaces between the cobblestones in the drive. In front of the house a summer storm had split a branch from a massive oak. It lay pointing down at an unnatural angle, still attached to the main trunk by a twisted section of bark and splintered wood. The mishap evidently had occurred some time before—the leaves on the broken branch were brown and dead— yet the damage had been left unrepaired.

"No servants came out to meet us as we pulled up in front of the main entry and I decamped. The coachman, taking in the absence of the usual footmen and the general atmosphere, grabbed the gold coin from my hand, hastily turned the horses around, and fled, using his whip.

"I suppose I might have shared my driver's apprehension, but I was too filled with smug certainty that I understood the situation. I was not ruled by superstition; just the opposite, in fact: I, the Khlysty faith healer, had made it my business to prey upon the superstitions of others.

"I had in my mind a picture of the woman who had summoned me. She would be the image of innocence, with just the hint of whore about the way she frankly appraised me with her wounded eyes. A bawd who had ruined many men, she would not be shy once we got beyond the usual formalities. Yet, at the same time I expected there was a worm of guilt turning inside her heart: the chaste insect was the agent that had turned her into a repentant sinner—though still troubled enough by her 'urges' to seek my help.

"The only light in the villa was a dim one from a distant inner room. I climbed the front steps, lifted the heavy iron knocker, and rapped on the door. No answer. I repeated my action.

" 'Hello!' called a voice from the distance somewhere behind me. I turned to see a woman emerging from the trees, carrying the sort of basket used to gather wildflowers. As she drew nearer, I saw that that was exactly what she had been doing: gathering wildflowers in the forest at night by moonlight. A peculiar thing to be doing, I thought. Even today there are wolves in the Krymskije Gory mountains.

"When she came close enough to me to see her face, I realized that the countess was one of the most enchanting women I had ever seen. I found myself instantly infatuated with her. I shall try to describe her to you," Rasputin told us, "even though words are inadequate to relate her rare beauty.

"Today women prefer to have tanned skin, but in those days only peasants who labored all day beneath the sun had bronzed bodies. Ladies had fair skin. The countess's skin was more than fair: It was a creamy white alabaster that seemed to be almost translucent. But not her lips: They were the deep reddish purple of fully ripened cherries. I had to restrain myself from an impulse to take her in my arms and press my mouth against hers as she led me into the darkened villa.

"Her mother was German, she told me, and she had inherited her mother's rich blond hair, which she wore long. Her eyes were the iridescent shade of blue you see when you look at the western sky at dusk, painted by the dying day just between the black of night and the red corona left behind by the sun. She was a tall woman, standing a full six feet, but with long, delicate bones and smallish breasts that kept her height from detracting from her femininity. Indeed her stature greatly enhanced her beauty. I have never been attracted to small women.

"We sat together on a sofa in front of a small fire in a salon's massive stone fireplace. It was the only illumination in the room, and it reflected in her eyes, making it necessary to study her face closely to follow her expressive features, which told me as much as the words that fell like petals from her rosebud mouth.

"Countess Katerina Trifonov had heard of my powers as a healer, but she had also heard other stories about me. A friend in Petrograd wrote her that I once had stayed up all night long satisfying a dozen women in a brothel.

"I usually have no trouble understanding what someone is trying to say, even when the intention is at odds with the words, but I was unable to guess the intent of the lovely woman sitting so close to me that I could feel the heat of her body against mine. Was she reproaching me or offering me an invitation? Both, perhaps. I could not read her.

" 'One hears many stories in Petrograd,' I said, deciding to be evasive. 'In the capital, one has friends as well as enemies. Both tend to be equally interested in gossip.'

"She smiled and said she did not doubt the stories she'd heard about the starets were true. She seemed to be impressed with me. I guessed she was attracted to me because she believed I had experienced something like her own struggle between the sacred and profane.

" 'I invited you here, Rasputin, because I think you can help me.'

"I promised sincerely to try.

" 'I must confess something to you,' she said. 'Since my husband died, I have been subject to unmentionable urges.'

" 'So you wrote me,' I said, smelling the perfume she'd put on her neck and wanting to lick it off. 'We all have such urges. The flesh is powerful.'

" 'No one knows that more than I.'

"She rearranged her hands in her lap.

" 'There are two ways you might help me, Rasputin.'

"I nodded for her to continue.

" 'We could get down on our knees together and pray.'

" 'Yes, we could.'

" 'Or we could . . .' Her eyes were smouldering when she raised them to meet mine. 'As I said, there are two ways you can help me,' she repeated.

"I said nothing to discourage her but kept my eyes locked onto hers. I felt no weakness in her will but, to the contrary, an unusual strength that I had seldom encountered.

" 'My question, my dear Rasputin,' the countess said, moving her face almost imperceptibly nearer to mine, 'is which is the stronger in you: the debauchee or the holy man?'

"I slipped my fingers into her hair and drew her gently toward me, looking down into her half-closed eyes, lowering myself toward her mouth.

" 'I will show you the force that controls Rasputin,' I said, and kissed her.

"Katerina Trifonov was the only woman I'd ever known who could match me in bed. No, I must confess that is a boast. She was more than my match. We gave each other pleasure many times, but when I finally fell back on the sweat-soaked sheets just before dawn, more exhausted than I'd ever been in my life, her gasps for breath quickly turned into pants of renewed desire.

"When she climbed on top of me, I felt a moment of panic: I knew I was not physically capable of continuing, not without rest. The countess put her hands on my chest and, moving her hips against mine, looked into my eyes with hers, which seemed to glow red in the candle-lit bedchamber. To my amazement I felt myself stir beneath her writhing body. She was using *her* mind to control *mine*!

"No wonder she had taken the trouble to learn so much about me: She, too, was a mesmerist! I burst into laughter. This was a woman of my own kind, one who could match me move for move, trick for trick—the first woman I'd ever met I could say that about. She *was* my equal."

Rasputin lapsed into silence and stared out the window.

"I knew at that moment that I loved her," he said, still following the moving shadows outside our train.

He glanced at me, then at Mozart, and back again.

"I decided it was my turn. I narrowed my eyes and reached into her mind.

*"Slam!"* Rasputin said loudly and clapped his hands together, making me jump in my seat. "It was like a steel door slamming shut. Katerina Trifonov had shut herself off from my suggestion just as quickly as that. She had not only resisted it, but, it seemed, knew what I was trying to do before I did it. Her power of mind was frightening. I was used to being in control, but there was no question that she had a considerable advantage on me.

"Countess Katerina Trifonov smiled down at me, still rocking back and forth, back and forth, with a rhythm that took the sharpest edge off my panic. Her eyes remained locked on mine, and then she began to smile in a curious way. I felt my spine stiffen as my arms and legs slowly extended until I was spread-eagled beneath her gyrating body. My joints were locked, and while my mind was perfectly conscious, I was unable to move or cry out or resist in any way. Her mind was *that* powerful. I was that helpless.

"I watched with mounting horror as Katerina Trifonov's lips parted and two gleaming blood teeth slipped down from their cavities inside her upper gum. At that moment I thought the tavern keeper had been only part right: The countess was something much worse than a witch.

"Still she rocked her body against mine, back and forth, back and forth. I experienced the most unusual mingling of sensations: sexual pleasure mounting toward climax; primordial terror; love; the dread fear that I was about to die at the hands of a beautiful monster. At once wonderful and terrible, it remains the single most remarkable experience of my entire life.

"Countess Katerina Trifonov moved her body more quickly against mine. We were getting very close, and our breathing came in short gasps. She thrust her sweat-soaked body next to mine with frantic urgency, running her tongue up and down the side of my neck.

"An explosion of pleasure that seemed to vibrate every cell of my body shook through me. But it didn't stop. My rapture soared higher and higher, far beyond the limit of anything I'd ever experienced.

"It was at that moment that I became aware my blood was spurting into her mouth from the wound she had bitten in my neck during our mutual climax.

"I didn't care. As my body went slack, I felt myself carried away on a warm stream of the most indescribable bliss, a river that flowed toward a pool of darkness, where my consciousness grew dimmer and dimmer until nothing remained but the sound of our two hearts beating together."

# Chapter 32

**J**ACHENAU, JULY 8, 1989—I have not seen Rasputin or Mozart since last night. Their rooms were empty when I looked for them earlier this evening. The concierge said they were gone when she came on duty, meaning they went out before sunset.

I think I would rely less upon their strength if I were more self-assured about my own powers, which are insignificant next to theirs. I've been practicing hard. I must waste no opportunity to sharpen my skills. I'm a stranger in a strange land—and the strangest time of all is yet to come.

It's four in the morning. The sun will rise soon.

I've mastered my latest exercise. The object is to remain completely calm and pay the closest possible attention to whatever it is I'm doing—which in this case was levitating a four-hundred-pound walnut dresser around the room using nothing more than the force of my mind.

Rasputin said it's like baking bread: You pay attention to the ingredients, don't hurry, and mix everything exactly right. If I'd let my attention wander or failed to maintain the correct mental attitude—which Rasputin describes as being "a fire burning so pure, it creates no smoke and leaves no ashes"—I would have sent the dresser crashing through the ceiling of the room below.

I've also made good progress in learning to hide my presence. The maid came into my room earlier and looked straight through me. Of course deluding a mortal is hardly an impressive feat. However, last night I walked into the reading room downstairs without Mozart noticing—or at least he pretended not to notice.

My practice has left me tired and ready for sleep. I'll work on my journal for another hour, and then to bed.

\* \* \*

*Rasputin:*

"The countess had invited me to her villa to be her lover—and her victim. But when she realized, as did I, how perfectly we were suited to each other, she decided to transform her 'holy satyr' into a vampire so that I could be with her forever.

"Countess Katerina Trifonov had been a vampire less than a year when we met. She had not adapted well to the life. With very clear tendencies toward what Freud would have described as nymphomania, she was unable to keep herself from being carried away by the sensuality of feeding. She had met a handsome Gypsy after her husband's death, and he gave her the gift of vampirey. She became death's agent, spreading his shadow wherever she went. She inevitably took men as lovers but left them as corpses.

"When I emerged from the transformation weak and hungry, I experienced the customary horror. Katerina Trifonov could do nothing to reassure me. She was less than ideal as a teacher for a novice vampire; in fact, the only way she could have been worse was if she had been openly evil, a point she had yet to reach. Despite my character flaws, I had never been cruel, and I could not imagine myself killing every fortnight.

"During my first feeding—in the midst of an orgy the countess arranged with the assistance of two young maidens from the village—I somehow perceived that I required but a small amount of blood to meet my needs. Like other vampires who possess the necessary degree of self-control, I intuitively understood why it was best to leave my hosts without permanent injury.

"But Katerina Trifonov had no such control, nor could she be made to understand the risks she took.

"By the time she unfastened herself from the neck of the girl she had taken first to show me how, the poor girl was as white as milk and completely lifeless. I had taken but a little blood from my girl, after putting her into a trance so that she didn't even know what I'd done to her. When Katerina Trifonov saw the girl in my arms was still living after I'd taken what I needed, she forced her naked body between mine and the girl's and bit into the helpless young woman's neck with a savagery that shocked and repulsed me. She sucked in the poor girl's blood greedily, as if she had found water after being lost in a desert for many days without drink. She did not stop until the second girl was as dead as the first."

A shadow of the horror showed in Rasputin's eyes as the train passed by a lonely farmhouse and the lights around the outbuildings momentarily illuminated our railroad car.

"When I asked her why she needlessly killed, she only laughed.

"I stayed with Countess Katerina Trifonov nearly six months, learning what I could, trying without success to convince her to moderate her behavior. I would not have stayed so long, except that I thought I could change her, although her fate was easy to see every time I looked into her eyes."

Rasputin shrugged.

"Love makes you do irrational things.

"I tried to convince her we should return to Petrograd, that it was foolish to remain at her estate, where the superstitious peasants had little better to do than relate rumors about the mysterious Black Widow. They already called her a witch, and I knew it was only a matter of time before they became frightened enough to take action, especially if the countess continued to seduce and murder the most handsome young men—and women—in the province.

"She refused to listen," Rasputin said, smiling sadly. "Katerina Trifonov was an enigma. I found her both fascinating and frustrating. I had at last met a woman who was my equal in life and love, but I was totally unable to make her see the end that was coming. She was the one woman I have ever loved, and yet the powerful Rasputin was powerless to save her from her own self-destructive tendencies."

The giant Russian sat in silence for a moment, as if still pondering the baffling Countess Katerina Trifonov ninety years after he had known her.

"When we made love, she spoke of dying in my arms and the killing bliss of our shared pleasure. She had a morbid fascination for the dead. She would spend hours in graveyards, wandering among the tombstones, reading the sad inscriptions and weeping over them. I once saw her linger over the corpse of a victim, stroking his cheek as if she were enthralled with the inexplicable disappearance of the life force from the empty and useless husk of a human being.

"Katerina Trifonov was in love with death. Sex and love and death had become so woven together in her mind that she could no longer separate the three intertwining strands in order to let go of the one that was dragging her toward the grave.

"It was hard to leave her. I learned several months later that a mob had burned her to death in her villa. I suppose she was fortunate, in a way, to have come to such an end. It was what she wanted. Besides, she was much inclined toward the dark side of vampirey; it would have taken little coaxing for her to have surrendered to the narcotic of unbridled evil. She was already more than halfway there. I have no doubt she would have already fallen in with Borgia by the time I knew her if she hadn't lived in such a remote part of the country.''

Rasputin looked at me with baleful eyes.

''And so you see, David Michaelovich, love between two vampires does not always have a happy resolution.''

''I returned to Petrograd, where life proved easy for a vampire.

''The sick still came to Rasputin to be healed, and my new powers proved surprisingly effective. I had unexpected successes with illnesses that had always resisted treatment with mesmerism.

''The power to do good was a wonderful tonic. It filled me with a spiritual energy that turned me away from the dark side of vampirey and burned away the lust for money and power that had fogged my soul for so long.

''It was a snowy night in early November when a royal emissary summoned me to the palace for a medical emergency.

''Before I was introduced to the patient, the man who had been sent to fetch me, a cossack captain in the imperial guard, made me take a formal oath of secrecy concerning the nature of my visit, my patient, and my patient's illness. If so much as one word of it were whispered outside the palace, he threatened, I would learn for myself why enemy soldiers preferred to kill themselves rather than fall prisoner to cossack troops.

''With so much secrecy I expected the patient to be the czar. It was, in fact, his child, the Tsarevich Alexis Nicolaievich, Grand Duke of Russia and Sovereign Heir. Little Alexis Nicolaievich was Czar Nicholas and Czarina Alexandra's only son and first in line to the throne after his father. The Romanov dynasty's future ultimately depended upon the boy.

''Alexis Nicolaievich suffered from the bleeding disease, hemophilia. A genetic imperfection had left his body unable to manufacture the clotting factors that stop wounds from bleeding. The smallest paper cut can turn into a fatal hemorrhage for a hemophiliac, and the ordinary bumps and falls that are part of growing up can become agonizing, life-threatening injuries, with the body incapable of controlling the internal bleeding.

"I was uncertain whether I could provide any relief to the poor child. The bleeding disease was not uncommon in European royalty, due to the interbreeding that tended to bring out the worst traits—witness England's Prince Albert Victor. There was no known cure for the disease, and its unfortunate victims rarely lived to adulthood.

"Czar Nicholas was skeptical that I could help his son, and it required only a glance into his mind to know he had argued against summoning me. It was the boy's mother who had decided to see if Rasputin could help. Czarina Alexandra was desperate to help her child—so desperate that she was willing to turn to the disreputable starets for help when the court physicians failed to ease her child's misery.

"Historians have painted a picture of the Czarina as an unstable neurotic who lacked the capacity to understand the difference between a faith healer and a legitimate doctor. Nothing could have been further from the truth. Alexandra was a rational, sober woman. She did what any other mother with a sick child would do under similar circumstances.

"The czar stood in the shadows, frowning while the boy's mother explained her son's condition.

"I insisted on seeing the boy alone. He was in bed in great pain. One leg, which he had bumped, leading to the current crisis, was elevated on a pillow and wrapped with cold, wet towels, which seemed at least consistent with good common sense. You never knew what to expect in those days, when the doctors were often worse than the quacks.

"I told the boy to look into my eyes. I began to tell him a long story about a youth who went into the forest alone to search for a wolf that had been killing his family's sheep. Gradually the child began to relax. I spoke in a low, hypnotic voice, using my skills as a mesmerist and vampire to put suggestions into his mind. The tension went out of his small face. He fell asleep before I finished my story.

" 'I do not know whether I have helped your son, or whether I can help him,' I told Czarina Alexandra. 'I was, however, able to ease his suffering, and he's sleeping now. Please call me again if I can be of any assistance whatsoever.'

"Czarina Alexandra was effusively thankful. One of her court functionaries tried to force a bag of gold coins on me, but I refused. Which was a mistake, of course. In refusing payment, I'd insulted the incompetent court doctors, who'd been only too happy to enrich themselves in the employment of the crown.

They immediately started a rumor that I was going to hold the royal family up for a great ransom the next time they called on me to help Alexis Nicholaievich. They couldn't have been more wrong. I never accepted a single ruble from the family.

"Before I left the palace, the czar's chamberlain explained in the indirect language of diplomacy what I already knew. With the empire teetering on the brink of dissolution, the perilous condition of the tsarevich's health was among the government's most carefully guarded secrets. The boy was the heir to the throne, and without him, the Romanov dynasty's already dim future became dark indeed.

"I promised again to be discreet. The next night a coach bearing the Romanov coat of arms arrived at my door and took me again to the palace to see Alexis Nicolaievich, who was much improved and insisted on hearing the end of my story about the boy and the wolf.

"My success treating Alexis Nicolaievich made me an instant member of the Romanov inner circle. I visited the palace every evening, and when they traveled, I traveled, too.

"In a country ruled by an emperor, even proximity to the king brings with it incalculable power. Serving as the tsarevich's personal medical adviser made me overnight one of the most important individuals in the empire. I could no longer go out in public without petitioners trying to bestow upon me gold and jewels and every imaginable favor for the mere chance that I might help them gain the czar's ear.

"Unlike most others at court, my intimacy with the royal family was not a commodity I was willing to sell. I refused to let myself become a tool in one faction's intrigues against another's. I realize now it was a mistake to have refused these bribes. It would have been more prudent to accept a few gratuities to make it seem as if I were accessible, and then do as little as possible to advance the sponsors' causes. But I was new at politics, and in behaving in an honorable and honest fashion, I made a grave error. Rather than passing myself off as a cog in the corrupt engine of the empire, I had behaved in a way that drew attention to myself.

"I found it difficult to keep one step ahead of the sudden crop of enemies that grew up around me after I became a casual member of the Romanov court. And once the evil vampires in Petrograd joined forces with the aristocrats who sought to eliminate me, it became inevitable that I would be defeated. If only the *Illuminati* had been there to help—but that was a time when the *Illuminati* had been driven from the East, and I had yet to make their acquaintance.

"Von Plehve vowed to destroy me. Everywhere I looked I began to see vampires lurking in the palace corridors, shadowing my movements; not one of them with so much as a demitasse of goodness in him. The only way to find allies of my own race, it seemed, would be to manufacture them, which I was reluctant to do for all the obvious reasons."

Rasputin's eyes fastened on to mine.

"I resisted doing this until very near the end, when my only hope of saving the tsarevich required me to transform a young girl." He was talking about Tatiana, I knew; I was finally beginning to see how it had all happened such a long time ago.

"The struggle continued even after I'd eliminated von Plehve. The creature who assumed von Plehve's role—after personally murdering a handful of his rivals—was Archduke Dimitri Pavlovich. And Dimitri Pavlovich was every bit as evil as his predecessor and more dangerous because of the privilege afforded him by his royal blood."

"In treating Alexis Nicolaievich, I simply followed my instinct and was lucky enough to have some success.

"The illness caused great suffering, and controlling pain is one area where hypnotism can be more effective than drugs. I was able to provide the tsarevich with relief, which, while it didn't stop the bleeding, relieved the stress and made recovery easier. I also discovered, in working with the child over time, that his mind could be used to actually stop his bleeding. He could not do it on his own, of course, but working with me, deep in a hypnotic trance, he could use my suggestions to reduce circulation in the affected area, gradually closing the capillaries until the flow of blood was arrested.

"The irony of the situation did not escape me," Rasputin said with a bitter laugh. "I, a vampire, was responsible for the health of a boy whose body bled at the slightest provocation. Forgive my mysticism—it's part of the Russian soul—but I cannot help but observe the striking symmetry that we sometimes discover in our lives. It was as if there was a balance that brought the blood-drinking monk and the boy with the bleeding disease together so that the one could help the other."

"Through all of this the political situation in the country rapidly deteriorated. It became increasingly plain to me that the

Romanovs were doomed. If I had the mental control I do today, I might have changed the course of history, saving the czar and his family and the millions who perished during the revolution and in Stalin's purges. But I failed.''

Rasputin sank back into his seat. I listened to the sound of the rails beneath the train. He looked too depressed to continue his story, but presently he gathered his energy and went on.

''I made treating Alexis Nicolaievich my entire reason for being. Countless times I stopped his terrible bleeding at the last possible moment before it would have been fatal—while all around us the nation bled. The secret that continued to elude me was how to stop the bleeding *before* it began. This, I thought, was the key. If I could do that, little Alexis Nicolaievich would live to be a man—in whichever country his family went into exile.

''I left no stone unturned in my search for a cure. A locked room in the basement of the palace became my private laboratory. I retreated there to work on my research into blood and blood abnormalities, sometimes staying up a week at a time without sleep, working in the subterranean chamber.

''What was it that kept the tsarevich's blood from clotting? It seemed obvious the boy's blood lacked some vital ingredient— an insight that came from knowing my own vampire's blood was deficient in some substance that made it necessary for me to drink raw human blood every two weeks.

''I made more than a few discoveries. I was years ahead of other researchers. My findings defined the early limits of hematology. I later leaked my data to deserving mortal colleagues, letting them claim the advances as their own, much as Mozart has done with his insights into quantum mechanics.

''Although the breakthrough I sought continued to elude me, the work was intellectually exhilarating. Microscopes did not exist at that time sufficient for my needs, so I spent several weeks learning about optics and designing my own. As I bent over the instrument of my design and manufacture to look at living blood cells swimming before my eyes, I witnessed things I knew no mortal eyes had ever seen. It was as though I were lifting the lid of life itself and peering inside. I was unraveling secrets known to God alone.

''If I only had sufficient time, I thought, I would make the discovery that would enable me to cure Alexis Nicolaievich.''

\* \* \*

"It was easy for Archduke Dimitri Pavlovich to enlist young aristocrats in his death plot against me. They all were shocked to see someone of common birth wielding such apparent power with Czar Nicholas and Czarina Alexandra. And all the while these idiots were bickering with each other about who would sit closest to the czar and how to best murder the debauched monk Rasputin, their real enemies—the revolutionaries—were planning to take over the country and put us all in front of firing squads.

"I watched the two groups of conspirators' rings being drawn ever tighter, one around me, one around the czar and the entire aristocracy.

"The czar recognized the many threats confronting him. I know because I had many long talks with him. He realized that the incompetent aristocracy had failed the country, and that rabid lunatics like Vladimir Ilyich Lenin waited in the wings, salivating for the opportunity to return to Russia and institute a reign of terror against the upper classes that would make what the French did with the guillotine after their revolution seem mild in comparison. The czar tried his best to steer a course amid these killing rocks, but whichever way he turned, a new and more deadly obstacle sprang up.

"Czar Nicholas went to the front to take command from his worthless generals in September of 1915, but it was already too late. He was a good man. He was ill-served. Left alone, he would have seen what needed to be done, and, I believe, done it.

"I remained in the capital with the Czarina and Alexis Nicolaievich. Czarina Alexandra had very little talent for public administration, I must admit, and she found herself increasingly surrounded by the parasites who are always present in a royal court but who become especially noxious during times of war, ever ready to take a profit where there is one to be taken.

"Things began to fall apart quickly. Food and wage strikes became common in the cities. Archduke Dimitri Pavlovich commanded the garrison in Petrograd—keeping himself far from the fighting and close to the sensual pleasures of society, in the tradition established by his master in Italy. When the strikes reached the capital, Dimitri Pavlovich called out the cossacks to put down the protest. It was the worst thing he could have done, both for our country and for our secret race. Using shock troops against unarmed civilians was the final blow. Troops mutinied and joined the workers. The revolution began in earnest, and in the end, the totalitarian state it brought into being proved as hostile to vampires as it did to aristocrats.

"Not long before the cossack massacre, I had tried to convince Czar Nicholas to abdicate, to keep the country from completely disintegrating.

"He refused, brave to the end, although I came this close to getting him to agree," Rasputin said, holding his thumb and forefinger a fraction of an inch apart.

"I think I might have eventually succeeded, if Dimitri Pavlovich hadn't managed to persuade a group of mortals that their only hope of saving the czar was to kill Rasputin."

# Chapter 33

**J**ACHENAU, JULY 9, 1989—Rasputin told me tomorrow is *the* day. I suppose I'm as ready as I will ever be. I hope, for the sake of Tatiana and the others, that I'm equal to the task.

Mozart asked me if I felt sufficiently prepared for Burg Wolfsschanze. That is the kind of friend he is: always courteous, thinking of my well-being. Rasputin, who has been in charge of this phase of my education, burst into laughter before I could answer, slapped me on the back and said that of course I was ready.

"It's simply a matter of focusing yourself," Rasputin said. "As Dr. Johnson so eloquently put it, 'The knowledge that he is to be hanged in the morning concentrates a man's mind wonderfully.' I imagine your mind will be *quite* concentrated, David Michaelovich!"

Mozart started to frown, but I have grown used to the Russian's sense of humor and found it easy to laugh at his joke. When Mozart saw I was not offended, he joined in the general amusement.

Rasputin had brought a bottle of Stolichnaya to my room. He poured drinks, and the three of us relaxed for the first time since meeting in Paris. Mozart and Rasputin are the wittiest characters I have ever had a drink with, and the jokes and stories they told made me laugh so much that I had no opportunity to worry about the Ripper and General von Baden. Which was no doubt as they intended.

Toward midnight we went downstairs and sang German drinking songs, with Mozart at the piano, acting a little drunk for the benefit of the mortals who watched us finish off the Stoli. Before I said good-night, Mozart asked me to play the piece I was to have ready for him in Paris.

I hadn't played in days, and my fingers were as stiff as if I'd just come in after an hour in the cold without gloves. Somehow, though, I managed to play the piece without embarrassing myself. To my surprise and joy Mozart actually liked it!

If only Tatiana were here, my happiness would be complete.

The last thing I have to finish in my journal is the entry on Rasputin's tale. I shall complete it before I go to sleep—if I can sleep, knowing what will start tomorrow.

I'm leaving this journal here in my room, along with a note to Mozart asking him to pass it on to Tatiana if I do not return from Wolfsschanze castle.

If neither Tatiana nor I make it, Mozart may burn it or do whatever he pleases with these notes on the life of a novice vampire.

*Rasputin:*

"The funny thing about what happened—although it wasn't really funny at all, of course—was that Archduke Dimitri Pavlovich succeeded only because I knew what he was up to and thought I could beat him at his own game.

"I was ready for a confrontation—*too* ready. I let my ego get the better of me, and in doing so allowed myself to be crudely manipulated in a plot that should have had no chance whatsoever of succeeding.

"Never let emotions get in the way of your intellect, David Michaelovich," Rasputin told me. "It is the surest way I know of to manufacture trouble for yourself."

Our train pulled into a station. The sign outside the window was in German. We were at the border. All of the other passengers in the observation car departed; after they shuffled out, a sleepy policeman entered. He glanced briefly at each of our passports, returning them with a polite *danke*.

We would remain in the station another twenty-eight minutes, the policeman told us, Mozart acting as translator. It struck me as odd, the characteristic German preoccupation with exactitude, that the policeman should say the train was leaving in twenty-eight minutes, instead of a half an hour or about a half an hour.

We were completely alone in the car, the three of us, after the policeman left. Mozart and I both politely waited for Rasputin to resume his story.

"Knowing Dimitri Pavlovich's arrogance, I assumed he would

want the pleasure of defeating me personally—of course with the necessary reinforcements to ensure it was I, and not he, who ended up dead. I already knew my powers were greater than his or his subordinates', and I was sure the vampires could not harm me.

"I couldn't have been more mistaken. In one of his few moments of true inspiration, Dimitri Pavlovich devised an assassination plot that involved only mortals. It was the last thing I expected, and it was so inelegant, so undeserving of our rivalry, that it surprised me enough to succeed in part.

"Prince Felix Yusupov was put in charge of the conspiracy. The archduke told Prince Felix that he, Felix, would be put on the throne once the hopeless czar was out of the way. But before the czar could be forced out, the power behind the czar—Rasputin—had to be removed.

"Prince Felix invited me to Moika Palace, using his wife, Princess Irina, to bait the trap. I had never met the princess, who was one the most beautiful women in the empire, and Prince Felix believed I would be unable to pass up the opportunity to meet her. His invitation called for me to arrive at midnight to have tea with the princess after she returned from a ball.

"Dr. Lazovert, one of the conspirators, was sent to pick me up in an open car. Dr. Lazovert—whom I had met on several occasions—arrived at my apartments disguised as a chauffeur, complete with uniform and false mustache—as if I wouldn't know him!

"I wore my costume, too, dressed as the striking, mysterious starets. My beard and hair were quite long then, and I wore my best embroidered shirt and black satin trousers tucked into the top of riding boots. I looked like Satan's own emissary—and I could see from the look in Dr. Lazovert's eyes that my appearance was as intimidating as ever.

"I sat alone in the backseat, wrapped in my cloak, while Dr. Lazovert drove me through the mostly deserted streets of Petrograd, with snow swirling through the darkness. He left me at the door of Moika Palace.

"The doorman admitted me, and a servant led me down into Prince Felix's cellar. This was no ordinary cellar, but a luxurious place, Gothic in design, that had been done over to serve as the site of drinking parties for the prince and his blue-blooded friends. The ceiling was low and vaulted, with stone-block walls and polished granite floors. Huge logs burned brightly in the massive fireplace. Bearskins and Persian rugs covered the floor.

"Along one wall stood a beautifully inlaid ebony cabinet of sixteenth century Italian design, a cabinet I had heard contained secret compartments where Prince Felix concealed his opium. I could smell the narcotic quite plainly, the aroma something between the smell of hot tar and rotting flowers. Bottles and glasses were arranged on the cabinet and, on its raised center, a single adornment: a gold crucifix.

In the middle of the room was a table holding a steaming samovar of tea and cakes laid out to appeal to my sweet tooth. I could smell the poison in the food, and saw the unburned part of one of the rubber gloves Dr. Lazovert had used while handling the deadly substance sizzling on the hearth.

Dr. Lazovert, whose expertise as a poisoner was well known (I later learned Dimitri Pavlovich had arranged for him to be tutored by Lucrezia Borgia herself), had been engaged by Prince Felix to engineer my death by dosing the tea cakes with cyanide.

"Poison didn't fit in with Dimitri Pavlovich's typically violent way of doing things. The poison might mean the archduke was not going to attend our little party, I thought, but in the end I decided the cyanide was part of the vampire's effort to delude Prince Felix.

"Prince Felix greeted me warmly and led me to the table with the treats, explaining that we would have to wait for the princess to return from the ball. I looked around curiously, wondering when Dimitri Pavlovich would arrive. Although I detected the presence of others upstairs, all were mortals.

"Prince Felix casually offered me refreshment. I refused. I had not been poisoned before with cyanide, and I didn't think it wise to take needless chances. The prince, however, became insistent. He picked up the silver tray and held it toward me, urging me to eat.

" 'Rasputin, my friend,' he said, 'I know these tea cakes are your favorite. I will be most insulted if you don't try one. I had them prepared especially for you.'

"Yes, I knew he had.

"I impulsively snatched up one of the poisoned tea cakes and devoured it in two bites.

"The cyanide made my stomach tingle, but the sensation quickly passed. I smiled angrily at Prince Felix. He took a step backward and withered visibly. He unsteadily put down the tray and offered me wine. I took up the decanter and poured myself a glass of Madeira. There was cyanide in the wine, too.

" 'No, it's not my drink!' the prince said a little too loudly and stopped me from pouring him a glass of Madeira. It was a farce, really. Prince Felix's reaction would have made even the most stupid person suspicious that there was something in the Madeira, but I pretended to notice nothing unusual. Instead of drinking wine, he nervously fixed himself a large vodka from a decanter behind the other bottles.

" 'To our mutual good health,' I said, toasting the prince. I fixed him with my eyes as I drank down the wine, releasing him from my stare only when I saw him sway and knew that he was about to faint with fear. I helped myself to a second glass of poisoned wine and settled into one of the chairs.

"My eyes kept going to the stairs, looking for Dimitri Pavlovich, but still Prince Felix and I remained alone together in the cellar. I was beginning to get irritated. I had not come to Moika Palace to demonstrate my powers to a harmless mortal clown.

"To relieve some of the tension in the air, I finally asked him to play some Gypsy songs for me while we awaited Princess Irina. He was notoriously conceited about his abilities as a musician, yet his hands were shaking so badly when he took up his flamenco guitar that he could hardly play. We sat in the cellar for more than two hours while Prince Felix sang every Gypsy love song he knew, waiting in vain for the poison to take hold and kill me. Meanwhile I drank up the Madeira and ate all the tea cakes, which actually were quite tasty, with a distinctive almond flavoring from the cyanide.

"I watched Prince Felix's agitation grow with each minute that passed, until at last it became more than he could bear. Abruptly excusing himself, he nearly threw down the guitar and dashed upstairs to meet with his fellow conspirators. I reached out with my senses. The vibrations were indistinct, but I knew that Archduke Dimitri Pavlovich was not in the palace.

"Dr. Lazovert was so frightened at the news that the poison had failed to harm me that he fell to the floor in a swoon. Brave assassins! When he was revived with smelling salts, the doctor and Prince Felix decided they had already had quite enough of the affair. Vladimir Purishkevich, a wealthy arms merchant who was in on the plot, was the only one of them who had the nerve to continue. He had a Browning revolver with him, and he forced it on the reluctant prince.

"I was standing in front of the ebony cabinet when Prince Felix returned to the basement, my back toward him to hide my

rage. A gun! How dare he presume that something as insignificant as a gun could stop the vampire Rasputin!

"'Grigori Efimovich, you had better look at that crucifix and
say a prayer,' Prince Felix said, his voice shaking and high-
pitched from fear.

"I should have made him turn the revolver on himself, but I
was so angered to realize that Dimitri Pavlovich had toyed with
me without daring to show his wretched self that I hesitated a
fraction of a moment too long. It was, however, all the time it
took for the cowardly prince to shoot me in the back.

"I screamed and fell to the floor, writhing with pain as my
blood pumped out onto a white bearskin rug. I shut my eyes,
depressed my respiration, and turned all my attention to the
wound. I had saved young Alexis Nicolaievich's life many times
by helping him stop his body's bleeding. Now it was time to
save myself by the same means.

"The bullet had hit an artery, and I lost a great deal of blood
in a very short time. I heard distant voices. Someone picked up
my arm, held it at the wrist for a few moments, then let it fall
limply back to the floor.

"'He's dead!' Dr. Lazovert cried from what seemed to be a
place far, far away. 'We've done it! We've killed Rasputin!'

"Hands lifted me roughly and carried me to a table, where
they laid me on my back. Footsteps receded. I was alone. The
hemorrhaging had stopped, but I was extremely weak.

"I became dimly aware of the sensation of pressure in the
upper part of my mouth—my blood teeth beginning to distend.
The Hunger came upon me, not in its usual slow, steady way,
but instantly and powerfully, an urge that screamed for satisfaction within every molecule of my being. I *had* to feed! My body
needed fresh blood to rejuvenate itself.

"There were footsteps again on the cellar stairs: two sets, one
heavy, one light; a man and a woman. Sounds and vibrations
came to me as if through a bale of cotton, but I could *see* the
scene clearly even with my eyes closed. It was Prince Felix,
pumped up with foolish exultation at the heroic deed of having
shot me while my back was turned, and his beautiful wife, her
reaction a mixture of fear and morbid curiosity. He had dared
to bring Princess Irina downstairs to impress her with the dead
body of the Mad Monk!

"'We have done a great thing tonight,' Felix said as they
drew near. 'The czar has been freed of a most noxious parasite.'

"He did not dare mention that Dimitri Pavlovich's plan, at

least as he understood it, called for him to be made czar. Felix did not have the nerve to utter such an absurdity to his wife, even when he chose to believe it himself.

"I listened to the rustle of silk against silk and breathed in the sweet, delicate smell of French soap and expensive perfume—and hovering beneath it all, beckoning sweetly to me, the river of life, the rich, pure, steamy richness of Princess Irina's blood.

"I opened my eyes and sat up straight on the table.

"The princess screamed. Prince Felix turned his back and ran, abandoning his beautiful wife to Rasputin. I kept my eyes on hers. I even smiled, listening to the sound of the prince's frantic footsteps scrambling on the stone staircase. I reached out with my mind and slammed the cellar door shut before he could reach it, holding it with my will so that it couldn't be opened from either side.

" 'You idiot,' I said to Prince Felix in a controlled voice. 'You have no conception of the powers you are dealing with. Come here!'

"A step at a time, his legs moving stiffly against his conscious command to remain motionless, I forced him to come back into the main room, where he found me, seated on the table, no more than a few meters from his lovely princess.

" 'You could never kill Rasputin.' I mocked him. 'Now stand where you are and witness the price of your folly.'

"Prince Felix shook with terror. He could not run. He could not look away. I had silently commanded him to watch what was to come next, and nothing short of his dying from fright could have spared him.

" 'Do not be afraid, my lovely,' I told Princess Irina in a soothing voice. The horror drained out of her face. I stood and walked the few short steps between us. Unlike Countess Katerina Trifonov, she was not tall, but small of stature and feature, like a well-made doll. I brushed my hand against her face. Her eyes closed, and she nuzzled my palm, smiling sleepily, her moist lips parting.

" 'I will bring you a pleasure you have never known,' I said and shot a glance at her husband, smiling so that he could see my blood teeth jutting below my lip like two tiny sabers drawn from their sheaths. The air stank of ammonia. Prince Felix had wet himself.

"I enfolded Princess Irina in my arms and lowered my face to her neck. Without any of the usual preliminaries, I pierced her satin skin and felt the delicious rush of hot blood splash against my mouth. She moaned with pleasure as I fastened myself to her neck and began to suck greedily. The strength flowed back into me with each swallow, until at last I was whole again.

"I have a confession to make: I was tempted to drain her dry, both to satisfy my body's need and teach Prince Felix the harshest sort of lesson. But that would have dragged me down to his cruel level. And so for her, but also for me, I let her live.

"Princess Irina's complexion was the color of milk when I finished. 'Sleep, my darling,' I told her, carrying her to a sofa. 'In the morning, you will remember nothing.'

'I turned to Prince Felix, again feeling the pull of a dark, powerful temptation. The urge to drain him and leave him shriveled and dead was almost too strong to resist. I had already taken the blood I needed, and I have never felt comfortable feeding from members of my own sex, but still—you sometimes meet a person so vile that your instincts tell you to strike him down while you have the chance.

"The flush of fresh blood in my system restored my sanity. I knew Archduke Dimitri Pavlovich was not coming to Moika Palace; I had been drawn into a mortal plot that I had not taken seriously. The archduke had played me for a fool, and I was lucky it hadn't turned out worse.

"I told Prince Felix to forget what he had seen transpire between me and Princess Irina, but to remember well the terror it inspired in him. I told him I would have no mercy if he crossed my path again, then snapped my fingers and set him free. As I had guessed, he did not move to protect his wife but again sprinted for the stairs with all the speed he could muster.

"I followed and heard him throw open the door.

" 'Rasputin is alive!' he screamed. 'The monster is alive!'

"They all were too petrified to react when I emerged from the cellar. I smirked in their direction, as if they were not worthy of my anger, and went toward the front door, ignoring the burning pain in my lower back, where the slug from Purishkevich's revolver still lodged.

" 'Shoot, Felix!' Vladimir Purishkevich shouted. 'Damn it, man, shoot Rasputin before he escapes and we all are undone!'

"I'd left Prince Felix with the gun! But there was nothing to worry about from him. I knew he would never have the nerve to lift his hand against me again.

"I opened the door and stepped out into the swirling snow. Behind me Vladimir Purishkevich snatched the revolver from the prince's hands and rushed to the door. 'For the emperor!' he shouted, and shot at me. He missed.

"Vladimir Purishkevich again fired and again missed. My hands were on the gate when he fired a third time. The bullet hit me in the spine. I felt my body falling toward the snow in slow motion. When I opened my eyes, Vladimir Purishkevich was standing over me, a fanatical look in his eyes.

" 'Purishkevich—' I said, pointing at the revolver as I began to push myself up with my other arm. 'Don't . . .'

"He shot me in the head."

"The conspirators were wrapping me in a blue curtain when I woke up and moaned.

" 'My God, he is *still* alive!' Dr. Lazovert gasped. I heard his footsteps running away through the snow. The others maintained their composure, though thoroughly terrified that the satanic Rasputin could not be killed. Grasping desperately for whatever thoughts I could pick up, I perceived with horror that Dimitri Pavlovich had instructed them to dismember my body. Fortunately the dawn was not far off, and the cool-headed Purishkevich ordered the others to pursue a more hasty course.

"The conspirators wrapped my body with chains and weights and took me to the Neva River. A hole was chopped in the ice. They dropped me in.

"And so the 'end' of my life was curiously symmetrical to my beginning. The icy waters of a frozen river had given me mortal life, and now they took it away.

"My body was never recovered, although they later exhibited another corpse to stop the rumors that Rasputin had been seen alive, hurrying through the dark streets of Petrograd near the czar's palace.

"Rasputin was, indeed, alive. But I could not openly help Tsarevich Alexis Nicolaievich and his family any longer, not with the conspirators bragging about how they had killed me. So, while the vampire Rasputin had been removed from the scene, Archduke Dimitri Pavlovich remained in action, and that spelled certain disaster for Czar Nicholas. The czar needed to have someone to counter Dimitri Pavlovich, I thought, somebody close to the royal family who could treat the tsarevich whenever the terrible bleeding started.

"And so I decided to do something extreme. It might not have been the right thing to do, but I had to do something.

"I had been greatly impressed with the intelligence and composure of the czar's second-eldest daughter, Tatiana Nicolaievna. She was bright, independent, fearless, serious. I went to her one night and explained the peril her family was in, and that she was the only hope for keeping her brother alive. The next morning, she was ill with a fever. She was delirious for days, and her family feared she would die. She recovered, but had two more relapses, each worse than the one before. And when the last traces of the malarial disease disappeared, she was left with a curious sensitivity to direct sunlight that caused her to refuse to leave her room except between sunset and sunrise.

"Although she agreed to being changed, Tatiana Nicolaievna hated me for a long time afterward. It's hard to make the transition. You know what it is like as well as any of us, David Michaelovich. She finally stopped loathing me the first time her brother's bleeding started and she was there to save his life.

"Even a vampire princess, working in concert with the ghost Rasputin—whose specter was seen haunting the palace deep in the night, moving from room to room in the vast complex of secret passageways—was unable to stop the unstoppable. The February Revolution overthrew the czar. The Bolsheviks took over in October, ousting the provisional government and bringing with them the perverse and ruthless notion that entire classes of Russians were guilty of treason and had to be exterminated, down to the last man, woman, and child.

"The Romanovs were arrested, and disappeared. When I found them, only Tatiana remained alive, although she was barely alive and wished she were not.

"The Bolsheviks had taken the family to Tobolsk in the Ural Mountains. They were herded into a semibasement room early in the morning of July 18, 1918. With Czar Nicholas were his wife and children, the empress's parlor maid, Demidove; a cook named Kharitonov; the valet, Trupp; Dr. Botkin, the family physician, and one of the family pets the children had been permitted to keep, a spaniel.

"The communist in charge of guarding the family marched them into a room at the front of a Cheka squad armed with revolvers. 'Nicholas Aleksandrovich,' he read from a dirty scrap of paper containing his instructions written in smudged pencil. 'By order of the Regional Soviet of the Urals, you are to be shot, with all your family.'

"The czar, in disbelief and outrage, shouted a single word: 'Chto?—What?' It was the final word spoken by the last emperor of the Russian Empire. One of the Cheka shot Czar Nicholas in the head; he fell to the floor, dead.

"They shot the rest of the family as they stood there, too paralyzed with shock to react. Then they got rifles and shot everybody a second time. The Czarina's maid, twice shot but still alive, ran around the room screaming until they stabbed her repeatedly with the bayonets. The dog, poor, innocent animal, escaped the bullets but was beaten to death with rifle butts. Anastasia fainted when her father was shot and miraculously escaped injury in the first two fusillades. She awoke after it was over and screamed. The guards fell on her methodically with bayonets and rifle butts, not one of them betraying the least remorse as they coldly and brutally murdered the innocent girl. The czarina covered her son's body with her own when the shooting began. They shot him twice in the head to be sure that the vile deed was done with the requisite thoroughness.

"Only one witness survived the slaughter, a young woman whose life continued to burn deep within her despite the terrible assault on her body that caused her attackers to believe she was dead.

"They carried the bodies to the shaft of the Four Brothers Mine and threw them down. Their orders were to cut the bodies to pieces, soak the remains first in acid, then in gasoline, and burn them. They actually began, but the first body—the doctor— was as far as they got. They didn't have the stomach for it. Tatiana Nicolaievna, still dimly alive, and the others were thrown down into the darkness. She dragged herself out the next night, and I found her. She would sooner have been dead.

"Archduke Dimitri Pavlovich suffered a similar fate, incidentally. The Reds shot him without a trial in the middle of the night and threw his body on top of a pile of corpses in the courtyard of Lubianka Prison just before dawn. The sunrise took care of the rest."

Rasputin looked at me and asked bluntly if I were curious about what became of the men who killed the czar and his family.

"The Soviets rewarded the head of the death squad by making him ambassador to Austria before the Second World War. I strangled him slowly with my bare hands. It was one of the most satisfying experiences of my life. Between the two of us, Tatiana Nicolaievna and I, we got them, one at a time.

"There is little remarkable to tell about the two of us after the revolution. We escaped across the border and went to Paris, where a friend, Olga Koklova, helped us. She was from a family of Ukranian aristocrats; her father had been a colonel in the Imperial Russian Army. She danced in Diaghilev's Ballet Russe until she fell in love with Pablo Picasso and married him, although I tried to talk her out of it.

"Tatiana Nicolaievna cut her hair and dyed it blonde. I, too, cut my hair and shaved my beard except for a mustache. No one ever suspected us; there were so many Russian exiles roaming about in those days that two more scarcely attracted notice.

"Olga Koklova was the only mortal who ever guessed what Tatiana Nicolaievna and I had become. That might have been partly responsible for what happened to her. She went insane, you know. Personally I blamed Picasso. It was Olga Koklova who introduced Tatiana to dancing. Tatiana still has a pair of Koklova's dancing shoes.

"I think those years in Paris were the only thing that kept Tatiana Nicolaievna from going mad herself with the grief. We traveled in a circle of scintillating people: the dashing impressario Sergei Diaghilev; Stravinsky; the dancers Nijinsky and Pavlova; writers Jean Cocteau and Gertrude Stein and Apollinaire; Matisse, whose art I was passionate about; Braque, the cubist; the absurd and amusing Dada artist Tristan Tzara; and Picasso, who could be quite charming when he wasn't being cruel.

"The years since Paris have been boring by comparison. Tatiana came to America in the 1950s. I remained in Europe. She had been living in Chicago about ten years when she met you, David Michaelovich. You know, you are her last and best hope at happiness. Without you she would have died of loneliness. Without you she *will* die of loneliness."

The three of us sat in silence as the train gently rocked its way through the dark German countryside, carrying us closer to Burg Wolfsschanze and the object of my quest: the assassinations of Prince Albert Victor and General von Baden and the freeing of their prisoner, Princess Tatiana Nicolaievna Romanov.

If this proves to be the last entry in this journal, I pray you survive even if I don't, Tatiana.

If I do not return from Burg Wolfsschanze, do not give up hope, my beloved. You will find someone else to make you happy. It is my last wish that you continue your search until you find someone who brings you the peace you have sought for so many years.

I was the best man I knew how to be. I've been the best vampire I could be. In this life that's the most you can hope for—that and love.

I love you with all my heart and soul, Tatiana. Remember me.

Your beloved,

David

Jachenau, 4:42 A.M., July 9, 1989

# Chapter 34

**B**URG WOLFSSCHANZE, JULY 11, 1989—The concierge came to my room the next evening just before nine.

I'd heard her the moment her foot first touched the stairs. Filled with impatience, I threw open the door before she could knock. The startled woman nearly screamed but almost immediately recovered her proper German composure and handed me the black vinyl suit bag she carried with her left hand.

The note taped to it was in Mozart's handwriting. It said simply:

*You will need this for tonight's party.*

I thanked her and, as soon as I'd shut the door, unzipped the bag. Inside was a black tuxedo, with a wing-collar shirt and a bloodred cummerbund. The purpose behind the formal clothing was a mystery to me, but I went ahead and changed, struggling a little bit with the bow tie to get it right.

An hour passed with no Mozart or Rasputin. I did not go looking for them. When it was time, they would come.

I slipped off my jacket and shoes and sat cross-legged on the floor. I took a deep breath and slowly released it, gently rocking back and forth until my body centered. I fixed my mind on nothing, a meditation technique Rasputin called *shikan taza*. It's a difficult exercise. The object is to keep your mind absolutely clear of thought, a blank slate. You are aware of only what you see and feel and hear at that precise moment; *shikan taza* brings you completely in the *now*. Try it for ten minutes, and you'll understand what makes it so hard to do.

It was important for me to keep my mind at least relatively calm. I was naturally keyed up, but I would need complete command of my faculties during the coming ordeal. I still had no idea how to keep the sunlight from burning me; Rasputin had left that for last. Whatever trick he had up his sleeve, I knew it would involve mind control—my mind, my control, my *skin*.

After I'm not really sure how long, a knock at the door summoned me to the surface of the pool of tranquility where I had been floating. Through the window the stars told me dawn was not far away.

It was Mozart. He wore a tuxedo like mine except for the red tea rose in his lapel. I picked up my jacket and looked at him with raised eyebrows while I pulled it on.

"The *Illuminati* are rather old-fashioned about these things," he explained. "Formal attire is a matter of pride, of culture, of refinement during"—he smiled thinly—"official acts."

"Official?"

Mozart nodded. "Yes, quite official. I have the death warrants for Borgia and the others, if you care to see them."

"Cesare Borgia will be at von Baden's castle?"

Mozart shook his head. "He is much too cautious for that."

I exhaled. I'm sure Mozart took it as a sigh of relief, which was exactly what it was.

"The particulars are these," he said, running one hand over his red-haired head, straightening the ponytail over the collar of his black dinner jacket. "Borgia made his last major assault on the mortal world a half century ago. His primary agents, the Nazis, were controlled from the beginning by a vampire elite— if *elite* is the correct word. They might have succeeded, if it were not for their worst excesses—and the fact that the *Illuminati* made sure it was the Americans, not the Germans, who first developed atomic weapons. Neither conventional nor nuclear weaponry plays a part in Lord Borgia's current scheme, which, unlike his others, actually involves a degree of elegance. Can you guess what his weapon will be this time?"

I shook my head.

"Economics."

I must have stared at Mozart with a particularly stupid gape because he repeated himself.

"Economics. Money is the weapon of the nineties. The OPEC oil embargo and the chaos it caused in the United States in the seventies was Borgia flexing his muscles, a small-scale exercise. There have been other examples since. He has become very interested in program stock trading and was heavily involved in the crash that shook world markets in October 1987.

"His thesis is simple: Control enough of the world's credit, and you control the world. But even Borgia is not ready to take on the entire world. He'll be satisfied to gain control of Western Europe."

"How, exactly," I asked, sliding into my shoes as I buttoned my jacket, "is he going to do it?"

"By precipitating an economic crisis that will make Black Thursday look like a profitable trading day. If the crisis becomes acute enough—and he means to assure that it will—certain political realignments will become necessary as governments scramble to keep themselves and their economies afloat. Borgia already controls the one country that will have the necessary liquidity after the crash to pull the others back from the brink of total financial chaos—and the massive social upheaval that will go along with such an economic disaster.

"Imagine Europe completely bankrupt, Herr Parker, its currencies worthless, millions of people out of work, food and supply systems completely disrupted, transportation and trade brought to a dead stop, governments falling like dominoes as a result of cataclysmic socioeconomic failure. You see, a genius bent on conquest no longer needs an army of soldiers to wreak devastation. All it takes are a few computers, a long line of credit, and a good enough understanding of economics to create a financial Hiroshima."

"Except," I said when Mozart paused, "that we are going to stop them."

"We are going to *try* to stop them. The simple fact, Herr Parker, is that Borgia has come up with an extremely complex scheme that will be impossible to halt once it begins. Even if he is only partially successful, there is no telling what the market will do. Investors and their bankers are blown by every wind and wet by every rain. Even fractional success could trigger the critical mass that brings the entire system crashing down.

"However," Mozart said, fixing me with deadly earnestness, "a single individual, acting alone, could take the key players out of action. Prince Albert Victor is to be in New York next Monday at the beginning of trading, and General von Baden in Zurich. Eliminate them, and Borgia might be forced to postpone his plan."

"I have the weapon Rasputin gave me."

"Violence is no solution, but sometimes it is the only option available."

I went to the dresser and took out the pistol.

The weapon was too large to conceal in my pocket, but I'd already thought about that. I'd found a ring-bound appointment book with a zippered nylon carrying case in a bookstore near the inn. The binder was just the size of the gun, and removing the paper made room for the weapon. Once the case was slipped over the binder and zipped shut, the pistol was perfectly concealed—at least from mortal eyes.

Rasputin was waiting in front of the inn, seated behind the wheel of a black Mercedes sedan. Almost imperceptibly the sky was beginning to lighten in the east. I looked from the Russian to the sky and back. He did not acknowledge my unspoken question.

Mozart opened the back door. I slid into the sedan, the concealed weapon under my arm. He climbed in next to me, and Rasputin stepped on the accelerator.

"It's really a very simple matter," Rasputin said without preface. "Even as a mortal you realized that to a certain extent you made yourself hot or cold by thinking yourself so."

"Yes, but getting burned up in the sun is more than just perception," I said a little anxiously. "I might be able to ignore the chill in a room where the air conditioner had been turned down too low, but if I were lost in a blizzard without a coat, I'd freeze regardless of what mental tricks I played on myself."

"You might freeze, David Michaelovich, but I would not. I have the power to control my body's reaction to extreme conditions, and so do you."

The sky in the east was turning the color of wine. This was the latest I had dared stay outside unprotected in the year I'd been a vampire.

"There's nothing complicated about it," Rasputin said, turning to flash me a brilliant smile that made his entire beard move. "You tell your body not to *let* the sunlight burn you."

"Would you please be serious?"

"But I am!" Rasputin protested, seemingly wounded by the implication that he was not taking his role as my teacher with the utmost seriousness. "Our skin is sensitive to only a small portion of the spectrum. Obviously we are not harmed by light in general, or we wouldn't be able to turn on a lamp or stand beneath a streetlight without discomfort. It is only certain wavelengths of radiation that affect us. We can control our reaction to the harmful portion of the spectrum, given the proper mental discipline.

"The way to do it, David Michaelovich, is to simply *do it*. Concentrate on not letting the sunlight burn you. Seal off your body from the harmful ultraviolet radiation. Shield yourself. Do not let the rays penetrate your skin. If it helps, imagine yourself surrounded with a transparent but impregnable armor of light-reflecting material."

"It is true, Herr Parker," Mozart said. "You can keep yourself from being burned by *willing* it. Incidentally you have nothing to worry about until we arrive at Burg Wolfsschanze. The windows in this automobile are tinted with a special photosensitive film that screens out the bands of radiation we are sensitive to. One of my inventions."

"You will only be in the direct light for a short time," Rasputin said. "You will go from the car into the castle. General von Baden has taken the necessary precautions to ensure the interior of his home is protected from the daylight."

"Then they are unable to come out in the sun?"

"Von Baden and Albert Victor?" Rasputin said with great contempt. "Not those weaklings."

"They lack the serenity and the control required to progress beyond the most basic realms of power," Mozart said. "It's what you Americans call catch-22: If they possessed the self-control necessary to master the vampiric arts, they would by definition be incapable of criminal activity."

As we drove out of Jachenau, the conversation reached a lull. I sat back and tried to relax, ignoring the impulse to keep talking as an outlet for my underlying nervousness; doing that would only drain my energy.

The night was fading fast by the time we reached the mountain Burg Wolfsschanze sits on, crouching like a beast on its hunting perch. The sky had become the steel-gray color it turns before changing to iridescent predawn blue. The trees, which swayed gently in the soft morning breeze, were a silvery green that would deepen several shades once the sun climbed above the horizon.

Rasputin braked. A fox ran across the road and disappeared into the ferns that grew in the short space between the road and the forest. We crossed a bridge spanning a stream of fast, sparkling water that looked as if it probably were filled with trout.

On the mountain itself, the road became steeper, and the trees closed in until we were driving between two towering green walls. The narrow band of sky overhead was brilliant blue, but

I still had not seen the sun, which remained hidden by the trees and the mountain.

It was easy to lose myself in the experience of my first dawn after a year of believing dawns and the days that followed them were lost to me forever. Trying to remember my last sunrise started me thinking about the life I'd left behind. My decision to make a clean break from it had worked more smoothly than I'd had a right to expect. Except for a few letters to my parents, I'd broken contact completely.

I wondered about Clarice. I don't know why, but I felt vaguely as if I'd abandoned her, although it had been just the reverse. I hadn't spoken to her since the divorce, and it had been months since I'd even thought about her. Poor Clarice. She had been so unhappy when I was part of her life; I wondered if she were happy now, and decided the answer was probably no.

However, it was Tatiana who occupied the central place in my thoughts as I watched that gorgeous morning ignite into day. She was my life and my future. I was quite ready to die rescuing her from Burg Wolfsschanze, if that was what fate required, since my life had no purpose without her.

The road abruptly emerged from the mountain forest, clinging to the side of the cliff, suddenly no longer wide enough for two cars to pass. Outside the windows on the left, the treetops quickly fell away below us. Still high above us on the other side of the Mercedes, the stone ramparts of Burg Wolfsschanze were just visible as the road curved, the incline markedly steeper as we approached the end of our journey.

The road twisted around to the east side of the peak.

Suddenly there was the sun! The burning golden orb was just beginning its ascent over the Bavarian landscape. I laughed out loud with irrepressible delight. The sun! I'd seen the sun before, but I'd never really *seen* it! I vowed to have proper appreciation for it and other simple pleasures in the future, if I, in fact, had a future.

The road continued to curve, carrying us past a crumbling guardhouse. One marble griffin remained on its roof, but its twin had pitched off the decayed structure and lay beside the road, staring at us with blind stone eyes. Ahead loomed towering stone walls and the massive main gate, which stood open— a detail that made me curiously concerned. It was almost as if they expected us, I thought, but then realized that the gang of vampires who made Burg Wolfsschanze their home probably thought they were beyond such precautions.

My fingers found the zippered case beside my thigh. I squeezed it for reassurance, but felt no sign of the weapon it contained. The huge pistol with its armor-piercing, exploding bullets had looked so lethal the first time I saw it; now, with the Mercedes fast approaching the medieval fortress that was von Baden's ancestral home, it seemed small and inadequate.

I pushed those thoughts out of my mind.

There was no time left for doubt. The moment of confrontation with my enemies was at hand.

The vampires the *Illuminati* represent may stand for the highest expression of earthly culture, but for me at that moment outside Burg Wolfsschanze, being a vampire meant having to kill or be killed.

# PART V

# Wolfsschanze

# Chapter 35

**B**URG WOLFSSCHANZE, JULY 12 1989—It's impossible to get a sense of the massive space the von Baden castle occupies without visiting it. Viewed from below in Jachenau, you get a sense of the mood, of the fortress's malevolent atmosphere, without gaining any real appreciation for its tremendous size.

It's easy to see why Teutonic knights chose this place for a citadel. The dense forest that carpets the mountain is stripped away to reveal naked rock for the final few hundred feet before the summit. The last part of the road is chiseled out of the cliff face; it twists its way around the mountain for nearly a mile before reaching the top, making nearly one complete circuit of the mountain on its ways to the peak. Invaders would have had to battle their way up the precarious road, which could have been easily defended below as well as from above, before even starting to lay siege to the battlements of the fortress proper.

The mountaintop itself also was barren of vegetation. I saw not a tree, bush, flower, or blade of grass. What grew instead was rock, which thrust upward in unusual, twisting formations. The castle complex appeared to grow out of this tortured rock, the towers and spires flung skyward as though they were giant crystal formations reaching up out of a freakish rock garden.

The summit was not truly flat, as it seemed from below, but continued to rise toward a thick knob of rock at the center. Little evidence of the natural formation remained, for it was on this prominence that the citadel had been built.

The heart of Burg Wolfsschanze, the citadel, evidently was one of the more recent constructions in the complex, if *recent* is a word that can be stretched to cover such an expanse of centuries. The squat and plainer aspect of some of the surrounding towers indicated they had been put up in the early Dark Ages. The citadel itself was at least several hundred years younger, dating from the high-medieval period, I guessed, judging from the Gothic architecture.

Since the highest part of the summit clearly was the most defensible, it seemed probable that the citadel had been rebuilt any number of times as the von Badens' fortunes as feudal barons rose during the Dark Ages. The existing citadel clearly had been designed to suit two intentions. Half palace, half fortress, it was the place the lord ruled from his throne, but also where his soldiers would fall back for the final to-the-death stand around their master.

Nowhere was the the significance of the fortress's name— Wolf's Lair Castle—more evident than in this final redoubt. The spirit of the wolf, the rapacious predator, breathed from every block of the towering stone structure. The style of the place was a discordant echo of the Gothic cathedrals built throughout Europe, with vaulting arches, gargoyles, and intricate stonework. But what the builders of Burg Wolfsschanze worshiped a god of war, not of peace.

Above the entry was the von Baden family crest, the central figure in the coat of arms, a wolf. The artisan who had carved it had chosen to emphasize the beast's predatory characteristics, ignoring any potentially beneficent elements in this symbol of the von Baden clan.

As I sat in the Mercedes, witnessing this disconcerting scene reveal itself outside the windows, I decided the vampires I sought most likely would be found somewhere within the central complex. But *where* within the citadel? There would be scores, if not hundreds, of rooms. And beneath the main level, there would be subterranean crypts, torture chambers, dungeons, and storage chambers honeycombing the rock below Burg Wolfsschanze in a maze bewildering enough to rival the Roman catacombs.

We sat in the Mercedes in the stone-paved courtyard for several torturously long minutes before I broke the silence.

"How will I find them?"

"Follow your instincts," Mozart said simply, sounding for once like our cryptic Russian friend.

"Do not worry," Rasputin said. "If you don't find them first, they'll find you."

"*That's* a relief to know," I replied. "How many do you think there are in there?"

"It's impossible to say," the Russian answered.

"Logic argues against a great number," Mozart said. "They wouldn't be able to feed—at least not according to their usual habits—without attracting attention."

"My guess would be von Baden, Albert Victor, Tatiana, and perhaps two or three others," Rasputin said.

"Remain calm, and you will be all right," Mozart said.

"Remember," Rasputin cautioned, "A high spirit is weak, and a low spirit is weak, also. Never let your enemies see your spirit. Remain calm but determined."

"Do they know we're here?"

"Not yet," Mozart said. "We cannot shield your presence once you leave the car. However, that should be no problem for you. Just don't forget the sun."

"The short time you will be exposed will be long enough to cause considerable injury unless you're careful," Rasputin warned, "so concentrate. It will be extremely dangerous for us all if we have to return to the inn and stay there while you convalesce before coming back up here a second time."

"I'm sure I can handle it," I said, thinking that one visit to Burg Wolfsschanze was as many as I wanted to make.

"Good."

"Remember, David," Rasputin said, "follow your instincts. Keep your mind from becoming cluttered with needless thoughts and fears. Simply act."

"All right."

"Don't let anything you see turn you aside from your purpose. Their powers are weak compared to yours, although they know many tricks," Mozart said.

"Deal with von Baden and Albert Victor before you free Tatiana, if at all possible," Rasputin said. "Otherwise you risk their playing you into a position where you have to choose between protecting her and eliminating them."

"I cannot emphasize how important it is for you to kill General von Baden and Prince Albert Victor," Mozart said. "But be brave. If your spirit is strong and good, you will succeed."

I focused my eyes on the back of the car seat ahead of me and quieted my presence until so much silence echoed from where I sat that I almost wondered myself if I were really there. I imagined an invisible armor enveloping me, starting at my feet and moving up my legs and body until I was entirely encased. I did not wonder whether Rasputin's suggested imaging was going to work; I knew if I doubted it even that much, it would fail.

Clutching the concealed pistol in my right hand, I flung open the door and quickly climbed out.

I stood with my eyes closed. The sun did not burn, but the naked light was too much for my eyes. There was a peculiar tingling on my face, neck, and hands—the parts of my body directly exposed. I was not burning up, but I knew that at least some of the rays were getting through. It was pleasantly painful, like the feeling of the hot sun burning on bare skin the first day at the beach after a long winter.

Rasputin tapped on the car window with his finger, encouraging me to get moving.

I smiled a little in spite of myself and cracked open my eyes. The nightmare vision of Burg Wolfsschanze's massive bulk looming in front of me abruptly ended my reverie. I hurriedly crossed the courtyard and went up the steps, which had smooth depressions worn in them from centuries of foot traffic.

I did not go in through the main door, which looked as if it might have taken several strong men to open, but through a much smaller entrance, which was unlocked, cut into the corner of the larger door.

I found myself in the midst of an enormous hall. A table almost a city block long ran lengthwise through the middle of the room, and pulled up to it were enough leather-thong-backed chairs to seat a hundred men. The fireplace on the wall opposite the entry was large enough to park a van in; upon its massive andirons were piled entire tree trunks that had been neatly sawed and stacked. Identical fireplaces stood against the side walls to my left and right.

The windowless chamber was decorated with a museum's worth of weapons. Shields, swords, spears, and a variety of arcane killing tools were on permanent exhibit, along with the hunting trophies brought back by generations of von Badens. The heads of huge stags and bears, the likes of which had not been seen in that part of Europe for hundreds of years, hung on the walls, accompanied by a variety of every other game that could be bagged between Finland and North Africa.

This was Burg Wolfsschanze's great hall, the place where the von Baden lords had feasted the knights who pledged to die, if need be, in their service. The room seemed strangely empty without a band of warriors seated at the table, filling the air with a subdued roar of masculine conversation. The quiet was, in fact, eerie.

It would be difficult to grow up a von Baden in such a place and not yearn for the olden times and the power that went along with that era. The romance—the *false* romance—of that violent earlier age must have shaped von Baden as a boy, contributing to the makeup of the man, and the vampire, he had become.

But what of Prince Albert Victor? I had no similar insight into what had turned him into the monster he was. The Ripper had been raised with every privilege in the most civilized culture in the world, yet he had turned, following the twisted nature of his perverted soul, to butchering women.

I put the travel case on the table, unzipped it, and removed the weapon.

I was overintellectualizing, I told myself. I did not need to understand von Baden or the Ripper; I only had to kill them.

A dozen different doorways led out of the great hall. Narrow stone steps along the back wall climbed to a gallery that ran the circumference of the room, with scores of doors off of it.

Damn, I thought, how would I ever find them? Mozart's words came back to me: *Follow your instincts*.

Skirting the table, I went through one of the doors in the far wall. I do not know why, but it seemed like the *right* door. It led into a smaller reception chamber—small only relative to the great hall—and to another selection of doors; the one I chose opened onto a darkened hallway that seemed to extend forever.

I adjusted my vision and moved silently past the suits of armor and age-cracked oil portraits of the von Badens and their thanes. Then I felt it far off in one of the rooms. "It" was two things, actually: the first, a vampire; the second, a mortal man, or what had been a mortal man before he was murdered.

I stopped and listened with my entire being. The vampire gave no sign of being aware of my presence. I redoubled my stealth and continued toward the room.

There was something familiar—and deeply disturbing—about the vibrations I sensed. The other vampire, a woman, was some-one I knew well, even intimately. And yet she was greatly changed. I knew her, yet I didn't.

The experience with Anna Montoya was still fresh in my mind. The thought that the Ripper might have transformed Ariel Niccolini or Rachel Weir into one of his twisted slaves sickened me.

But I knew it could be worse, for this woman's vibration

touched my soul in a special way. I had to force myself to maintain control in the face of my appalling suspicion that the vampire I'd find in the room stinking of death was Tatiana, my angel, tragically fallen from the luminous beauty I had known and loved, changed by Prince Albert Victor into something I could scarcely recognize.

The exercises Rasputin taught me proved their worth. Concentrating on my breathing, I forced my mind to empty itself of all thought, of all emotion.

I stopped outside the room where the vampire and her victim were long enough to make sure the weapon's safety was turned off. Then, holding my breath, I stepped through the door.

The room once had served as an armory for the castle, and it was packed with swords, spears, crossbows, and other antique weaponry. A single torch burned in an iron holder on the wall, the stone behind it blackened from the accumulation of soot.

The corpse's physical beauty remained even in death. He must have been an athlete, judging from the almost perfect musculature in his body. He had longish blond hair and what might have been a handsome face, although it was impossible to know for sure because of the way he'd been disfigured.

The wound in his neck was savage, and the pallor of his still-warm body told me that he'd only recently been drained of blood. His body leaned against a rack of spears, so that he appeared to stand; the bloodied point and shaft of one lance protruded through the opened mouth of his upturned face. From the rigid way his body stood, it was evident that he had been impaled, that the spear had been run up through his entire torso—a form of execution popular in medieval times, and known for the extreme agony in which its victims died.

The amount of blood on the end of the spear indicated that he had been impaled before, not after, being drained—a cruel, savage death.

I had to force myself to turn toward the female figure sunk to the floor in the dark corner behind the door, her own senses still reeling from the intoxicating excess of the blood she had consumed.

I expected to see Ariel or Rachel or even Tatiana, but I was not prepared for it to be Clarice.

I stumbled backward as my former wife looked up at me, her mouth smeared with blood and her eyes burning with a passion I dared not name. She wiped her mouth on one sleeve of the velvet gown she wore and smiled. And then she *laughed*. It was a sound filled with insanity, with murder—with an insatiable lust for blood.

Clarice came toward me, crawling across the floor on her stomach like a sex slave groveling for her master.

"I've been waiting for you such a long time, David," she said, her voice a slurred whisper.

"Who did this to you?"

She pulled herself slowly to her feet and stood swaying in front of me like someone who has had too much liquor and is about to pass out.

"Someone rich and powerful."

"Albert Victor?"

She smiled wickedly. "It's the dream of every American girl to be fucked by a prince."

"You don't understand any of this, do you? You don't know what he is or have any appreciation for the boundless evil he represents."

"You only call it evil because you're weak."

"If you knew how mistaken you are, Clarice."

"Don't take that damned superior attitude with me!" she shrieked. "I had enough of it when we were married. I was your equal then, and I'm your equal now!"

"Do you know Prince Albert Victor is Jack the Ripper? Can you imagine how that monster has manipulated you?"

"You don't know him."

"No, *you* don't know him."

Clarice moved a step closer, her eyes filled with hatred.

"You had something wonderful, but you wouldn't share it with me, would you? You were so infatuated with your princess. You and she would be immortal together, and Clarice could shrivel up, get old, and die. But you had it wrong, David darling. It's Tatiana who is going to be dead—and soon—and I will be his queen."

"He's lied to you, Clarice. It's Tatiana he really wants. He's lied to you and used you."

She tried to claw my face, but I was too quick and moved out of the way.

"You son of a bitch! You know, I visited that little tramp you were screwing in Chicago. The one you gave my town house to."

I felt as if she'd just plunged an icicle into my heart.

"*He* let me do it. He held her on the bed so she couldn't

move, but her mind was aware of every detail. She was my first! Prince Albert Victor wanted to kill her, but I told him it would be much more fun my way. Did he tell you it was my idea to transform her?''

"My God . . .''

"Not that I'm squeamish about killing.'' She giggled and nodded in the direction of the corpse. "My first was your friend from Daddy's firm. Surely you remember your chum Michael Byron.'' Her eyes flashed. "He said he was bored with me, but there was nothing boring about our last night together!''

"How could you have ruined Anna Montoya?'' I asked, not really caring much what she'd done to the man who helped break up our marriage.

"I intended to visit your parents . . .'' She paused to let that sink in. ". . . to say good-bye, but I didn't have the chance. Perhaps I'll see them when I'm back in the States next week. In fact, I'm going back to Chicago. Did you know I've become quite good at making money? It's not at all like when we were married, and I only knew how to spend it. The general has helped me buy a seat on the Chicago Board of Trade. They're open for night trading now, you know. The world market never closes.''

Behind her grin she looked capable of anything.

"I have some special investments to make next week. I'm managing a large portfolio that belongs to someone *extremely* important who lives in Italy. I'm not at liberty to disclose his name, of course, but I'm sure you know who I mean.''

"If you bother my parents . . .''

"I thought I'd do Mother first,'' she said, her eyes wide. "What do you think? Should I ask the general if I may borrow one of his spears? It does rather add something to see them beg for death. It almost makes me wish I'd listened to the prince and done something creative with your little Gypsy whore.''

My fury seemed to flow into my head and form a ball of white-hot energy.

Clarice looked at me first with surprise, then alarm.

I didn't just want to kill her: I wanted to obliterate her.

Clarice shook as if she were having a seizure. I hated her for what she'd done to Anna Montoya—and what she'd promised to do to my parents. The Ripper had made a particularly brilliant choice in transforming Clarice, given that his motivation was to spread evil. She had all the right weaknesses, her soul polluted down to its essence. I'd known it even when we were married.

Blood was running out Clarice's nose and ears now. There were black circles around her eyes.

Anna Montoya—she had been so pure, so filled with creative fire. Enslaving her to Borgia was a crime for which Clarice and Prince Albert Victor deserved eternal damnation, if there was such a thing.

I felt as if my brain were on fire. Anger was burning me up. The emotion would destroy me if I didn't gain control of it. I had to concentrate, to focus on the task I'd come to Burg Wolfsschanze to perform.

With one explosive effort, I forced all the pent-up fury from mind.

Clarice flew backward, slamming into a rack of shields. They clattered to the floor together, where she lay very still, staring at me with unseeing eyes. A welter of blood covered her face; it even seeped from under her fingernails.

I was sorry to see her dead—and more than a little surprised at the power I had brought to bear against her—but it could have been no other way. Clarice had become a monster in the truest sense of the word.

"Bravo!" said a voice behind me.

I spun around to see a tall, lean man, his head perfectly bald, standing in the doorway, applauding me in a slow, measured way. I did not need to be introduced to know it was General von Baden, the lord of Burg Wolfsschanze.

"I am sure many men would enjoy killing their former wives, but few have the pleasure of actually doing it," he said with a stiff smile. *"Ich gratuliere!"*

I was suddenly aware of the gun in my hand, which I'd quite forgotten about. It felt solid and heavy.

"Forgive me for not welcoming you, but I only recently realized you were here," von Baden said in a self-amused tone I found highly irritating. "You are indeed as strong as Albert Victor said. He was right about the black woman, too, you know. He said she would be no match for you. I should have listened."

I glared at the German, holding my finger against the trigger, pulling it to nearly the pressure point so that the weapon would fire the moment I lifted it.

"You are *ein begabter Mann*—a man of talent," General von Baden said. "Unfortunately you have been traveling in the company of old women. You need to begin associating with men, *mein Herr*. The world is there to be taken, for those bold enough to seize it. You will be a fine asset to our organization."

"I have no intention of joining you."

"But listen to reason, *mein Freund*. Your only other option is death. It would be a shame for me to have to exterminate so *einen talentvoller Mann*."

I think the way General von Baden's eyebrows rose was a sign that he knew what was about to happen, although I did not give him time to react.

The blast was deafening in the stone-walled room. There was a second, almost simultaneous, explosion as the charge in the bullet burst.

The shot tore von Baden in half. The middle portion of his torso simpy disappeared in a spray of red mist. For a second the two portions of his body, upper and lower, seemed to remain in place, as if the missing part in the middle had crept off without being noticed. Then, with the awful shriek that accompanied von Baden's exhaling his final breath, the two pieces of the general's body collapsed to the stone floor in a fast-spreading puddle of blood and gore.

I took a step forward and forced myself to look down.

Von Baden's face was frozen in a grimace, the eyes rolled up in their sockets so that only the whites showed. Rasputin's weapon had done the trick. Even a vampire could not survive being blown in half.

After tucking the pistol under my belt, I lowered Clarice's victim gently to the floor. I did not have the nerve to pull the spear out of his body, but I took a swath of age-yellowed linen off a table and used it to cover the corpse.

I went to Clarice and closed her eyes, feeling the tears forming in my own. She'd had a miserable life and a miserable death. I wished I could have done something to make it easier for her, but now it was too late for anything except regrets.

Behind me came a loud sucking noise that made my skin crawl.

I spun around, grabbing for the pistol.

Bits of von Baden's torn intestines were slithering across the floor like great bloody white worms, intertwining themselves with their mates from the opposite half of the divided torso.

Paralyzed with a combination of disgust and fascination, I watched von Baden's bowels drag the separated halves of his body toward each other.

It was astonishing to watch the damaged flesh repair itself, like seeing a body being created from the inside out. The intestines shifted and quivered like a nest of snakes until they were in the proper position, then a glistening sheath of tissue covered them. The abdominal muscles regenerated a layer at a time, building themselves up in rippling cords until they were complete, enclosed at last by layer of pink new skin.

The entire process could not have taken much longer than a minute.

And in the next moment, von Baden was on his feet, laughing.

"Did you seriously think you could kill me?" he asked, falling suddenly serious. There was murder in the vampire's eyes, as unmistakable as the stink of death that filled the room.

I fired wildly, not even aiming. Part of von Baden's left arm, perhaps two thirds of it, was shot away and fell to the floor, twitching spasmodically where it lay, as if it might at any moment fly up and reattach itself to the general's body.

*"So was kriege ich als ihn zu überzeugen suchen mit einem Amerikanischen Schwein!"* General von Baden spat. "You have made a fatal error, Herr Parker, and it's going to cost you a slow and supremely painful death."

The force of von Baden's will hit me like a brick in the forehead as he tried to force his way into my mind. I doubt it was my mental strength as much as a physical reaction to the assault—reflexively tensing my mind and body to resist the attack—that caused me to pull the trigger again.

The bullet struck General von Baden just above his left knee, severing one leg and doing terrible damage to the other. Von Baden, his feet literally shot from under him, fell to the floor, his face a mask of agony, cursing me bitterly in German.

*"Schweinhund! Ich werde dich schlachten! Ich werde deine Familie schlachten!"*

He tried to get inside my head again, but the pain distracted him too much to be effective.

*"Meine Beine!"* he screamed, clutching at his legs with his remaining hand.

Von Baden managed to get into a sitting position. He pointed at me with his right hand while he summoned up the energy for one last assault on my mind.

I leveled the pistol, this time taking careful aim, and squeezed the trigger.

A tiny black hole that looked hardly serious enough to kill a vampire appeared in the center of von Baden's forehead. Then I noticed the wall directly behind him. It was splattered with the greater part of his brain and skull.

There was a look of surprise on Von Baden's face as he toppled forward. The entire back half of the general's head, and most of what had been inside of it, were simply gone.

Without a moment's hesitation, I dragged Clarice's lifeless body across the room and piled her on top of von Baden, whose various pieces continued to quiver with unnatural life.

I wasn't about to make the same mistake twice.

There was a kerosene lamp sitting unlit nearby. I smashed the top off it and poured the contents of its vast reservoir over the bodies. With stone floor, walls, and ceilings, there was little risk of setting the castle on fire. Backing out the door, I took down the torch and threw it toward the bodies.

The fire would do the rest, I hoped.

Holding the pistol in front of me, I set off to find Prince Albert Victor, the fiend who had contributed so much to the destruction of Anna Montoya and Clarice Luce. After the gunshots, though, I thought it likely that he would also be looking for me.

It was not difficult to follow von Baden's trail. A dim green phosphorescence just outside the mortals' visible spectrum lingered in the dark hallway, showing the direction he had come. The path took me to a spiral staircase. I looked over the railing. The stairs corkscrewed down past the castle's many subterranean levels. One, two, three, four—I counted five stories chiseled into the stone beneath the citadel's ground floor.

Slowly and silently I descended the stairs. The faint glow von Baden had left lasted until I reached the bottommost level, growing progressively more faint until it finally flickered out entirely. I had a choice among five passages that led away from the lowest landing. I reached out with my senses, but I was unable to determine which hall the general had come down.

Then I caught a distant flicker, almost imperceptible but unmistakable: Tatiana!

She was alive but far away, hidden somewhere in the labyrinth. Her presence was faint. She was either very weak, or guarded by someone very powerful.

Perhaps it wouldn't be so easy after all.

Somewhere in the pitch-black maze was my lover, but the Ripper was out there, too, and I knew from previous experience that he could hide from me until he chose to show himself—or until I devised a way to *force* him into the open.

I took a step in the direction of my lover but immediately stopped. Going straight toward her was hardly the cautious thing to do.

I turned in a slow circle, examining the passageways. I had to trust my instincts, Mozart said. I stopped at the one that looked right and set off down it, the weapon extended before me, feeling Tatiana's presence shrink behind me, trusting I would find my way back to her nevertheless.

The passage twisted and turned, going up and sometimes down, following the contours of the rock. Many of the doors along the hall were open or stood ajar, revealing tiny cells with stone benches that had once served as beds for prisoners awaiting the ax. There were still rusted shackles attached to the walls.

I reached another intersection and chose the one of three passages that seemed likeliest to lead back toward Tatiana.

The stink of death—old death—slowed my progress. It came from a room filled with devices designed to inflict pain and death in various ingenious ways. The equipment had been used somewhat recently. Stretched upon the rack were the decomposing remains of a woman. She had been there several months, I guessed, though it was hard to tell because the cool subterranean air had turned her sunken skin black, mummifying the corpse.

I moved on.

Down one of the hallways at the next junction I saw a dim red glow. Cautiously, almost reluctantly, I went toward the light, like a moth to a candle, the weapon ready.

I was in a different section of the cellar now, and the surroundings were considerably more refined. The ceiling came to a carefully finished arch overhead, and the floor was covered in a series of narrow carpets that once had been rich but were now disintegrating with age. Small alcoves were carved into the stone on either side of me, and within each sat a bust upon a pillar. These heads belonged to the von Badens who had gone on to their just rewards. There was even a bust for the general, I saw with some surprise, then remembered that as far as the mortal world was concerned, he had died with his führer in 1945.

The light came from the funeral chapel outside the family crypt beneath the heart of the citadel. The sanctuary lamp, an ornate gold antique with red glass walling in its single candle, hung above the altar from a silver chain that was turned black with tarnish.

The altar was stone, like the pews, and the cross and chalice upon it gold—everything covered with a thin blanket of dust that gave the room a vaguely out-of-focus appearance. The walls were decorated with enameled wooden panels depicting scenes of medieval court life: noblemen paying homage to their king, bloody battles, victory celebrations where the vanquished were laid out, headless, in long rows before the knights in armor on prancing war stallions.

"I've been waiting for you."

I did not know the woman who came toward me out of the shadows—nor had I noticed her until she spoke in her husky voice.

"Your powers"—she closed her eyes a moment and held out her opened hands as if to feel the warmth of my fire—"are *very* strong."

I lowered the gun. Something told me she would not harm me. There was nothing wicked about her eyes. Just the opposite, in fact. Could she be one of the *Illuminati*? She seemed so strong, so filled with inner light. If she were a gem, I thought, she would have been a ruby.

"You killed Clarice and General von Baden."

I nodded.

"You had no choice," she said sympathetically.

"No, I did not."

The delicate shape of her body and her facial features reminded me of a painting by a Renaissance master. Her beauty was of the bewitching sort; there seemed to be the distilled essence of grace and loveliness of many women concentrated in her short, slight frame.

"You like poetry, don't you?"

I smiled.

"There are so few men today who do. When I was young— a very long time ago—all my suitors wrote poetry for me. It was a romantic time."

The message her eyes flashed made my heart melt.

"You remind me of a poem."

"What is it?" I asked, entranced with her rare, antique beauty. There were no masculine edges in this woman. She was of a time when women of good birth were *ladies*, in every way the embodiment of a femininity that had become extinct in the modern world.

She beamed—her smile itself was a poem—and began to recite:

*"But oh! that deep romantic chasm which slanted*
*Down the green hill athwart a cedarn cover!*
*A savage place! as holy and enchanted*

*As e'er beneath a waning moon was haunted*
*By woman wailing for her demon lover!"*

I blinked.

*"And all who heard should see them there,*
*And all should cry, Beware! Beware!*
*His flashing eyes, his floating hair!"*

I took an involuntary step backward, shrinking from the woman, my momentary infatuation replaced by an entirely different emotion.

*"Weave a circle round him thrice,*
*And close your eyes with holy dread,*
*For he on honey-dew hath fed,*
*And drunk the milk of Paradise."*

"The milk of Paradise," I echoed, startled at the sound of my own voice. Why had I spoken? *Had* I spoken?

"The blood of Paradise, my love, the *blood* of Paradise," she said, tilting her head to look up at me with a shyness that was incongruous with the subtext hidden within her words.

"I was mistaken."

"About what, my darling?"

"I thought you were one of the *Illuminati*."

Her smile was radiant. It brought a blush of color to her alabaster-white face.

"Not I," she said, drawing out the words into almost a sigh as she pulled the golden clasp away from the neck of her cloak, letting it fall open to reveal the soft curve of her perfect breasts. She was naked beneath the robe.

"I am Lucrezia Borgia."

I was too terrified to move. But her body—I *burned* to touch it!

Looking at me though her eyelashes, she pulled the cloak away from her shoulders and let it fall to the floor with the hushed rustle of velvet sliding across bare skin.

"My brother has given me to you, David Parker, if you will only join us. Rule a country. Rule a continent." The fire in her eyes was of a sort that frightened me. "Be a *god*!"

"Why—" I had to swallow before I could speak. "Why," I repeated, "offer me this when I've just killed two of your friends?"

"They do not matter." She came a step closer. "They were weak, but you have a rare strength, my love. There is steel in your soul, and I am the one who has helped you to find it.

"I have gone to a great deal of trouble to get you to the point where you would realize what you really are, David Parker. Losing General von Baden will inconvenience my brother, but what is a small inconvenience next to gaining an ally like you? I could transform a thousand mortals without finding one who has your *will*. You are different. You have the sensitivity required to become truly powerful, if you are properly nurtured."

I said nothing.

"Help us to save mankind."

"What?"

"We want to save the world, David Parker. If mortals are left in control, how much time do you give them before they annihilate life on the planet? Twenty-five years? Fifty? The vampire is the Earth's last and best hope. Without our guidance, humanity will perish, and everything else living with it."

She reached up and touched my cheek lightly, like a butterfly, but her fingers were cold.

"I do not deny that some of us have been bad. But the so-called *Illuminati* have all but exterminated us. In self-defense we've been forced to transform individuals poorly suited to vampirey. We've had to take desperate measures to defend ourselves."

I couldn't think. I tried to clear my head, but the only thing I knew was how badly I wanted to run my fingers across her silky skin, to wrap her small body in my arms.

"We are not evil," she said, stroking my face.

I tried to speak but couldn't.

"Do not fight it, my love. Surrender. Join us and serve my brother. Give in to the sweet temptation, and I will make love to you as you have never been loved before. Women, I know, have always been your weakness."

Something about hearing those words from Lucrezia Borgia cleared the fog from my mind. She was exactly right, I thought, driving the sense of confusion out of my mind: Women *had* been my weakness. But I could no longer afford to let them influence me to such a degree. I had to think for myself, to act in accordance with my own instincts. Tatiana was the only woman I truly loved, and she was not a weakness but my strength.

I raised the pistol until its barrel pointed at Lucrezia Borgia's head, but I could not bring myself to pull the trigger. She had not threatened me. She had no weapon. And while I knew in my heart that it was not true, I rationalized that she was only the tool of her evil brother, that without Cesare Borgia, Lucrezia would not have been drawn to the darkness.

"I am so very disappointed," she said, backing away. Without taking her eyes off of me, she knelt and picked up her cloak, drawing it tight around her as she stood, fixing it shut with the golden pin, which I noticed was decorated with the head of the snake-haired female monster Medusa.

"There won't be any need for that," she said, indicating the pistol with a nod. "The person you seek is in there." She pointed at a doorway in the shadows.

When I looked back, Lucrezia Borgia was gone.

The far reaches of the low-ceilinged crypt beneath Burg Wolfsschanze were obscured by endless pillared arches and side chambers, each filled with the orderly clutter of the von Baden family's stone sarcophagi.

Many of the vault lids had horizontal statues carved in them, as if the sleeping lords and ladies within had lain down on top of their coffins many centuries ago and turned to stone.

I followed the well-traveled path through the cobwebs and dust until I came around a corner and saw an ornate wooden coffin that was quite out of place among its marble counterparts. The lid banged open, and its occupant scrambled out.

The face that leered back at me through the darkness was unmistakable. It was Prince Albert Victor, better known to the world as Jack the Ripper. He spent the daylight hours reposing in a coffin, probably the very one his royal family believed they had buried their young lunatic in.

He was one vampire I would not allow to escape. I raised the gun, but he was already gone, ducking away in the blackness.

I felt a flush of exultation. *He* was afraid of *me*!

Lucrezia Borgia had again confirmed what Mozart and Rasputin had been telling me. I *was* more powerful than these creatures of darkness—perhaps even more powerful than the ancient vampire Lucrezia Borgia, for why else would she have let me go?

I raced after the Ripper, following him through the crypt until a stone wall blocked my way. He had gone *through* the wall. Some trick of transference?

My fingers quickly searched the wall until I found a loose

piece of mortar. I pressed it, and discovered it worked back and forth, like a toggle. I pushed it all the way to one side and the wall swung silently away from me, revealing a narrow stone stairway that climbed almost vertically for what seemed like ten stories.

My eyes found the small landing where the stairs finally ended, in time to see the Ripper's distant form disappear through a doorway.

I flew up the steps and dashed through the doorway without pausing, stopped in my headlong pursuit only by the overwhelming presence of death that crashed into my senses once I got into the room at the top of the stairs.

# Chapter 36

**B**URG WOLFSSCHANZE, JULY 13, 1989—The room at the top of the stairs had been designed in the same Gothic fashion as the rest of the citadel. Almost twice as long as it was wide, its windows were high and peaked and covered over with what looked like miles of wine-purple drapery. As if to make up for the lack of sunlight, a dozen massive chandeliers hung from the ceiling, each holding a hundred flickering candles, from which the dripping wax had formed thick white stalactites.

The furnishings were greatly in contrast to the room's medieval architecture. General von Baden had gone to great lengths to make over the room as a sort of Turkish seraglio. Everywhere were daybeds and large, body-sized silk pillows, all spread out on the Persian carpets that overlapped one another, many layers thick upon the stone floor.

Several dozen mortals, some men, some women, all noteworthy for their exceptional beauty, were scattered about the room in various stages of undress. All were quite dead, but not long dead.

It was easy to picture what had taken place there the night before. The vibrations still hung heavy in the room, like smoke in the air after a battle. The memories of the perverse pleasure—and sick fear—tainted the atmosphere, like the smell of cheap perfume mingled with excrement in the apartment of the dead hooker in Paris.

In my mind's eye I saw the depraved Lucrezia Borgia, sister and lover of the greatest criminal the vampire race had ever spawned, presiding the night before over an orgy of sex and death, a murderous bacchanal where blood flowed instead of wine.

Here by the stairs, Clarice had drained this handsome youth of his blood. Bored with the pedestrian level of violence at the party, she'd taken another young man by the hand and led him to the armory in search of more exciting diversions.

Nearby lay the bodies of two astonishingly beautiful women. Von Baden had lingered with them at the end of the night, I could tell; he'd left them, dead in each other's arms, to look for Clarice.

At the far end of the room was a raised platform, a sort of dais, and upon it two thrones: one large for the lord, a smaller one for his lady, both carved of shining black granite set off by copious amounts of gold leaf.

On the throne intended for the lord of Burg Wolfsschanze sat Prince Albert Victor, leaning back, legs crossed, the usual sardonic smile playing on his thin, bluish lips.

He had not been afraid of me after all when he ran from the crypt. Another of his games. It hardly mattered. I soon would be finished with Albert Victor's malevolent pranks.

"Court etiquette requires subjects to genuflect when they approach us," Prince Albert Victor said, adopting the annoying royal contrivance of referring to himself in the plural. "We don't suppose you know that, though. You Americans are all barbarians."

"I'll not kneel before a psychopath."

"Oh, you'll bow down to me, Mr. Parker. One way or the other, you'll pay me the respect I'm due."

An unseen door behind the throne opened and closed. I heard a woman's footsteps. Tatiana, dressed in a silk gown the color of midnight, emerged and sat next to Albert Victor. She looked at me, her expression blank, her eyes seeming to go right through me.

"Tatiana!"

She did not respond.

"Do not speak to the queen unless she has first spoken to you!" the Ripper shouted, gripped by one of his unpredictable mood swings. Then, more equably, he added in a lecturing tone: "You're manners truly are wanting, Mr. Parker."

"So?" I challenged.

There was murder in the smile that returned to his face.

"So, do not worry. I will give you the necessary *correcting*."

"What have you done to Tatiana? She seems drugged."

"Drugged? Not at all. I've merely helped her understand her natural allegiances. As self-possessed as women seem these days, I've discovered that what most of them really want is to submit to a male's stronger will."

"That's utter nonsense, like most of what you have to say."

Prince Albert Victor wagged his bony finger at me as if correcting a disobedient child.

"Only the king's ministers are permitted to disagree with him, and then always indirectly. Try to remember that for the few brief minutes you have left to live. Not to change the subject, Mr. Parker, but I owe you a debt of gratitude," he said with mock politeness. "You have ever so conveniently got General von Baden out of the way. I must thank you for freeing me of the necessity of doing so myself."

"I would have thought you were allies."

"Oh, we were, of a sort. In the game of power, it is quite common to have allies who are also rivals. Allegiances form because they are expedient; when they no longer are expedient, they are dissolved."

I was suddenly aware of another presence in the room. It startled me enough to make me foolishly take my eyes off the Ripper, although I kept his presence fixed with my other senses when I looked away.

Ariel Niccolini entered the throne room through a side door.

Prince Albert Victor had a smirk on his face when I turned back to him. Tatiana's expression remained completely blank, as if she were asleep with her eyes open.

"Ariel, stay by me," I said softly as I felt her approach from behind.

She did not respond.

"It's me, David. I can help you."

The beautiful Italian walked past me as if she hadn't heard a word I'd said. With her head bowed, she climbed the dais steps. Keeping her eyes lowered, Ariel unfastened her dress and lowered it until she was naked to the waist.

I pointed the pistol at Albert Victor.

"Get out of the way, Ariel," I said, not wanting to risk hitting her or Tatiana. There was no telling what would happen if the exploding round went through Albert Victor and hit the stone behind him.

"Your assumption is quite mistaken, Mr. Parker. I quite had my fill last night. It is Queen Tatiana who needs to feed."

Ariel shuffled to her right and dropped to her knees in front of Tatiana.

With the same blank expression, Tatiana ran a hand through

Ariel's black hair. Lowering her lips to Ariel's neck, Tatiana opened her mouth until I could see the ivory gleam of her blood teeth.

"No!" I shouted, but Tatiana did not seem to hear me, or even be aware of my presence.

Ariel Niccolini's body trembled with orgasmic pleasure when Tatiana bit into her neck.

I pointed the gun at Tatiana, but I could not make myself pull the trigger. There were tears in my eyes, and my ears burned with the Ripper's mad, hysterical laughter.

I lowered the weapon and watched, helpless.

Tatiana remained fastened to Ariel Niccolini's neck for what seemed like an eternity, drinking far more blood than she needed to keep the Hunger at bay. The color ran out of Ariel's body as Tatiana sucked the life out of her.

When Tatiana was finally satisfied, she looked up at me with the same blank stare, wiping a little blood from her lips with a lace handkerchief. Ariel's limp body rolled onto the floor, stopping on its back, her arms flung out on either side, her eyes staring blindly at the ceiling.

"You bastard!" I said to the Ripper. "This is your fault."

"I wanted to finish her myself," he said to Tatiana, with what I took as genuine disappointment.

"Where is Lucrezia?" I asked, looking slowly around the room, knowing I could not trust my higher senses to detect her. The Ripper was not powerful enough to have put Tatiana under such an evil spell without Lucrezia's expert help. I should have killed Cesare Borgia's sister when I had the chance.

"That opportunity is long past, old boy," the Ripper said, reading my unguarded thoughts. "Lucrezia's gone back to brother. And about time, I might add. She tends to meddle. You still haven't figured it out, have you?"

I stared back at the fiend.

"Lucrezia Borgia has been your protectoress these past months. She had great plans for you." He laughed merrily. "However, she has quite washed her hands of you now. You failed to meet expectations."

He put his hands on the armrests and slowly raised himself to a standing position.

"A silly thing, these affairs of the heart. Lucrezia entertained such fantasies about you. You angered her more than you can imagine by proving her charms are not, as she likes to believe, irresistible. Of course, I told Cesare it would never work out between you and his sister, but she has him wrapped around her finger. However, Mr. Parker, that is all water under the bridge, as they say in America.''

His voice became quiet, almost gentle.

''And now, old friend, it is strictly you and old Jack. Your patrons—neither the good ones nor the evil ones—can no longer help you.''

He gave me his most charming smile.

''The time has come, Mr. Parker, to settle accounts before moving on to new business. And big business it is. It's a shame you won't be around to see me bring Europe to her knees.''

I raised the gun.

''Oh, no! A simple trick will fool a simple mind, but you're no longer dealing with von Baden.''

''Tatiana! Get down!''

She ignored me.

I squeezed the trigger, but it would not budge. The gun began to grow hot—so hot that I could not hold it. The pistol had turned a glowing pink by the time it hit the carpet, fast becoming red around the edges. Smoke curled up from the impression the metal was burning into the soft blue-and-cream-colored rug.

I knew what was coming next and managed to take several quick steps backward before a half dozen ear-splitting explosions went off in quick succession as the shells in the weapon's magazine burst. The force of the explosion was directed harmlessly downward into the floor by an invisible shield of energy the Ripper created to surround the pistol.

''I have lived with the threat of assassination from genetically inferior dwarfs like you all my life,'' Prince Albert Victor said.

His face started to change as he spoke. His upper jaw elongated, the lip bulging from the growth of teeth beneath it. He lowered his face for a moment as a shudder rolled through his body. When he looked up at me again, his face was no longer recognizable as anything human.

The metamorphosis he had undergone in the Paris restaurant was mild compared to this. Albert Victor was giving outward shape to the inner cancer that had long since devoured any small bit of goodness that ever existed in his demented soul. Hell itself could offer no more repulsive an image of hatred, of jealousy, of pride turned inward to feed on itself until there was nothing left but a burning, insatiable hatred for all of creation.

The Ripper's hands had become claws, with long, pointed

black nails at the end of each digit. His spine twisted forward at an unnatural angle midway up the torso, then bent again vertically, making two nearly right-angle turns. His chest was a mass of enormous muscles, the transformation ripping apart his shirt and jacket, leaving them clinging to his body in shreds.

"In the next few years, Mr. Parker," he hissed, "we will see a rebirth of the Age of Kings." The words were difficult to distinguish, coming from the deformed architecture of his mouth. "That is, those of us who are still living."

Another spasm bowed Prince Albert Victor.

The vertebrae in his back had become grotesquely enlarged and began to break through the skin. Leathery appendages extruded from above his shoulder blades, extending a dozen feet or more on either side; the growths seemed to be extra arms, although they more closely resembled tentacles. I was wary lest they grab for me, but they lay rigid and apparently useless on the floor, covered with glistening mucus.

The Ripper's breath came in harsh gasps now. He was clearly in excruciating agony; I wondered why even someone as boundlessly perverse as he would undergo such pain for the express purpose of making himself more horrible.

"Only a few weak fools now stand in our way," the Ripper hissed, panting, holding his chest as if it were about to burst open. "Soon we will wipe the *Illuminati* off the face of the Earth. Then mankind will witness the dawn of the new millenium."

The Ripper doubled over from the pain, his control momentarily exhausted by the change his body was undergoing. I looked around the room, trying to mass my energy to fend off the attack I knew was coming. There were swords and other weapons scattered around the chamber as decorations, but what good would they be against such a creature?

As if having read my thoughts, the fiend raised his head and roared with laughter. The appendages fixed to the Ripper's back lifted off the floor and began to swell and stretch. With a loud crackling sound, he unfurled a pair of enormous leathery wings.

The fiend raised himself to his full stature now, swelling his wings. His misshapen body was huge, and every movement bespoke tremendous strength.

Lifting his wings and bringing them down with a force that blew the death-tainted air in the chamber against my face, he soared upward, using the wings as a sort of parachute to brake his descent as he floated back down onto the balcony that over-

looked the room, his three-toed feet clutching the stone banister.
Where minstrels had once sat and played lutes now stood the
angel of mankind's destruction.

"I am going to slit your belly open and slowly draw out your
entrails. A beautiful necklace they'll make, something truly fit
for a vampire queen to wear about her neck."

My eyes flashed to Tatiana, who continued to look at me with
the same impassive stare. If she had been unable to defeat the
fiend, how could I?

I forced myself to focus on my breathing. In, out. In, out. I
*had* to maintain control. This was all a ruse to frighten me, to
make it impossible for me to see through Albert Victor, and to
defeat him.

"Rasputin's mind control tricks won't save you now!" the
creature shouted. "What you see is real, and what is about to
happen to you will be real, too."

He unfolded the black wings, ready to swoop.

"Your time has come, David Parker. I am here to commend
you into the hands of sweet Satan."

"I compel you to stop!"

Mozart stood in the doorway, pointing his finger at the beast.

"You have proven your superior power," Mozart shouted.
"Let my apprentice go unharmed."

"Why would I do that?" the beast asked, cocking its head to
one side.

"Because I offer you a bargain," Mozart said, lowering his
voice. "Let Herr Parker go, and you can keep Tatiana Nicolaievna."

"No!"

"Silence," Mozart ordered me. "You were sent here to do a
job and failed. Now we must accept the consequences of your
failure. Tatiana knew the risk. She was willing to stake herself
in the gamble. Unfortunately, she—we have lost."

The beast shrieked with laughter.

"Tatiana is already mine, you old fool. She would not go with
you if she could."

The look on Mozart's face seemed to confirm it was true.

"Then let us go in peace to avoid a needless confrontation,"
Mozart said. "I warn you that my powers are strong."

"And if I refuse?" the creature asked.

"Then you shall have to deal with me," Mozart said. It was
the closest thing to a threat I have ever heard him make.

*"You?"* the beast thundered contemptuously. "What could *you* do to *me*?"

Mozart's smile enraged the beast. It flew at Mozart so fast that I didn't have time to react. The two collided, and both were enveloped in the leathery wings. A moment of struggle was followed by a terrible stillness. Then, like the moment a nightmare begins to unfold in your dreams, I heard the sound of the beast's wheezing laughter.

There was a suit of armor against the wall between where I stood and the place the beast rejoiced over his latest and most noble victim. I managed to snatch the battle-ax from the steel figure's hands before the Ripper let out a second angry screech and wheeled toward me.

I had no time to think, only to act.

Rising quickly in the air with a stroke of its wings, the beast banked sharply and came straight at me, dripping Mozart's rich purple blood from its daggerlike teeth.

I hurled the ax. It turned over once in the air and struck the monster's wing at the place it joined the body.

The creature veered sharply to the left and crashed into an oak table, smashing it to pieces.

I dashed to the ax and grabbed it up again, ignoring the severed wing, which trembled as it disgorged putrid bile from its open veins.

The thing was almost upon me as I stood. I raised the ax high above my head and brought it down with all my strength, splitting the Ripper's deformed skull to the neck.

It would not die, but grabbed frantically at the ax handle, which I still held firmly in my own hands. I jerked the weapon free, backing away.

The creature continued to come at me, clutching blindly with its claws, its eyes lost in the mass of bloodied, pulverized flesh.

I took several quick steps backward, planted my feet and let it come. There was plenty of time. I stood with the bloody ax at shoulder level, its steel blade almost touching my right arm. When the thing that had been Prince Albert Victor came another step closer, I swung the battle-ax a final time, severing the smashed head, which fell to the floor in two halves.

The creature's body stood there, shaking, its claws continuing to clutch at the air. I swung the ax again, hitting it full in its deformed chest.

Albert Victor finally collapsed and was still.

Exhausted, I turned away.

The gates of Hell crashing open to disgorge the souls of the damned in one screaming mass could not equal the banshee wail that sliced the air.

I turned to see the monster, its body regenerated in an even larger and more hideous shape, rise up off the floor on spreading wings that blocked out the light and cast me in the shadow that I knew would soon cover all of Europe.

Prince Albert Victor had not been killed. In that terrible moment I realized that perhaps nothing I could do would kill him. The weapon had not been made that could knock the infernal life out of his diabolical form. Each time I struck him down, he would only rise up again, more powerful than before.

The monster was falling at me, dropping down from the room's vaulted ceiling with an ear-splitting wail that made me want to cry out in pain.

*DIE!*

My body jerked as if I'd been plugged into a high-voltage line the moment I projected that simple thought. Such a peculiar feeling! It was as if I'd become a lens that gathered stray particles of goodness from the atmosphere and projected them in a powerful, laser-strong beam of light.

A halo of yellow lightning formed around the creature as it hovered over me in the air, its attack arrested. The monster itself then began to glow with the light that became blindingly brilliant, consuming the creature with its fiery luminescence.

A moment later Prince Albert Victor was simply gone, consumed by the cleansing fire I'd projected at him.

I felt the change immediately in my soul. The world had been freed of a very great evil.

I did not know whom to run to first, my friend Mozart, who had lost his life because of my weakness, or Tatiana. But Mozart, to my considerable surprise, was picking himself up off the floor, straightening the torn remains of the front of his tuxedo as best he could. Nothing remained of the lethal wounds the Ripper had inflicted on him.

"Thank God you're all right!" I said, running to his side and grasping him by the shoulders to reassure myself that I wasn't hallucinating.

"He couldn't actually hurt me. Of course he didn't know that. And neither did you. Forgive the deception. I wouldn't be a very good friend if I'd left you to face the Ripper alone."

"Help me with Tatiana."

"But why?"

I turned to my lover, who was looking at me, smiling.

"Dah-veed," she said. "You were magnificent. Please do not think—Ariel . . ."

Ariel Niccolini got to her feet and began to fix her dress, moving as if she were in a dream.

"Her death an illusion," Mozart explained. Ariel's unsteady legs carried her behind the thrones. The door opened and closed.

I began to laugh.

"Then, all's well that ends well," I said, delighted at last to understand how well the pieces of Mozart's puzzle fit together. "When it comes to devising initiation exams for novice vampires, all I can say is—"

*"You!"*

The thunderous pronouncement came as the main doorway to the throne room burst off its hinges. The entire castle shook as the stone wall surrounding the doorway was smashed when the scaled abomination forced its leviathan form into the chamber.

"General von Baden," Mozart said without a hint of emotion.

"No vampire dares boast powers greater than mine!" the thing von Baden had become roared.

The stink of burning sulphur filled the air, and wisps of blue flame trailed out of the monster's mouth every time it exhaled. The creature closely resembled the dragon St. George frequently is pictured slaying in medieval art. For all his evil von Baden lacked Prince Albert Victor's twisted originality; the general had to copy other monsters when he wanted to make himself horrible.

"Now you will see what it is like to kiss the fire you tried to use to destroy me!" the creature roared, and shot a trailing arc of blue flames toward the ceiling, where it ignited the rafters.

I looked toward one of the tapestries hanging from the walls and nodded. The covering fell to the floor, revealing the old lumber used to cover a cathedral-sized circular window. I snapped my fingers and one of the boards ripped free, allowing a single shaft of golden sunlight to pierce the chamber's gloom.

"Not the light!" the dragon howled.

I waved my hand and the remaining timber came crashing down, uncovering a magnificent round stained-glass window. A rainbow of light erupted through the red and cobalt and amber and crystalline panes, suffusing the entire room with the heavenly glow of morning sunshine.

"The burning! The burning!" the creature screamed, but there was no escaping the sunlight.

The purifying flame consumed von Baden with a blinding flash that left behind neither smoke nor ash nor any trace of the German's carefully nurtured evil.

Tatiana came down the steps toward me and put her hands on my arms. I lowered my face to hers.

"I hope you are not angry, *liubov' moya*. We wanted, finally and completely, to awaken your power and at the same time to rid the world forever of two very great evils. We—and you—have succeeded on both counts. I only pray you can find it in your heart to forgive me for deceiving you today. If you could do that, the *Illuminati*'s victory would be complete."

"Forgive you for what?" I said, and lowered my lips to Tatiana's.

My year-long apprenticeship had ended, but I knew that my education as a vampire had only just begun.

# Epilogue

**B**AYREUTH, JULY 16, 1989—We remained in Burg Wolfsschanze four days. It took that long to unravel the intricate financial arrangements von Baden and the others had made and to ensure that it would be a long time before Cesare Borgia could put a similar scheme into play.

We discovered that one tower of the citadel had been modernized. The windows had been sealed, electricity run, and a climate control-system installed to keep the temperature and humidity constant. The central room in the tower was filled with computers and telecommunications equipment linked to banks in places like Montreal and Milan and brokerages as far away as Hong Kong and Tokyo. This was the nexus of Borgia's European financial network, the war room that would have been the heart of his operation if we hadn't arrived at Burg Wolfsschanze in time to stop it.

Mozart's interest in higher mathematics served us well. He broke into General von Baden's computer codes and unraveled the intricate money system, tracing the credit channels, asset chains, blind trusts, dummy corporations, and holding companies many times around the globe. And more important, he defused the computerized trading program that automatically would have pushed the world into a financial panic even with von Baden and Albert Victor dead.

I'd never worked with computers before, but Mozart coached me, and I was amazed at how fast I picked up the nuances. He put me in charge of dispersing the assets Borgia had amassed to bring his economic bomb to critical mass. Once I found his organization's numbered Swiss bank accounts, it was relatively easy to tap into the computers in Zurich and transfer Borgia's money to various charities.

(At the same time, Rasputin and Tatiana were busy selling off Borgia's stocks and bonds and transferring the money to Switzerland for me to spend!)

I gave enough money to the United Nations to feed Ethopia for a decade. I also made substantial contributions to the American Cancer Society, the International Red Cross, the United Negro College Fund, the Safer Foundation, the University of Iowa—I awarded anonymous grants as quickly as I could think of a charitable group or nonprofit organization and trace its bank account number.

We'd won a double victory. We'd prevented Borgia from bringing the world considerable misery, but then we went a step further and used the means by which he'd intended to inflict hardship and employed it instead to ease suffering.

I've seldom felt as satisfied as when I got up from the terminal of that Macintosh computer after giving away the last of Borgia's billions.

I wish I could say the rest of the work at Burg Wolfsschanze was as enjoyable.

The four of us—Mozart, Rasputin, Tatiana, and I—had the odious job of cleaning up any traces of the bloody diversions that had occupied von Baden and his guests before our arrival.

"I wish there had been some way we could have prevented this," I said to Tatiana as we fed the last corpse into the crematorium that was part of the vast Burg Wolfsschanze complex.

I was touching on a sensitive point. In the back of my mind I kept wondering why Tatiana hadn't stopped them from the night of murder that took place even as I was preparing to come to the castle.

"As do I, my love. Unfortunately innocents are sometimes hurt. It is the way of the world."

"There was nothing you could have done?" I said, finally putting it in the open.

"Prince Albert Victor kept me locked in the north tower in a room surrounded by negative energy. He and von Baden came there and worked on me for hours at a time, trying to beat me down mentally. To convince Albert Victor I was submissive to his will, I put myself in a semitrance. I was aware of my surroundings, but just barely."

"So, you didn't know?"

"I knew no more than you did from your room in Jachenau. Albert Victor did not trust me. To be certain I was truly under his spell, he brought me in front of you and silently ordered me to kill Ariel Niccolini. It was my final test.''

"I'd say you passed," I said, rolling down my sleeves and buttoning the cuffs. "I was certain you'd murdered her."

"All an illusion," Tatiana said with a sad smile. "You must trust what you feel, not what you see."

"I'm sorry," I said. "I know you were incapable of hurting Ariel."

"It is all right, *moi dorogoi*. But what will become of her? Even with her memory altered, it would be dangerous for her to return to Florence."

"Mozart said he wouldn't be surprised if she had a job offer in Bonn that would be too good for her to turn down. He has friends in Bonn."

"Then, as you said earlier all's well that ends well."

"Yes," I said, and sighed, still feeling vaguely responsible for the poor mortals killed by the Ripper, von Baden, Lucrezia Borgia, and Clarice—and also for the mortal Clarice, Anna Montoya, Ariel Niccolini, the absurd blonde prostitute from Chicago, and all the others who had suffered after coming in contact with the bittersweet vampire world. "All's well that ends well, for the survivors."

Tatiana took my hands.

"You are a survivor," she said. "Mortal or vampire, that is the best you can hope for. It's a distinction that should make you proud."

We left Burg Wolfsschanze and took the Mercedes for the drive to Bayreuth.

The Wagner Festival was not to begin for another day. We checked into our rooms and unpacked, with apparently nothing in particular to do until the next day. My questions about the *Illuminati*, who were supposed already to have gathered in Bayreuth, brought only noncommittal responses from my three friends.

After supper, Tatiana took me to a concert hall where there was to be a preview concert for the music lovers who'd arrived early for the festival. As we took our seats, which were exactly in the center of the hall, a little bit back from the middle, I caught Tatiana looking at me with a smile that seemed to contain a hidden message.

"What is it?" I asked.

"Nothing, *liubov' moya*."

"No, please, what?"

"Be patient. You will see."

The orchestra members, who had been tuning their instruments, fell silent as the conductor walked onto the stage from the wings. The crowd applauded politely. I'd started to clap, too, before I realized the smallish figure—whose red ponytail went strangely well with his black tie and tails—was Mozart.

I looked at Tatiana, filled with excitement.

"I didn't know *he* was going to perform!"

"A special surprise he arranged for you, *moi dorogoi*. Hush. They're about to begin."

Mozart raised his ivory-white baton. When he brought it down, the orchestra began the dramatic opening allegro vivace movement of the *Jupiter* Symphony.

I have heard Mozart's *Jupiter* performed by the best orchestras in the world under the most brilliant directors, but never had I experienced anything as electrifying as hearing it played under the composer's direction. The orchestra performed not as a collection of individuals working together but as a single entity, with one mind and one soul.

At the beginning of the third movement, the menuetto, something strange began to happen as the tempo picked up and Mozart's musical themes became more involved, more complexly interwoven.

Occasionally—and seemingly quite at random at first—other members of the audience glanced my direction, then quickly returned their attention to the orchestra. These brief moments of eye contact were long enough to establish the spark of recognition that informed me these were not merely strangers, but other vampires.

But there was more.

There is a place in the final movement of the *Jupiter* Symphony where Mozart's divergent themes begin to come together. It is a stunning moment of genius that has a virtually cosmic effect, the musical equivalent of the planets aligning themselves in the night sky, the universe in harmony, the planets and stars wheeling through the heavens in divinely choreographed dance.

At that *precise* moment, the entire orchestra and audience gave me *that look*. I could even feel the vampires behind me looking at me.

In that fleeting, fragmentary moment—less than a second, no longer than the time it takes to blink—I realized the entire orchestra was made up of vampires (No wonder they played like angels!), as was the audience.

I had met the *Illuminati* at last, and they simultaneously delivered a single message: *Welcome*!

The symphony ended. The audience jumped to its feet as one, applauding and cheering wildly. Everyone in the hall knew we'd been blessed with a musical miracle, that the *Jupiter* Symphony had never before been performed so perfectly, so sublimely. Even the orchestra and conductor joined in the euphoric celebration.

But the vampires in the concert hall were not just clapping for the heavenly music.

They also were applauding the newest member of the *Illuminati*.

# About the Author

Michael Romkey is a newspaper editor who lives in Bette·
dorf, Iowa. This is his second novel.